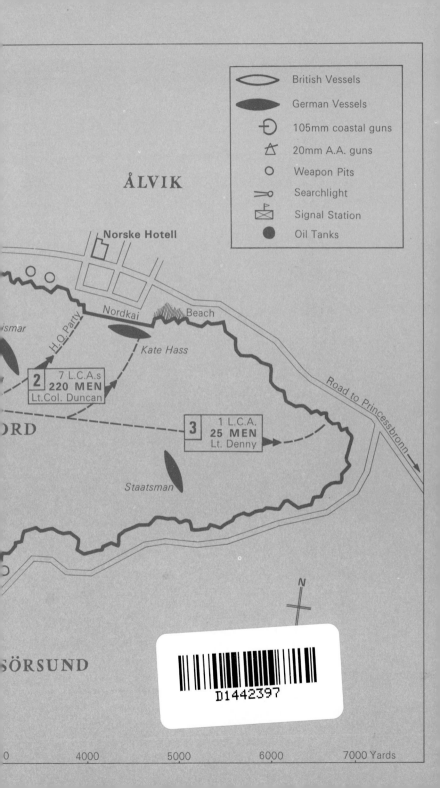

ÅLVIK

Norske Hotell

Legend:
- British Vessels
- German Vessels
- ⊖ 105mm coastal guns
- △ 20mm A.A. guns
- ○ Weapon Pits
- ⤚ Searchlight
- ⊠ Signal Station
- ● Oil Tanks

Nordkai

Beach

ismar

H.Q. Party

Kate Hass

2 7 L.C.A.s
220 MEN
Lt.Col. Duncan

ORD

3 1 L.C.A.
25 MEN
Lt. Denny

Staatsman

Road to Princessbronn

N

SÖRSUND

D1442397

| 0 | 4000 | 5000 | 6000 | 7000 Yards |

The Dawn Attack

Brian Callison

THE DAWN ATTACK

COLLINS
St James's Place, London, 1972

William Collins Sons & Co Ltd
London · Glasgow · Sydney · Auckland
Toronto · Johannesburg

First published 1972
© Brian Callison 1972

ISBN 0 00 221036 3

Set in Monotype Imprint
Made and Printed in Great Britain by
William Collins Sons & Co Ltd Glasgow

The Ålvik Raid never happened. The people and the places I describe are entirely fictional. But there was a war. And there were raids like this one – on St Nazaire and the Lofoten Islands and on tragic Dieppe. And, particularly, on Vaagso, Norway, where many gallant men fought on both sides – German as well as Allied Forces.

I have deliberately kept the preliminary planning and preparations for the Ålvik Raid to a minimum – I am writing not for the pundit strategist but of men. This is a story, not a military thesis. Many of the incidents described here did actually occur, but I have done my utmost to avoid portraying any of the real personalities involved – only the spirit and the courage which motivated them.

Tentatively I offer this novel as a tribute to all of them – raiders and defenders – but, in particular, to the officers and men of that proudly select group, the British Commandos.

I hope they will forgive me if my research has proved, in any detail, inadequate.

Prologue

'Wind speed in knots – 12, from NNE; Waves, height
in feet – 4, from ENE; Corrected barometric pressure
in millibars – 1002.6; Air Temperature in degrees F – 28;
Sea temperature in degrees F – 36; Visibility –poor. . . .'
Extract from Escort Force Commander's log,
time hrs: 05.30

The raindrop was first conceived five miles above the North Sea,
out of the frigid womb of the tropopause. In its infant state it
materialised only as a minute sliver of ice, slowly descending
through the upper layers of cumulonimbus which, while they
had given the raindrop life, could not afford immunity from the
forces of gravity.

As it fell, the temperature of the turbulent air enclosing it
began to rise at a steady rate of $5\frac{1}{2}$ degrees Fahrenheit for every
kilometre of altitude the baby raindrop sacrificed. It was then
that the embryo first started to grow. That moment when the air
temperature rose above $-40°F$, and the water vapour forming the
anvil shaft of the thundercloud intimately enveloped and con-
densed around the little stick of ice causing it to mutate, instead,
into a perfectly formed globule of supercooled water almost five
millimetres in diameter.

And the now adult raindrop tumbled faster and faster towards
the black void of the waiting North Sea until it was descending
at its maximum velocity of seven metres per second.

It finally terminated its brief, twenty-seven thousand foot life-
span as a wet little star on the upturned forehead of the youngest
occupant of the gyrating yellow liferaft below. He didn't notice
the impact though, because he had died quite a long time before
the raindrop was born. It was very cold on the surface of the
North Sea in November of 1941 – much too cold for a twenty-
year-old boy who'd only lived under a warm, loving Dresden roof
until the day he'd first joined the Luftwaffe.

Within minutes the now disintegrated raindrop had reverted

7

to its original crystalline state under the chilling caress of a wind recently brushed by the frozen mountain peaks of Norway. The patina of ice shrouding the dead face glistened slightly, indetectable from the dull glaze of the sightless, open eyes, but inexorably gaining volume and density from countless other falling raindrops, sandwiching to form a below-zero blanket which fuzzed and deformed the features of the golden-haired young upper turret gunner from Dresden.

A looming, hissing sea cast a momentary wash of phosphorescence over the dinghy, illuminating the slowly swelling iceman and causing the second, and last, survivor from the ditched bomber to stretch out his hand tenderly and, somehow, awkwardly in a futile attempt to stay the monstrous cocooning of his comrade.

It took the Pilot – for it was he – some little time to understand why he couldn't really move his arms, and also why they didn't look quite right with the sleeves of his flying suit all slipped down and wrinkled in great, soft folds around his wrists. And then he realised with a certain element of rueful detachment that it wasn't the sleeves of his flying suit at all, but that it was the flesh and charred skin of his forearms which had formed into slug-white bracelets above the claws of hands, and that it must have happened as he strained to hold the nose of the burning JU86 from dipping too soon, and too positively, into the waves of the North Sea.

It was funny how you didn't notice even the important things. Not when you were trying hysterically to stay alive, even if it was only to be for another few hopeless hours.

He slumped back, letting the melted arms trail uncaringly in the crackling slush forming on the rubberised canvas floor of the raft. They didn't hurt. Not really. Certainly not as much as the hurt his only son would feel when he learned that his Papa had gone forever, and that the tall man in the Luftwaffe walking-out dress with the love in his eye and the model Junkers in his hand wouldn't be coming home any more to kiss him and whirl his mother around in mighty glee. . . .

The black anvil of the cumulonimbus cloud towered thirty thousand feet above the Cooked Man and the Ice Man in the microscopic yellow dinghy. As the atmospheric turbulence increased, the millions of raindrops tumbling through to earth were arrested and fragmented, and the smaller droplets whirled back aloft, freezing again as they soared into billions of icy spicules. And this process caused the accumulation of a massive charge of positive electricity in the upper layers of the billowing monster while, suspended at the base of the cloud, the larger, more hardy raindrops created an equally gargantuan negative charge.

When the insulation of the dividing air finally broke down, the two opposing forces met. The Pilot smiled fractionally into the eye of the lightning flash – now this was a truly Wagnerian finale for any Teutonic warrior's dying. Borne on a golden pneumatic bier, sharing the stage only with a pure Aryan cadaver as consort. A present-day *Junker*, accoutred in his armoured cosmetic of ice, returning homewards from the battle across the heaving flanks of the German Ocean . . . *Götterdämmerung* . . . The Twilight of the Gods. . . .

Shit!

He started to vomit into the charred black space between his legs. . . .

A second river of lightning hung shimmering against the hurrying clouds, branching into smaller rivers and tributaries and streams, jigsawing the night with sodium-bright fingers, etching momentarily through the eyelids and into the retina of the Cooked Man's sight. And then another, and another.

As the discharge slashed seawards through the heart of the cumulonimbus the air in its path became – for a few milliseconds only – superheated. An infinity of molecules expanded into the surrounding refrigerated atmosphere until, cooling almost as quickly, they tumbled and contracted back into the void left by the lightning's passing. The sound waves set up by this tropospheric friction reverberated grumblingly, following and extending in duration down the course of the parent electricity. They took fifteen seconds longer to reach the Pilot in the dinghy than the flash had done, because he was three miles away from the true source. . . .

Not that he gave a damn. But he did hear the thunder though, and he smiled painfully again, which showed that he was a very brave man as well as being a connoisseur of Richard Wagner. This booming, overwhelming magnificence was undoubtedly the first few bars of the final movement – *his* final movement – and he'd always favoured a slightly stronger element of percussion than was, perhaps, generally acceptable. There was only one

9

question left unanswered now, and he rather hoped he wouldn't be too long in finding the solution.

Wann ist die Aufführung zu Ende . . . ? When does the performance end?

Please?

The dinghy slid down the side of a black, green mountain then crazily skated across the trough and clawed up the face of the next foam-streaked sea. It raised the survivor's height of eye by less than five feet, but it happened to coincide with the next flash of lightning, illuminating the suddenly revealed seascape with a flickering, searching brilliance which sculpted every wave and fleck of spindrift into a magnesium-bleached image.

It also revealed something else. Something even more ridiculous than the concept of a thunderstorm playing Wagner over a spit-roasted, marinating Luftwaffe Flugzeugfahrer because – just for a moment – he thought he imagined a line of ships . . . long, low, silent ships. Ships stealing predatorily eastwards across the jagged line of the black horizon. Grey ships, with the silhouettes of cruisers or destroyers and, even more impossibly, infantry assault transports. . . .

Then Thor switched the light out again, and the dinghy spiralled sickeningly into the next infinite pit. And the flotsam Pilot forgot all about phantom ships which couldn't be there and dreamed instead of a lovely, lonely Bremen girl and a happy, proud little boy who just sat and played with his model aeroplanes until his daddy would come home with another one. . . .

Imperceptibly the crackling glaze spread over the open, wistful eyes, and the ice surreptitiously commenced to join the two comrades together. And very soon the Pilot didn't think about anything any-more.

But he was still the first German to have seen the coming to Norway of Number 22 Commando, Special Service Brigade.

Chapter One

'Against all the rules I propose to attack an enemy who is many times superior. . . .'

Frederick the Great

On 9th April, 1940, the Armed Forces of the Third Reich crossed the Norwegian Border.

On 12th April a motorised *Aufklärungsspähtrupp* of the German Wehrmacht entered the small North Sea coastal town of Ålvik and, by noon on the 13th, a detachment of field engineers had commenced to prepare weapon pits to house the coastal battery allocated to Oksenes Point.

The only Norwegians who welcomed the new protectors were the seven Ålvik members of Vidkum Quisling's *Nasjonal Samling* Party.

Between May and July 1940 the Ålvik Garrison had increased steadily to embrace a total of some three hundred and twenty infantrymen from *Armeekorps H*, supported by sixty-five members of the Labour Corps, forty cooks, orderlies and clerks, and a further forty-six ratings and petty officers from Number 265 Naval Artillery Battalion.

The troops' regulating function was carried out by two sections of Wehrmacht Militarpolizei, on detachment from Princessebrønn twenty-three miles inland.

On 21st September, 1940, the coastal trader *Martha Schiller* went alongside Ålvik's only heavy lift crane at the Nordkai and unloaded three additional self-propelled guns to bring the Garrison's artillery capability to full establishment.

They were commandeered Czechoslovakian type TNHP'S. The Germans re-titled them *Panzerkampfwagen 38(t)'s* in the way which victorious armies have with these things, but it still meant that the Ålvik Area Military Commander now had a further trio of 3.7 cm. portable weapons to consolidate his defences.

The winter of 1940 and spring of 1941 passed uneventfully. Coastal convoys came and went from the sheltered grey waters of the Østersfjord while, occasionally, the Ålvik Garrison stood-to as the muzzles of their two solitary flak guns hopefully followed the high-flying passage of R.A.F. bombers en route for the more strategic targets around Trondheim and Namsos. The general consensus of opinion among the troops was that Ålvik was a pretty good billet – except that those Norwegian *frøken* were undoubtedly the original Norse icemaidens, the way they could stare right through you like you weren't there at all.

At dinner-time on 3rd September a single Royal Air Force Mosquito screamed in from the North Sea at wave-top level. At the entrance to the Østersfjord the pilot gunned his Rolls-Royce Merlin engines viciously and the plane snarled skywards in a soaring half-roll which not only shattered the morale and aim of the gunners in the flak towers but also laid the sights of his underslung reconnaissance camera squarely over the Ålvik dock area and the camouflaged fish oil tanks surrounding the Sørenson Factory at Sörsund, just across the fjord.

The Mosquito then made a wide, leisurely banking turn which placed it on a homeward course and vanished across the North Sea again, fractionally ahead of a somewhat delayed scattering of ack-ack bursts plotting a straight line towards R.A.F. Sumburgh in the Shetlands.

On 4th September the Military Commander, Major Rhöme, stated in his incident report, '. . . an entirely new mark of British fighter bomber . . . obviously on a trial harrassing mission with questionable practical value. . . .'

But on 5th September, 1941, Number 22 Commando were ordered to prepare to attack the town of Ålvik, Norway.

*

And – on the morning of 31st November, 1941 – they did.

H-HOUR minus 60 MINUTES

There were, in point of fact, very many more men sailing to war aboard that nocturnal fleet than the four hundred and eighty-six soldiers of Number 22 Commando.

For instance, there were the crews of the ships themselves – the one thousand, three hundred and seventy officers and ratings of the Royal Navy, whose specific task it was to deliver the raiders to the designated place of mayhem.

There were the key individualists – a Rear-Admiral who had first gazed wide-eyed at the flash of guns as a midshipman in a battle-cruiser at Jutland, many years before. And a Brigadier who had, more recently, devoted two days to winning a D.S.O. by standing, for virtually that length of time, up to his chest in the Channel and shepherding a large proportion of the battered British Expeditionary Force aboard small boats off a beach near Dunkirk.

They were submerging something else this time, the Admiral and the Brigadier. For theirs was the awesome responsibility – as Joint Operational Commanders – of stifling a tradition of inter-service rivalry which had flourished since before the embryonic navy of King Edward III.

It had been done before, in an earlier war, at Gallipoli and at Zeebrugge, but it was still a relatively new precept. The British even created a special department to nurture it – Section MO9 of the War Office.

And Section MO9 christened their baby – 'Combined Operations'.

There was an ex-Highland Regimental officer who had been a captain until a man from Section MO9 had suggested he might find a more succulent field in which to employ his talents as a Special Service volunteer. Then they made him a Lieutenant-Colonel, and gave him Number 22 Commando to lead.

Slightly farther down the structure of command, but equally indispensable, roosted a Royal Air Force liaison Flight Lieutenant with his attendant brood of sea-to-air communicators. Indispensable because, without them, there couldn't be any air support to handle the Herdla-based ME109's, and anyway, you had to combine to become a Combined Operation.

There were twenty places allocated in the assault craft for twenty quite special, and singularly determined men. They were all soldiers too, and out of much the same mould as the British Commandos but with, perhaps, an even more personal interest in the mission ahead.

They operated under the control of a sub-branch of the Ministry for Economic Warfare, and they were called Norwegian Independent Company A.

They wanted very much to be allowed to kill Germans.

*

The twenty-first Norwegian wasn't a soldier of any kind, and he was still vaguely surprised to find himself there at all. In fact, less than ten days ago he had been in bed with his wife, lying listening bitterly to the measured tread of patrolling jackboots outside his suburban house in Occupied Kristiansund. And then the telephone had rung and a man's voice had inquired if it was true that, before the outbreak of war, he had been employed as a ship's pilot for the approaches to Østersfjord. . . .

He had been disembarked at Sollum Voe in the Shetlands two mornings later, by courtesy of the Flag Officer Submarines and, since then, had huddled shoulder to shoulder with the Assault Force Navigator while preparing the passage plan to the landfall. That S.O.E. agent who had nocturnally, and somewhat incredibly, recruited him into the Allied ranks, had also promised that, by this time to-morrow, he would be back in his berth alongside Fru Grönaas, and amply supported by a suitably documented alibi for his temporary absence.

Joss, but it was to be hoped that the British proved as reliable as they appeared to be homicidally aggressive.

There was a Press Unit of five accredited news agency correspondents sailing with the force. There were two British Army cameramen, an R.A.M.C. Field Medical Team, and an R.N. Surgeon Commander plus fourteen extra R.N. sick-berth attendants.

There were – on the crew muster lists – thirteen Canadians, eight Australians, seven New Zealanders, five Indians, five South Africans, two Rhodesians, one Fijian, one White Russian Count and one German Jew.

There was one American. He wore the uniform of a United States Ranger Captain and he was attached to the landing force as a military observer. But it was noticeable that he did seem to carry rather a lot of weapons for just a plain, pacifist bystander.

There was even an inter-denominational contingent from the Royal Army Chaplain's Department. They offered cigarettes to many and comfort to some, but it was generally felt that their real usefulness would be acknowledged when the Commando sailed for home.

After the killing had finished. And the dying was still going on.

*

'Rear gunner to Skip. . . . Permission to test guns?'

'Go ahead. But f'r Chrissakes watch out for Mister Evans down astern.'

The Blenheim shuddered imperceptibly and P/O Prescott smelt the faintest whiff of cordite seeping forward through the odour of stale urine, oil and obscure things which always seemed to cling to aeroplanes.

Fourteen thousand feet. He caressed the airscrew pitch controls delicately and levelled off, watching as he did so the popping blue exhaust flames which pinpointed D for Dog up ahead and Ben Davidson's crate out to port. Fifty-four minutes to the target, and bloody rain, rain, rain as usual. He sucked the skinned knuckles of his right hand ruminatively.

'Undercarriage lever again, Johnny?'

Prescott stopped sucking and grinned at his navigator through the darkness. 'Yeah! It took some professional sadist a long time to design that bloody mousetrap of a spring-loaded cover flap.'

A soft chuckle. 'So wear your gloves next time an' save me using up all my sympathy.'

The Blenheim lifted sharply on a belly punch of turbulence and Prescott felt the butterflies move in his stomach. Usually they went to sleep after take-off . . . he glanced at the green, luminous fingers of his watch – now 07.18 hours – and settled back into the collar of the Mae West.

'Take a quick count for a V.H.F. back-bearing on Wick, Ian. I want to check our drift. . . .'

The four bombers droned on towards Ålvik. They were far too far away yet to see the high cumulonimbus off the entrance to the Østersfjord.

Or the ships of the Assault Force which were approaching it from seaward.

*

The ships really were long and low and grey, just like the German pilot had thought he'd dreamed as he swirled, isolated in his yellow dish, grilled over a white hot spray of Luftwaffe aviation fuel and basted by the salty stock of the North Sea.

Or at least, three of them were. The fighting ships of Force King – the cruiser and the two sinuous destroyers. Finely bred from centuries of British maritime supremacy and reared out of the skeletal stocks of the world's finest shipyards.

His Majesty's Six-inch Cruiser *Hystrix* leading. . . . Temporarily seconded by the Commander-in-Chief, Home Fleet, and serving as Flagship to the Naval Force Commander, Rear-Admiral Arthur Braddock-Tenby, C.B., R.N.

Also functioning as floating S.S.B. Headquarters for Brigadier John Aubrey, D.S.O., and his staff. Also as Intelligence Flag Plot, Bombardment Co-ordination Directorate, Communications Centre, Reserve Force Holding Base, Navigation Leader and Mother Figure.

And primary target for those 105 mm. coastal batteries long since dug in on Oksenes Point.

H.M. Fleet Destroyers *Salamander* and *Muscadin* flanking. . . . Lt. Cdrs. Oddiham and Bradbury. Mounting six 4.7-inch guns, ten 21-inch torpedo tubes plus depth charges aft. Capable of proceeding at thirty-seven knots on the crest of forty thousand shaft horsepower. On detachment to Force King from the 12th. Destroyer Flotilla to provide passage anti-submarine cover and close escort to the L.C.A.s on the final assault. Their secondary mandate – to seek out and destroy any enemy naval or mercantile shipping taking refuge in the cleft of the Østersfjord.

To the captains of *Salamander* and *Muscadin* the operation suggested open season on the Kriegsmarine – with the Royal Navy playing away.

To Rear-Admiral Tenby in *Hystrix* it meant the appropriate culmination of a quarter of a century of training and tradition. And, to Brigadier John Aubrey, the completely logical and inevitable conclusion to forty-eight hours of blaspheming, steeping in brine, and pledging that the very next time his troops got wet they'd be damn well going in and not out. . . .

And finally, there were the Prince Consorts to Force King. Or two Princes in point of fact – in the less flamboyant but equally utilitarian Infantry Assault Ships *Prince Rupert* and *Prince Michael*.

Fast, shallow-draft vessels chosen for the quietness of their engines, they carried the khaki-clad in-fighting virtuosos of 22 Commando to that debarkation point within the pincers of

Oksenes and Hæl-en whence they would board the lightly armoured Higgins Craft for the final run-in to the landing area.

In halcyon days gone by they had plodded on their peacetime calling as cross-channel ferries. Now, garbed in the grey overalls of war and with the box-bowed L.C.A.s clustered like monochrome lobster spawn under the claws of their davits, they surged just as purposefully in the wake of the maternal *Hystrix*.

Still civilians, though. Underneath the battledress. Like most of their complements. . . .

H-HOUR minus 56 MINUTES

The submarine had lain on the bottom all night. Her position, by periscope observation, was precisely two thousand yards due west of the entrance to Østersfjord.

Her name was H.M. Submarine *Foiler*. She was also the biggest signpost in the North Sea that morning.

The duty watch Asdic Rating suddenly stopped chewing his last breakfast bacon sandwich and glanced up at the First Lieutenant, one hand absently caressing his head-set. 'Hydrophone effect, Sir! Bearing Red Two Thuree. . . . A fair gaggle. Turbine an' reciprocating.'

The Number One placed his kai mug on the ledge of the chart table, carefully avoiding the hazards of pencils, rubbers and dividers. 'Thank you. That should be them now. . . . Call the Captain. Hands to diving stations in five minutes.'

Looking up at the bulkhead clock he reached for the log. The time was exactly 07.14 hours G.M.T.

H-HOUR minus 50 MINUTES

Gefreiter Scherer really enjoyed his duty at the Hæl-en Signal Station. Partly because watch-keeping in the lonely hut kept him well out of the way of that bastard, Oberbootmann Schwarzhaupt, and partly because, as the leading hand, he was senior to that very ordinary ordinary seaman, Leichtmatrose Balke, who kept him company.

In fact, on reflection, he was the senior Naval representative on the north-west shore of the Østersfjord, seeing that the crews manning the northern flak tower and searchlight battery were all Wehrmacht blokes and really only garrisoned in Ålvik as support for the Navy's proper guns over there on Oksenes Point.

Not that Herr Major Rhöme's infantry squaddies would entirely agree with him. To hear them talk you'd think the only things keeping the British away from Norway were their three clapped-out Czech Pz.Kw. 38 (t)'s and the scatter of light weapon pits around Ålvik harbour.

Mind you, it was all academic anyway. The British had shot their bolt and it was only a matter of time now. Though probably the *Führer* would make a tilt at the bloody Americans right after . . . sort of keep on going right across the Atlantic.

The field telephone shrilled. It was the harbourmaster, Lieutenant Rex, informing him that the coastal convoy forming up the fjord would be sailing at 08.00 hours. . . . 'Four general cargo and one fish oil tanker under the escort of the armed trawler *Patzig*. . . . Advise me when they have cleared the fjord, Scherer.'

He saluted the receiver, thinking that this was real taut Navy co-operation. None of your Army inefficiency and Prussian bull. '*Jawohl, Herr Hafenmeister!*'

Then Gefreiter Scherer swung his boots back up on the desk and lit a cigarette. So let young Balke stand out there on lookout in the cold for a bit longer. I mean, what's the point in carrying the rank if you can't have the privileges to go with it?

And it was good to get away from that selfish bastard, Petty Officer Schwarzhaupt. . . .

H-HOUR minus 47 MINUTES

There was the very faintest swirl on the surface of the sea, hardly perceptible from the sucking draw of the waves rolling in from the nor'west. Then like some great, stalked Cyclopean eye, a metallic finger rose out of the maelstrom, coldly reflecting the yellow dawn blush from the hooded prisms within.

Slowly, carefully, predatorily it swivelled. Seeking and probing with suspicious, optical stare. Hesitating fractionally at what might have been the flare of a match from the blacked-out signal station on Hæl-en, then continuing its wary circumference.

18

Two thousand, one hundred and seventy yards from the place where Gefreiter Scherer held court, H.M. Fleet Submarine *Foiler* was commencing to surface.

And three thousand yards west sou'west of *Foiler* the oil-bright gun muzzles of the closing assault ships glistened delicately, throwing the palest suggestion of the light from the stars back to trace the tensed white, anti-flash hooded forms of the steel-helmeted gun crews.

A further two miles out to sea towered the great black thundercloud, spindly high tension webs still occasionally searching seaward, rain drops still shedding icy cold tears on to the uncaring eyes which gazed unflinchingly upwards from a skating, cavorting yellow raft.

Eighty-six miles away, and fourteen thousand feet above a track linking Wick in Scotland to the Østersfjord, the Bristol Mercury VIII engines of Johnny Prescott's Blenheim Group carved 840 h.p. tunnels through the darkness.

And behind them came the Hampdens and the Beaufighters, and other Blenheims from Sumburgh. . . .

It all suggested the dawn of a busy day for the Ålvik Garrison. And the assembling ships of the Bremen-bound *Geleitschiff* XJ23, still anchored at the head of the fjord.

And the Herdla-based ME109E-4's of *Luftwaffe Jagdgruppe 77*.

Not that Ålvik hadn't had a lot of busy days in its time. And more especially since that sombre morning of the 12th April last year, when the first of the field grey protectors had bumped down the valley road from Princessebrønn, looking slightly discomfited and undignified in the bath-shaped side-cars of the recce troop motor cycle combination.

Though, from that day on, the discomfiture had been largely on the part of the Norwegians as, with undoubted Teutonic efficiency, the strategists at German Naval Group Command West under the notable Admiral Saalwächter had designated, and thereafter implemented, the institution of a coastal convoy assembly anchorage in the sheltered waters of the Østersfjord.

But they hadn't lost their dignity because of it. Not the Norwegians.

And Occupied Ålvik suddenly found it had a lot of other factors which were of considerable importance, especially for a small town with only one main street.

For instance, there was the Sørenson Fish Oil Factory just across the fjord at Sörsund. Before the war it had provided ninety per cent of Ålvik's employment, if you included the support it gave to maintaining the Østersfjord fishing fleet, and also a substantial contribution to the Norwegian economy. But, to the military mind, fish oil has an even greater priority – in that it contains a very high proportion of glycerine. And glycerine is one of the primary bases for the manufacture of explosives such as dynamite, gelignite and T.N.T. Or link it with alcohol, marry the names to Glycol, and you have a highly efficient aero-engine coolant.

Sørenson's fish oil even had another, less apparent, rôle to play in the advancement of the Nazi war machine – in the U-boat campaign. Because another of the by-products is in the form of the sunshine vitamins A and B. And with the ever-increasing efficiency of the Allied convoy escorts in the North Atlantic it meant that the crewmen of Hitler's patrolling *unterseebooten* were being forced to spend more and more time submerged in their steel chariots and, accordingly, growing more and more pallid and vitamin-starved.

Then there was the geographical location of the Østersfjord itself, in that it was one of the most northerly German bases which remained ice-free all the year round. This meant that Ålvik provided an ideal secondary refuelling and logistics port for those same U-boats with the white-faced crews, and it was to this end that a substantial stock-pile of sea-mines and torpedoes was maintained near the Sörsund Pier.

Unfortunately Ålvik wasn't very much of a tourist centre before the war, which rather restricted the availability of the type of large comfortable building favoured by the Wehrmacht as military headquarters in Occupied Areas. There was, in fact, only one tolerable structure in the whole of the Østersfjord – a timbered inn known, with a certain lack of originality, as the Norske Hotell, and it was here that the Garrison Commandant, Major Rhöme, had established his base.

The Norske Hotell did, however, have another function which made it doubly interesting from a British Intelligence planner's point of view.

Shortly after the Germans arrived in Ålvik, and while the coastal batteries were still under construction on Oksenes Point, a Kriegsmarine signals section tramped ashore on the Nordkai and, following a preliminary survey, erected a high, spidery radio mast over the commandeered hotel.

A few days later several Naval Officers disgorged from two Naval Group Command West Mercedes and, having selected three rooms within the Norske Hotell, commenced to set up a sub-section of the *Seekriegsleitung*.

And the *Seekriegsleitung*, or S.K.L, was the branch of the German Naval Staff responsible for Planning and Operations. This task they performed after having derived the positions of Allied Naval Forces from intercepted radio traffic.

Which was why there was a radio mast on top of the Norske Hotell. And why – among all the other reasons – a British Commando Force was approaching the Østersfjord at such an ungodly hour on that November morning in 1941.

H-HOUR minus 45 MINUTES

The submarine now lay like a great black whale under the lee of the cliffs of Oksenes. Trimmed down on the surface with her main decks still awash, only the angular, menacing finger of her 3-inch deck gun and the high slabside of her conning tower rising to form a taut bowstring out of the jumping stay, invisible from bow to stern.

Ignoring the captive salt water still dappling the bridge rail, *Foiler*'s Captain struggled futilely to pierce the gloom to seaward, even with the aid of the night-coated Barr and Strouds. He rubbed his eyes irritably and sniffed.

'D'you reckon, Charles?'

The First Lieutenant chewed his lip briefly, wishing he could damn well stop the uncontrollable shivers which still racked him despite the thick, oiled wool sea jersey and the oilskins he'd struggled into before they surfaced. Roll on the close humidity of the boat down below. This sea spray and foam type of sailoring was strictly for the destroyer and corvette brigade. Like Willie Bradbury out there in *Muscadin*. . . .

. . . if it *was* Willie Bradbury, R.N., and not Kapitänleutnant Hans Schmidt in a bloody great Kriegsmarine hunter-killer with those Mk. IV depth charges like the ones which had rattled them round *Foiler*'s belly like peas in a tin can five weeks before, off Brest.

'My money's on them being our crowd, Sir. Only alternative would be a Jerrie convoy coming in, and they'd be showing the Hæl-en Light on half power if it was.'

The Captain grinned sardonically into the darkness. 'I sincerely trust, Charles, that you are the luckier brand of betting man.'

He turned to the signalman standing with the red-hooded Aldis at the ready. 'Make the recognition signal, please, Scott. . . . How's her head, Charles?'

'Two eight five, Sir.'

'Thank you. . . .' Moving to the voice pipe, 'Bridge, Asdic! Target bearing, please?'

'H.E. bearing Green Oh Wun Two, Sir, and closing!'

It was very quiet off Oksenes Point. Only the soft sigh of the wind playing with the wave crests, and the steady clack of the Aldis shutter disturbed the night, now that the thunder had gone.

It was cold, though. Damned cold. For a submariner, anyway.

*

Fliegerhauptmann Paul Fichte was cold too. And *he* was still in bed.

Not that being cold was anything new in this bloody Godforsaken country. It just went to prove that the Luftwaffe employed as many sado-humourists in their appointments section as every other airforce. Nine weeks ago he'd been riding the bucket seat of a *Jagdgruppe* 26 109E-4/N Variant, beating up the North African desert – and the British troop convoys crawling across it – ahead of Rommel's Afrika Korps. For seven interminable months he'd tolerated sand in his coffee, flies in his beer and centipedes like armoured cars in his bloody boots, and he'd beaten them all. Finally he'd become fully acclimatised.

And then they gave him a Knight's Cross, 2nd Class, loaded him on to a beat-up Dornier and flew him back to Berlin as Heroic Exhibit 'A' at one of Paul Joseph Goebbels's '*Ein Volk, ein Reich, ein Führer*' rallies. Standing there all ponced up alongside those super-human *Liebstandarte Adolph Hitler Waffen S.S.* bastards.

'One people, one State, one Leader. . . .' *Sic itur ad* bloody *astra.* . . .

Crap, little Corporal Adolf! I'm a professional flyer, not a Nazi propaganda specimen in a bottle labelled 'Master Race'. *And* I, for one, don't go for that line they shoot up at *Luftabwehr* H.Q. about the R.A.F. scraping the bottom of the barrel for fighter pilots nowadays. I mean, they said that all before – when the 11 Group boys from Biggin Hill and Tangmere and Hawkinge came up to welcome our JU88's from *Luftflotte II*. And *they* knocked the hell out've us.

And if the Englishmen I met piloting those clapped-out Hurricanes over North Africa, if they were the worst, then God help me when I ever meet their cream. But if I ever do, then please God – give me a Spitfire to do it in!

Cautiously he turned over in bed, wincing as the cold areas of mattress touched his drawn-up legs. And, after Berlin, had they sent him back to where he was experienced? Back to the land of Lili Marlene and great black beetles and indecently warm schnapps – if you ever got it . . . ? No! Because with the perverted obtuseness which only the military mind can muster, they'd posted him instead to Herdla Fighter Base where the pilots of JG 77 eternally struggled to lift their 109E's off a permanently snowed-in runway . . . or so it seemed.

He lit a cigarette and flopped back on the pillow, staring moodily up at the ceiling and feeling the coarse grey fuzz of the blankets irritating the underside of his chin. 'Watch it, Paul boy, or one of these days you're going to say something out loud in the mess about this carnival of cretins we're backing. And then see that little sod Leutnant Söhler take off to tell his *Geheime Staatspolizei* mates they've got another non-conformist candidate for the hose pipes and electrodes. . . .'

Glancing at his watch he stubbed the cigarette out abruptly and closed his eyes. Still twenty minutes before breakfast and he wasn't flying until the evening patrol, anyway. And what else was there to do up here in the frozen north, except sleep. And think.

Eicke's *Schwarme* roared down the runway outside, the four Daimler-Benz engines slamming the windows in their frames with twelve hundred horsepower fingers. Dimly Fichte heard them climbing away into the darkness over blacked-out Bergen, then the yellow glow shining through the cracks in the window screen died as the runway landing lights were cut.

Soon even the sedimentary drone of the departing 109's faded and the silence clamped down again over Herdla Airbase. The time on Fichte's watch, greenly luminescent against the pillow, said 07.25.

*

In the Hæl-en Signal Station Naval Gefreiter Scherer nipped the tip of his cigarette carefully in the tin lid which served as an ashtray and, even more carefully, placed it in the breast pocket of his jacket then – after adjusting the Signal Log fractionally to keep the duty desk proper Navy fashion – reached for his watch-coat hanging on the back of the door. Maybe he'd better go out and relieve young Balke for ten minutes. It got pretty cold out there when you'd been standing around on your own for the last hour with nothing to do except stamp your feet. Only for ten minutes, though. I mean, who's the Leading Hand around here. . . . Lucky for him I'm not that bastard Oberbootmann Schwärz-haupt. . . .

Directly across the four hundred yard width of the entrance to the Østersfjord, Soldat Kruger was also serving his *Führer*. Perhaps not quite as willingly as Gefreiter Scherer but, still, quite placidly. In fact, Soldat Kruger was quite a placid man, which might account for the fact that he was still a private as well. The only thing Joachim Kruger couldn't quite reconcile himself to, as he shrugged a little bit deeper into the field grey collar of his greatcoat and eased the band of his steel helmet a fraction, was why – if the Navy were so damn chuffed with these antiquated coastal guns of theirs up here in the Oksenes Battery – then why the hell didn't they guard them themselves instead of sitting like snug bugs at the bottom of their bunkers . . . bunkers which the Wehrmacht had built for them in the first place!

One and a half miles away from Scherer and Kruger, in the Ålvik Military Commandant's quarters on the top floor of the Norske Hotell, Herr Major Otto Rhöme was also up and about. A pleasant, even a gentle man for an officer from a Prussian military family, he intended this morning to embark in one of Hafenmeister Rex's somewhat unstable launches and cross the fjord for an informal, morale-stiffening visit to the guard detachment at the Sørenson Factory. He thought it would be nice if he took his dog, Cuno, with him as well, but he hoped alsatians weren't sick on boats. He rather hoped Majors weren't either, for that matter.

Four minutes' walk from the hotel Leutnant Sur See Rex was operating in his dual capacity as Ålvik Harbourmaster and Naval Control of Shipping Officer. At this moment he had his N.C.S.O.'s hat on, which meant a never-ending struggle with convoy manœuvring signals, air attack formations, surface attack formations and the exact name and antecedents of any particular ship's cat. . . . Eternal damnation to the luck that nominated him as one of the few junior officers of the *Deutschland* to be wounded by the *Rawalpindi*'s guns before the poor bloody Britons felt their under-armed ship blow apart beneath them. But they'd still left him with a permanently crippled leg, though. And a desk command in the capital of nowhere.

Out in the fjord itself deckhands Katzmann and Strobe leant over the bridge rail of the ex-Baltic trader *Wismar*, idly waiting for the standby whistle in preparation for leaving harbour. Strobe was a bit worried about his mother and sister back in Nienburg, but Katzmann didn't think he needed to. Strobe still wasn't too sure, but perhaps that was because Hans Strobe was a Jew.

Three cables off the *Wismar* rode the escort to Convoy XJ23, the Armed Trawler *Patzig*, Leutnant Sur See Lohemeyer Commanding. And Werner Lohemeyer was very proud indeed of his ship. Maybe she did only have the one solitary main armament forward plus her bridge-wing mounted, ex-Wehrmacht MG 34 machine-guns – which didn't exactly put her in the *Scharnhorst* and *Prinz Eugen* league – but she was still his alone, and God help the Royal Navy if they ever came within range.

He had a last glance in the mirror, noting the glint of pristine braid on the monkey jacket sleeve with a flush of pleasure, then opened the door of his tiny cabin and stepped out into the biting chill of the Østersfjord. It was time to prepare for sailing.

It was also 07.25 and 30 seconds.

H.M. Submarine *Foiler* had been flashing the homing signal towards Force King for half a minute precisely.

*

'Red flashing light, Sir. Dead ahead!'

'Thank you.'

Braddock-Tenby glanced briefly into the eyepieces of the binoculars, then allowed them to fall into the folds of his duffle-coat conscious, at the time, of a mounting excitement perhaps unseemly in an officer of his maturity – but it didn't really matter, not as long as this latent juvenility remained concealed from the others who were stood-to on the *Hystrix* compass platform.

Nodding to where the Force Navigator, Captain Rutleigh, leant alongside Pilot Grönaas, he deliberately kept his voice flatly conversational. 'Congratulations, Peter, on an impeccable landfall.'

Rutleigh's silhouette didn't move an inch. 'Thank you, Sir. But I seem to be two minutes behind time, according to D.R. With your permission I should like to reserve judgment until we arrive on station.'

The Admiral smiled broadly into the darkness. It was quite strange, really, how Peter Rutleigh seemed to feel the need for a forcedly casual tone as well. . . .

*

Aboard the two Assault Ships the muffled throb of the engines, uninterrupted since they cleared Sollum Voe the day before yesterday, suddenly cut to a whisper as the revolutions tumbled. Almost silent now the Prince Consorts sighed through the last few cables of sea between them and the beckoning submarine.

In the shelter decks black-faced men in steel helmets and oddly pummelled Balaclavas looked at each other expectantly and smiled. Some of the smiles were nervous, some anticipatory, and – in one or two cases – some were smiles of sheer unadulterated relief at the prospect of getting off this bloody nauseating roller-coaster of a boat.

Some of the soldiers didn't smile at all, because they suddenly found they were more frightened than they would ever have believed possible. But there weren't very many of them and they, perhaps, were the bravest men of all aboard Force King that morning. Because – like the Admiral's excitement and the Captain's professional pride – they kept their fear to themselves, and didn't say anything, not even to their friends.

Quietly the word was passed down from the high bridges.

'Lower assault craft to embarkation level . . . !'

*

The only thing now left was the implementation of the task itself. And the planning of that had been completed, for better or for worse, many weeks before. Shortly after a Mosquito Recce plane had returned from one of that aircraft's first operational sorties of the war. It proved that the gentle Major Rhöme had, in fact, been partly correct when he reported '. . . an entirely new mark of British fighter-bomber'.

But that he had been terribly wrong when he added the conclusion, '. . . a trial harrassing mission with questionable practical value'.

It was to be hoped – from the British point of view – that the strategists of Section MO9 were a little less complacent, and a little more . . . well . . . aggressive!

During 1941 the various Commandos which constituted the Special Service Brigade were further sub-divided into Troops of sixty-two other ranks under three officers, there being six Troops and one Headquarters Troop per Commando.

For the Ålvik Raid there was one added operational change to the make-up of 22 Commando. In order to cater more properly for the anticipated and varying degrees of resistance, and for the priorities of the various targets scheduled, the attacking force was to be re-formed into Assault Groups – each with its specific objective and task.

GROUP ONE, under the command of Lieutenant Gordon Courtenay, would break away from the main assault force even before the landing craft came within the pincers of Hæl-en and Oksenes. They would land at the base of a thirty-foot rock face and, having scaled this, proceed to demolish the Naval signal station, the Wehrmacht-manned anti-aircraft gun position and coastal searchlight, and also the Hæl-en Light itself.

Having accomplished this, Courtenay's Group would then repair inland to join with GROUP TWO, the largest and, possibly, the most vital force. This consisted of two hundred and twenty men, including the main body of the Norwegian Independent Company, and would be under the direction of 22 Commando's C.O., Lieutenant-Colonel Dougal Duncan, D.S.O. and Bar – the most senior British Officer to enter the Østersfjord that day.

GROUP TWO's mandate was a two-pronged assault on the town of Ålvik itself and then, having established a beach-head, the destruction of the Nordkai installations, the seizing of the Military Commandant's and *Seekriegsleitung* Headquarters in the Norske Hotell – and particularly any codes and documents therein – the

27

killing or capturing of the German Garrison in Ålvik and, finally, the seizing of all Norwegian Quislings and the recruitment of any willing townspeople into the Free Norwegian Forces.

GROUP THREE, Lieutenant Denny, would proceed to the head of the Østersfjord and establish an ambush on the Princessebrønn Road, the only access into Ålvik for *Wehrmacht Armeekorps H* reinforcements.

GROUP FOUR was scheduled to steam ashore behind Major Bert Stenhouse and effect the ruination of the Sørenson Fish Processing Factory over at Sörsund, and of the five storage tanks flanking the fjord.

GROUP FIVE, consisting of fifty-nine men and Captain Mike Seely, would circle in behind the Oksenes Battery, land on the eastern side of the Point and attack the three 105 mm. coastal positions, the southern flak gun and searchlight, and mortally savage the duty members of 265 Naval Artillery Battalion plus any other Occupation Troops they may find.

And GROUP SIX – somewhat frustratedly – would temporarily remain under the custodianship of a nail-biting Captain Cyril Tennent aboard the Cruiser *Hystrix*. Their seventy-man fire-power was to be retained as a fluid, floating reserve to be dispatched *tout de suite* to wherever the going got rather rougher than the planners anticipated.

It was all a very taut skeleton of strategy.

On paper.

H-HOUR minus 44 MINUTES

Men moved like silent, thoughtful ghosts along the shelter decks of the two *Princes* as the word was passed along. Occasionally the cold sheen of the stars picked out the fleeting glint of burnished Thompson sub-machine-gun muzzles and tenderly caressed .303 Lee Enfield 4/Mk.1 rifle butts.

There were other weapons too, like throwing knives and cheesewire and blackjacks, and dull bronze knuckle-dusters and – incredibly – a two-inch mortar which had, if the owner be believed, 'fallen off've the back of a lorry, Sir!' But none of those were strictly legal, and the first people to see them properly would be the Germans.

'. . . all troops muster at embarkation stations!'

Someone said, vaguely surprised, 'Does that mean it's really on, then?'

And someone else, unquestionably a man of sublime faith. 'I told Sheila we'd meet 'em outside the Regal, half-five, Friday. . . .'

Far below the level of the sea the telegraphs tinkled a muffled command. Abruptly the reciprocating shudder of the slowly turning engines ceased and, ever so gently, the ships coasted on towards the low, black shadow that was Occupied Norway. It was all quite pleasant, really. Now that the wind had faded, as well as the rain.

Chapter Two

'Close Fire Support for the assault craft within the confines of the Østersfjord will be provided by H.M. Destroyer *Muscadin*. . . .'
Operational Orders. Force King.

There were the ships of the Assault Force, and there were the key individuals. But, somehow, being a keystone in anything seems to make a man just a little less of a personality and just a little more of a figurehead. And there were also personalities by the score in the ships which crept across that alien sea. Important men and not quite such important men, each one embodying countless permutations of the foibles and fallibilities which go to make up a real live human being. Each one combining his own private recipe for the making of a man – spiced with a *soupçon* of pride or avarice, or perhaps quite a measure of love and joy, or hatred, pessimism, even fear.

Or just the sheer delight of existing. Like the specification for the Creation of Lieutenant-Commander William Bradbury, Royal Navy.

*

Actually, one of the most irritating things about Willie Bradbury was that he was such a vain man. In fact, probably the most consistently infuriating factor about service in *Muscadin* was that – while her officers and ratings attended to their watch-keeping duties around her exposed, open bridge and, meanwhile, huddled miserably and untidily into the soggy cocoons of hooded duffle which Their Lordships of the Admiralty had so providently afforded – their Captain Willie seemed to weather the harrowing hours with the phlegmatic aplomb of a Fifty Shilling Tailor's dummy. Clad snugly in a privately commissioned duffle-coat of the finest camel hair, he would still retain, after twice as long as anyone else, a crease in his doeskin trousers fit to slit his fingers open should he slip while tying his shoe-laces.

It was that which made you mad, while the freezing rain found its way past the towel round your neck and your collar gradually disintegrated into a noose of wet grey rope. That and the incredible way he seemed to always produce an elegantly folded, whiter than white hankie no matter how many times he waved it in the style of a pomander under that somewhat disdainfully beautiful Grecian nose while you, of course, just sniffed and snorted bad-temperedly into your own private scrap of limpid waste. And muttered. Under your breath.

That, and the Georgian Silver coffee service, complete with salver, which contrasted sneeringly with the one pint WD-issue cocoa mugs manipulated by the rest of the peasants. And the bloody ostentatious hand-worked, Javanese filligree-encased cigarette holder. . . .

But one of the nicest things about Willie Bradbury was his unswerving loyalty to you, and his barely concealed love for every last matelot in his ship's Company. That and his little boy sense of immaculate timing for the bizarre.

Like the recent occasion when *Muscadin* was selected to receive an official visit at her anchorage in Scapa Flow by a notoriously critical Member of Parliament. A fire-eater whose current crusade was that the Navy at War allowed too little emphasis on the minor humanities of welfare and the maintenance of the individual. In fact, the very last thing the Commander-in-Chief had said was: 'Now remember, Willie. Be solicitous with the damn fellow – let him see the Navy isn't only concerned with the greater issues. That we also have time for a genuinely deep interest in people an' in the little things of life. . . .'

The great day came and *Muscadin* gleamed like a freshly painted star among the other ships of the fleet. Chief Petty Officers and Leading Hands adopted strangely concerned and kindly voices along the lower decks. And the Distinguished Visitor duly arrived alongside aboard a specially tiddleyed-up fleet tender which – oddly enough – appeared to be crewed entirely by Admirals, Vice-Admirals and Rear-Admirals for the short crossing from Flotta Pier.

But then, as is the inevitable way with these things, disaster struck. At the very moment when the Distinguished Visitor began to negotiate the companion ladder to whence Willie and *Muscadin*'s complement were stiffly and shinily awaiting his arrival, the measured pom, pom, pom of ack-ack fire from the east heralded the simultaneous approach of a solitary, entirely unco-operative, hit-and-run Heinkel bomber.

The boat-bound Admirals, Vice-Admirals and Rear-Admirals sheered off in a welter of threshing foam while the destroyer's reception committee dissolved in a cacophony of controlled fire commands, alarm bells and the clatter of expertly handled ready-use ammunition. Willie, however, noted with some apprehension while pounding towards his bridge that the enemy plane appeared to be heading dedicatedly and unerringly for H.M. Destroyer *Muscadin* – and *Muscadin*'s altitude-seeking guest, still only half-way up what must have suddenly seemed an ever-extending ladder.

The Heinkel dropped one bomb. It exploded seventy yards from *Muscadin*'s starboard side, and sixty-nine and a half yards from a still frantically scrambling Member of Parliament garbed, rather unoriginally Willie thought absently, in striped trousers with brief-case, umbrella and bowler hat.

Willie completely ignored the downward slam of the raider's slipstream, as he also ignored the spatter of machine-gun rounds which dappled shiny little holes along the wing of his bridge and the gracefully rising column of cordite-stained Scapa Flow towering above him. Instead he watched as his late visitor took off vertically from the ladder before describing an immaculate parabola back into the sea.

Then he said thoughtfully, 'Oh Jesus!' And started running again.

Three minutes later a somewhat bewildered V.I.P. found himself back aboard the destroyer for the second time, apparently unharmed apart from the saline bath and – due to the vagaries of blast – the loss of every stitch of clothing other than the brief-case and umbrella still clutched in a vice-like bureaucratic grip.

It said a great deal for the standards of discipline maintained by the Royal Navy that not one member of *Muscadin*'s complement seemed to notice anything amiss at all.

Willie stepped smartly forward from a sweating ship's company now hastily shepherded together again, rubbed a little apologetically round the rim of the Distinguished Visitor's rescued bowler with the sleeve of his Gieves monkey jacket, then – still dogmatically conforming with C-in-C's insistence on establishing the niceties of life – placed the sodden hat squarely over an otherwise denuded Member of Parliament's brow while saying, in a terribly interested voice: 'But apart from that, Sir, did you have a jolly good trip out from the pier . . . ?'

Which was why Willie Bradbury's ship's company also loved Willie very dearly too.

*

Troop-Sergeant Arthur Henderson had sailed aboard the *Prince Rupert* before. But that seemed a very long time ago now, while he'd still been plain Mister Arthur Henderson who had the green-grocer's shop along Salford's Eccles New Road.

She'd been doing a different job in those days too. Carting weekend trippers across the Channel to Ostend, which was why he and Ginny and the kids had been aboard. It had been the first holiday they'd ever been able to take – two whole days plus the early Friday closing – and, God, it was still the most precious forty-eight hours of his whole life.

That had been in June of '39. Before the War.

Standing quietly ahead of the line of waiting troops he watched as the flat bottom of L.C.A. Three dropped jerkily into view from the boat deck above, descending soundlessly under well-greased blocks. As the chipped gunwale reached embarkation deck level a young sub-lieutenant said quietly, ' 'vast lowering!' and the box-boat stopped moving and just lay there, wide and slightly forbidding, twenty feet above the cold black sea.

He shivered fractionally and turned away. He didn't like the sea, not when it was so dark and almost evil looking. Though that day they'd gone over to Belgium had been all right, with the sun and the warm breeze blowing over from the bows. A small oblong board caught his eye just along the alleyway from the sub-lieutenant. It said, in faded lettering, FIRST CLASS PASSENGERS ONLY FROM THIS POINT.

He smiled softly into the darkness. Wistfully. So the Army had finally made him a Gentleman. The last time he'd seen that sign it had been from the other side, and Ginny had said it didn't matter, Arthur, we'll just give the children their orange drinks on the deck, right there. So they'd all squatted round that ventilator in the corner, just where Bob Saunders now rested the section Bren, and smiled at each other like excited school kids, and been very, very happy. . . .

Of course with him being in the Territorials he'd been whipped off to France the moment Chamberlain cocked it all up; Ginny had kept the shop going, though, and they'd seemed to manage as well as everyone else in Salford. Even when Jerrie had booted the B.E.F. back home he'd just stepped straight from the truck on to a destroyer without any of that standing around on the beach under the bloody Stukas.

Then it was home to a Ginny crying with relief, and to Barbara and little Tommy yelling with delirious anticipation about the German helmet Daddy had promised to bring back, which Daddy had thought was pretty damned ironic seeing some big Nazi stormtrooper was probably giving *Daddy*'s helmet to *his* kids right at that moment. Then a five ration-book fatted calf of boiled ham and jelly and strong, sweet tea, and a quick nip down to the pub with his brother-in-law Jim. . . .

Hell, they hadn't even stayed to finish their pints when the sirens had gone. Just slammed them down on the counter with quick apologetic grins at the barmaid, and out into the street under the spangle of stars covering the city.

Under the bombers too. Because they could hear them already, homing in from over Glossop way. He remembered shivering slightly then, too, at the memories those droning, de-synchronised *Jumo* 205 diesels brought back.

Jim had said, 'Shelter?', and he'd grinned back, 'Not bloody likely, lad. Not when I've got a warm bed an' Ginny waiting.'

They'd got to within a hundred yards of the shop, and the little flat above, when they heard the bomb coming.

He'd said sickly, 'Oh dear Christ!' and started running with the scream of the bomb running too, higher and higher up the scale until all he could hear was the shrieking agony of displaced air above. Then Jim's shoulder had slammed into the back of his knees and they'd both gone down in the filth of the gutter with his brother-in-law on top, and the misery in Jim's face etched forever on his mind by the stroboscopic flashes of the ack-ack gun from the next street.

Then the screaming stopped, and his whole life stopped, as he watched the roof of the flat lift off all in one piece like a Sunday School teacher's hat, and a great, silent red ball of fire popping out of where the living-room had been, and the walls slowly falling inwards on to the shop below.

34

And the roar of the explosion hit them just as he was shaking his head up at Jim and whispering that it couldn't really be happening. Just before the left half of Jim's shocked, white face was sliced neatly away by a spinning scalpel of plate glass still with the letters FLUKIST etched across it in bright gold leaf.

He found seven-year-old Barbara still in bed, except that the bed was now sitting neatly in the street in front of the house. And he wasn't absolutely sure it was Barbara, really, except that the larger of the two incinerated, charcoal forms on the red hot springs still bore an ever so slight resemblance to the great big teddy-bear he'd won for her on a shooting stall in Blackpool that time.

He never found little Tommy at all. The A.R.P. blokes did later, of course, though they wouldn't let him see what was in the pathetically small groundsheet. He didn't argue very much with them. Not after having been standing there watching blindly for sixteen eternal hours. But he did have to know that there wasn't any hope left to cling to.

Ginny had been alive for the first few moments after he'd scrambled frantically towards her across the volcanic rubble that had been their life. He smiled again into the darkness that framed L.C.A. Three when he remembered how beautiful she'd still looked as he'd tried to reach her, but he was glad she'd died before he got there because she must have been terribly mutilated below the waist where the bricks had swallowed her. . . .

Then the softly spoken command rustled along the embarkation deck. 'All troops to board landing craft. . . . Pass the word!'

The young sub-lieutenant nodded towards him. 'Can you start moving your chaps, Sergeant?'

And Troop-Sergeant Henderson A. became a soldier again. But he didn't forget Ginny and her brother, and the kids. Or those who were responsible for taking them away from him.

But that was why Mister Arthur Henderson, Grocer and Florist, had become a Commando in the first place.

H-HOUR minus 43 MINUTES

'Just like black paper cut-outs,' Braddock-Tenby thought idly as he glanced along the row of silhouetted figures lining the

35

Cruiser's bridge. 'Almost as if we're not really people at all, just vague shapes drifting on through history. . . . I suppose Nelson was simply an insubstantial wraith to those watching him in the dawn light before Trafalgar. And Jellicoe before Jutland. And Raleigh and Drake and Frobisher. . . .'

Then the Admiral started feeling silly about the idea of his suddenly becoming a middle-aged romantic, and was glad when one of the silhouettes turned towards him and regained a three-dimensional quality by virtue of the faintest green tinge from the master gyro compass reflecting around the rim of the oversized steel helmet.

'The troops are embarking in the L.C.A.s now, Sir,' the midshipman said.

Braddock-Tenby nodded courteously. 'Very good, Mister Todd!' And wondered if *he'd* had quite such a squeaky, child's voice on that morning before his first great battle, almost twenty-six years ago.

＊

Captain Michael Joseph Seely had fought a great battle too, on that particular November day twenty-six years before. Or perhaps it would be more accurate to say that Mike Seely's mother had done most of the fighting, because to-day was his birthday and he couldn't help thinking, with just the faintest trace of apprehension, that this was one helluva way to throw a party.

But, like everything else Michael Seely tackled, if he was going to do it, then he was going to do it damned well. That was partly why he'd got up at 04.30 hours instead of the stipulated five a.m. reveille and, after scrubbing fastidiously over every square inch of his body, had donned scrupulously clean underwear because the *Prince Michael*'s First Lieutenant had told him over dinner the previous evening that some Navymen did the same thing before going in to action in order to minimise the risk of infection.

Seely had retorted cynically that personally he considered the best protection against germs in open wounds was not to be bloody silly enough to get hit by a bullet in the first place. But then again, Mike had never heard a shot fired in anger before and, deep down, wasn't really convinced that bullets hit anyone other than the Germans on the other side, or the chap from the next Troop on your flank.

Still, he wasn't leaving any more to chance than absolutely necessary, and it was a curious reflection on the instability of the human mind that, because of the First Lieutenant's gloomy caution, he'd spent the first four and a half hours of his birthday lying wide awake and just staring up at the rust-mottled deckhead above his bunk, and thinking – for the very first time – about the possibility of being wounded.

Even more inexplicable was the way in which his imagination had escalated from mild acceptance, through growing apprehension, to the eventual sheer horror of what might happen. At midnight he had virtually resigned himself to the fact that his personal legacy of Ålvik might include a small nick or cordite-pitted graze, but at two a.m. the nick had become a shrapnel-jagged slash and the graze a blackened, gaping cavity in the flesh itself, while by four in the morning, Mike Seely was virtually shuddering with revulsion at the looming spectre of white, sinew-trailing dismemberment, the muscular spasms of H.E.-shattered limbs and – dreadfully taking precedence over all – the almost physical anticipation of his own castration through the supersonic slam of a white-hot ricochet. . . .

Which was the real reason why Captain Michael Joseph Seely had risen early from his warrior's couch. And started scrubbing.

*

The ships now lay rolling gently in the slow swell, only the slightest mutter of throttled back engines and the warm cascading of ejecting coolant making them detectable, even to an anticipatory ear. But Soldat Kruger, the nearest of the Defenders, was still a good two thousand yards away and you can't hear such delicate sounds over that distance without an electronic aid. And the Germans hadn't installed hydrophones around the Østersfjord. Not at that time anyway.

From the shore, you couldn't really see the silhouettes either. Not when you were bored and cold and thinking about breakfast, and when the planners who had considered this eventuality had purposely selected one of the darkest mornings of the winter when whatever first light there would be would steal across from the east, acting as an ally to the raiders instead by picking out those inland peaks and crests so beloved of navigators.

There was, however, just enough of the embryonic dawnglow

already in existence for the watchers on the ships to detect the pallid swirl of foam still lingering on the surface just ahead of the high flaring bows of *Hystrix*. They continued to gaze, many of them, intently at the fading patchwork of bubbles until they merged and identified with the colourless sea, because that healing scar marked the place where H.M. Submarine *Foiler* had submerged – the first unit of Force King to have accomplished its part in the business of the day.

With *Foiler* there went a silent prayer for good fortune, and the smell of frying bacon and diesel and body sweat. And a First Lieutenant who gratefully sniffed at it all, thinking how lucky he was to be warm and snug inside his steel shell with nothing to offer discomfort – apart from the considerable odds against the survival of those curious men who chose to fight the war in submarines.

Indeed, they were almost as formidable as those against the men who wore the *Commando* flash upon their shoulders and voluntarily sallied forth seeking to joust with the enemy within the confines of his own bastions.

Men like 668497 Trooper Williams, D.H.

*

Not that Trooper Williams, D.H., would ever have thought of himself as a bastion breacher. No, in Danny's own eyes he was more of a sloth-brained bloody half-wit ever to have got trapped into joining 22 Commando's mad bastards in the first place.

Leaning gingerly over the assault transport's sanded teak rail, the one with all the hearts and initials scratched in it by countless passaging lovers of years long past, he gratefully eased the webbing straps away from the grooves they'd already worn into his shoulder blades, and spat moodily. Then he watched the ball of spit as it spiralled downwards through the still fitful gusts of wind until it disappeared into the white welter of foam breaking against the grey slab side of the trooper.

'Fuck it!' he said to nobody in particular.

Then somebody in particular hissed, 'Gerrin the bloody boat, Williams!' and he looked up a bit startled to see Troop-Corporal Hanson staring irritably at him from across the space between Danny and L.C.A. Eight.

A disembodied voice – Charlie Smart's voice – giggled, 'Bloody

Norah! Danny's changed his mind about comin'!' but Williams just gave them all a hard stare back, muttered 'Yes, Corporal!' and picked his rifle up from its resting-place.

Norah! Yeah, it was bloody Norah, all right. Or maybe the start of it all was that she wasn't . . . if you see what I mean? Because it was a Norah who'd got him into this in the first place. A Norah with over-large breasts and long legs and a penchant for anything in battledress walking out of the Carlisle Infantry Depot. Until the third month her period didn't arrive and, oh yeah, everything was bloody different then, all right, what with Norah yelling everythin' but 'rape' an' him elected Daddy of the bloody Year. . . .

The ship rolled unexpectedly just as he was stepping across into the boat, and the L.C.A. snubbed away from her side, pulling against the gripes restraining her. He glanced down nervously and saw the white water right below his straddled legs, and muttered 'Oh Jesus!' Then hands gripped him reassuringly, pulling him down amongst the rest of the section, and he felt the close warmth of men's bodies shielding him from the bitter chill of the morning.

But you couldn't help grinning a bit, really. Not when you looked around and saw where a few frantic, fumbling minutes behind a bus shelter could land you – like in the middle of a bath tub in the middle of an ocean. In the middle of a bloody nasty war. Those few synthetic magic moments had really thrown Danny Williams's custard pie right in the fan . . . them an' that War Office letter, anyway.

That was the one which had been circulated to all units in the field, and had arrived on his company notice board just when Norah was really putting the squeeze on about telling Dad so's the wedding could be laid on early. It had been a bit vague actually, that letter, with its welcome assurance that any volunteers for 'Special Service' would not be required to make parachute jumps but that they should be able to drive, be physically fit, above average in intelligence, good swimmers and possess strong initiative.

The latter quality of which Danny Williams undoubtedly had him having arrived at the Regimental Sergeant-Major's office three minutes after the notice being posted.

But the odd thing was that, despite the veneer of cynicism, he was a good soldier. He was one of the first applicants to be accepted, in fact. And it was thus that he obtained his ticket to bachelordom.

As well as to the town of Ålvik, in German Occupied Norway.

And that was the reason why 668497 Trooper Williams, D.H., really became a Commando.

H-HOUR minus 40 MINUTES

Aboard *Prince Rupert* the Colonel glanced briefly up and down the almost deserted embarkation deck, conscious of the blackened faces of his men watching him from the row of out-swung assault craft. Just for a moment his features softened fractionally – they were grand lads, all of them. . . . Och hell, man – they were the best!

A movement from aft and Bertie Torrance came into view, leading a party of heavily laden Naval ratings. Stopping at each craft in turn, Bertie superintended the placing aboard of two large, steaming dixies of cocoa. The Colonel nodded approvingly. As a second-in-command Bertie hadn't an equal, and it was going to be a long, cold run for the thirty-eight minutes before his troops could stop being passengers and become soldiers in their natural element again.

Bertie said happily, 'That's all the important things done now, Colonel. There's only the fighting left before we can all go back to our beds.'

The Colonel grinned at the Major's broad back as he swung over into L.C.A. Five and called, 'Aye, and you'll be getting the Germans organised too, just as soon as you get there, I've no doubt.'

Bertie Torrance hesitated and looked back quite seriously. 'No, Colonel,' he murmured quietly, 'I'll be killing the German laddies!'

But Torrance was a Highlander too, and he still remembered what had happened to the Black Watch at St Valéry.

Then the *Prince Rupert*'s First Lieutenant coughed diffidently behind the Colonel, and said, 'It's nearly time, Sir.'

The Colonel nodded again. 'Aye, Number One, but it is. Probably for quite a lot of people.'

Slinging the haversack containing the Verey Pistol and the three green flares across, he climbed over the gun'le of L.C.A. One. The last man for the Ålvik Ferry was now aboard. The First Lieutenant looked at his watch and raised his hands.

'Start the falls. . . . Lower away together!'

The time was 07.31 hours G.M.T. The attack on Ålvik had commenced.

＊

On the Flagship's bridge there was only one order passed to mark the occasion. Rear-Admiral Arthur Braddock-Tenby gave it.

'Hoist Battle Ensigns!'

＊

In the surgically white main galley abaft the seamen's mess deck of *Hystrix* yet another order was passed to the line of aproned men standing poised before the long, scrubbed wooden table. Cook Chief Petty Officer Lumley gave it.

'Right, lads. Get tore in!'

And the first of four thousand sandwiches destined to victual the Flagship's complement during the forthcoming hours at action stations was expertly sliced, buttered, slabbed with cold beef, seasoned, dappled with chopped pickle, topped and – in the twinkling of a matelot's eye – stowed neatly in its stainless steel tray.

The electric urns were brought to the boil to provide the basis for the two thousand, three hundred and fifty pints of tea which would be drunk that day by cordite-reeking leading seamen already stood-to in their gunlayer's seats and – equally pleasurably – by sterile-coated operating teams waiting quietly beside their instrument trays for the Commandos to return. And by sweating, swearing ratings labouring in high explosive packed magazines far below the waterline or by their Troglodyte oppos, the E.R.A.s and stokers on watch in the cruiser's twin-engine spaces.

Because, as Cook Chief Petty Officer Lumley confided to his friend and assistant, P.O. Chalk, 'They got the Padre to keep a listenin' watch on their minds, Herbert, an' the Master-at-Arms for their morals. The Doctor fixes up their physics an' Jimmy The One plans their routine. But they need us, Herbert, to look after their bellies 'cause that's where a matelot gets 'is fire . . . an' where the guts is!'

It proved that Cook Chief Petty Officer Lumley was a psychologist as well as a somewhat earthy anatomist. He had also been – until the Wehrmacht marched into Poland – one of the most brilliant *Chefs de Cuisine* on the London hotel circuit. An artist of whom the Commander (Supply) once remarked, borrowing the words of Désaugiers:

> '*Un cuisinier, quand je dine,*
> *Me semble un être divin*
> *Qui, du fond de sa cuisine,*
> *Gouverne le genre humain.*'

'A cook, when I dine, seems to me a divine being, who from the depths of his kitchen rules the human race.'

With all of which Cook Chief Petty Officer Lumley – and Herbert – most heartily acquiesed.

*

Sandwiches were the current subject for discussion in yet another supporting element of Force King. In a Blenheim bomber still many miles away over the western horizon.

'Bloody spam again!'

Johnny Prescott grinned at the green dials winking up at him from the panel. 'There's a war on. Maybe someone should've told you.'

The Navigator's dim figure moved irritably in the right-hand seat. 'There's going to be bloody two, mate. Just as soon as I see the catering mob . . . want one?'

'Uh! Uh . . . ! Not 'til we're through the target. Pass over the Thermos when you're organised, though.'

Prescott was aware of his Navigator's eyes watching him curiously across the flight deck but he pretended to ease the scarf around his neck. Yet there *was* something different about tonight. Something . . . a feeling of deep unease which kept those damn butterflies twitching and made his mouth go dry at the merest thought of food. Ah, hell, Johnny boy. It's the same as every other night, except instead of an H.E. bombload you're carrying smoke. . . . Just wait for the three green Vereys, then it's in at fifty feet, lay the screen to cover the poor bloody pongoes

as they paddle ashore, and Home James into the wild blue yonder
. . . or rather the slushy greyness of Royal Air Force Station Wick,
God help us . . . !

'*Dive*, Johnny! Dive left, f'r . . . !'

And he felt the sickness flood into his throat as the rest of the
scream was lost in the hammering vibrations of Alley's turret gun,
then his foot automatically hit the rudder bar with a frenzied
jab of terror and the blue exhausts of D for Dog shot up and were
lost above the top of the screen as the Blenheim dropped like a
stone.

The gas-operated slam of the Vickers K stopped abruptly as
Alley lost whatever it was and Johnny dimly heard Ian yelling
through the intercom, 'What was it, for Christ's sake?'

He started to haul the stick back, feeling the vibrations of the
battered air tearing at the Blenheim's undersurfaces, then the
turret gunner's voice, breathless and distant over the electronic
bridge. 'Dunno! There *was* something, sliding in from astern
high. . . . I didn't stop to get the bloody I.D. chart out,
Nav.'

Ian said petulantly, 'I got a cup of coffee – somewhere up there
on the cab top.'

Johnny snapped, 'Shut up . . . see anything more, Alley?'

A pause. 'No. . . . No, nothing. Sorry, Skip!'

He glanced at the altimeter dial. One two three zero. . . . Hell,
they'd lost seventeen hundred feet in that panic-stricken opt-out.
And the rest of the flight, which meant that from now on they were
on their own. A trickle of sweat tickled at his eyebrow and he
wiped at it savagely, then he said quietly, 'That's O.K., Alley.
Just keep looking. . . . Ian?'

'Skipper?'

'What d'you reckon?'

'About the spook . . . ? I dunno. It's hardly likely a JU88 would
try a squirt all on his own, and I can't see the MEs operating this
far out. . . . Maybe it was cloud.'

Alley's voice. Peevishly. 'Clouds don't cruise at three hundred
knots, Nav.'

Prescott shivered slightly and leaned forward, attempting to
peer upwards to where the rest of the flight must be – unless
they'd seen the same phantom too, and in that case they'd all be
running their own private airforces for the rest of the trip to

Ålvik. He said, 'Yeah, well, give me a revised heading for the target, Ian.'

'Come right three degrees. Better add five knots to our A/S as well, to maintain the E.T.A.'

He caressed the throttles gently, feeling the vibrations increase ever so slightly as the bomber lifted to a sullen updraught from the invisible sea below. Could it have been clouds? Or Jerrie night-fighters a long way from home? Either way they'd lost whatever it was now, but it wasn't the best omen a bloke could ask for.

Something rolled across the deck as the Blenheim lifted one wing spasmodically and he saw Ian's figure lean forward awkwardly against the straps. 'The Thermos. I lost it when you dived.'

The intercom clicked on with a tinny splurge of static. 'Turret to Navigator. . . .' Johnny grinned softly, Alleycat had gone all formal and hurt about his cloud. '. . . I can see a star at two o'clock high. *If* you're interested, that is. Over!'

Ian pointed. 'There she is, Johnny,' and the Pilot leaned forward parallel to him, craning his neck upwards. Thank God for a break in the overcast, maybe enough to let Ian get an astro-fix. Vaguely he heard the Navigator's deliberately precise tone saying, 'Navigator to Turret Gunner. I have it now. Thank you terribly, terribly much for your kind assistance. Over and out!'

Alley muttered 'Shit!' back into his throat mike just as Johnny raised the star too. It looked awfully bright and near against the blackness, almost as if it were only a thousand feet above them instead of a thousand eternities. Ian started fiddling for his bubble sextant. 'That bright it must be Pollux, or maybe Procyon. . . .'

Then the star grew into a planet, and suddenly became a great, red sun with flames spurting and cartwheeling out of it. And the turret intercom blurted, 'Oh dear *Jesus* . . . !'

But Johnny just watched hypnotically while the burning plane fell lower and lower until they could see every detail of the underside of it as it neared, still beautifully trimmed in its normal flight attitude but with no apparent forward motion, just spinning slowly like a flaming, airborne Dervish with bits and pieces of molten, super-heated alloy tearing off and floating away in long, arcing fingers.

Then a man slowly fell out of the burning Blenheim – because

44

it *was* a Blenheim – and he was burning too, and they could actually see him tearing at his smoking flying suit though it all seemed a bit unnecessary because the sea was only twelve thousand feet below him and it wouldn't take very long to get down because he didn't have a parachute. . . .

Ian suddenly screamed, 'Bank left, Johnny!' and Johnny did so just as the fireplane filled the sky ahead, then tried to climb in on top of them through the starboard window, and he was only conscious of the closing shriek of run-away Mercury VIII's before the Thermos jumped up from the deck and fragmented the dial of the turn and bank indicator before him.

He closed his eyes and thought, 'Ben! Poor bloody Ben David-son, 'cause Alley's bandit made a pass over me from the starboard side, an' Ben was the next sitting duck out to port. . . .' Then he felt the bomber roll almost over on her back until the red glare snapped off through his closed eyelids so he reopened them, feeling the straps cutting into his shoulders, and started to fight for control of the bloody aeroplane again.

Ian's voice started to run down the altitude scale in a flat, almost resigned, monotone. 'Twelve thousand! Eleven five . . . eleven thousand! Ten five . . . ten thousand feet! Nine. . . .'

They weren't flying anymore. They were falling.

The time was now precisely 07.35 hours G.M.T.

Not that Pilot Officer J. Prescott gave a damn. Not when he was speculating on whether his Blenheim's wings would tear off before – or after – they dived into the North Sea.

H-HOUR minus 35 MINUTES

Yet another aviator was diving uncontrollably, inevitably, at that specific moment in time. But he was still in bed, and his dive was merely the product of the kind of nightmare which only combat flyers can experience, where the controls are like slop in your hand and the whole world below starts inexorably spinning faster and faster while the Black Angels gibber and snarl through bloodied muzzles. Until you wake up screaming, with your arms across your face . . . !

The Angel's voice snapped, 'Wake up, Paul!' again, and Fichte finally regained altitude through the cumulus of horror to discover that it wasn't an Angel at all, but his very good friend the Squadron Adjutant, Gerhard Lusser.

Fichte groaned, 'What the . . . ?' and struggled to keep his eyes open long enough to look at his watch. It read twenty-five to eight. He'd only been asleep for ten minutes.

Lusser handed him a lighted cigarette and grinned cheerfully. '*Guten morgen, Herr Fliegerhauptmann* . . . and get your ass off the bunk because you're flying in thirty minutes!'

Fichte blinked uncomprehendingly for a moment, then sat up abruptly. Protestingly. 'The hell I am, pal. My name's on the duty roster as from 18.00 hours. An' that means *to-night*, not this bloody God forsaken morning . . . !'

'Twenty-nine and a half minutes!' Lusser pronounced succinctly.

Paul grimaced as the raw smoke caught the back of his throat. 'Pass my trousers . . . why?'

'There's a flap on up at *Luftflotte Funf* Operations. They've monitored an increase in R.A.F. signals traffic to Scotland. Mostly for Wick and Sumburgh. And we've just had a contact reported eighty miles nor'west of Solund – some cheeky bastard in a JU Recce claims to have downed one of the Tommies. . . .'

Fichte grimaced sardonically. 'What did he do – ram the sods?'

'. . . so arise, Pegasus, and do an extra turn for the *Führer*.'

Paul stopped grinning at the thought of it. 'What's happened to Bernie Eicke's patrol, or have they surrendered?'

Lusser started to look irritated. 'Fliegerhauptmann Eicke has been diverted to cover the area south of Björne Fjord. You're to make up the northerly patrol – Sectors Gustav Dora to Quelle Paula as a *rotte* with Söhler for your wingman.'

'Söhler?' Fichte glared up at the adjutant, 'I'd rather go alone than have that creepy little Gestapo tit-licker behind me.'

'Just get up, Paul boy,' Lusser muttered wearily. 'And do try to keep that big mouth of yours shut about Leutnant Söhler . . . even if he *is* a creepy little bastard, at that.'

H-HOUR minus 33 MINUTES

The flaming bomber and the falling bomber were still flaming and falling. In fact, it might have seemed, to an onlooker, that the two tumbling specks were competing in a race to see who could get down to the beckoning North Sea first.

Then, rather unfairly, the burning bomber just couldn't stand the competition any longer, and allowed its starboard wing to fold vertically upwards from the root, then the wing ripped away altogether in a suspended gout of spurting, igniting fuel. And then – as if pleased by the increased efficiency of the cleaner fuselage – the dying Blenheim shed its other wing, and the nose tipped forward until the red hot, now aerodynamically perfect cigar carried on down to victory.

But Pilot Officer Prescott was too busy to be a sportsman. And he didn't want to die like Ben Davidson had done only a few milliseconds before, so he just closed his eyes and hung on to the stick and waited for *his* wings to rip away too, while all the time the cold, hypnotic voice from the navigator's seat offered, 'Six thousand . . . Five five . . . five . . . Four five. . . .'

Dimly, over the intercom, he heard Alley starting to cry and a voice within his own mind kept shrieking, 'Thass it! That's your bloody lot, chum. And you often wondered what it would be like, din't you? An' now you know why those butterflies wouldn't go back to sleep this trip out. . . .'

Ian's catalogue went up a plea-filled octave. '. . . Thuree . . . Five . . . Thuree. . . .'

'. . . c'm*on*, you bitch, pull out. Pull *out*!'

The Blenheim started to shudder in agony and Johnny thought, what a bloody funny thing but even the sweat's running diagonally across my face with the centrifugal pull. . . . Then Ian yelled, 'Two thousand and levelling. . . .'

The vibrations increased to a racketing, slamming judder – and then stopped! Abruptly Prescott felt the stick nuzzle back into the belly of his Mae West with the passive acceptance of a blind man's guide dog and he started to grin foolishly at the orderly, completely reasonable set of instruments in front of him, but it wasn't until he felt the first droplet of perspiration hang in its proper place under the point of his chin that he finally knew they were flying again.

The A.S.I. read 880 feet. The bomber rocketed above the surface of the North Sea leaving a booming blast of expended power from the blurring airscrews as its only calling card. Three miles astern floated a spreading, placid patch of aviation fuel and – right in the centre of it – a rabbit's foot. And it must have been the luckiest rabbit's foot in the world, because there wasn't anything else left of a whole bomber.

Nothing else at all.

Johnny listened to Alley retching into the intercom and said thoughtfully, almost conversationally, 'That was Ben. That flamer?'

The Navigator hadn't moved since they passed through the six-thousand foot marker. Now he shifted cautiously, slightly disbelieving. 'Yeah . . . and the flask's gone for a burton too.'

So had the butterflies. But that was because Pilot Officer Prescott knew he should have died several seconds ago. Any time he had left was merely a bonus from God.

Or the Luftwaffe.

*

The small waves seen from the assault ships seemed larger, more menacing, from the fourteen landing craft as they circled and meshed into formation. To the sailors manning them it was all old hat except that this time it was for real instead of just another bloody nocturnal jolly off some Godforsaken Scottish beach. To the soldiers it was the last, and possibly the most gruelling, stage before they came into their own and practised the trade to which they had been apprenticed.

To the defenders of Ålvik it didn't mean a thing. Because they still didn't know it was even happening.

H-HOUR minus 30 MINUTES

It was then that one of the most insignificant but, at the same time, one of the most critical events of that day took place.

When a soldier gave a sailor a lift.

Or two sailors, to be precise. Leading Seaman Hopp and Ordinary Seaman Specht, en route to relieve their opposite numbers, Scherer and Balke at present on duty at the Hæl-en Signal Station.

Unlike their oppos, however, Hopp and Specht were very good friends, having served together in Hamburg before their transfer to 265 Naval Artillery Battalion. It was for this reason, and for their love of walking through crisp, clean snow, that they had decided not to use the bicycles provided for duty men but instead to stroll pleasantly and conversationally along the narrow track leading to the Point.

Since leaving their billet in Ålvik some twenty minutes before they had, consequently, strolled and conversed most intelligently, happy in the warmth of their friendship and in the knowledge that they were surrounded by many more good chums amongst the Garrison.

Except for Gefreiter Scherer of course, who was a right rotten bastard altogether. And far too masculine to be attractive, anyway.

They'd talked about quite a lot of things during their walk. From the most curious phenomenon of the suicidal Lemmings and their apparent affinity with those British Tommies of the Allied 8th Army who were launching yet another futile attack on the impregnable Feldmarschall Rommel's Afrika Korps – to the rather distressing shortage of silk stockings in the Berlin shops, as evinced to Leichtmatrose Specht during his last leave.

Of course, they stopped holding hands the very minute they first heard the motor cycle engine approaching from behind. In fact, if the Wehrmacht Corporal hadn't been quite so handsome and with such strong white teeth, they might never even have accepted his offer of a lift as far as the Signal Station.

And – if they hadn't – things might have turned out very differently on that cold, dark morning in the Østersfjord . . . . .

The gilded lattice doors of the lift slid erratically open on to the ground floor of the Norske Hotell to reveal the erect, immaculate figure of the Commandant in company with the squatting, haughty figure of the dog, Cuno.

Rhöme murmured gently, 'Come, Cuno,' and, together, they strode into the lobby just as the duty N.C.O., Unter-feldwebel Oehlschläger, swung shiny boots from desk to floor and slammed upright to rigid attention in one smooth, practised movement.

'*Guten morgen, Herr Major!*'

Rhöme smiled pleasantly. It was good to have such an efficient and polite reception first thing in the morning, and he hadn't actually *seen* Under-Sergeant Oehlschläger's feet up on the table. The Major firmly believed in the axiom that it's not what you do wrong that counts – it's if you get caught doing it which calls for the embarrassing necessity of a reprimand.

'Good morning, Unter-feldwebel. . . . Is my car waiting?'

'*Jawohl, Herr Major*! Your driver is outside also, *Herr Major*!'
Oehlschläger almost fell over himself rounding the desk to hold
the door open. Rhöme nodded politely and said, 'Come, Cuno,'
again, then strolled outside into the cold air thinking what a creepy
little toady the Unter-feldwebel really was. But efficient, though.
Damnably efficient.

He settled back into the rear seat of the open Mercedes, but not
too far. It was necessary to maintain a certain military bearing
when on view to any of the local townspeople. In fact, if it had
not been for the need to keep up appearances by using the official
car, he would very much have enjoyed the short walk down to the
wharf with Cuno. He didn't know that the Ålvik residents smilingly
referred to him as *Første Gir Major* – the First Gear Major.

Among other things.

In the port headquarters office a few hundred yards away,
Leutnant Sur See Rex glanced at his watch and, levering himself
to his feet, reached for his cap. It was nearly time for that silly
old woman, Major Rhöme, to arrive for the boating party. Trust
him to pick a morning when he had a convoy due to sail and when
the bloody paperwork was days behind schedule. God help them
all if the British ever decided to attack the Østersfjord. Unless, of
course, the Tommies obligingly gave them a couple of days'
notice. . . . Leutnant Sur See Rex, having already fought against
the Royal Navy, had never felt quite so secure in the knowledge
of the Third Reich's invincibility ever since.

Not like Naval Gefreiter Scherer, impatiently waiting for those
two poofs, Hopp and Specht, to relieve him for breakfast. Thank
God they were the exception. Mind you, they did say there were
more homosexuals than fighting men in the so-called British
Armed Forces, though – especially amongst their fighter pilots
and senior Naval officers. By God but he'd kick the poncy bastards
around a bit when he finally got drafted to London or Liverpool.
A gutless, decadent race like the Anglo-Saxons were a slight on
any Aryan true to the *Führer*. Worse than those stinking Jews . . .
or as bad as the Jews, anyway.

He peered through the window, trying to see if the kid Balke
was still on the ball out there. Balke worried him a little, sometimes. Maybe he was a bit queer too, which would account for
his quiet, passive acceptance of all the crap Scherer slung at him.

Hell, maybe he even *liked* it . . . ? The Gefreiter started to grin pleasurably at the idea. Perhaps he could have some real fun with young Balke sometime – but off duty, of course. A real navyman never let personal enjoyment interfere with watchkeeping. Not like those red-hot boys in the Waffen-S.S. and the Gestapo, able to mix business and pleasure while entertaining a few Jews or suspect Commies. He leaned back comfortably and began to think about his chances of applying for a transfer to where the real action was . . . by Christ but he'd like to have a few minutes with one of those fruity little Tommy *Kommandos* though. Like those bastards who'd sneaked ashore on the Lofoten Islands last March and set a few ineffectual fires before scuttling away like hell. . . .

Soldat Kruger, across the entrance to the fjord, wouldn't have minded a fire right then, not even if the arch-villain Winston Churchill himself had suddenly materialised to light it. Tentatively he tried to wiggle his toes inside the snow-encased boots – they said frostbite crept up on you before you knew it and, even though the snow of the past few days had turned temporarily to a sleety rain earlier on he was still nervous about losing a foot, or even a few numbed, useless fingers.

He peered at the luminous hands of his watch – still nearly an hour to go until his relief arrived. He'd arranged to do an extra turn for his mate, Hans Arndt, this morning in exchange for a similar favour from Hans to-morrow evening. There was a good film on at the Garrison cinema and Soldat Kruger didn't want to miss it. Errol Flynn was one hell of a fellow, even with sub-titles – he hoped they never had to fight the Americans. Not if they were all like Flynn.

He glanced wistfully over to the finger of yellow light marking the Wehrmacht guard bunker. Hitching his rifle sling higher on to his greatcoat shoulder he allowed his eye to traverse casually along the skyline, out past the three levelled, menacing silhouettes of the Navy guns in their sandbagged emplacements, and out to sea where an occasional fleck of white blinked fleetingly from the dark backcloth of the west.

It was funny, he mused distantly, how your eyes could start playing tricks when you'd been on guard a long time. Like that almost luminous shred of white water momentarily materialising over there – now to a man with imagination that could have suggested the bluff bows of an approaching craft buffeting into the

51

short chop of the waves. Except that he knew there weren't any arrivals scheduled for the Østersfjord that day. And, if you really let your imagination run riot, then what about those apparently more solid shapes farther out? That mist? The biggest patch over to the left – how about that for a battle-cruiser, eh? And the smaller, lower forms could almost be E-boats, or maybe even destroyers . . . ?

He grinned to himself and turned away, starting to think about Errol Flynn again. But then, Soldat Kruger had always been an unflappable, placid man.

So had Warner Lohemeyer. Or at least he'd always considered himself so . . . until he'd been given the responsibility of Bremen Convoy XJ23 to escort.

'What the hell . . .' he snarled at the *Patzig*'s second-in-command, Chief Petty Officer Krupinsky, 'What the bloody hell are they playing at over there?'

Krupinsky breathed heavily on the lenses of the ship's only pair of binoculars and, after polishing them with the thumb of his glove, leaned over the rail of the armed trawler's bridge. Young Lohemeyer still had a lot to learn if he expected the merchant service to be ready to sail the minute some kid of a Kriegsmarine snot dropped his hat.

Of the two ships anchored between them and the wharf only the nearest, the *Pökel*, showed any indication of life with the whisps of steam from her windlass rising into the cold air to signify they were ready to weigh. Aboard the beat-up Baltic trader farther away there wasn't a sign of anyone – not unless that was a couple of blokes lounging up there on the *Wismar*'s bridge.

'Maybe we should give them a flash-up?' he suggested indifferently. He wasn't in any hurry personally. Bremen wasn't his favourite port.

Lohemeyer glared at him. '*Leutnant* if you please, Oberbootmannl'

'Herr Leutnant Sur See!' Krupinsky acknowledged wearily.

'Yeah! Well, we'd better call her up on the lamp. Now.'

'*That's* a good idea . . .' Krupinsky said admiringly. '. . . *Herr Leutnant Sur See!*'

*

It all indicated 'Situation Normal' in the port and surroundings of occupied Ålvik. The strategists and planners of MO9 waiting around a radio set nearly a thousand miles away hoped it would remain so.

For another twenty-five minutes, anyway. Until His Majesty's Ship *Hystrix* opened fire.

Chapter Three

'Troops will land simultaneously at 08.10 hours G.M.T. (B.M.N.T.). . . .'

Operational Orders. Force King.

H-HOUR minus 27 MINUTES

B.M.N.T. . . . Less than half an hour away now.

The critical time. The time when the night first begins its retreat from the inevitability of the advancing dawn. That moment of every day – long before the actual rising of the sun above the distant horizon – when the velvet anonymity first surrenders its intensity, and when the blacks ever so delicately become formless but visible greys. When a running man can be detected farther than a stone's throw away. And when the tip of a fore-sight can first be centred in the leaf of a back-sight. . . .

. . . Beginning Morning Nautical Twilight.

The time when the killing was planned to start. And the Being Killed.

＊

The double column of landing craft were now entering their tenth minute of the run-in to the beaches. At a buffeting, cork-screwing six knots that placed Lieutenant-Colonel Duncan's L.C.A. One precisely two thousand yards from their release point.

And bisecting a theoretical line extended from the tip of Gefreiter Scherer's cigarette on Hæl-en to the frozen condensation ringing the muzzle of Soldat Kruger's 98k Carbine, across the fjord at the Oksenes Battery.

The Østersfjord was one and one-tenth of a mile wide at this, its narrowest seaward point. The other duty rating at the signal station – the lookout, Leichtmatrose Balke – saw nothing at that particular time. Had his senior rate, Scherer, only been a little more willing to take his proper turn of duty out in the cold then it was just possible that the now frozen ordinary seaman might have stopped shuddering for long enough to keep a careful watch – but still highly unlikely that he would have seen anything. A Landing Craft Assault is a very insignificant sliver when over half a mile away. And it wasn't even near B.M.N.T. yet.

Willie Bradbury's *Muscadin* wasn't exactly insignificant, though. Not even to a numbed, disinterested onlooker. And the destroyer was due to enter the Østersfjord in another three minutes and thirty-five seconds. Very slowly too, for a destroyer capable of thirty-seven knots, but you can't use your speed as a defence when you're dawdling solicitously in the wake of fourteen plodding shoe boxes.

But if Scherer and Balke were ignorant of the close proximity of the Royal Navy at that moment, then the Royal Navy most certainly knew precisely where the nearest branch of the Kriegsmarine were serving their *Führer*.

In fact, the Royal Navy was pointing the anticipatory and highly lethal muzzles of *Muscadin*'s multiple pom-pom right at the Signal Station on Hæl-en. Just to prove it.

✳

Not that Willie Bradbury, sitting coolly on the destroyer's exposed, open bridge, actually knew that messmates Scherer and Balke were out there to port. All he was concerned with was that the R.A.F. recce photographs had betrayed the existence of some form of observation post and, as his sole function at this stage of the jolly was to provide cover for the L.C.A.s, then cover them he most emphatically would.

And Christ help any Hun astute enough to blow the gaff.

It wasn't even that Willie grudged Leading Seaman Scherer the acknowledgement of a piece of weaponry larger than the midships pom-pom. In fact, had it been within Willie's power, the gallant Gefreiter could have had a 4.7-inch naval shell all to himself, the Captain of *Muscadin* being nothing if not a generous man. But there were also the vital and more threatening guns of the Oksenes Battery on his starboard hand to consider, to say nothing of the cinema-struck Soldat Kruger. Which was why *Muscadin*'s 'A' and 'B' Turrets slowly traversed aft as the greater menace crept abeam.

Nobody moved aboard the destroyer as she nosed silently between the rocky pincers of the entrance. Flash-hooded and steel-helmeted seamen chewed thoughtfully and tensely with eyes screwed tightly against rubber-cushioned gunsights or night-coated binocular lenses. Other men stood waiting amid the warm brassy gleam of stacked ready-use ammunition, or in the hot, oily atmosphere of the gently vibrating engine-room where a spanner had to be clutched tightly so that it couldn't drop deafeningly to the chequered steel plates below.

A lot of them were frightened. Yet others among them were starting to experience a sense of exhilaration unlike anything they'd ever felt before. Some were actually happy.

Very, very few of them were bored.

Softly, unexpectedly, a slight, keening wail broke the silence surrounding the bridge. Eerie at first in its remoteness, almost inhuman in its quality, then gradually becoming more and more familiar as the source was noted.

Tautly strained faces became smoother suddenly, and nervous men smiled gladly into the no longer quite so frightening darkness.

'Om! Tiddely om, pom . . . tiddle iddle om pom . . . !'

Willie Bradbury was beginning to enjoy himself.

*

That same rain which had fallen on to the faces of the Ice Man and the Cooked Man in a far-away rubber dinghy had also, for a very short time, provided an equally unwelcome change to the fitful snow showers which had dappled Ålvik for the past week. It hadn't lasted long anyway, and those puddles which formed had almost immediately frozen again and become lost in the hollows and clefts of the terrain.

So it was with the slight dip formed in the track from the town to the Hæl-en searchlight and flak posts. And to the Naval Signal Station.

But before it had returned to its frigid, crystalline state that rain which had fallen had first trickled and crept downwards, seeking its lowest level. And this it had succeeded in doing some twenty paces from the eighteenth field telegraph post east of the Point. After a short, sharp battle to retain its fluidity the rain had finally succumbed once again to the dropping temperature. But not before it had smoothed and dissolved the original snow blanket to a glistening mirror-like surface.

It meant that that particular section of the track was now a super-efficient skid-pan.

But neither the very good friends Hopp and Specht nor the handsome Wehrmacht Corporal with the strong white teeth were aware of this natural phenomenon as they approached the dip behind the weak yellow beam of the motor cycle combination's shuttered headlamp.

At the start of the downward gradient the speedometer registered forty-eight kilometres per hour. A very safe and commendable speed.

For a dry surface.

*

Every man in 22 Commando had been issued with one hundred rounds of ammunition. They also carried, between them, fifty magazines for the Brens, two dozen cases of Mills Grenades, twenty illicit 2-inch mortar bombs for the equally illicit mortar and – in the case of the demolition teams – 280 pounds of plastic explosive, 150 pounds of ammonal, 1000 pounds of guncotton, 150 incendiary bombs, 80 primers and 1500 feet of fuse.

Troop-Sergeant Arthur Henderson also had an eight-inch double-edged knife. He hadn't been a violent or a vicious man in peacetime but, then again, he hadn't been a widower either.

He was now crouched forward, up in the bows of L.C.A. Three, the second craft in the port-hand column and directly astern of the Colonel's boat. It was a good place to see what was going on about him. It also meant that he would be one of the first soldiers of Group Two to meet the enemy defences as they went up the bamboo assault ladders and on to the town's Nordkai. He hoped he wouldn't be killed at that stage, and let Ginny and the kids and Jim down after all.

Corporal Loomis, kneeling beside him, nudged his shoulder and pointed over to the left with the barrel of his Tommy Gun. For a moment all Henderson could see was the black shape of the land, broken occasionally by sickly patches of lighter snow. Then he saw the light moving jerkily out from the town, a tiny glow-worm gradually creeping past the secret men in the middle of the fjord.

Loomis whispered, 'A car?' and the Sergeant shrugged. Nobody was talking very much in the boat. It was a time for private thoughts for most of them.

But he couldn't help gazing across the cold dark water to where the slowly travelling glimmer occasionally disappeared from view, presumably as it passed behind the mask of a rocky outcrop. And he couldn't help wondering, either, about the man who was driving that anonymous vehicle. Was he tall or short? Was he dark or was he fair and blue-eyed in the finest traditions of the pre-war pro-Nazi journalist's sunburned Teutonic youth.

And would he, Troop-Sergeant Arthur Henderson of Number 22 Commando, have to kill that far-away man before the day was out?

He watched the light blink out and then reappear once again, and chewed his lips uncomfortably. It was such a bloody simple question – but it suddenly created such a lot of problems, when you once allowed yourself to think about it. Because if you did kill him, then how many other people were going to die a little, or maybe an awful lot, along with the man behind the yellow lamp?

Maybe that passaging enemy had a Ginny too. Except in his case she'd be a Hilde or a Berta or an Ilse . . . and that meant kids perhaps, with happy expectant faces and all the unfettered love a child could show for a daddy who was at least twenty feet tall . . . !

He swallowed hard then, because it suddenly reminded him that all he had now was a hole in a tenement block, and a lot of unforgettable memories. That made it a bit easier, somehow, to stop asking too many questions about the first man to appear in the peep sight of his rifle.

But to destroy all those people face to face? Like a predatory animal? Without any compassion or remorse?

He drew the eight-inch knife from his gaiter and, after a moment's hesitation, dropped it over the side of the landing craft. Just for a moment the icy touch of the wind lifted from his face and he smiled at something or someone no one else would ever see. But that was his secret – his and Ginny's.

It was also why Arthur Henderson could never be a really bad man. Not even after all the bombs in the world had been dropped.

Trooper Williams, sandwiched between Charlie Smart and a stack of grenade cases in the stern of L.C.A. Eight, saw the light too, but as far as he was concerned all it meant was that one distant field grey bastard was going the other way, and that was O.K. with Danny.

Gloomily he fingered the satin-smooth skin of the contraceptive Charlie had given him to put over the muzzle of his Lee-Enfield – 'Keeps the barrel dry an' stops it gettin' V.D. at the same time, mate!' – and brooded that, if he'd had one of those that night behind the bus shelter with Norah, then he wouldn't have been riding with this bloody boatload of homicidal maniacs right now, f'r Chrissakes . . . !

Charlie muttered anxiously, 'I'm gonna be sick,' but Danny just glared at him out of the corner of his eye. 'And I got sick a helluva long time ago, mate. . . . Swop around so's you can get it over the side.'

There was a silence, then Charlie's shadow bent forward abruptly as the L.C.A. took another sharp drop into the trough of a wave. The involuntary revulsion on Danny's face was wiped off instantly when the spray flew back in the wind, needle-like in its icy flail.

Charlie wiped his mouth shakily with a khaki handkerchief. 'It doesn't matter,' Charlie said. 'Not any more!'

Danny felt the warm wetness of bile soaking through to his right thigh and thought viciously, 'That's what *you* bloody think, mate!' while pondering on the further caprice of fate which had placed a seasick chatterbox right next to him in this seagoing sardine tin.

But that got Danny started on thinking about the result even one large calibre round would have amongst the tightly packed bodies if it penetrated the lightly armoured sides of the landing craft. Gradually he stopped feeling aggrieved about Norah and, instead, began conjuring up skin-crawling images of a drifting slaughterhouse of corpses with him, Danny Williams, trapped and suffocating on the blood-slimed bottomboards. . . .

He began to feel frightened. For the very first time in his life.

*

Strangely enough Captain Michael Seely, even now still pink and tingling from his labours over his cabin washbasin, didn't feel at all nervous any more. In fact, ever since he'd climbed aboard L.C.A. Twelve besides its Leading Seaman Coxswain he'd only felt a slight surge of anticipation at what lay before him and the other fifty-nine men of his Group Five after they'd splashed ashore on Oksenes, behind the Battery emplacements.

Ahead of him, into the fjord itself, everything seemed quiet. Ålvik proper lay somewhere over there on the port bow, about two miles off now, but the Jerrie blackout was pretty good. No lights at all showing from the town. Farther over to his left, almost at right angles to their track, there was one twinkling light – a vehicle of some kind heading west – and, just for a brief moment, the dim golden glow silhouetted the steel-helmeted heads lining the length of L.C.A. Nine in the other column.

There was another glimmer of yellow over there to the right. That must be coming from the Sørenson Factory at Sörsund. It didn't seem to be very high above the water so perhaps it escaped from a vessel lying alongside the jetty there. Bert Stenhouse would make very sure that wasn't the only light burning by the time he and his eighty-odd Troopers pulled out. Fish oil tanks should burn bloody lovely, and the Mad Major had enough incendiaries to set the Østersfjord itself ablaze.

Just for a moment Seely felt a slight pang of jealousy – maybe there's a little bit of the arsonist in everybody – then he grinned cheerfully. Spiking the guns of Jerrie's coastal battery wouldn't exactly be a dull job either and, if it came to a choice, Mike had a leaning towards blowing things up rather than burning them down anyway.

Glancing astern he looked over the dimly perceptible bulk of Sergeant Knox's following craft – containing the other thirty men of his group – and tried to make out the shape of *Muscadin*. For a second he thought he could make out a momentary flash of phosphorescence just about where the destroyer's bows should be, then it vanished and no one could have guessed there was a ship there at all.

He swivelled forward again. Just as well too. The one thing they didn't need right now was advertising. If, by any mischance, the assault force was detected before H-Hour then *Hystrix*, *Salamander* and *Muscadin* would commence firing immediately –

and the pin-pointed Commandos would have to press on to their
objectives in the full glare of a naval bombardment. He swallowed
quickly and tried to think about something else . . . his Mae West,
for instance. At first it had seemed bulky and uncomfortable but
now he was glad of the warmth it afforded his chest. Even two
vests and three jerseys didn't seem to be very successful at keeping
the Norwegian winter at bay. And the fold of the lifejacket also
provided a handy little pouch for the three Mills Grenades he'd
stuffed inside.

But, please God. Don't let them see us. Not just yet . . .

'I think we're on our holding station now, Sir!'

Seely nodded gratefully to the Cox'n, still only a vague shape
beside him. 'Thank you . . . we'll break off then.'

The landing craft heeled slightly as the Cox'n put the helm
down and, trailed anxiously by Knox's Fourteen, they swung away
from the line of the column. And safely out of the path of *Muscadin's* knifing bows. Mike caught a glimpse of a white blob of a
hand raised in salute as L.C.A. Eleven plodded straight on towards
Ålvik, then they were gone into the dark future which lay ahead.

The Leading Hand cut the engines and the silence shuttered
down over the two crafts as they lay silently side by side, linked
together by a tenuous umbilical cord of manilla. Seely peered at
his watch – it said a quarter to eight.

It seemed very quiet and very peaceful out there. And a very
long twenty-five minutes ahead of them, when all you could do
was think.

✳

Out on the Hæl-en observation platform Leichtmatrose Balke had
never felt so utterly frozen in all his nineteen years of life. It was
so cold he was nearly crying with the pain in his hands.

That was why, when he quite ridiculously imagined he saw the
denser black form of a ship out there in the fjord, he couldn't even
get his fingers round the cylindrical lenses of the Zeiss binoculars
slung around his greatcoat neck.

Not at first, anyway.

✳

Muscadin's First Lieutenant watched the delicately glistening
barrels of 'A' and 'B' Turrets train the last few inches until they

were traversed precisely abeam then said, with only the very slightest trace of resignation, 'Well . . . we're right in it now.'

'The fjord . . . or the shit?' retorted the Navigating Officer.

Number One pulled a face under his steel bowler. 'Take your pick, they're both one and the same really.'

'Um tiddely om pom . . . !' said the Captain.

*

Just before the motor cycle reached the bottom of the dip Leading Seaman Hopp, snug in the bouncing, rattling combination, felt Specht's warm gloved hand sneak surreptitiously into his. He smiled happily and squeezed just a little to reassure his very good friend up there on the pillion that he wasn't really jealous of the broad-backed Wehrmacht Corporal who chauffeured them so ably to their place of duty.

Though he did think Willi had kept his arms around the Corporal's waist just a *little* longer than had been completely necessary to maintain his balance when they mounted.

But it really was most pleasant just sitting here comfortably as the snow-covered sides of the mountain echoed the engine's brisk note, and the telegraph poles carrying the lines from Hæl-en to the Norske Hotell flashed past like stately, erect lances, reflecting the beam of the headlamp. . . .

The patch of frozen, burnished snow at the bottom of the dip reflected the glow too, but by the time he'd seen it and throttled back it was far too late for the Corporal to do anything other than stamp involuntarily on the motor cycle's footbrake pedal . . . though at any speed above a crawl it is most inadvisable to do anything other than pray when you're already broadsiding down a glassy, frictionless bitch of a hiiiiiiiiill . . . !

The waltzing combination's speedometer was hovering un-decidedly between the forty-nine and fifty kilometres per hour mark at that specific moment when the nearside front wheel collided shatteringly with an unyielding granite slab bordering the track. Hopp was already screaming when he felt the sidecar lift beneath him and propel him with awful force high into the air.

Leichtmatrose Willi Specht stayed with his very good friend until almost the last moment as, still holding hands as tight as could be, they flew together into the night.

Their devoted togetherness ended only when Hopp's skull,

shoulder blades and most of his spinal column were driven into a bloodied pulp on colliding with the stout Norwegian Fir forming the eighteenth field telegraph post east of the Hæl-en Signal Station. Whereupon little Willi Specht completed the last milliseconds of his short but perverted life as a lonely, arcing bullet which stopped shrieking only when the waters of the black Østersfjord closed ever so finally over his head.

He never came to the surface again.

The handsome Corporal didn't die for quite a long time after the accident, but when he finally did he was probably glad to. The blued-steel barrel of his Schmeisser MP38 sub-machine-gun had been driven completely up through his stomach as far as the base of his right lung.

Of Field Telegraph Post Number One Eight, only a stump remained erect. The rest of it lay amid a tangle of ruptured telephone wire and shattered insulators across the monstrosity which had been Kriegsmarine Gefreiter Hopp. The only other immediately recognisable protrusion was that of an arm and a hand.

There was no apparent explanation as to why the hand should still be fondly clutching someone else's blue woollen glove.

There was now no longer a telephone link existing between the Hæl-en Signal Station and the Garrison switchboard in Ålvik's Norske Hotell either.

*

From the bows of L.C.A. One the Colonel noticed the wandering light on the north shore suddenly blink out, but he didn't think anything more of it.

He was still trying to determine whether to have his one personal whim – in the awe-inspiring and kilted form of Pipe-Corporal McLusky – play 'The Black Bear' or 'The Barren Rocks of Aden' as he led the Commando ashore.

The Colonel finally decided that, while the latter had merit in its association with the local physiography, 'The Black Bear' still had the more traditional and blood-stirring edge to it.

And the very skirl o' it would scare the bloody wits out of any defending German within half a mile of the Nordkai.

'Where?'

'Over to your lef . . . to port, Herr Gefreiter! And still moving into the fjord.'

Scherer grabbed the binoculars in disgust, fumbling irritably with the knurled focussing wheel. It was cold out here, damned cold, and it wasn't even as though he hadn't given that creepy little fairy, Balke, a ten-minute break a little while ago. But now the selfish bastard was grasping at straws – anything to while away the last few minutes of his watch. Like pretending he thought he saw a *ship*, f'r God's sake. . . .

Even the rubber eye-pieces of the Zeiss 10 × 60s felt like ice-cubes against his brow as he began to scan the gap between them and Oksenes. Hell, but if he hadn't had a most highly developed sense of responsibility towards his juniors he'd have kicked young Balke's arse for him on the spot, and told him to get back out on watch like a proper sailorman. Instead – like the superlative senior rate he was – he was doing his duty.

And *then* he was going to boot the little cretin's ass. But good!

Through the lenses of the binoculars the peaks of the far-away mountains seemed so close Scherer felt he could almost reach out and touch them with the tip of his finger. He noted, with a slight twinge of disappointment, that the eastern sky was already beginning to lighten as the first flush of the new day approached. Scherer was a man who liked the night. You felt bigger, somehow, when it was all dark about you. Bigger, and more of a secret, powerful person.

He levelled the glasses until they covered the fjord itself. Bloody Balke! It was like staring into a pot of tar in a blacked-out coal cellar. He swivelled along towards the Sørenson Factory, getting more and more disgusted and more and more frozen by the second.

'Listen, you! You give me any more of your imaginary shi . . . !'

Scherer stopped dead. Stopped talking and stopped moving.

He saw a ship, too, now. Almost directly abeam of where he stood. And immediately he knew without any doubt that something terribly wrong was about to happen to Ålvik.

*

The car flying the Commandant's pennant stopped in front of the Harbour Office. Herr Major Rhöme waited with great dignity for his driver to run round and open the door then, with Cuno following passively, stepped on to the ice-speckled quayside.

The Major acknowledged the driver's salute with a friendly wave from the peak of his cap and strode into the office calling cheerfully, 'Come, Cuno!'

Cuno came. But only after a warning growl at the driver, who had never quite managed to capture the animal's affection.

The driver snarled 'Fucking dog!' right back. But he didn't like Cuno either. Or think all that much of the terribly nice Major Otto Rhöme, for that matter. You had to hate an officer to really admire him.

Leutnant Sur See Rex waited fractionally as his assistant, Chief Petty Officer Döring, slammed to attention, then stepped forward to greet the Commandant. The Major smiled, generously waving Döring back to his seat. Informality must be the keynote of his relations with the Kriegsmarine – let them see the Army didn't have to rely on pompous frivolities to maintain discipline. You had to like an officer to really admire him.

'Good morning, my dear Hafenmeister.'

Rex noticed that the Major's salute was a military one and not the outstretched arm of the Nazi. Acknowledging, he thought, 'Good for you, Herr Kommandant! Perhaps there's more to that placid exterior than meets the eye.'

He said, 'Good morning, Sir! Your launch is waiting. My deputy, Oberbootmann Döring, will be your aide for the Sörsund trip.'

Döring lifted his Schmeisser and steel helmet from the rack and moved impassively towards the door. The Major smiled cheerily then winked with great camaraderie at Rex, indicating the sub-machine-gun. 'It would seem I am in capable hands, Leutnant. The Oberbootmann is obviously prepared to take on the whole Royal Navy by himself.'

The C.P.O. held the door open respectfully. 'I should be grateful for the opportunity, Sir . . .' he said, '. . . but not *too* many of them all at one time!'

But Döring was not only a sound and dependable seaman. He was also endowed with great good sense.

Three miles to the west, on the gently heaving bridge of the Flagship, the Admiral and the Brigadier had been standing side by side just gazing inshore for the past few minutes, each lost in his own thoughts and responsibilities. Each praying, in his own secret way, that nothing would happen at this critical juncture to alter the minutely pre-planned sequence of the attack.

Braddock-Tenby eased the tired muscles of his calves and momentarily switched his gaze to the hunched figures of the two Army signallers, both waiting intently for the first break in the static mush from their field radio headsets to indicate an incoming transmission from the assault troops.

And that – at this stage – could only mean premature discovery. Strictly observed radio silence was to be maintained by all units until the very second of H-Hour itself . . . unless they came under direct fire from the enemy ashore.

Rather unnecessarily, for he already knew every chronometrical tick of the operational schedule, Braddock-Tenby murmured, 'Where are your chaps now, John?'

The Brigadier smiled inwardly at his opposite number's polite formality in asking the Army where the Army was. He slipped the wrist of his glove back. Nine minutes to eight.

'Dougal Duncan's main force will still be making for the town and the ambush point, roughly three thousand yards to go. . . . Stenhouse should now be lying off the Sørenson Factory while Groups One and Five have already been waiting on their holding stations off Hæl-en and the Battery respectively – that's Lieutenant Courtenay and Captain Seely. . . .'

'Seely? Isn't that the young man who's celebrating his birthday to-day?'

Aubrey glanced up in surprise. One didn't really expect a Rear-Admiral to reveal an interest in the strategically irrelevant details of comparatively junior Commando officers, albeit ones within his own command. His respect of Braddock-Tenby – already considerable – climbed even higher.

'Twenty-six, actually. Seely's twenty-six this morning. . . .'

The Admiral raised his hand politely. 'Then please excuse me, John . . . Chief Yeoman?'

'Sir?' A vague figure detached itself from the huddle at the after end of the bridge.

The little boy twinkle in the Admiral's eye was lost in the darkness. 'A signal to *Prince Michael*, please. As soon as communications are de-restricted . . . IMMEDIATE UNCLASSIFIED . . . DISPATCH BOAT TO COLLECT ITEMS ONE AT . . .'

The Admiral frowned momentarily. He wasn't quite sure how long one took to bake a birthday cake. '. . . AT 13.00 HOURS ZULU OR AS SITUATION PERMITS . . . ACTION ADDRESSEE FOR CONSIGNMENT CAPTAIN SEELY . . . ahhh?'

'Michael Joseph, I understand,' the Brigadier ventured, straight faced.

'. . . SEELY letter M letter J! And send it with my compliments, Chief Yeoman. . . .' Braddock-Tenby rubbed his hands pleasurably, 'Oh, and perhaps you would ask Commander Supply to be good enough to come and see me as soon as he's free?'

The Brigadier waited until the Chief Yeoman had gone, then murmured, 'A cake, I presume? Very decent gesture, Arthur. Thank you.'

'It's not a lot.' The Admiral looked wistfully over to where the mouth of the Østersfjord had swallowed 22 Commando. 'Not in return for what they're doing for us. I do hope he enjoys it.'

But what he really meant was – 'Dear God, please let him and the others come back from there. Just so that they can start afresh to enjoy *all* the good things in this life. . . .'

Though he already knew, when he asked, that a great many of them wouldn't.

*

Scherer jiggled the telephone receiver for the twentieth time and snarled nervously, 'Christ but the Wehrmacht couldn't string the lamps on a bloody Christmas tree without a fault. . . . *Achtung! Achtung*, switchboard!'

Angrily he slammed the handset into its already battered cradle and chewed his lips worriedly. Suddenly he noticed his hands were shaking and viciously dug them into his pockets so that Balke wouldn't see. God only knew what that was out in the fjord, but if she'd been German she'd undoubtedly have been flashing the day's recognition signal. And there most certainly weren't any arrivals logged as expected. . . .

An' where the hell had relief Gefreiter Hopp an' his pansy pal got to? This was one burden he desperately wanted to share – even with a couple of poo . . . !

Balke entered the room diffidently, tugging at his gloves with frozen fingers. 'It's out of sight, Herr Gefreiter. The ship. She's too far down the fjord to follow with the glasses.'

Scherer snapped desperately, 'When she was first abeam . . . did you see *anything* to suggest what type she could have been? Anything at all, man?'

The kid hesitated and Scherer could see the unwillingness to commit himself written all over the stupid, oafish face. It never occurred to him to wonder why. All he could think of was those great big brown cow's eyes staring back at his so bloody vaguely.

Suddenly he couldn't stand the fear that was twisting in his guts a moment longer. He took one step forward and struck the boy angrily, full across the mouth. Balke slammed back against the door and just leant there, half crouched like a terrified animal with one gloved hand dabbing ineffectually at his bloodied lip.

'*Anything at all*, you *dümmling* landlubber . . . ? *Anythiiiiiing . . .?*'

Unbelievably, the kid started to cry and Scherer felt a black rage overpowering him. Something was wrong, terribly wrong, and all that blubbering imitation of a real sailorman could do was worry about Number One! He drew his foot back, only wanting to kick, smash, batter the need for urgency into Balke.

Then the youngster sobbed, 'No . . . *please*! It . . . she seemed to have something up forr'ad. One, maybe two . . . I think they were gun turrets. I think she was a warship . . . !'

Scherer froze, foot still raised, like a ridiculous statue cast in Kriegsmarine blue.

For suddenly he realised – with unchallengeable perception – that he didn't need to hunt for action with the Royal Navy any longer. Instead, the Royal Navy had brought it all the way to Gefreiter Scherer. In person.

And he couldn't even phone anyone to tell them!

✳

For one unit of King Force it was almost broad daylight – as seen from the cockpit of Prescott's lonely Blenheim, now droning steadily towards its target at a comfortable, and it was to be hoped, safe twelve thousand feet. To Johnny it was one of the nicest times to be flying, when all the world below was still wrapped in black tarred paper while, high above it, you hung in a great multi-hued vault with the blues and yellows and mauves stroking the main-plane with ever so sensitive washes of constantly changing colour.

Except that you didn't have time to sit back and really savour the sky's infinite loneliness, because the war made those same vast reaches not quite so empty. And the towering, fleecy banks of cumulus hanging so placidly across the southern horizon could also spew forth the terror of the pouncing Heinkel or Messer-schmitt.

Nobody aboard O-Orange had said much since that last time when Ben Davidson's crew had ridden the flamer right into the North Sea. Johnny was glad in a way – he still couldn't shake off the bad feeling which had stayed with him all the way from Wick. He was also worrying about how the hell he was going to lay smoke over four separate targets when there was only enough in the bomb bay for his scheduled one . . . the beach to the east of the Oksenes Battery, and one other in an emergency.

Unless they picked up the other two members of the flight in the next few minutes. The two remaining ones, that was. He hoped.

Ian stirred abruptly. 'We should be raising the Norwegian Coast pretty soon. . . . I estimate eighteen minutes to the release point.'

Prescott nodded. 'We'll pull the plug now, then. I'll take her down to one thou until you can pinpoint, then we'll make our run-in at . . .'

'Fifty!' Ian muttered gloomily. 'Fifty feet! It's engraved on my bloody heart.'

Johnny grinned tiredly. 'You're just upset 'cause you missed your morning coffee.'

The Navigator shook his head positively. When he spoke it sounded a bit more like the old Ian Johnny knew.

'No!' he said succinctly. 'No, it's more my afternoon tea I'm hoping to be in a position to bloody enjoy.'

Then Alley's taut voice came down from the upper turret. 'Two o'clock starboard . . . I see an aircraft.'

Oh my God, Lohemeyer thought bitterly. It's not escorting this convoy that's going to be difficult. It's getting the bastards together and sailing in the first place. . . .

Krupinsky ambled towards him from the wing of the tiny bridge, grinning broadly. 'The *Wismar*'s acknowledged readiness at last, Leutnant. An' the *Pökel*'s fair snubbing at her cable to get away. . . . Now all we got to worry about is the *Staatsmann* arriving on time from the head of the fjord an' that whatsit tanker. . . .'

'The *Bluthund*!' Lohemeyer muttered, suddenly glad of the Chief's capable, if somewhat irreverent presence aboard.

'Yeah, her! Well, if she's ready to get under way as we go down past the Sörsund jetty, then we're full ahead for Bremen.'

'You've forgotten about the *Käte Hass* alongside the Nordkai, Oberbootmann,' Lohemeyer said, childishly pleased at catching his second-in-command out on something. Anything.

Krupinsky stared at his Commanding Officer as if utterly shocked by his lack of faith. 'Oh, her? Hell, but she's been ready to sail for *ages* now . . . Herr Leutnant Sur See!'

*

On the Nordkai itself, and just ahead of the bows of the *Käte Hass* in question, yet another Chief Petty Officer was providing moral support to a Commissioned Rank.

'It's really quite large, Herr Kommandant. Completely seaworthy, I assure you.'

Major Rhöme looked doubtfully from Oberbootmann Döring's patiently attendant figure and down over the edge of the wharf to where the sullenly heaving launch lay alongside, the white faces of her three crewmen gazing upwards respectfully. Farther out, despite the slowly increasing dawn light, all the Major could see was black, evilly beckoning water with an occasional white cap as a wave, slightly larger than its companions, reared fitfully and excitedly out of the smother.

He shuddered – discreetly, of course, so that the Navy people wouldn't notice. More than ever he regretted his momentary bravado in suggesting a water-borne visit to the factory guard.

And it could have been such a pleasant, relaxing trip in the back of the Mercedes, all the way round the head of the fjord.

The Major drew himself up and took a deep breath. 'Come, Cuno!' he said. And started down the weed-encrusted steps.

It was not for nothing that Herr Major Otto Rhöme was a proud holder of the Knight's Cross, Second Class.

Even if it *had* been awarded during the First World War.

*

Scherer said desperately, almost pleadingly, 'Look, kid. Get on your bike an' get down to Ålvik fast . . . straight to Hafenmeister Rex at the Nordkai. D'you understand?'

He hesitated, watching the young Leichtmatrose closely while, all the time, his guts churned acidly with tension. Scherer now had two worries to cope with. Firstly the anonymous warship which was still moving inexplicably, and to all intents and purposes undetected as well, into the fjord – and, second, the charge he knew was hanging over his head from that very moment he'd lashed out at his junior rating.

And to Scherer the hypocritical wrath of that narrow-minded bastard, Oberbootmann Schwarzhaupt, was even more terrifying a prospect than the arrival on Ålvik's doorstep of the whole of the British Home Fleet.

Then he started wondering if maybe the whole of the British Home Fleet *was* out there anyway, and started to feel even more desperate . . . while having to force himself to be uncharacteristically solicitous in the hope that the *dummkopf* Balke might keep his somewhat ravaged mouth shut about his, Scherer's, minor breach of the regulations – *that* wasn't helping his twanging nerves hellish much either.

Balke sniffled a bit more, then seemed to pull himself together, spurred by the urgency of the threat. Hating himself for every reconciliatory gesture, Scherer stepped awkwardly forward and sort of brushed the kid's coat with a huge hand, then set the flat Kriegsmarine cap at the regulation angle – while all the time a frustrated voice in the Gefreiter's brain kept on screaming, 'It's over five minutes since you first raised that ship out there, an' all you can do is ponce this gutless little bastard up like a Hamburg tailor's dummy . . . ?'

He twisted his mouth into the travesty of a reassuring smile.

'Now you nip off like a good lad . . . report to Leutnant Sur See Rex himself, mind.'

The youngster hesitated and Scherer's heart sank. Now what?

'Excuse me, Gefreiter, but . . . would it not be quicker if I ran over to the searchlight post, or the ack-ack gun? They have a telephone, maybe even a field radio link with the Commandant's office. . . .'

Scherer's tortured patience snapped for the second time within five minutes. 'I said the Harbourmaster, dung brain . . . !' he bawled uncontrollably. '. . . that's an Army post over there, an' this is a *Navy* matter . . . an' anyway, I wouldn't ask the Wehrmacht to post a bloody letter . . . !'

He stepped towards the door and hurled Balke's rifle after the fleeing figure. If it did get jammed with snow and mud, so what – the ignorant little sod wouldn't know what to do with it anyway.

Then he returned to the arms rack and took down his own 98k Carbine. Flicking the safety lever to the vertical he pulled out the bolt stop on the left of the receiver and withdrew the bolt itself. He started to clean it carefully feeling, as he did so, the tension draining out of him and, instead, that pleasant sensation of power which handling a weapon always seemed to give him. He rather hoped it really was the British out there.

Gefreiter Scherer was a proper bastard in anyone's navy. But he wasn't a coward as well.

H-HOUR minus 15 MINUTES

At long last the Convoy was going about the leisurely business of getting under way.

In the *Wismar*'s antiquated wheelhouse Hans Strobe lounged behind the varnished mahogany wheel, idly watching the dimly lit compass card swing gently in its alcohol suspension. From forward the windlass on the foc'slehead rattled excitedly as it dragged the anchor cable protestingly into the open maw of the hawse pipe. Strobe noticed a steam line was leaking, spurting little white suspended clouds from the deck gland to wreath Katzmann's legs as he stood at the windlass controls.

Hans Strobe liked Katzmann very much. Oh, maybe he wasn't all that close a friend in many respects – for instance, he seemed strangely diffident about going ashore with Hans, especially in a German home port – but at least he was talkative. And even that was something nowadays, ever since the Jews had become second-class citizens in the eyes of the Third Reich.

He still couldn't stop worrying about his mother and sister back in Nienburg, though. And it all seemed a bit ironic, really – seeing he was more concerned about what the S.S. or the Gestapo might have done to them than the British. . . .

Up in the bows the First Mate's features gleamed momentarily as he turned to face the bridge. His right hand pumped up and down – the anchor was off the ground. Strobe gripped the spokes of the wheel with practised anticipation, the first helm order of the voyage was due.

Beside him the Second Mate toyed with the brass handles of the telegraph. Strobe noticed the ring of a pyjama collar peeping from above the Second Mate's blue roll-neck jersey and grinned surreptitiously at the compass card. Herr Bögel was quite a decent bloke too, for an officer – not that a couple of gold rings on a man's sleeve meant much aboard this broken-down hulk of a ship, but at least the Second didn't put on any airs about it.

Bögel smiled back. 'Going home out of the cold, eh, Strobe? To warm women and strong beer.'

The Captain's voice, with its rough Silesian accent, called from the starboard wing. 'Dead slow ahead. . . . Starboard ten!'

Hans leaned on the wheel spokes with his right hand as the Second Mate swung the telegraph back, then forward. Below them, from the grimy, dust-laden engine-room, the reply jangled back and the ship started to shudder gently.

'Ten of starboard wheel on, Herr Kapitan!'

'Ease to five.'

'Ease to five the wheel!'

The compass card spun slowly to the left, away from the lubber line, as the *Wismar* churned round in a wide circle with the blacked-out buildings of Ålvik falling away astern through the port wheelhouse door. Strobe noticed a few shaded lights on the deck of the *Käte Hass* as they singled up her lines, ready to join the convoy. Alongside the jetty steps and overhung by the merchantman's bows a Kriegsmarine launch seemed about to leave with a party of V.I.P.s, judging by the way the bowman was going through some pretty flashy boathook drill up forr'ad.

The windlass stopped clanking abruptly from the foc'slehead and Strobe watched as Katzmann screwed her down tight. The vagrant whiffs of steam died to a somnolent trickle, almost as if cowed by the ferocious scrutiny of First Mate Krupp as he bent down to inspect the gland. Strobe almost felt a ridiculous sense of sympathy for the steam – Krupp was the one man who really scared the hell out of him. But the First Mate had a son serving with the *1st S.S. Panzerdivision Leibstandarte Adolf Hitler*, and you couldn't get more anti-Semitic than *that*.

The Old Man wandered into the wheelhouse accompanied by a choking cloud of smoke generated in the charred bowl of his permanently clamped briar. The *Wismar*'s Master was, without doubt, the smelliest man Strobe had ever known. He positively reeked of tobacco and tar, and hemp and cabbage and Munich beer.

But he still didn't stink of Jewry. If he had, then he'd never have stayed a Captain.

'Half speed, Bögel.' Puff . . . puff . . . puff. . . .

The telegraph flashed again, verdigrised brass reflecting only sombrely the light from the binnacle. Above the wheelhouse the *Wismar*'s stick of a funnel puttered frenziedly as the revolutions built up under her counter. One of the wheelhouse windows began to rattle and a fine powder of dislodged snow speckled the glass as the wind veered from ahead to abeam under the turn.

The Old Man leaned out of the starboard door, watching critically as the ship's head swung on to the escort, now also under way. Strobe could see the stubby, unwarlike silhouette of the armed trawler quite clearly now, with the shapes of her wing-mounted machine-guns and foredeck main armament contrasting oddly with the rest of her. As the light from the east gradually straddled the mountains he could even make out her name and numbers, painted in bold white letters against the grey hull – 236 . . . *Patzig*.

'Midships the wheel!'

'Midships . . . wheel's amidships, Herr Kapitan!'

'Steady.'

Strobe deftly corrected the swing, laying the ship's head square in the centre of the dark blob that formed the seaward end of the fjord. Just for a moment he thought he saw a fractionally darker patch right in the middle – almost as though there was another ship there – then he dropped his eyes to the binnacle to read the course.

'Steady on . . . nor'west by west, Herr Kapitan.'

'Puff. . . . *Gut!* . . . Puff, puff!'

Patzig . . . ! Strobe smiled bleakly to himself. *Cheeky!* What a hell of a name for a warship, because that's just about all they could be if they ever met the British on one of these coastal hops . . . not that they were ever likely to. Not this far north. Not when what was left of the Royal Navy was now too busy in the North Atlantic trying vainly to combat the super efficient U-boat offensive. He didn't think there'd been a British ship near the Norwegian coast since . . . oh, since the Narvik affair. And that was pretty damned cheeky too, when you thought about it. The way the enemy had created utter havoc, sinking seven German destroyers after chasing them nine miles into the fjord. . . . But he only knew about that from a friend who'd been wounded while serving his gun for the *Führer*.

And *that* was pretty ironic as well, really. Because his friend – now a one-legged cripple – *he'd* been a Jew too. As well as a patriotic German.

Which got Hans Strobe back to wondering, and worrying, about his mother and sister back in Nienburg.

H-HOUR minus 12 MINUTES

The Officers' Mess at Herdla Airbase was beginning to fill up. White-coated mess waiters scurried urgently among the Luftwaffe uniforms dispensing basketfulls of hot rolls and steaming pots of indifferent coffee to – so it seemed – those extroverts who shouted loudest and most diligently.

Fliegerhauptmann Fichte glanced at his watch and pushed his chair back stubbing his cigarette into the saucer before him. From across the room Leutnant Brandt waved cheerily and bellowed 'Overtime, eh? Tell me, Paul, do you just like flying or are you trying to impress the Reichsmarschall?'

A roar of laughter went up as Paul grinned back. 'All I want to do for the Herr Reichsmarschall, Brandt, is line that big fat ass up ahead of my prop an' . . . !'

The mess suddenly went quiet. Everyone seemed to stop talking all at once as even the waiters hesitated in their frantic haste. Fichte felt his voice trail off and turned slowly, aware of a vein in the side of his forehead pulsating angrily.

The handsomely arrogant features of Leutnant Söhler stared curiously at him from the doorway. Söhler murmured, 'Please continue, *Herr* Fliegerhauptmann . . . I am sure the Tommies will wait while you expound on your plans for Herr Reichsmarschall Goering's discomfiture.'

Fichte took a step forward, the flush of temper burning his face in tiny red patches. He was aware of the tension in the room but he didn't give a damn. No junior officer was going to challenge him before the whole squadron, and there was something more in Söhler's attitude – a thinly veiled threat?

He forced himself to speak slowly and deliberately, choosing his words with extreme care. 'Get your little black notebook out first, Söhler. The one your *Geheime Staatspolizei* bosses issued you with. . . .'

A teaspoon fell to the floor with a tinkling echo. No one moved to pick it up again.

'. . . an' I'll state, precisely and succinctly, just exactly what I think of our pasty-faced, pudgy little Commander-in-Chief, Leutnant.'

Fichte took another pace towards Söhler who stood, tensely drawn, less than a roundhouse swing away from him. 'It's spelt with a "B", Söhler . . . B . . A . . S . . T . . ARD! Write it down . . . it's a word the Gestapo should be more than familiar with.'

The youngster in the doorway was white as a sheet, Fichte could see the sweat varnishing the forehead under the yellow hair. That's it, Paul boy, he thought wearily – that's you scheduled for an intimate little chat with the boys in the black suits. He grinned viciously, defiantly, right into Söhler's pale blue eyes.

'There's an adjective to go with it, Leutnant . . .' Paul said softly, '. . . it probably suits you too, on reflection. And that word, you good little Nazi ponce, is . . . *Queer*! Queer as a nineteen Mark note!'

Someone laughed nervously from the back of the room. Another voice, he thought it was Brandt's, muttered, 'Easy, Paul, for God's sake.'

But Söhler didn't move. He just stared bleakly back at Fichte with the thin lips compressed into a straight, bloodless line.

'Don't make too many plans for your future in the Luftwaffe, Fliegerhauptmann. The State may consider you need . . . a rest.'

Paul nodded thoughtfully. Then he smiled at the kid. It was a lovely, promising smile.

'And don't, Herr Leutnant, forget you are *my* wingman for this morning's patrol. It means you have neither the rank nor the skill to be anything other than the obnoxious little shit which you undoubtedly are. . . . Now go and wind your aeroplane up before I smack your tight little bottom, there's a good boy.'

The thin lips quivered fractionally as Söhler's eyes opened wide with disbelief. 'I'm not surprised,' Paul thought ruefully. 'I've just presented you with a public confession of dissidence, Söhler boy. Like Christmas Day in the bloody dungeons. . . .'

He drew himself up, staring at the fair-haired Leutnant with haughty Teutonic arrogance. It was the only approach Söhler would understand. 'I gave you an order, Söhler. . . . Now, *get out!*'

Just for a moment he could see the hatred mingling with the ruptured pride at the back of Söhler's eyes, then the kid's arm shot out in a viciously presented Nazi salute. Fichte caught the low, strangled, *'Jawohl, Herr Fliegerhauptmann!'* just before the Leutnant spun on his heel and practically ran out of the room.

A movement at his shoulder made Paul turn. Gerhard Lusser was gazing at him strangely, rather sadly. Behind him the mess was still a sea of watching faces. The Adjutant muttered uncomfortably, 'I warned you, Paul. About tilting at Söhler.'

Fichte gazed at his friend coldly. 'You heard?'

'I couldn't help it. We all did.'

'And you still allowed him to threaten me? A senior officer?'

Lusser's face was ashen. 'He's not like other. . . . Damn it, it isn't just a simple question of rank, Paul. Don't you understand?'

Fichte nodded slowly, bitterly. 'Yeah! Yeah, I understand only too clearly. . . .'

He turned towards the door, then hesitated. '. . . God help the Luftwaffe, Lusser. In fact, with your kind of fear, then God help Germany . . . because us poor bloody Germans won't!'

He strode out of the mess unseeingly. Deep down in his belly he felt the first delicate touch of death. Somehow he knew now that it was to come, and very, very soon, too. The only questions which remained were when. And how?

And by which side?

*

In the Østersfjord itself they were a bit short of white china cups aboard the L.C.A.s – either with or without a glazed Luftwaffe Eagle crest and the accompanying silver teaspoons.

But they did have sixty gallons of sluggishly thick, steaming cocoa and, to a man taking the early morning winter air in a boat off the coast of Norway, a hot drink is equally acceptable whether it's from a pewter tankard, a galvanised bucket or a W.D. – issue mess tin.

Especially if the flavour of the kai is surreptitiously bolstered by a measure of Navy Rum passed on from illegally bottled matelot's tots. For while the British sailor is notorious for his antipathy to a khaki uniform he is equally renowned for his hospitality and generosity to a Pongo on passage.

Which was why quite a few of Number 22 Commando's members felt the pleasurable warmth of real Jamaica Spirit seeping through numbed bones on that bleak November morning.

That Navy cocoa, laced with the delicate sunshine-promise of molasses, was the thing which, for many of the soldiers, put the big 'C' in Combined Operations.

*

In Blenheim O-Orange a sardonic voice from the Navigator's seat put the 'C' in a rather shorter, four-letter word.

'Silly what?' Prescott queried, glancing up from the altimeter now hovering on the one thousand foot marker.

'Him,' Ian grinned, relief showing through the nervous creases around his eyes. 'Dai Evans down there . . . they haven't even seen us yet an' we're close enough to spit down his collar.'

Johnny eased the Mae West which had started to rub the back of his neck uncomfortably and levelled off, looking at his watch. Two minutes to eight. They should be picking up the Norwegian coast any moment now. . . .

'Who's riding the upper turret with Dai to-night?'

'Bernie Glass. New kid, replacement for Taylor.'

Johnny nodded silently. Flight-Sergeant Taylor had been killed in the most ridiculous way possible – on the ground, and riding a *bicycle*, for crying out loud. Johnny had actually seen it happen, four days ago out on B Flight dispersal. The ground crew were running a mag test on a factory-fresh kite – full boost with the plane leaning forward against her chocks like a raging, tethered bird and the powdered snow shrieking and whirlpooling a hundred yards astern under the blast of her slipstream – when Doddy Taylor had cycled, head down and legs pumping like pistons, round the corner of the crew hut.

One of B-Bertie's crew, lounging outside the hangar door, had shouted something after the furiously pedalling air gunner. Something about being late for his own ruddy funeral. . . . Taylor had half turned in the saddle, grinning like an overstuffed Teddy bear through the muffler wrapped around his neck, then the bike skidded uncontrollably on the runway ice.

And Doddy, still with that frozen, ghastly grin on his face, had wobbled unerringly into the spinning prop of the Blenheim's starboard engine.

Prescott gripped the stick involuntarily as he remembered how the shimmering disc had turned abruptly to pink, then bright contrasting red, then back to a shimmering, insubstantial silver halo again as the bottom half of Flight-Sergeant Taylor finally stopped pedalling. . . .

And how the hell d'you tell an elderly couple in a little Somerset cottage that their only son has been killed in the war. But not by a bullet, Dad. In defence of Freedom. No! Run over, actually, and by a bloody aeroplane!

Alley's disembodied voice floated down. 'He's seen us at last, Skip. Or maybe he had his alarm clock set for eight, anyway.'

The Navigator dryly sucked a hollow tooth. 'He'll never make it 'til half-past then. Not unless he learns to see properly.'

Johnny leaned across Ian and stared down at the other Blenheim. Thank God it *was* another of the boys and not a patrolling *Schwarme* of 109s from Herdla. A white face gleamed briefly through the port cockpit window – Pilot Officer Evans making rude gestures – then Ian stuck two retaliatory fingers up while Prescott flopped back in his bucket seat.

'Pilot to Turret. . . . We're ten minutes from our aiming point. I'll be taking her down low in a few moments, Alley. When I do, you keep watch astern. . . .'

Ian pointed. 'I have the coast now.'

'. . . Roger! There shouldn't be too much flak. Not from two towers.'

Ian muttered gloomily, 'There doesn't bloody have to be. Not if it smacks us on the nose.'

Johnny eased the stick forward and O-Orange dipped gently, heading for the sea in a long, shallow glide. Out of the corner of his eye he saw Dai Evans's kite float, apparently vertically upwards. Then his opposite number started his descent too, and the two Blenheims temporarily lost sight of the coast again as their horizon distance decreased.

Less than eight hundred feet below them at that point they passed over their first German.

But the yellow dinghy was an almost white dinghy now, and virtually indetectable from the creaming wave caps that supported it. And the tall, horribly burned Luftwaffe Flugzeugfahrer couldn't possibly have seen them either, not even if he'd still been alive.

Not with a half-inch blindfold of ice encrusting his open, empty eyes.

*

Ice was also forming aboard the big ships lying patiently off the entrance to the fjord. Hardly apparent, only the very faintest patina deposited by the millions of particles of frosted glass drifting out to sea on the off-shore wind, but still there nonetheless. Still forming a natural hazard for unwary sea boots hurrying along iron decks or gloved hands reaching over-hastily for steel ladder rungs.

The cold had another side effect too, in that it provided a visual indicator to reveal the coming of the dawn. Admiral Braddock-Tenby noticed it first as he allowed his eyes to roam restlessly over the silent, silhouetted figures on the cruiser's bridge.

Now, for the first time, he could detect the fuzzy wreaths of condensing breath-clouds hanging momentarily under steel helmet rims. Just before the north-easterly airs captured, dissipated, then bore them triumphantly away above the snatching fingers of the covetous North Sea.

He glanced up, turning slightly aft to where the angular profile of the six-inch director tower reared bleakly above the open bridge.

And above that, the high tripod foremast spiralling in erratic whorls against the shredded sky.

But he could also see something else – other details which had been, up to this time, lost in the camouflaging darkness of the November night. He could now make out, quite clearly, the swing of W.T. aerials and signal halyards, the latter rising in tautly tethered array from cleats to their individual blocks suspended from the crosstrees.

And above everything, presiding over the ship like a great white flapping bird, *Hystrix*'s Battle Ensign streaming and rippling proudly from the masthead itself – the Red Cross of Saint George arrogantly, defiantly even, inviting the laying of enemy shot towards them. That same Flag which had flown over sturdy, plunging British Ships of the Line at Barfleur and St Vincent, and Trafalgar.

'But not yet.' The Admiral thought anxiously, 'Please God, not quite yet. Not for another seven minutes . . . until those young men are in position, and I can fire first!'

H-HOUR minus 10 MINUTES

Leutnant Sur See Rex stepped awkwardly out of the Harbour Office door and on to the quayside. Glancing at his watch he noted gloomily that it was precisely eight o'clock and, as ever, the convoy was still swanning about, trying to find its formation for leaving harbour.

Straining his eyes to pierce the gloom he could just make out the vague shapes of the *Wismar* and the *Pökel* cruising stolidly and unco-operatively off the anchorage, waiting for instructions from *Patzig*. He grinned broadly to himself – Werner Lohemeyer was the worrying kind anyway, and now they'd given him that broken-down armed trawler to command, along with a handful of extra-bloodyminded merchant masters, the officious Lohemeyer was well and truly embarked on a one-way voyage to the burble house.

Even as he watched a signal lamp started blinking from *Patzig*'s toy bridge. Directed up the fjord in the vague direction of the still invisible reserve anchorage, where one hoped against hope that the *Staatsman* might be more or less ready to leave, the shaded light ordered plaintively . . . TAKE UP POSITION ASTERN PORT COLUMN . . . IMMEDIATE . . . IMMEDIATE . . . IMMEDIATE EXECUTE!

A splash made Rex turn. The last line from the *Käte Hass* had been cast off, winching up through the stern fairlead like an ever-decreasing length of spaghetti. The space between the ship and the Nordkai began to widen as the bow swung out into the fjord. From deep inside the belly of the freighter Rex could hear the muffled tinkle of engine-room telegraphs and, with a creamy swirl of disturbed water, she started to move slowly ahead – her last link with Ålvik severed.

He glanced up towards the bridge. The lumpy shape of the *Käte Hass* skipper leaned over and out, critically observing and assessing the clearance of his stern. He saw Rex and raised a hand in grudging salute. Rex smiled again – it was that age-old reservation which created a barrier between mercantile and fighting seamen of all nations.

Waving back he called, 'Give my regards to Bremen, Herr Kapitan. I trust you have a good voyage.'

'*Auf wiedersehen, Herr Hafenmeister!* No doubt we shall, God willing . . . and the Tommies!'

Leutnant Sur See Rex turned away, back into the warmth of his office. He couldn't possibly have known then that – while God's intentions were still, at that time, somewhat obscure – those of the British were quite positively tending towards the aggressive.

H-HOUR minus 9 MINUTES

Leichtmatrose Balke was still running. In fact, the young seaman hadn't stopped running since that moment when Gefreiter Scherer summarily dispatched him on his errand of warning. Balke was not, however, a particularly fit young man and already his lungs were pumping agonisingly, dragging in great sobbing gouts of air to fuel tortured muscles.

His back hurt where the butt of his rifle had caught it, just under his left shoulder blade. And now the four-kilogram dead weight of the 98k Carbine was sending stabbing pains up his arm

82

to knot neck muscles in agonies of strain. And his boots were hurting too. Chafing his heels with sadistic persistence. . . .

At least he was warm though. Too damned warm under the heavy bridge coat. Feeling the sweat smearing his brow and trickling in jerky rivulets down the side of his nose, he started to drag the coat off as he ran, only vaguely aware of the road ahead.

Just as he struggled to get the first arm out of its sleeve the snow-powdered surface under his pounding feet commenced to slope away downhill. Involuntarily Balke ran faster, a weird bat-winged figure flying uncontrollably through the night under the stately canopy of the Norwegian Firs. Like some monstrous legendary Troll from the folklore of the Ice Country's nightmare past. . . .

. . . until his greatcoat tails wrapped with devilish ingenuity around pumping, runaway legs and Very Ordinary Seaman Balke completed his descent as an avalanching octopus of flailing arms, legs and obstinately clenched rifle.

For a few dizzy seconds Balke just lay there on his back, staring up at the nodding branches above and feeling the cold wetness of clinging snow as it succumbed to his body heat. There was another factor which his addled brain couldn't at first reconcile – a harsh, rasping keen rising above the sigh of the trees. Then he realised it was his own tortured breathing.

He sobbed, 'Shit!' with feeling, knowing that it was a bad word but not really caring any more.

Then he struggled painfully up on one arm, half turning for support.

And froze. Rigid!

Because Leichtmatrose Dieter Balke had never looked deep into the open, reproachful eyes of a dead man before.

Not from an intimate, flesh-crawling distance of six inches away.

*

At 08.01 Hours Greenwich Mean Time someone else was having trouble with his eyes too. And that was the placid Soldat Kruger, still standing lonely watch over the 105 mm Heavy Battery on Oksenes Point.

Except that Kruger wasn't feeling quite so placid now, not

when the light from the east was gradually feeling and probing over his shoulder, piercing the heavy grey blanket to seaward and uncovering the previously secret, shifting surface of the ocean.

Because those patches of mist which Kruger had idly catalogued into battle-cruisers and E-boats and destroyers . . . they were still there. But the strange thing was that there were only four of them altogether, almost directly abreast of where he stood, while on either side of him the dark line of the horizon appeared clear and unbroken. Not even the faintest concentration of suspended fog above the restless wave caps . . . *and* there was a wind now. And wind blew all the mist patches away together, didn't it . . . ?

But it didn't do a damn thing to *warships*, f'r God's sake . . . !

Kruger started running towards the beckoning light from the Wehrmacht guard bunker. His shrill, disbelieving voice was snatched by the wind and overpowered under the steady crash of the North Sea as it clambered and swirled frustratedly against the foot of Oksenes cliff.

'*Feldwebel Voss . . . ! Kommen sie hier. Schnell! Schnell . . . !*'

It struck him then that Errol Flynn wouldn't have hurried. Not one bit. But, come to that, Herr Flynn wouldn't have needed Feldwebel Voss either . . . !

*

'A cake . . . ?' Cook Petty Officer Chalk exploded. 'Whaddyou mean . . . a *cake*?'

The supply rating shrugged uncomfortably, eyeing with barely concealed amazement the long line of white-garbed men still slicing, buttering, pickling and all the rest of the assembly line expertise which went into producing the *Hystrix* complement's picnic lunch – if a hurried sandwich swallowed in the cordite-reeking aftermath of a six-inch salvo could be described as a picnic.

'A birthday cake, P.O. . . .' the supply rating muttered again. 'Twenty-six candles . . . an' it's gotter have "Michael" on the lid.'

'Jesus *Christ*!' Chalk echoed disbelievingly.

'No, P.O. . . . *Michael*,' the supply rating corrected helpfully.

Chalk stared at the youngster accusingly, then shook his head slowly as if hardly able to credit the kind of mentality which could call for a birthday cake to be baked less than four minutes before the ship was due to go into action.

'Who wants it?'

The supply rating shuffled awkwardly. 'I got told to see you by P.O. Blantyre. . . . He's Petty Officer Supply.'

Chalk stared at the kid heavily. 'I know *that* much already. In fact, it's surprisin' how many petty officers I do know aboard this boat, seein' I bloody *am* one . . . an' who told him?'

'Chief Petty Officer Supply, P.O. . . . His name's . . .'

'McClusky!'

'Yes, P.O.'

'Ah! So who told . . . ?'

'Him . . . ? Commander Supply, P.O. . . .'

Chalk nodded. 'An' we all know *his* name, so you don't need to say it even. You wouldn't happen to know *why* he wants a birthday cake too, would you?'

The supply rating shook his head positively. 'Oh, he doesn't, P.O.'

It was just too much for Herbert Chalk. Four thousand beef sandwiches – they were O.K. Just a dawdle. But a birthday cake? And now, apparently, for nobody . . . ? He looked appealingly along the line of bread stackers towards his friend and senior colleague, Cook Chief Petty Officer Lumley who – noting the S.O.S. glint in Chalk's eye – approached comfortingly.

'. . . the Admiral does, P.O.,' the supply rating finished rather lamely. 'It's the Admiral wants the cake.'

'What cake?' asked the newly arrived Lumley interestedly, wiping his hands on his snowy apron.

'Oh, not again!' moaned the frustrated Herbert.

'A birthday cake, Chief P.O.,' repeated the supply rating with the patience of a man with nothing else to do anyway. And everybody knew they weren't quite the same as other people, down here in the heat of the galleys. 'It's the Admiral. He wants a birthday cake.'

Apprehensively Chalk waited for the explosion. Lumley could be a terrible man when roused – especially in the middle of four thousand sandwiches and two thousand, three hundred and fifty pints of tea. Figuratively speaking, of course.

Lumley drew himself to his full, majestic height and smoothed his apron with great dignity. He skewered Herbert with a steely, professional look.

'Then we'll require half a pound'v butter, half pound castor sugar, ditto currants an' candied peel . . . an' was it green, white

85

or pink icing the Admiral wanted, lad? An' how many candles . . . ?'

But that was why Cook Chief Petty Officer Lumley *was* a Cook Chief Petty Officer in His Majesty's Royal Navy.

H-HOUR minus 8 MINUTES

Apart from birthday cakes, the one factor that the planners of the Ålvik Raid couldn't possibly have anticipated was that the Bremen-bound convoy XJ23 was scheduled to sail at the precise moment when the seven landing craft of the H.Q. party were also due on their waiting station off the Nordkai.

Not that it would have mattered all that much even then – if it hadn't been for the additional fact that the outward bound course of the German ships coincided exactly with the inward track of two hundred and twenty-odd slightly trigger-happy British and Norwegian Commandos.

Not to mention His Majesty's Destroyer *Muscadin*.

In fact, it was one of *Muscadin*'s bridge lookouts who saw the vague, swinging shapes of the sheep-like merchantmen first. The young ordinary seaman, crouched well down into the enveloping folds of his duffle, stiffened as the dark silhouette of a vertical-stemmed ship swam into the range of his binoculars, the faintest smother of water under her forefoot visible even from that distance through the Barr and Stroud night-coated lenses.

'Ship, Sir! Bearing red zero zero five!'

The still, seated figure of the Captain was already bringing his own glasses on to the bearing. 'Thank you. . . . Guns.'

'Sir?'

'Target for 'A' Turret. She may be a warship.'

The First Lieutenant moved urgently at Willie's elbow. 'She's slap in the L.C.A.s line of approach to the jetty, Sir. . . .'

Both bridge lookouts called together this time. 'Two ships now, Sir!'

'Three . . . *four*!' said the First Lieutenant a few moments later.

'. . . knock on the door. Thank you everybody,' murmured Willie thoughtfully, his mind racing to cope with this new and rather inconvenient problem. But Willie Bradbury's philosophy of life was that you couldn't make an omelette without breaking a few eggs – now all he had to ensure was that the eggshells were

Kriegsmarine blue wherever possible, and not khaki worsted, W.D. weave.

He lowered the binoculars. 'Midships . . . ! Stop both engines!'

Almost immediately the vibration cut below the bridge as the red and green painted revolution indicators sank back to zero. The Captain glanced at his watch then at Number One. 'Three minutes before the bombardment commences. Chances are that Jerrie down there'll be too busy sailing his boats to watch for anyone coming up the garden path. I propose to sit it out for now.'

The First Lieutenant jerked his head forward. 'What about the assault group, Sir? We can't risk signalling towards the town.'

'Hobson's Choice, Number One. If we hold them back at this stage, then they'll have that much farther to run the gauntlet when the balloon does go up. Continuing as they are, there's still a good chance they'll remain undetected.'

The First Lieutenant chewed his lip, eyes fixed on the faint white tails of foam trailing behind the receding landing craft. So this was what a Combined Operations was all about. When a sailor made a decision which involved the lives of soldiers . . . and based, in all probability, on a plan formulated partly by an airman.

But he was damned glad he wasn't that particular sailor right then, all the same. Though he did agree with Willie's reasoning – that the L.C.A.s would see the distant enemy ships before they themselves were detected, being that much lower in the water and that much more alert.

He just hoped to God the Germans would go along with the assumption too.

And if they didn't . . . ? Well, there was always 'A' Gun to attract their attention. Unless *Muscadin* was pulverised into a flaming coffin first. Drifting heedlessly under the command of a dapper corpse, and manned by a roasted crew of dead men. . . .

*

Which was pretty close to the line of thought currently being pursued by Trooper Danny Williams, still hugging his Durex-capped Lee Enfield in the gyrating after-end of L.C.A. Eight, now lying waiting off the Sørenson Factory jetty.

He was getting a bit browned off with Charlie Smart being sick all over everything in the ruddy boat too. Not that Charlie was the only one suffering, judging by the peculiar retching sounds coming from farther forward. Hell, it wouldn't be quite so bad if they were allowed to raise their heads above the level of the thinly armoured sides, just to have a look-see shorewards. But the Mad Major out there in Number Six had ordered them to keep down – as if it was going to make the slightest difference should some cat's-eyed Jerrie range in on them from the beach.

Charlie vomited again, a dried-up, exhausted spatter of misery. Danny glared at him nervously. 'That's that cocoa, knothead. I told you you shouldn't've had the bloody cocoa!'

Charlie raised his head wearily, black-camouflaged face a steel-helmeted blob of chalky mosaic in the darkness. Danny noticed absently that, for the first time, there was enough light to give a sparkle to a man's eyes. Even a man as ill as Charlie. Or was it tears he could see . . . ?

'Oh Gawd!' Charlie groaned faintly. 'How long to go, mate?'

Williams shrugged. He had a watch on but he was damned if he was going to struggle through a woollen mitt, a shirt cuff and three jersey sleeves just so's Charlie Smart could know the time.

'Dunno! Maybe a coupl've minutes. You in a hurry then?'

'Jus' thinking. With a bit of luck some kind bastard might shoot me soon as we hit the beach. . . .' Then Charlie's head tipped forward abruptly and it was eyes down for Private Smart as usual.

'Spew your ring over me again, chum, and you won't need to wait 'til you get ashore!' Danny turned away, partly in disgust and partly to prevent his own stomach churning in sympathy. Then the full import of what he'd just told Charlie Smart – about there only being another couple of minutes or so left before the assault started – hit him, and all the fearful images began to crowd back into his mind.

Anxiously, almost desperately, he craned his neck to see forward, looking for something – anything – to distract his thoughts. Anything at all, apart from a sea of backs and packs, and weapons and steel helmets and webbing shoulder straps. . . .

Troop-Corporal Hanson, for instance. What was he peering at with such intense concentration? Something white . . . ? Then Hanson tipped it awkwardly to one side to catch whatever light there was, and Danny saw it was a *book*, f'r crying out loud.

The Corporal noticed Danny watching and grinned sheepishly. 'That Norwegian phrase book they issued. Full of fascinating conversation pieces. F'rinstance, here's one you just *got* to keep on the tip of your tongue ... Kan yay faw chope ... Oh hell! ... Noh-en ... prohspehkt-kort!'

'Meaning?'

Hanson smiled again, teeth white against the black mask. 'Can I buy any picture postcards?'

Danny tried to smile back but didn't quite manage it. 'Maybe they should've given us another edition. Like how you say – "Don't shoot, I've already surrendered" ... in German.'

Hanson stuffed the book back into the breast pocket of his B.D. blouse, then glanced at his watch and gripped the blued barrel of his Tommy Gun just under the foresight. The casual, matter of fact way he did it made Danny glad he wasn't a German.

'Doesn't that depend on whether you want to understand what Jerrie's saying, Williams ... or so's you can *tell* him?'

Then Charlie was sick again.

Christ, but it was a bloody awful way to fight a war.

*

Still down on his hands and knees at the foot of Field Telegraph Pole Number One Eight, Leichtmatrose Dieter Balke was thinking much the same thing. Except that, in between uncontrollable spasms of revulsion, he was trying to solve an additional problem – of whether to pull the barrel of the Schmeisser out of the Wehrmacht Corporal's belly or not.

The trouble was that, having already inspected the casualty's blue-tinged features from close range, Balke was fairly certain that the man was already dead. Yet if, on the other hand, he still retained a spark of life then, indisputably, being skewered on the muzzle of an MP 38 wasn't going to help him far along the road to convalescence.

But young Balke hadn't seen a corpse before – apart from when Father had held his hand so very tightly in that darkened, hushed room a long time ago. And, even then, his mummy had still looked pretty in the eyes of a curious, bewildered little boy. Not like the Corporal. . . .

He clambered shakily to his feet and stood looking down, with the short hairs at the back of his neck crawling with the horror of it all, and wondering, if he sort of half closed his eyes, would it help to diffuse just a little of the detail.

Then he forced himself to ignore the cold sweat streaming down his face, and gripped the stock of the machine-gun firmly with both hands while all the time whispering, 'Sorry, Herr Korporal, but I will be gentle. . . . Sorry, Herr Korporal, but I will be. . . .'

A tail-end of the dying gale sneaked over the mountains and shook the tops of the black trees with impish fingers. A faint wail of anguish swept the forest, brushing the young sailor's shoulders with a fine dandruff of powdered snow. He looked up fearfully, closed his eyes. . . .

. . . and pulled! Ever so gently.

But nothing happened. Only the wide eyes of the butterfly-pinned cadaver staring up at him incredulously, almost as if unable to credit this final fumbling desecration of its person.

Balke let out a shuddering explosion of pent-up breath, bit his lower lip until the pain brought tears to his already swollen eyes, and pulled again. But this time in a frantic, rather than a gentle, way. Like a mother desperately picking a fat-bodied spider from her sleeping child's face.

Until as the probing Schmeisser foresight compressed the long dead lungs, the corpse in the military shroud belched. The slackly grinning mouth opened until purple lips drew back from yellow teeth – and a gush of foetid air exhaled in a long, keening shriek of despair.

Balke let go of the gun butt as if it had been suddenly transformed into a deathly cold maggot. Eyes wild, he stumbled back, arms held protectively before him.

'Jesus . . . Jesus *Gott*!' he whispered through the bile that flooded his throat.

And then he fell backwards. Clean over the impacted half body of the man who'd flown into a telegraph pole.

Actually, it was the first time Dieter had ever met Willi Specht's very good friend and companion, the late Leading Seaman Hopp.

*

The bulkhead-mounted clock in the cruiser's six-inch director tower said 08.04 hours zulu.

Beneath it, leaning forward in his padded swivel chair, the Gunnery Officer spoke quietly into his telephone headset.

'All guns! One round star shell. . . . Load!'

Ålvik only had one minute left.

In the bows of L.C.A. One the Colonel was practising loading
the Verey Pistol for the twenty-third time. It had become an
obsession with him that he had to get those three green flares up at
just the right moment – in those few exposed seconds before the
assault craft took the ground – in order to signal to *Hystrix* to
lift her bombardment, and for the R.A.F. Blenheims to place their
smoke bombs ahead of the landing areas.

He was wishing now that a little more foresight had allowed
him to bring three ready-charged pistols. . . .

Tyndal, the Bren-gunner, said urgently, 'I see a ship, Sir.
Away in front of us.'

The Colonel forgot about Verey Pistols and stood sniffing
searchingly, like a pointer on the scent. 'Good Man . . . where-
away?'

Tyndal gestured over the bell-shaped muzzle of the Bren.
'D'ye see yon dark patch that's the town, Sir? Well, she's over to
the right, maybe a hundred yards off the shore . . . it looks an
awfy big boat, Colonel.'

'It's only if she's got awfully big guns that I'll be worrying,'
the Colonel thought grimly, straining his eyes to pierce the gloom.
Tyndal had damned good night vision, all the same. Not – the
Colonel smiled softly despite the worry he felt – that it was surprising, really. Brigade rumour had it that Tyndal had been a
professional salmon poacher on the Tay, before the Army had
poached *him*.

He saw her just as the Bren virtuoso said irritably, 'Och, now
there's bloody two . . . three . . . Jeeze, *four* boats now, Sir!'

The Colonel's mind raced, trying to assess the situation just
as Willie Bradbury had done two minutes before. He gazed forward
again. The four ships were suddenly quite clear now, even their
masts visible against the dark mass of the mountains forming the
inland end of the fjord.

He glanced aft, towards where *Muscadin* lay and, seeing nothing,
immediately grasped the strategy behind her Captain's reasoning.
He nodded thoughtfully, absently watching as a wave, bigger than

the rest, reared above the side of the plodding L.C.A. in a glinting, white-streaked hummock. 'Aye, Commander. You stay back there like a big, secret grey ace in the pack . . . but keep yon wee guns o' yours pointing down here, if you please.'

He knew that, in the next sixty seconds, *Hystrix*'s star shell would flood the fjord with light, right across the entrance and the Oksenes Battery. All he could do now was hope the glare wouldn't spill too far and reveal the assault craft carrying Groups Two and Three strung out like ducks in a vast shooting gallery.

Tyndal cuddled the butt of the Bren into his shoulder and said with supreme confidence, 'It's all right now, Colonel. Ah'm ready to have a go anytime ye want.'

'Thank you, Troop-Lance-Corporal,' the Colonel answered with extreme gravity. 'But we may be as well to wait for the cruiser to fire first. . . . Just to give you support, of course.'

Tyndal considered his Colonel's request in silence for a few moments, then nodded generously. 'Aye, all right, Sir. But just so long as they're no' expecting us to leave *all* the skilled work for they Navy lads.'

*

As Fichte snapped the buckle of his safety belt and patted the emergency ration kit stuffed into his knee pocket into a more comfortable lie, the ground crew chief below the ME's wing-tip held up a thumb.

Paul glanced shortly to starboard – Söhler's plane was ready too, but the little bastard was just sitting in the cockpit, staring straight ahead like a spoilt kid. Fichte treated him to a haughty, cold glare of open contempt and swung back to the ground chief. He changed the glare to a friendly grin and nodded.

The inertia starter began to wail, the note rising higher and higher in protest against the sub-zero temperature.

'Contact!'

A flight mechanic, muffled to the eyes in a great red woollen scarf, slammed the canopy to and slid nimbly off the wing. Paul threw the ignition switch and, immediately, the already run-up Daimler-Benz engine slammed into life, clouding a great white fog of glistening snow to blind the men on the ground.

The ground chief signalled, leaning forward and clutching the lapels of his greatcoat against the slipstream. . . . 'Chocks away!'

Paul opened the throttle, listening as the twelve cylinders roared healthily. Unexpectedly the plane leaned forward too and, just for a moment, Fichte wondered if they *had* left a chock in place, after all. Then the wheels broke through the crust of snow which encased them and the ME started to roll forward.

Trailing a whirling dervish of ice particles, the two planes taxied bumpily from dispersal to the end of the planked runway. The ground crews were already gone, back into the dubious warmth of the hangar coke stove. Fichte kicked the tail round, lining the Messerschmitt's yellow painted spinner on the dimly seen line of stunted trees across the horizon. As the plane jolted to a halt the flarepath flicked on, bathing the two fighters in a warm orange wash of colour.

Paul snapped the switch on his R/T mouthpiece. 'This is Jumbo-One. Request permission to take-off!'

A crackle of static in the earphones, then the voice of the duty flight controller. 'Jumbos-One and -Two. Victor, Victor. Clear for take-off!'

He glanced briefly over the instrument panel. Coolant temperature, oil pressure, fuel gauge at full – which meant he was now astride eighty-eight gallons of high octane petrol. . . . He eased the throttle forward, feeling the exhilarating anticipation that swept over him during every take-off he'd ever made, and the fighter began to gather speed.

The revolution counter read 2400 r.p.m. Fichte felt the plane gradually lighten and pulled the stick back into his belly. Twelve-hundred horse-power lifted five and a half thousand pounds of fighter aircraft into the air. He glanced back to see Söhler rising and falling gently out of his starboard wing-tip, and suddenly Paul didn't feel exhilarated any more.

They banked round to the north, engines snarling irritably for altitude. As they increased height it gradually became lighter, with the black void of the ground below merging into the purple richness of the clear dawn sky.

The R/T spluttered again. 'Jumbo-One. Jumbo-One!'

Paul adjusted the oxygen mask. Christ, it was bloody cold. 'This is Jumbo-One. Pass your message.'

'Heavy babies in Berta Kurfürst. Hanni-one-zero!'

Fichte snapped out of his depression. So there *had* been something in the JU88s report, after all. This was more like it. Sector

Berta Kurfürst was out to sea . . . assuming the Tommies were approaching from Northern Scotland that meant they'd be heading for . . . the area around the Østersfjord? He frowned. Not much there, not really. Still. . . .

'Victor, Victor. Message understood.'

A few moments later. 'Heavy babies now in Berta Ludwig!'

'Victor, Victor!'

Fliegerhauptmann Paul Fichte set the grid on his compass to give him a heading for the sea, then he gestured through the cockpit perspex to the blue-eyed young man in the other flying machine. A hand grudgingly waved back and suddenly they weren't enemies any more. Just two fighter pilots doing the job they were trained for – to kill bombers, or be killed by bombers.

It was only on the ground that the Gestapo took a hand.

Or so Paul Fichte thought at the time.

*

So far the first stage of the attack on Ålvik had gone almost exactly as the tacticians of Department MO9 had hoped. In this, the final minute of secrecy, all assault craft were either on, or approaching, their holding stations. And those holding stations were precisely – on a strict speed and distance formula – four minutes and fifty-nine seconds of an L.C.A. ride from the designated landing beaches.

All the ships of Force King were in position – except, of course, for Willie Bradbury in *Muscadin* who was being a bit sneaky and holding back. But there *was* a reason for that, and anyway, to Willie, the very stuff of life lay in knowing just how far you could bend a rule without actually breaking it.

Johnny Prescott's Blenheim group was still quite a long way out to sea, but still on schedule according to its E.T.A. of H-Hour minus five seconds. This element of the attack was, however, the one factor in which bad luck had taken a hand – and even *that* depended largely on whether you were a German . . . or a dead man called Davidson, still sitting at the controls of a cremated aeroplane on the bottom of the North Sea.

Or the crew of the second missing bomber, D for Dog. Because nobody, British or German, knew where they were.

But there was another factor – perhaps the most critical element of all – which was, as yet, unknown. Yet without it even the most impeccably laid plans of all would prove irrelevant. It was a nebulous, indefinable thing which had already dictated the conduct of many great battles through history, from the moment when the tops'les of the Spanish Philip II's Armada were first sighted by the sailors of Howard's Channel Fleet to that mad, futile death of the Light Brigade under the Russian guns of Balaclava.

It was called, 'Fighting Spirit!'

Fortunately, for the British, it is the one asset they ever seem to have in any quantity at the start of a war.

*

The Commandos had it. Bucketfuls of it. But that was largely why they were Commandos in the first place.

In fact, most of them were suffering more from the effects of half an hour's stomach-heaving instability in the wallowing boats than they were from the anticipation of whatever fate lay ahead of them on that snow-covered enemy shore.

To some of them, as with Trooper Charlie Smart, the certainty of shortly coming under German fire was nothing compared to the present limbo of misery they were enduring. To them, the keening phosphorescence of a homing tracer bullet paled into insignificance beside the curling glow of the next foam-capped wave.

For others, the morning held no more discomfort than just another exercise – except that this time an umpire wouldn't be coming along when you made a mistake, to tie a red tag to your battledress blouse and say scathingly, 'You're a casualty, Trooper. Out of the game.'

In this, the last long minute of waiting, a few Commando veterans were grinning fiercely, and thinking it was a bloody welcome change from the last time they were afloat off that equipment-strewn beach outside Dunkirk. But they were the men who'd already been under fire, and had found out that the German soldier was a pretty ordinary bloke too. And that Hans, or Fritz or Gunther, got just as shit scared when a mortar straddled him; and that he bled his life away just as freely on to the dirt floor of an aid post.

And that he, too, could start to cry with the utter terror of it all when his little bit of the war got just too close for courage.

Like it seemed to be doing to Soldat Kruger.

*

It had taken him almost three minutes of practically incoherent babbling before Feldwebel Voss even half started to get the message. Not that Voss could really have been blamed for the delay, having been nodding pleasantly in the comfortable glow from the Oksenes Guard Bunker stove when a now anything but placid Kruger had burst into the Sergeant's reverie.

Kruger had struggled frantically with his carbine, which had somehow got itself jammed across the angle of the anti-blast entrance, while all the time yelling hysterically, 'Ships! The Tommies . . . they got *ships*, Herr Feldwebel . . . !'

Someone sitting in on Woitke's card-school guffawed. They all knew of the young private's imagination, and of his affinity for the more lurid productions of the degenerate Hollywood Studios. Corporal Woitke himself, sitting with the buttons of his jacket undone as far as the paunch of a truly enviable *bierkeller* belly, slapped the scrubbed wooden table mightily and roared, 'Only until they meet our *Scharnhorst*, Little Soldier . . . !'

Then Kruger seemed to stop flapping, and he just looked at them with frightened, appealing eyes. And said quietly, 'The British Navy, Unteroffizier Woitke. I think they are outside. . . . Perhaps one thousand metres off the Battery!'

Voss and Woitke collided at the entrance. For the very first time in fourteen years of military service the Feldwebel didn't even wait to don his steel helmet, while Woitke's tunic still gaped as wide as a ravished fräulein's dress.

But they did need to hurry, under the circumstances. It took a long time for a man's eyes to get used to the dark. Even when it *was* relieved by the first glow of Beginning Morning Nautical Twilight.

*

Herr Kommandant Rhöme was in no position to suffer from night-blindness, having spent the past few minutes uncomfortably staring at anything which could distract his attention from the quite terrifying waves which seemed singularly determined to impede the launch's progress across the Østersfjord.

He was even a little jealous of the way in which Cuno sat, ears erect and nose sniffing the cold air, and obviously cut out to be the saltiest of natural sea-dogs.

Though he had to admit the experience did hold a certain interest. It was the first time he had actually watched a convoy sailing from the fjord, and the expertise with which those seemingly huge, slab-sided ships were handled was most reassuring. And Döring was an excellent host, the Oberbootmann giving a lucid running commentary on the manœuvrings of the swinging *Wismar* as she closed on the – to Major Rhöme's jaundiced eye – rather diminutive escort trawler. And on the way the master of the *Käte Hass* turned his ungainly vessel short round off the wistfully receding Nordkai.

The Kommandant glanced over towards their destination and pursed his lips disapprovingly. That tanker at the Sørenson Factory pier, she appeared to be showing a light in complete disregard for his blackout regulations. This was one breach of defence security which would have to be taken up with Leutnant Sur See Rex at a suitably diplomatic moment. Not that there was much likelihood of the enemy showing any interest in a stray glimmer from this particular backwater. . . .

The Major smiled wryly and gently fondled the furry hollows behind the dog's ears. He had no illusions about the strategic value which the High Command attached to the Ålvik Garrison and its outdated, perhaps even a little pretentious, Commanding Officer.

He swivelled his gaze towards the entrance of the fjord, where the seaward gap between Oksenes and Hæl-en was rapidly becoming visible through the pre-dawn haze. A slim, unfamiliar shape seemed to bisect the opening – much more streamlined and attractive to his untutored mind than the stubby merchantmen up here.

Partly out of polite interest and partly through a childish desire to show the Oberbootmann that his soldier's vision was still equal to any seaman's, he turned to Döring and pointed.

'I see they keep you fully occupied in the harbour office, Herr Oberbootmann. No sooner does one ship sail than another one arrives for your attention. . . .'

It took the Major some considerable time to understand why Chief Petty Officer Döring seemed to go so abruptly berserk. And why the launch swung round to retrace its course so violently that the dog, Cuno, was nearly ejected over the side with typical Navy disregard for the welfare of an inoffensive dumb animal. . . .

*

Now the waiting was over. And the secrecy. Because The War had finally come to Ålvik.

It came at precisely 08.04 hours and fifty-nine seconds Greenwich Mean Time, when Rear-Admiral Arthur Braddock-Tenby lowered his binoculars to his chest, glanced at the silent cluster of waiting men on the cruiser's bridge, and spoke five quiet words of command.

'Open the Line of Fire.'

Chapter Four

'Geneva Convention . . . ? Shit! Let's hit the
bastards hard, then keep on kickin' them while they're
down . . . !'
            Unknown Leading Seaman. H.M.S. Hystrix.

Saturation Gunnery – the science of pouring as many tons of high
explosive into as small an area as tactical requirements permit.
And as quickly as human and mechanical expertise can be prevailed
upon to do so.

The Royal Navy were very good at it.

They'd been practising since the year 1600, give or take a
decade or two. . . .

H-HOUR minus 5 MINUTES

The first indication that it was going to be an unusually busy
day for Ålvik came to the Norwegian and – it was to be hoped –
transient German residents when every window around the
Østersfjord rattled uneasily in its frame while a rumbling crash
from seaward announced the departure of *Hystrix*'s first flare
salvo.

Moments later a mystifying pop-pop-popping in the sky above
the entrance heralded its arrival, then the starshell burst in a
blinding, shocking swell of magnesium brilliance, etching every
shelf and angle of rock into a temporary black-and-white imprint
on the retina of a staring eye.

Most of the Commando soldiers in the landing craft didn't see
the instant daylight, because that was one of the reasons why
they'd been ordered to keep their heads down in the first place.
The few whose furtive curiosity – or sheer independent bloody-
mindedness – had still made them stare expectantly upwards, lost
the considerable advantage of night vision. And that, in turn, made
them just a little less efficient when they reached their respective
killing grounds.

99

A starshell can normally be regarded more as a spectacular rather than a lethal – weapon of war. But one German sailor still lost his life because of them – the first man in the Ålvik Garrison to die as a direct result of enemy action.

His name was Braun, Erik Braun, aged nineteen years and two months. He wasn't very bright. He didn't hate the British or the Norwegians or the Poles or even the Jews. He wanted to be a dairy farmer after Hitler had won the war, and he had a widowed mother living in permanent fear for her son's safety on the fourth floor of a Cologne tenement block.

Erik died quite suddenly and violently, largely because he forgot to look where he was going. You shouldn't spend a lot of time blinking stupidly and uncomprehendingly at lights in the sky ahead of you, not when you're on duty. And especially not when that duty is driving a seven-ton Naval stores truck along a winding road with a sheer fifty-metre drop into a fjord on your starboard side.

In a way those first pyrotechnics from H.M.S. *Hystrix* killed two people. A broken heart also compelled the bereaved Frau Braun to step out of her fourth-floor Cologne window a tear-filled twelve days later.

But you couldn't really blame the British for that.

Probably the only defenders who realised what was about to happen to them immediately after that first glaring moment of shock were the three groups of people who were already alerted. Herr Major Otto Rhöme's boatload of grim-faced Kriegsmariners, the Oksenes Battery Wehrmacht guard under the abruptly awakened Feldwebel Voss, and the lonely, frustrated Gefreiter Scherer still viciously working the bolt of his 98k Carbine in the Hæl-en Signal Station.

Young Balke was still too absorbed with his abrupt and macabre introduction to the late Leading Seaman Hopp even to notice the six-inch calibre sunrise over Ålvik.

From the buffeting launch now returning at full speed to the Nordkai, Chief Petty Officer Döring gazed bitterly up at the starkly illuminated fjord entrance, noted absently that the silhouette between them was that of an unmistakably British fleet destroyer and muttered hopelessly, '*Leuchtgeschoss, Herr Major . . . !* Star shell! The next salvo will be H.E. On the Battery . . . maybe the Sørenson Factory too.'

Rhöme stared at him through the uncanny, ever-shifting over-spill from the flares. Unnoticed by either of them a cloud of icy spray flew aft from the plunging bows, rattling like dried peas on the taut canvas screen forward of the cockpit.

'I must get back, Döring,' the Commandant said quietly. 'How long will it take?'

The Oberbootmann glanced at him in surprise. Maybe there *was* more to Herr Major Otto Rhöme than first impressions suggested. The whole bloody Royal Navy knocking on the front door for all they knew, and the old man just sitting there patiently, cold as the waters of the Østersfjord, already planning his first move.

'Four . . . five minutes, Sir. We're pushing this bucket fast as we can.'

The Major nodded. He hoped Döring couldn't see how sick he felt, and how frustrated at being a virtual prisoner out here while his Command was being attacked. Of all the damnable times to choose for . . .

Yet beneath all the disbelief and the concern, Major Rhöme was vaguely conscious of another, rather an unexpected, emotion – a feeling of pride. Of a somewhat two-edged appreciation that, out of all the isolated potential targets along the North Sea coast, the Allies had honoured *his* Garrison with whatever it was that they intended. It seemed to make him something rather special, in a sacrificial sort of way.

Like a white goat to a Moslem. Just before the creature's throat is cut!

None of the defenders in the motor launch realised that there were seven assault craft full of High Priests less than two hundred metres away. And that 22 Commando would be only too willing to assist with the sacrificing of as many offerings as Herr Hitler was prepared to place in front of a Tommy gun sight.

Another small detail not at that time apparent to the Kommandant of the Ålvik Garrison and his maritime hosts . . . that the Kriegsmarine launch was due to return alongside the Nordkai at almost precisely the same moment as Lieutenant-Colonel Dougal Duncan's Headquarters Party were scheduled to storm ashore.

Also on the Nordkai.

Meanwhile, back at the Battery. . . .

'Oh, Christ!' said Feldwebel Voss hollowly.

'It's starshells,' said the bare-chested Unteroffizier Woitke ungrammatically.

'It's *British* starshells,' said Soldat Kruger, both ungrammatically and unnecessarily.

'Oh, *Jesus* Christ!' shouted Feldwebel Voss again, lunging urgently for the hand-cranked air-raid siren beside the bunker entrance.

Voss was scared too now. Sick scared in his belly because he'd suddenly realised, for all his experience, that he didn't really know what to do or even what was happening, but it was the only way to alert the Naval gunners, no matter where the attack was coming from.

'Please, Unteroffizier Woitke. What will they do next?' pleaded a still stunned and disbelieving Kruger.

But fat Woitke didn't know either. And anyway – there didn't seem to be all that much time left for speculation.

Scherer knew, though. Or at least he had a pretty good idea. Having had nothing to do since young Balke had so abruptly disappeared down the long path to Ålvik – apart from fiddle nervously with his rifle and prowl the Signal Station deck like a helplessly caged lion – the Gefreiter had had more time than anyone else around the Østersfjord to debate the enemy strategy.

That warship the idiot kid had seen, f'rinstance – she wouldn't be the only one. And she must have had a more important reason for entering the keep-net of the fjord than to hit the Bremen convoy, even assuming that the Tommies were now desperate enough to squash grapes with a sledgehammer. Apart from which they could do that equally efficiently and a lot more securely as the merchantmen came out into the North Sea.

Yet she sure as hell wasn't berthing in Ålvik for a courtesy visit . . . !

Then the starshell went up and Scherer deliberately avoided gazing at them, instead staring hard out to sea to where he was almost certain that the balance of the enemy force would be lying. So, because the Gefreiter was a good seaman and knew his naval strategy, he was the second German to see the main element of Force King that day.

But unlike the Cooked Man in the tossing yellow dinghy, Scherer believed implicitly in what he saw.

In the arrogant, stately shape of the cruiser steaming one mile out to sea, with the sluggishly rolling topsides of her glinting as they reflected the light in the sky from the patina of ice varnishing every grey plane.

In the two smaller infantry landing ships, now bows on to the Battery to present a minimal target should things go wrong as they waited patiently for their fledgling L.C.A.s to return.

And, nearer to Hæl-en, in the lower, more rakish lines of the British Fleet destroyer leaning over in a skidding turn which would bring her broadside to bear on the land in a few more seconds.

While over all those menacing ships streamed that great white Battle Ensign of the Royal Navy, standing out from the dark horizon so proudly and so gallantly that even the reluctant Gefreiter felt a momentary surge of bitter admiration. . . .

. . . then the orange cordite flames stabbed from *Hystrix*'s guns. The greys turned to reds, and were obscured by a blast of rolling, wind-torn smoke. And the smashing roar of the first British broadside thundered and skipped over the rearing wave crests towards the anguished man on Hæl-en.

But before Scherer could switch his gaze to the Battery across the fjord, where he knew the shot would fall, a second ripple of flame caught the corner of his eye. And the sharper, more vicious slam of *Salamander*'s 4.7s added to the bewildering terror of that winter morning.

While the Gefreiter's little bit of The War suddenly became much more personal.

Because he knew that, this time, the Royal Navy was firing at *him*.

*

There was – during that initial frightening moment when the night turned into day and, for the first time since leaving the *Princes*, the troops saw the faces of their companions – a fractional time-slip of inactivity.

For even though this was the minute towards which they had spent so many months in training, and the one for which the savouring and the anticipation had been so strong that they could almost taste it in the dry, unnatural coating over the roofs of their mouths, they were still vaguely surprised – still momentarily disbelieving – that the waiting and the preparation were finally over. That they were now irrevocably committed to the attack.

Until the already poised arm of the Senior Officer in each group slashed downwards, idling engines roared into frantic life and, as the leading seamen cox'ns spun their wheels, the fourteen landing craft swung on to a buffeting, pounding heading for the last thousand-yard run-in to the attack areas.

The Colonel, constantly shifting his calculating gaze between the dimly discernible shadow of the Nordkai and the now more clearly visible ships of the assembling convoy, was conscious of a feeling of relief. While there was obviously an overspill of light from the flares above Oksenes he didn't think it was enough to reveal his L.C.A.s to any but the most astute and unruffled observer.

Or not for another two or three minutes, anyway. Until they passed so close under the high bows of the merchantmen that even a casual glance could give the game away. . . . Dougal Duncan smiled grimly. Maybe even then an ex-salmon poacher with a Bren Gun could give them just a little more time.

Also heading for Ålvik's Nordkai, Troop-Sergeant Arthur Henderson was experiencing something he never thought he would feel again – a sensation of great peace and . . . almost tranquillity. Oh, he still thought about Ginny and the kids – he'd never really be able to forget them completely – but in that moment when *Hystrix* switched the lights on over the Østersfjord something had also happened inside Arthur Henderson, Grocer and Florist. A presentiment, even a certainty, of approaching fulfilment coupled with a very small glimmer of understanding, and acceptance of the Ways of God.

It brought Ginny very, very close to him, even out there on that cold bleak morning off the coast of Occupied Norway. It also had the effect of making the Troop-Sergeant quite unique too. Because out of all the Commando Soldiers approaching that hostile shore, he was the only one among them who really didn't mind the Germans shooting at him.

Now he finally knew that, in his moment of dying, he would be with Ginny and the children once again. . . .

Trooper Danny Williams, currently heading towards the Sørenson jetty along with the rest of Bert Stenhouse's mad bastards, wasn't feeling at all like being shot at, though. In fact, as far as

Danny was concerned the German Army could have bloody Norway for nothing . . . though he had to admit, with a faint stirring of surprised pride, that now the flap had really started he *was* sort of looking forward to a bit of action when they finally got ashore.

If they ever made it. And as long as the action was reasonably restrained on Jerrie's part. He kept his head below the level of the armoured sides of the craft, not so much because he'd been ordered to as because he reckoned it was a helluva lot safer, and hoped that Jerrie might be even less keen to hold on to the lousy country than *he* was to capture it.

The funny thing was that, behind all the griping and the cynicism, it never once occurred to Danny Williams to do anything other than fight . . . in between moaning about the bull and the N.A.A.F.I. and the bloody weather.

It made him the same kind of man as those swearing, stumbling, bloody-minded legions who'd charged at Waterloo and suffered at Inkerman, and wallowed in the mud of the Somme and at Passchendaele and blood-soaked Vimy Ridge.

It meant that Trooper Williams D. was a pretty average British Soldier.

Just like Corporal Hanson, still trying to learn Norwegian but now with the aid of what must have been the biggest bed-light in the world.

And Charlie Smart. Still being sick.

And the two L.C.A.-loads of men curving round behind Oksenes Point, en route for the Battery assault. Being almost directly under the hanging luminescence of the shells they were the most exposed yet, paradoxically, they were probably the Commandos who also wore the biggest grins at that critically vulnerable time. Smiles which carved white, incongruous slashes across the features of men dappled black for the business of killing.

Because it knocks a lot of the drama out of any grim situation when the silence is broken by a tall slim Commando Captain humming softly, 'Happy Birthday dear Michael . . . Happy Birthdaaaay toooo meeeee . . . !'

Especially when you didn't know how frightened he really was, and how desperately he wished he could just curl up and hide anywhere at all that was dark and secret until that birthday was over.

And then the first six-inch salvo came over the Point sounding like an express train in the sky, and Mike Seely's voice was drowned by the thunder of high explosive as the Oksenes Battery started to blow up.

While the grins faded from the darkened faces as even those men who had been expecting the bombardment were stunned by the sheer violence and fury and the terror of it all.

Even though they were still half a mile away.

*

Down in the cruiser's galley, almost directly below the aircraft catapult deck, Petty Officer Chalk finished creaming the golden cake mixture with a final flourish and placed it on the stainless steel table beside a gradually mounting stack of sandwich-filled mess kits.

C.P.O. Lumley inspected it with a critical eye, prodding tentatively with the wooden spoon, while Herbert stood back and waited tensely for the master craftsman's verdict.

Suddenly a shiver ran through the ship and Herbert felt her lying fractionally over to starboard while the metal trays rattled excitedly and the serried ranks of hanging pots and pans gleamed even more brightly as the deckhead lights swung from the horizontal.

Just for a moment the assembly line of white-aproned ratings hesitated, looking meaningfully at each other or, in some cases, glancing upwards as if hoping to penetrate the steel decks above. Then the knives flashed again, and the buttering and slicing and pickling continued as though nothing had happened.

Chalk murmured quietly, 'We're in action, then.'

Cook Chief Petty Officer Lumley gave a last searching poke. 'More currants, Herbert. An' wait 'til the shoot's over before you bake or it'll never rise proper!'

The faintly disapproving lines around the corners of his mouth suggested that he'd never had so many time-consuming diversions to contend with at the Savoy. But, then again, the Savoy didn't often fire a six-inch broadside.

It was largely a question of priorities, really. . . .

*

Aboard H.M.S. *Muscadin* they knew it was only a matter of

seconds before they drew fire from the shore, now that the star-shell was lighting them up like a long flickering ghost ship under the magnesium glare. In fact, it was an evens bet that the British destroyer in the fjord would be the first element of the attacking force to be selected as a target by every bewildered German soldier frantically searching for whatever the hell had hit them so abruptly.

So as far as Willie Bradbury was concerned, *his* task was purely a matter of priorities too – to detect and destroy anything which appeared to offer the greatest and most immediate threat either to his ship or to the virtually helpless assault craft – and to do it with a speed and precision that would prevent them doing unto him first.

The First Lieutenant anxiously scanned along the slowly moving shapes of the ships lying off the Nordkai, now approximately three-quarters of a mile farther down the fjord. He hesitated as his lenses settled on the stubby, angular shape of the *Patzig*, then gestured to Willie.

'One point on the port bow, Sir. Looks like an armed trawler.'

The Captain switched his equally penetrating gaze from the potential targets in the still shadowed town nestling at the foot of the mountain. The trawler swam into his vision and he gently caressed the knurled focussing wheel until she fused into sharp clarity. Even in the uncanny light he could vaguely make out the white, upturned blobs of faces as two men on the tiny bridge stared at the sky in frozen astonishment.

'And if *that* surprises them,' Willie thought grimly, 'just wait for their expressions when we lob a coupl've rounds through her wheelhouse windows. . . .'

The Gunnery Officer spoke crisply into his headset. ' "A" Gun! Target . . . ! Range – wun thousand fife hundred yards! Bearing – thuree fife zero degrees. . . .'

The Leading Seaman gunlayer settled himself that little bit more comfortably in the padded seat behind 'A' Gun's lightly armoured shield and felt the turret swing fractionally as the traversing mechanism whirred softly. The German vessel almost filled the gunsight, they were so close.

' "A" Gun on bearing. Range set, Sir.'

'Thank you,' Willie murmured. 'We may need a quick getaway in a few moments.'

Then *Hystrix*'s first H.E. salvo landed on Oksenes, arriving with the same shock of displaced air as that created by an express train shrieking and roaring through a suburban station. Somebody on *Muscadin*'s bridge said, 'Christ!' in a hollow voice, and the Captain saw one of the young lookouts lifting his head in awe.

Number One snapped, 'Keep your eyes where they should be, Jackson!'

The first blast waves from the erupting Battery skittered and skipped across the wave tops towards the silvery grey destroyer in the fjord. Each wave caught and reflected the light from above as it reared and clawed playfully upwards, grasping for the slowly falling starshell with wet, undulating fingers.

A silver ship in a sparkling sea. . . .

Now all she had to do was wait. Until somebody started firing at her.

*

Wait like Vice-Admiral Braddock-Tenby who somewhat ironically – after having given the initial order to start all this in the first place – now found himself with very little to do other than watch.

Yet even watching was a little difficult from the bridge of a cruiser which was hurling broadside after broadside of shells as quickly as her sweat-streaming ammunition numbers and gun crews could handle and load the one-hundred-pound rounds.

The Admiral and the Brigadier stood together on the port side of the bridge with binoculars glued under furrowed eyebrows while, every few seconds, *Hystrix*'s guns voiced an ear-splitting crash and the ship moved fractionally sideways through the water. Then the muzzle-flash of the salvo switched off again and the men on the cruiser's bridge felt, rather than saw, the acrid cordite smoke drifting around them, making the eyes stream and the pulses quicken.

And almost immediately, along the line of the dimly seen shore, a rippling sparkle of dull orange flame which pinpointed both the fall of the British shot and – the Admiral sincerely hoped – the position of the enemy coastal Battery.

He caught sight of a slim figure behind him and turned to see the young Midshipman Tod staring silently and thoughtfully towards the shore. Something about the boy's tense gaze caught the Admiral's attention then, as he moved slightly, the guns crashed again and the flash lit up the white, little-boy's face under the big steel helmet. And the moist, shining glint over the smooth round of the cheek bones.

Suddenly Braddock-Tenby realised, with a surge of surprised concern, that the boy was actually crying and, just for a moment, he was conscious of a swelling irritation within him that one of his officers – no matter how junior and inexperienced – should betray such an immature emotion. He even opened his mouth to speak sharply to the child until, instead of delivering the appropriately scathing rebuke, he snapped it shut again and discreetly turned away.

The muffled form of the Brigadier moved awkwardly at the rail beside him and Braddock-Tenby guessed, with an unworthy sense of embarrassment and shame on the part of the boy, that the soldier had seen the fleeting incident too. Then his friend spoke quietly, ensuring that no one else on the cruiser's bridge would hear, just before the guns roared again.

'You were right, Arthur. He's just realised what a violent, bloody business this is. That there are real people being killed, over there – and horribly mutilated . . . and that's the one bit about war which the story-books never do emphasise. . . .'

But that wasn't quite the reason why the Admiral had turned away. Or not the whole of it.

Because he'd suddenly remembered another little boy with bewildered, tear-filled eyes who'd suddenly understood that dismemberment and pain and an unutterable sadness was the only real end-product of those guns he was helping to fire, as they thundered bravely from Jellico's Battle Fleet at Jutland, so long ago.

His name had been Braddock-Tenby too.

H-HOUR minus 4 MINUTES

One sea mile east of the Admiral, and precisely on the other end of the curving trajectory of *Hystrix*'s shells, stumbled Soldat Kruger.

And *he* was suffering the worst of both worlds because, not only did the once placid sentry have the bewildered tears in his eyes, but he was also in the middle of those poor bloody people who were being killed!

The first salvo had arrived on the Battery while he was still staring dumbly at Unteroffizier Woitke under the white glare of the starshell. Feldwebel Voss had hurled himself at the air-raid siren and, blue veins knotting in his neck with effort, had started to crank the red handle furiously.

As the siren started to wail – groaning at first and then, as the Sergeant's nervous grasp overcame the inertia, louder and louder with that eerie, spine-tingling howl – Kruger saw a sailor dressed in white trousers and the inevitable tailed Kriegsmarine hat amble sedately up the steps from Number Two Gun Bunker.

The sailor had sort of yawned, scratching furiously while staring interestedly around him then, as the impact of the unnatural daylight coupled with the swelling screech of the siren had slowly dawned, the gunner stopped in mid-scratch, gaped foolishly towards his empty weapon-pit fifty yards away – and disappeared back into the bunker yelling just as furiously as Kruger himself had done four minutes before.

Then the first explosive rounds arrived. Just as Voss finally hit the high note on the siren!

To the few men who actually heard them coming towards Oksenes they sounded just like a vast bolt of canvas, stretched across the sky, which was suddenly and violently ripped across by a gigantic hand. Then the tearing stopped abruptly and, just for a blink of time, there was a smothering blanket of utter silence. . . .

. . . before the shells exploded!

No one, and certainly not Soldat Kruger, remembered exactly what happened during that next uncomprehending flash of terror. All he knew was that the hand in the sky had let go of the canvas for a moment and reached down to pick him up and throw him away instead.

While, behind him, raced the shock-wave and the glare and the shrivelling heat from the explosions. Overtaking and tumbling and shaking him like a rag doll in the clutch of a hysterically violent child.

Until the compressing air got tired of playing with him and raced on ahead towards the men now pouring out of Number Three Bunker, while Kruger scrabbled in the whirlpooling snow to drag himself erect – just in time to be aware of a rumble out to sea, and the luminous sky tearing in half again as the next salvo dropped in on the Oksenes Battery.

The Naval Artillerymen from Three Bunker were nearly half-way to their gun pit, running and stumbling grimly under the hail of earth clods and falling, smoking rock. Two of them had fallen behind, fumbling dazedly on hands and knees where the splinter-laden blast from the first salvo had left them, but the rest just kept on going – until a shell landed squarely in the sand-bagged circle ahead of them. The 105-millimetre barrel seemed to jump vertically, spinning round and round parallel to the ground like a great steel flail, then, as Kruger watched through bulging eyes, the gun barrel literally cruised through the running men at chest height, neatly pulverising its own crew.

And then it was coming towards Kruger with, detectable even above the roar of the barrage, the swish of a juggernauting pro-pellor. But Kruger just stood and stared and tried to understand what was happening, and why he couldn't wake out of this high-explosive nightmare that wasn't at all like the kind of war Herr Flynn seemed to fight so gallantly. . . .

Then the rogue barrel tipped sideways when it was less than ten metres from him, and the breech dug into the frozen earth and the careering monster went leaping and cartwheeling down the slope towards the sea.

Just as a hand stretched out and a hoarse voice shouted, 'Ged-downyousillybastard . . . !' and his legs were yanked from under him before he hit the ground to see the wild eyes of Feldwebel Voss glaring down at him.

Voss wiped a hand across the sweat-streaked shine of his fore-head and spat. Kruger gazed in fascination as the blood oozed from a cut under the Sergeant's hairline and mingled with the dirt and the grime and the soot. He'd never seen Voss looking anything other than immaculately turned-out before – but then again, he'd never seen the Feldwebel when someone was trying to shoot him with a six-inch cruiser before, either.

He said learnedly, 'They're firing at us, Herr Feldwebel.'

Then he started to cry again.

Just as the next salvo homed in and the two of them – the old soldier and the young recruit – grovelled under the pounding roar of the explosions, faces jammed into the cold, frozen earth so

III

closely that every subterranean jolt addled their brains a little bit more, pushing them that little bit farther over the edge of the condition known as 'Shell-Shock'.

They didn't know what had happened to Unteroffizier Woitke, or any of the other members of the Wehrmacht Guard detail.

In fact, after sixty seconds of British saturation gunnery, nobody on duty in the Oksenes Coastal Battery knew where anybody else was. And didn't really care any more.

Because a target area is a lonely place, no matter who keeps you company.

*

Out in the middle of the Østersfjord, Major Rhöme watched the first shells land on his Battery with an unspeakable sadness which was only reflected, even to the closest observer, in the erect old gentleman's eyes.

Beside him in the launch Oberbootmann Döring gripped the polished walnut stock of the Schmeisser in an agony of frustration, his whole body leaning forward towards the distant Nordkai as if to encourage the boat to go even faster than the clanking, roaring engine was already driving her. '*Go*, you bitch! F'r Chrissake, go, go . . . go . . . !'

The dog Cuno allowed its head to rest, ears flat aback, on its master's knee. The big intelligent eyes stared trustingly up at him through the flashes reflected from Oksenes while sheer habit made the Major ever so gently caress the thick furry collar around the alsatian's neck.

The dog knew about the Major's misery, though. It could sense the agony of mind that made the loved hand tremble every time another salvo came in from the sea.

And the hand trembled very frequently, because the cruiser's gunners were very good at their profession.

*

Leichtmatrose Dieter Balke was trembling too. In fact, after having met two dead men in the middle of a forest, young Balke wasn't so much trembling as shaking uncontrollably, like a gazelle which identifies the scent of a stalking lion.

He hadn't even been aware of *Hystrix*'s starshell – all they had meant to Balke's swimming brain was that he had even greater light to record the more intimately horrible details of the half corpse which had been Leading Seaman Hopp.

Right down to that inexplicable blue woollen glove clutched in the stiffly set hand.

Until the dull thunder of the shelling rolled across the fjord while, even at this distance, the concussion shook the tops of the trees angrily.

Then Balke suddenly snapped out of the trance-like daze he'd so nightmarishly slipped into, and – realising with uncharacteristic perception that this was, in some way, connected with the appearance of that mysterious warship in the Østersfjord – started running towards the town once again.

For about twenty coat-tail-flapping paces. Before he stopped abruptly for the second time, looking a bit disgusted with himself, and returned for his forgotten rifle.

And doing a thing like that could demand a lot of courage. From most people.

But one of Dieter Balke's attributes was that he had the enviable capacity for totally enclosing himself within a protective mental shell. Once any problem had become too large to cope with or too distressing to face up to any more, then Balke could just switch out the circuit, isolate himself completely from that particular aggravation, and carry on as if nothing had ever gone wrong in the first place.

So not only had the beautiful, if slightly perverted, soul of Leading Seaman Hopp ceased to exist on an earthly plane, but his rather less attractive cadaver had also ceased to exist in Leichtmatrose Balke's fail-safe mind.

As had the once handsome Wehrmacht Corporal with the Schmeisser stake in his diaphragm.

Unfortunately, one of the disadvantages of Balke's mental blockading was that – once an enemy had become too threatening and too hostile for reconciliation – then they ceased to remain a danger and faded into limbo too.

Which was liable to prove a little disconcerting to any one of the four hundred and eighty-six super-aggressive, Tommy Gun-waving enemies who were likely to run across Leichtmatrose Balke during their day's visit to Ålvik.

And a little fatal for Balke, his protective shell being rather less than effective against nine-millimetre bullets.

He finally found his rifle beside the remarkably solid phantasy of the Corporal's body and had just started to continue down the tree-lined path towards the town when, close on the heels of the cruiser's opening shots on the Battery, *Salamander*'s first salvo landed on Hæl-en, less than a mile behind Balke.

Without any warning at all the tops of the trees, previously black against the white light in the sky, suddenly reflected red then orange and then went back to a waving black again just as the multiple ripple of the exploding shells raced over the running seaman.

He didn't stop this time. His eyes opened a little wider as the fear came back and the skirts of his greatcoat flapped even more erratically as he panted into top gear, but he still kept on running to tell people they were being fired at. . . .

In actual fact, anyone else who had received the treatment that the sadistic Gefreiter Scherer had been meting out to Leicht-matrose Balke would perhaps have been forgiven had they allowed themselves to hope, even a little wistfully, that one of the explosions behind them was occurring fatally close to their tormentor.

But the galloping Balke didn't think like other people, because he didn't feel any enmity towards the Gefreiter at all. Not now. Scherer had gone and got himself switched off from the moment that rifle butt had caught the young sailor's shoulder. . . .

H-HOUR minus 3 MINUTES

Actually, Scherer had damn nearly got himself switched off on a far more permanent and physically destructive basis than in the over-stretched mind of a fleeing idiot.

The trouble was that, even though he'd virtually anticipated the broadside of the racing British destroyer out there, he'd still been so taken-aback by the sheer bloody temerity of actually being shot at – and by what Herr Goebbels had proved beyond doubt must be a ship-load of decadent homosexuals – that he forgot to hit the deck.

Until he found out that, not only were the British sailors both degenerates and queers, but that they were also lucky *shots*, f'r Chrissakes – when the windows of the Signal Station blew in on him as the blast from a 4.7-inch shell landing fifty metres away left him standing otherwise unharmed amid the shambles of his first command.

And, to Scherer, his post held just as vital a place in the glorious structure of the Naval Forces of the Third Reich as did the *Scharnhorst* or the *Prinz Eugen* – even if it was a fraction smaller, and just a wooden hut.

So Scherer started to get angry. Bloody angry.

Not quite angry enough, certainly, to forgo the luxury of going to ground as the second salvo roared in from *Salamander*. Each projectile tunnelling several feet into the rock-strewn ground around the Army flak tower and searchlight position before its forty-pound charge converted instantly to a white-hot gas. This subterranean pressure then searching for release once again with roaring, expanding fingers.

The Gefreiter suddenly found himself burrowing into the ruins of the hut with astonishing enthusiasm, and if there were any traces of shame or of injured pride, then they hardly raised a ripple on the surface of his desire for self-preservation. Scherer may have been a confirmed Nazi, with nothing but admiration for Herr Doktor Goebbels and his legends of Teutonic invincibility, but he was also a realist. And two-hundredweight plus of T.N.T. exploding next door sounded a pretty damn convincing argument for converting to the British way of life.

For as long as it took for a Naval shell to explode, anyway.

The blast tugged excitedly at Scherer's back and he felt the pressure waves compress his eardrums agonisingly. Remembering a tip from an old Kriegsmariner of long ago, he opened his mouth and started to scream – shrilly and unashamedly and without the slightest trace of embarrassment. And then the pain went away as the pressure was released, leaving Scherer panting and wild-eyed with little shards of broken glass from the windows tinkling and fluttering in the wake of the invisible monster.

Gradually he became aware of a creaking, rending sound from the hill behind him and, awkwardly screwing round in the mess, he was just in time to watch the Wehrmacht flak tower beginning to topple.

Uncannily, almost dreamily, the high wooden structure seemed to sway tiredly against the lighter sky. Scherer watched with resigned interest as a man – a black, lonely silhouette of a man high in the air – tried desperately to swing a leg over the side of the tower and find the ladder. Then the spindly Norwegian Fir struts forming the frames of the *Fliegerabwehrturm* finally splintered on one side, and the displaced flak gun rolled down the weapon platform as the list abruptly increased.

Scherer continued to watch the scrambling man until the heavy machine-gun overtook him, then the screaming soldier jetted off the ladder before the two objects – the shrieking, animated one underneath – plummeted into the drifting fumes blanketing the Point.

The rest of the dissolving flak tower slowly collapsed like a fatigued skeleton under the probing of a drunken medical student.

Salamander flickered angry red again, just over a mile away.

Scherer said gloomily, 'Ah . . . *shit*!'

And went back to playing at being a mole.

*

In the warm, cosy atmosphere of the Norske Hotell's gilded lobby, Unterfeldwebel Oehlschläger hadn't seen the starshell. In fact, secure in the knowledge that his Lord and Master was by now firmly launched upon his voyage of adventure across the fjord, the Under-sergeant was once again relaxing in his standard horizontal position.

It was only the clatter of hurrying feet on the cobbles outside which finally made Oehlschläger frown and grudgingly lower his shiny boots once again to the carpet. Leisurely massaging the small of his back, he ambled to the hotel entrance and opened the door, bracing himself for the anticipated blast of freezing air. But the Under-sergeant had never been a man to put personal comfort before duty – not unless he could be one hundred carat bloody certain to get away with it, anyway.

It was so light outside that, just for a moment, he glanced at his watch, alarmed in case he had made the unforgivable error of remaining at his post after his duty had finished. Then he realised that his relief, Unterfeldwebel Schmidt, hadn't turned up yet and felt a bit better.

The road outside did seem remarkably well lit, though. So bright, in fact, that he could clearly see several groups of stunned, silent soldiers and a few equally mystified Norwegians staring up at the lights in the sky.

Then Oehlschläger realised nervously that they really *were* lights in the sky, and that they shouldn't *be* there . . . just as the first H.E. salvo speckled Oksenes with pretty golden flashes of colour, and the distant seaward rumble of *Hystrix's* introductory broadside arrived in Ålvik.

One of the Wehrmacht corporals standing near the door – a big man with a bicycle, presumably on his way to relieve the gunners in the weapon pits to the east of the town – muttered '*Jesus Gott!*'

Oehlschläger said disbelievingly, 'Explosions! Maybe the Battery magazines . . . ?'

Another soldier shook his head emphatically. It was funny how, at this stage, no one seemed to feel any sense of involvement. Ålvik's main street held only detached observers at seven minutes past eight on that winter's morning.

'That's starshell, mate! I was at Narvik when the British . . .'

The big Corporal held up a warning hand. 'Listen!'

Gradually another distant sound became apparent to the un-easily shifting group of watchers. A thin, eerie whisp of sound, only detectable as a link between the rumble of the explosions themselves. The Corporal started to mount his bike urgently. 'Air-raid siren . . . get moving, boys.'

Oehlschläger frowned doubtfully. They could be bombs, yeah, but wasn't there something missing. Something . . . ?

A dark figure came charging out of the hotel. 'What the hell's happening?'

Oehlschläger whirled irritably. 'If you'd use your bloody eyes f'r . . .'

The newcomer's bloody eyes glinted coldly above the navy-blue uniform of a *Seekreigsleitung Korvettenkapitän* – the senior officer of the S.K.L. Intelligence Section based in the Norske Hotell. Abruptly Oehlschläger slammed to attention and forgot about the men dying a few thousand yards away. '*Es tut mir leid!* I apologise for the indiscretion, Herr Korvettenkapit. . . .'

The Lieutenant-Commander snapped, 'Shut up and tell me what's happening, Oehlschläger. Quickly, man!'

The Narvik veteran said knowledgeably, 'Starshell, that is, Sir.'

The big Corporal spat. 'They're sounding the air-raid alert, *dummkopf.* You think *they* don't know who's throwing the shit . . . ? Beggin' your pardon, Sir.'

The cold eyes switched interrogatively back to a confused Oehlschläger. 'Well?'

Unterfeldwebel Oehlschläger didn't have a clue, but he didn't dare admit it. And for all he knew, the S.K.L. Officer might well be probing just for the hell of it – to prove that the Wehrmacht didn't know the difference between bombs, shells and fireworks. One thing for sure – the icy Korvettenkapitän would know. That gold braid on his cuffs said he would.

Oehlschläger took a deep breath as the second salvo shook the town – or was it the second stick of aerial H.E.? He had a fifty-fifty chance of being correct.

'An air-raid, Sir. The Battery is being bombed.'

The Korvettenkapitän nodded expressionlessly and Oehlschläger's heart leapt with relief. 'Then sound the alarm, man. Don't stand ogling!'

Oehlschläger saluted smartly and turned towards the door. The white light from the flares carved a black, foreshortened silhouette of himself on the steps before him. '*Jawohl!* If you will excuse me?'

He ran back into the lobby, heading for the red-painted switch behind the desk. Throwing it he listened gratefully as the infernal siren on the hotel roof started to wail its melancholy warning to the residents of Ålvik, then he began to reach for his steel helmet and gas mask hanging behind the door. He nervously hoped that Unterfeldwebel Schmidt would hurry and relieve him – the shelters in the hotel basement seemed infinitely more attractive right then than the Duty N.C.O.'s post in the lobby.

Unwittingly Oehlschläger had now sent all but a handful of air defence personnel down into the Ålvik Garrison air-raid shelters. And you can't see very much when you're in a hole in the ground.

It was only when the siren had completely drowned even the loudest of the explosions over on Oksenes that the Unterfeldwebel remembered what it was that had been missing from the illuminated sky – there hadn't been any complimentary sound of aero-engines. Not even the faintest suspicion of a drone, as one would reasonably expect.

He shrugged and exchanged his forage cap for the reassuring solidity of the coal-scuttle helmet. The interrogative Korvettenkapitän would soon have picked him up if his guess had been wrong. And *he* was only too obviously a seaman reared on the smell of salt and cordite – not a bloody interfering squaddie drafted in from Narvik who just happened to have heard a British gun firing, once upon a time. . . .

Of course, Unterfeldwebel Oehlschläger couldn't possibly have been expected to know that the Korvettenkapitän's question *had* been put in a sincere, if somewhat camouflaged, desire for advice. And that, until four months ago, the Korvettenkapitän had been a Professor of Philosophy at Hamburg University – until they called him up for Intelligence work.

And that he knew even less about Naval gunnery than he did about tying a reef knot. . . .

*

Consequently, outside in the flickering, illuminated street, a big Wehrmacht Corporal on a bicycle pedalled furiously in erratic tacks, bellowing excitedly in a stentorian voice, '*Fliegerwarnung . . . in Deckung gehen! Fliegerwarnung. . . .*'

And quite a lot of soldiers hurried down into bunkers and cellars who would otherwise have been hurrying even more urgently up *out* of them.

But all that did was to prove that War is just a series of little mistakes which, when joined together, make the biggest mistake of all.

H-HOUR minus 2 MINUTES

At fifty feet above the North Sea and the flat-out airspeed of a vibrating Blenheim bomber, you can't afford to make any mistakes. Not even little ones.

Especially when it's dark and you're not really sure whether your altimeter really means fifty. Or forty-five. Or something. . . .

The only advantage is that, under those circumstances, no one else can see the sweat on your face, or the death grin twist to your lips. Or the staring fear which varnishes your eyes with the dull patina of horror at what may lie ahead of you, past the next anticipatory second of incredibly precious life.

Not that anyone wants to look, anyway. Because, to them, it would only be like gazing into a mirror.

Ian was still hunched unmoving in the Navigator's seat. Johnny had decided to use the optional pilot's bomb release switch, thinking – hoping, dammit – that at least there wouldn't be any loss of co-ordination when they arrived at the aiming-point after this crazy beat-up of the fjord ahead.

He tried not to imagine how Ian must be feeling. He, Johnny, had the dubious advantage of being able to funnel all his concentration into keeping them just far enough above the deck to survive, and just low enough below any searching flak to . . . well . . . survive!

From the upper turret Alley was watching astern. Maybe he was scared to hell too, but at least he couldn't see what was ahead of them, in that black, featureless gap between the two erupting pincers of Hæl-en and . . . what was it? . . . yeah – Oksenes.

Ian was just watching.

The intercom crackled, sending an unexpected clutch of fear down Prescott's throat to grip his already taut belly muscles. Alley's voice was high pitched above the static mush. 'Christ, he's . . . no, he hasn't . . . !'

Johnny snapped nervously, 'Hasn't *what*, Alley?'

'P.O. Evans. They dipped their port wing. I thought. . . . Sorry, Skip.'

The Pilot hit his mike button in a fury of snapping tension. 'An' you . . . !' Then he hesitated, feeling the cold sweat trickle down behind his ear. Imperceptibly the plane lifted on a crest of air and without thinking he eased the stick forward fractionally, delicately, playing the thundering aircraft with all the skill in his fingertips. Then Johnny suddenly realised that, for the first time in his life, he was really *flying*. Oh, not by instruments or by mechanical conditioning, but by feel and by touch, and by becoming an extension of O-Orange herself.

And abruptly the fear had gone again, to be replaced only by a sense of exhilaration, because Johnny Prescott had finally become a pilot. It was the one thing he'd always wanted to be all his life.

He said calmly, 'O.K., Alley. Just try and watch the sky an' not worry about Dai. . . . Ian?'

Nothing. Only the occasional splurge of static. Johnny risked a quick glance sideways. The Navigator hadn't moved since they'd pulled the plug, he just seemed to be sitting there, staring hopelessly at the onrushing lights as they sparkled and frisked towards them across the tops of the blurring waves in glinting reds and blues and yellows.

Just waiting. And watching. And, maybe, thinking of a dark lonely bedroom above a cottage in Sussex. And about the girl, heavy with the child they'd made together but hadn't yet experienced.

And she would be waiting too. . . .

He said sharply, urgently, 'Pilot to Navigator!'

The hunched figure in the right-hand seat stirred. Slowly the hand came up and Prescott heard the tinny click of the mike. Another moment of silence with only the eerie whisper of the Navigator's breathing in Johnny's earphones. Then Ian's voice.

Cool, slightly irritable and almost petulant. 'Christ, but I've *brought* you here, chum. Now what d'you want . . . or maybe I should jump out and wave a torch where X marks the spot?'

Johnny blinked at the dials in front of him and felt just a little silly and, all at the same time, a sort of funny, warm glow inside. Then Alley's calculatedly resigned falsetto from above. 'If the flask's smashed, does that mean dry sandwiches on the way back then?'

Which was when Johnny started feeling proud too. Because not only did he have the best actors in the Squadron for company that night, but he also had something more incredibly precious than all the medals in the Mint.

He had the friendship and the loyalty of very ordinary, very brave young men. It was, perhaps, the only nice thing a man could ever get out of the bloody awful business of War. But maybe, just maybe, it helped to make up for all the fear and the terror of what lay ahead.

One hundred and fifteen seconds ahead.

It didn't seem very long, really.

*

At eight minutes past eight the leading assault craft of each group were approximately four hundred yards from their appointed landing areas.

In the case of the Colonel's Group Two, now heading directly for the Nordkai, this placed them some two hundred yards from the nearest ship of the assembling convoy and one hundred and sixty yards from the Kriegsmarine launch transporting Major Otto Rhöme back to Ålvik.

The nearest ship was the armed trawler *Patzig*.

A few hundred yards to the west, still moving slowly through the water, lay H.M.S. *Muscadin*. She presented a big target.

And even discounting the reflected white glare from the dying starshell, it was rapidly getting lighter over the Østersfjord.

The first retaliatory shots were fired by the German Garrison at 08.08 hours and sixteen seconds G.M.T.

*

They were fired by a Wehrmacht soldier who'd come from a small village outside Gelsenkirchen. His name was Walter Zentner and he was actually quite an Anglophile in his own way. Having worked as a commis-waiter in a Brighton hotel for several years before the war, Unteroffizier Zentner had many affectionate memories of elderly ladies and gentlemen from Coventry or Manchester or Birmingham who had treated him most kindly during their sunset years of gracious retirement.

Being rather good-looking in a blond, blue-eyed manner, Walter also had a few fond memories of some not so old English ladies who'd just . . . well . . . *treated* him.

There were two weapon pits situated on the Hæl-en side of the town, both commanding an excellent field of fire over the fjord. Described in the Wehrmacht Manual of Field Works as a type *Schutzenlach fur s.M.G. Gewehrfuhrer schutze 1 und 2*, these pits were designed to accommodate the gun commander and his numbers one and two.

To the fjord side of the trench was dug a shallow recess in order to lower the weapon's silhouette. The fire trench itself was one metre forty deep and excavated in a curve behind the weapon recess to facilitate traversing the gun.

The weapon was a bipod-mounted 7.92 mm. Mauser MG34. It was fed by a series of 50-round non-disintegrating ammunition belts linked together to form 250-round belts. This meant that, with a cyclic rate of over 800 rounds per minute, it was an extremely efficient general purpose machine-gun against normal infantry targets.

It wasn't very good against destroyers.

Unteroffizier Zentner had been sitting on the edge of his trench, idly smoking and talking in a low voice to the gun commander, when the starshell had gone up over Oksenes. He quite liked the early morning duty because everything was quiet and still and, apart from the bitter cold, nothing much ever happened to interfere with a man's solitude.

On this particular morning Walter had, strangely enough, been thinking about the British and, in particular, about a dark-haired girl called Edith Mollison. She came from Bradford – he still had her address in his notebook, discreetly buried at the bottom of the kitbag – and they'd met in a hotel on Brighton promenade.

It had been a good summer in '38. A happy summer. Walter had fallen in love with Edith in those few carefree weeks . . . and then he'd come home. And they'd written a few times. And then Britain had declared War on a disbelieving Walter just as he was planning to return for Edith.

And the letters stopped. And they'd taught Walter how to fire an MG34 instead, then sent him to Ålvik.

Which was why Walter had been wondering if he dared try and write to Edith again, perhaps even through the International Red Cross. Except that then he would be guilty of communicating with an enemy. But how the *hell* can you fall in love with an enemy . . . ?

And then, at that point, a British Admiral had said quietly, 'Open the Line of Fire!'

For a few moments the gun crews lounging in the Ålvik weapon pits had, like everyone else in the Garrison, stared curiously up at the sky. Then, as the first shells landed on the Battery, curiosity changed first to concern and then, rapidly, to a realisation that this wasn't going to be an ordinary day any longer.

Perhaps it was because they were already at their posts, and that their brains weren't still numbed with the remnants of sleep, but Zentner's detachment were manning their weapons and alert for an assault from the sea even before the bloody silly air-raid sirens had started to wail from the distant hotel roof.

Walter, still snuggling in behind the high-impact plastic stock of the MG34, had stared incredulously at the gun commander, his face under the steel helmet reflecting the ever-changing colours of the erupting Battery, and muttered, 'What the . . . ?'

The Sergeant snarled, 'Bastards! The stupid *bastards*! They think it's a lousy air-raid in progress.'

The first blast waves from Oksenes whispered up the shingle beach and bounced over the parapet of the trench, tugging fretfully at the blond hair which had escaped from under Zentner's helmet. He saw the heads in the other pit turn involuntarily sideways as, far to their right, the waving black tree-tops between them and Hæl-en stood stark against the shell bursts from *Salamander*.

The Sergeant bellowed, 'Watch your front, there!' and swung grimly back to Walter. 'They'll be coming, lad. The Tommies'll be coming any moment now.'

Walter grinned uncertainly. Not quite comprehending but, at the same time, feeling the first clutch of fear at what was happening to them. 'The Tommies . . . ? You mean, the *British*, Sergeant?'

The man in field grey kneeling beside him nodded. 'I've got a feeling, Zentner. That's ships out there, softening us up. Hitting the coastal battery . . . then the Tommy *Sturmtruppen* – like it was on Lofoten.'

The ex-waiter was dimly aware of his hands starting to tremble and, nervously, he cocked the gun. Once the bolt had been retained in the sear he automatically pushed the cocking handle forward again to prevent the risk of a malfunction. Unteroffizier Walter Zentner was a good machine-gunner.

But he was also getting frightened. Much too frightened to have a clear, cool head. And it was the really frightened people who made a lot of those little mistakes in a war.

A great orange and grey mushroom suddenly erupted over Oksenes. Zentner could see it reflected along the air-cooled, oil-smooth barrel of the gun. Sickly he gazed across the water to where the mushroom, now flickering a dull eerie red on its undersides, climbed slowly into the sky with little jetting spurts of smoke trails tracing vagrant tentacles from within.

The Sergeant jerked his head. 'Ammo!' he muttered tensely. 'They've hit one of the magazines.'

Zentner couldn't take his eyes off the obscene growth still rising above the Battery. There were men actually dying under that, ordinary decent blokes – blokes he knew, with wives and families and love-affairs and Christmas leave to come. He wondered if his friend Kruger was on duty just now. Poor bloody Kruger, if he was. Kruger, the *afficionado* of the Garrison Cinema . . . and now, maybe, just a wispy fragment of a rolling, climbing puff of fire-washed cloud.

Behind and to the left of them, down the snow-powdered road into the dimly seen town, a man was shouting excitedly. The voice sounded familiar to Walter – just like that of Corporal Rogge, his relief number, who'd never quite been able to master the ability to ride his bicycle in a straight line.

'*Fliegerwarnung . . . in Deckung gehen!* Air-raid warning . . . take cover! *Fliegerwarnung . . . !*'

Zentner started to shake uncontrollably and closed his eyes tightly. 'Please, God. Tell me what is happening to us? Tell me that the British won't really come, and that this *is* just an air-raid like the siren says. And that one day we'll all wake up to find there isn't any war and I'll be able to write to Edith again. . . .'

Then the booming, rumbling roar of the distant explosion swept over the soldiers in the weapon pits, blanketing the anguished wail of the siren on the Norske Hotell and drowning the stentorian warning of the furiously pedalling Rogge.

Unwittingly Zentner's finger slipped inside the MG34's trigger guard. The gun was already cocked with the safety catch off. Fifty of the two hundred and fifty rounds in the belt consisted of tracer ammunition.

There are two firing grips on the Mauser MG34. Compressing the upper part of the trigger allows the selection of single shots – pulling the lower extremity produces a fully automatic rate of fire of some fourteen rounds per second.

Unteroffizier Zentner's tensed index finger now curled almost abstractedly round the base of that trigger. The time was eight minutes past eight precisely.

Beside Zentner the Sergeant said sharply, '*Jesus Gott!* Look, out there. . . .'

Startled, Zentner opened his eyes again, feeling the muscles in his shoulders tense with shock. Ahead of him the waters of the fjord seemed to move and sway under the lights. Great, threatening shadows loomed momentarily on either hand until, as another salvo shrieked in from the invisible enemy ships, Oksenes glowed with unearthly brilliance once again while the shadows flickered and vanished.

All except one. But that wasn't quite the same as all the other shadows anyway, because sometimes it seemed darker than the surrounding water and then, paradoxically, as the glow flared again it became lighter.

A lighter grey, more angular form. Almost directly opposite the weapon pits and the nervous soldiers. Right in the centre of the navigable channel.

For a further few uncomprehending moments Walter found himself staring at the slowly materialising ship in the fjord, and listening to a madly pleading voice in his head whispering, 'Make it a friendly one. Make her a German boat, *please*. . . .'

Until a little bit more of the Battery blew into blazing, illuminating fragments just as the huge White Ensign above the shadow stirred arrogantly and invitingly. And the Sergeant's hand involuntarily gripped Walter's hunched shoulders. . . . 'Warship! Din't I say so, lad? It's a Tommy warship!'

One pulse of a racing heart later and Unteroffizier Zentner wasn't even aware of the Sergeant's white shocked face staring down at him in horror. Or of the too-late bellowed command to 'Hold your *FIRE*!'

He didn't realise that a man firing an MG34 against Commandos was a killer, but that the same man firing against a destroyer was merely a very heroic – or very stupid – volunteer for martyrdom.

In that split second, when his overstrung nerves snapped and runaway reflexes pulled the trigger, he'd even forgotten that – while tracer rounds are an excellent guide to a gunner's accuracy – they are an equally infallible guide to his whereabouts.

Especially when the gun crews aboard H.M.S. *Muscadin* had been keyed up for quite a long time too. Just waiting for someone like Unteroffizier Walter Zentner to shoot at them.

*

Ten miles to the south-east, and seven thousand feet above the Østersfjord, the two ME109-Es of *Jagdgruppe* 26 were still droning on an interception course for the intruders reported as passing through Sectors Berta Kurfürst and Ludwig.

At this time no one in the operations plot at *Luftflotte Fünf* had realised that there was more than one group of enemy planes approaching the Norwegian coast.

The planned diversionary British air-raid on the inland town of Princessebrønn began at exactly eight minutes past eight – two minutes before H-Hour but, due to an unexpected freak snowstorm which temporarily blocked the Sumburgh runways, three minutes later than the Operational Schedule demanded.

It still meant, however, that – as no reports had yet been received from Ålvik – the six Hampdens which were just beginning their delayed high-level bombing run over Princessebrønn were assumed to be that same intruder flight reported earlier by the pilot of the JU88 recce plane which had splashed Ben Davidson's Blenheim.

And that Johnny Prescott's dual formation, now slamming in above the wave tops, remained as yet undetected. . . .

'Jumbo-One, Jumbo-One!'

Fichte brushed the R/T switch. 'This is Jumbo-One.' Idly he flicked his eyes over the instrument panel. Revs, boost, oil and rad temperatures, all still O.K.

'Jumbo-One. Fiver plus heavy babies now over Princessebrønn. Raid in progress. . . . Vector to two seven five to intercept intruders homeward bound.'

'Victor, Victor! Message understood!'

Paul thought irritably, 'Bastards!' not really certain of whether he meant the Royal Air Force or those Berlin desk-flyers who'd devised a system of air control which must have been the world's most efficient method of closing the stable door after the bloody horse had bolted.

He called Söhler. 'You hear that, Leutnant?'

'*Ja!*' Short and abrupt. Maybe there *was* still a touch of the Gestapo clinging to his wingman's plane after all. Fichte grinned humourlessly.

'Then let's go.'

He allowed the port wing to dip and the Messerschmitt slid round towards the new heading. Below him the cloud banks formed a frothy grey canopy, preventing any sight of the fires which must now be sparkling around Princessebrønn. Over to the left there was a break in the overcast just above the coast and gradually, as the compass grid came on to two seven five, the cloud rift swung directly ahead of the shimmering propeller. Abstractedly Fichte noted that it lay just above the point where they would cross the coast, and about two minutes ahead.

And directly, according to the map strapped to his knee, above some Godforsaken place called . . . Ålvik.

*

To the stunned and battered mind of Soldat Kruger, still grovelling into the frozen rubble of Oksenes, it seemed as though God really *had* forsaken Ålvik.

Over fifty six-inch naval shells had landed within the Battery lines in the three minutes since the bombardment began. The entire area of the Point was now a thundering inferno with the ground convulsing with subterranean shock every few seconds and, above it, that rolling smoke which clogged the lungs and made a semi-hysterical man retch with its foulness.

When the first magazine blew Kruger had momentarily lost consciousness. He wasn't even aware of the great glowing cloud rising above them into the sky, or of the expanding pressure waves which had bowled half a sailor right across the hollow where he and Feldwebel Voss burrowed – appearing magically from one bank of cavorting fumes, spinning directly above them and then disappearing once again into another wall of cordite smoke without even touching the ground.

But when he did finally open bulging eyes once again he found that, at least, they'd discovered what had happened to Herr Unteroffizier Woitke. Because fat Woitke had now joined them too, only he wasn't fat any more, not since a white-hot splinter of steel had sliced clinically across his lower belly, allowing most of his intestines to uncoil wetly over splayed thighs.

The one thing Kruger didn't really mind about was the noise. Not that he could hear it very well anyway – not since the magazine had exploded – but in the few brief moments when a salvo wasn't erupting all you could dimly make out was the dreadful sound of wounded men screaming from behind that drifting wall, and someone nearby pleading in a tone of unutterable agony for '*Hilde . . . liebling Hilde . . . !*'

Something pasty white stirred feebly beside Kruger and, as he turned his head, he suddenly saw with a shiver of fascinated revulsion that not only was Woitke still alive but that the Corporal was actually *moving*, for the love of Jesus! And that, even more horrible, the pudgy, shiny-black face above the breached belly still wore the same kind of secret grin that Woitke usually reserved for a particularly devastating hand of Skat cards.

It took several seconds before he realised that fat Woitke wasn't really smiling at all, and that the Unteroffizier had merely lost control of his facial muscles, allowing his bloodless lips to contort into a ghastly travesty of humour.

Kruger said helplessly, 'Lie down, Herr Unteroffizier Woitke. Please lie down and rest.'

Which was a pretty bloody silly thing to say, even for one of Hollywood's less credible productions. But that was another thing which Soldat Kruger was rapidly losing – his celluloid illusion that, when a superfluous extra came to the end of his script, he exited with a neatly dramatic blemish on his temple and just the slightest suspicion of a gallant smile to soften defiantly composed features.

In only three minutes Kruger had learnt that a man really died screaming and writhing, and with quite a proportion of his vital parts either eviscerated or shorn to tattered stumps. And that those defiant smiles were merely the death's head convulsions of beings who had lost their humanity.

And then Soldat Kruger did a very gallant thing himself. The kind of thing that he'd just decided could only really happen on a cinema screen. He didn't even know he was *being* gallant, but maybe that's how it always happens in real life.

It all started when two grimy, swearing figures loomed out of the fog and literally fell over the equally vociferous form of Sergeant Voss. They were Kriegsmarine gunners, they were shocked and jumpy too. But they were also very, very angry men. Almost as angry and as frustrated and as full of hate as Voss himself.

They pointed towards where the sea must lie, and their lips moved urgently. Kruger couldn't hear anything other than the almost continuous gunfire until the Sergeant, quite incredibly, stood up and, hauling the unresisting Private to his feet by the lapels of his greatcoat, bellowed in his ear that he was to follow them to . . . !

Another salvo straddled the Point to the south of them, the flashes only momentarily piercing the chemical gloom. And when the flashes had gone Kruger found himself all alone again – except for Woitke. Then Woitke opened his mouth and a froth of bloodied, glinting bubbles ran down his chin, and Kruger couldn't stand the terror of it any longer so he painfully stumbled after the disappearing men.

There was one gun left untouched out of the whole Battery. If you had looked carefully along the length of it you would have seen a grey, repeatedly sparkling shape just over a mile away in the North Sea. That shape would have been H.M.S. *Hystrix* and it was beside this last surviving gun that Kruger finally found the Sergeant and the sailors.

They actually fired that solitary gun, those four men. Yet even that was only accomplished after nightmare moments of slipping and sliding over the blood-soaked mounds of earth which now heaped the concrete emplacement. And a revulsed struggle to remove the charcoal-black corpse which an earlier blast had left folded almost carelessly over the barrel of the scarred weapon.

Kruger even loaded the shell into the breech himself, feeling the satin-smooth brass of the round cold against his skin as he pushed it clanging home up the oiled and rifled bore.

There was another slight delay when, after the first of the sea-men gunlayers had climbed into the metal seat and spun a few wheels, he suddenly seemed to rest his forehead tiredly against the soft rubber eyepiece of the gunsight and not want to move any more.

Until they pulled him away and found that it wasn't so much a lack of motivation as a minute splinter of shrapnel which had burrowed into the base of the sailor's spine, and that he wasn't actually dead but only paralysed.

Voss finally squeezed the trigger grip. At that particular moment Kruger really did feel just as the gallant Herr Flynn must have done when he saved the British Colonel's daughter from the Pathan hordes. For the tenth time.

He felt a bit let down by Feldwebel Voss, though. The Sergeant *could* have spat something a little more dramatic than 'Bastard Tommies . . . !' just before the great 105-millimetre barrel slammed back in its mounting and the only shell to be directed from the Oksenes Battery that day winged on its way towards the British Flagship.

He even saw the hit – a brief orange flower registering only briefly and rather disappointingly, just below the aircraft catapult deck between the cruiser's two raked funnels – then the next salvo winked from the British guns a mile away, almost as if they hadn't noticed his efforts.

Then the next! And the next. . . . And the bloody *next* . . . !

Until Soldat Kruger was screaming too, as he finally lost his sanity. Just sitting like a drooling idiot child amidst the still warm bodies of a decapitated Sergeant Voss and a black folded cadaver, and a paralysed man and a sailor now spitted on a twisted gun breech.

Sitting howling like a mad dog, with the blood pouring from his shattered eardrums and freezing in black rivulets down the side of his shocked face.

But they didn't show *that* either.

Not on a cinema screen.

*

During those first few long-anticipated moments when Walter Zentner's over-nervous finger directed a phosphorus finger to betray the alien presence of H.M. Destroyer *Muscadin*, a lot of the Commandos in the landing craft ducked involuntarily.

It wasn't that they were surprised by it – in fact, if anything, most of the British soldiers felt only an abstract sense of wonderment that they hadn't been engaged before. But now the defenders had actually begun to defend, it did emphasise that the next round could have a man's name on it. And that name varied for each particular Commando who was rather ashamedly ducking at the time.

The Colonel didn't duck. For one thing he was far too proud a man to flinch, and his Regiment had two hundred years of tradition behind it which said that he musn't. And, secondly, he was too absorbed in assessing the precise moment when he should pull the trigger of the Verey Pistol already held vertically above a steady arm. That one critical time when the first of the three green flares must blossom over the Østersfjord and signal the bombardment to stop.

And, also on the Green, the Blenheims from R.A.F. Wick would come roaring over Ålvik to lay their protective smoke around the landing areas.

Tyndal, L.C.A. One's Bren Gunner, didn't duck. But he didnae hae time f'r yon nonsense, being too busy setting his immaculately polished sights to zero as the range between him and the Jerrie boat wi' the bluidy big cannon on its front closed until he felt he could reach out and knock on the hull.

None of the men ducked in Captain Mike Seely's Group either, now wallowing and slamming into the offshore wavelets just under the lee of the Oksenes Battery. In fact, they didn't even notice the tracer, as every single one of the sixty blackened, grim faces under the steel helmets stared up in appalled silence from this grandstand viewing of the end product of saturation gunnery.

Now so close that they could actually feel the heat of the shell-bursts on their skin, it was perhaps salutory that not one of Seely's Commandos felt even a flicker of apprehension that the Royal Navy might shoot less than one hundred yards over, and kill them instead.

Troop-Sergeant Arthur Henderson didn't duck when the MG34 opened up. But he didn't have any fear of anything any more.

Charlie Smart didn't duck. He was still being sick.

Trooper Danny Williams ducked all right – then grinned nervously at Corporal Hanson, expertly worked the bolt of his Lee Enfield until he now had one round chambered for ready-use, and said matter-of-factly, 'What's the word f'r "Watch it, mate"? In German?'

22 Commando had just over one minute left before they could drop in for the day.

*

Unteroffizier Walter Zentner didn't have any time left at all.

As the ex-waiter's stream of tracer spanged and screeched against the twelve-foot range-finder and fire control top-mounted above *Muscadin*'s open bridge, Willie Bradbury bent forward over the voice pipe and snapped flatly, 'Full ahead both engines . . . starboard twenty.'

Then the Captain leaned back and – if you hadn't been quite so occupied with that terrifying 7.92 mm. flail ricochetting just over your head – you might just have detected the note of intense satisfaction in Willie's voice.

'Open Fire!' he said.

The Gunnery Officer spoke clearly and deliberately into the fire control handset. 'Shoot . . . Shoot . . . Shoot . . . !'

Amidships, directly abaft the destroyer's single grey funnel, the gunlayer of *Muscadin*'s multiple pom-poms had already lined his sights squarely over the source of the swerving tracer stream which appeared almost to float towards him.

It never occurred to Leading Seaman Docherty that there was actually a man behind that distant machine-gun. As far as he was concerned it was a target, a generously signposted target, and *that*, as far as Alf Docherty went, was bloody that.

He felt the ship suddenly tremble under the 40,000 h.p. surge of the turbines, then the gun platform leaned over to port as the ship's stern slewed under the rudder action. Only vaguely aware of the rising breeze gusting in over the edge of the mounting as *Muscadin* leapt ahead, Docherty automatically readjusted the pom-pom's elevation until the lighter tide-line of the fjord again lay just below the horizontal hair of the gunsight.

The pom-pom's Communication Number tensed, the white folds of his anti-flash hood flapping fitfully and unnoticed against th ₂ square-set steel helmet.

Docherty squeezed the trigger before the kid had finished yelling '*Shoo . . . !*'

It was undoubtedly a macabre coincidence that, just prior to *Muscadin*'s being detached as escort to Force King, Leading Seaman Alfred Docherty had been married in his home town of Bradford, Yorkshire.

He had been wed to a girl called Edith Mollison. He first met her in the autumn of 1938.

Just after she'd returned from a holiday in Brighton.

*

In the bucketing harbour launch carrying the rigidly impassive Major Rhöme back to the Nordkai – now clearly seen less than fifty agonising metres away – the dog Cuno started to bark.

Chief Petty Officer Döring didn't take his angry eyes off the slowly building bow wave of the distantly accelerating British destroyer, and he didn't stop gripping the stock of the Schmeisser so tightly that it might almost have been mistaken for the arch-fiend Churchill's neck.

But he did wonder why in Christ's name the bloody animal was barking at irrelevant shadows. Even though they *did* seem to be creeping quite inexplicably under the lee of Lohemeyer's swinging escort trawler . . . !

*

From the *Patzig*'s postage stamp bridge wing Leutnant Sur See Lohemeyer didn't see the water beetle shapes of the approaching landing craft either. Largely because, after one incredulous glance

at a Royal Naval warship steaming towards him down the Østersfjord, he wasn't able to credit that the British *could* have anything
even more outrageous in mind for Ålvik.

Apart from which – when you're commanding an old fishing
boat with a single ex-Polish Army 3.7 cm. foredeck armament
plus two ex-German Army machine-guns, and you see a hostile
destroyer less than a mile away from you, with gun turrets bigger
than your own bloody foc'slehead – then you've already got
enough problems.

'Destroyer! She's a *destroyer* . .' Lohemeyer said stupidly.

'A *Tommy* destroyer!' pronounced Oberbootmann Krupinsky
succinctly and, more practically, starting towards the wheelhouse
for his lifejacket. But Krupinsky – like Gefreiter Scherer at the
Signal Station – was a realist.

'Oh Jesus, a destroyer!' the *Patzig*'s Commander muttered
again. They were probably the words most often repeated in
Norway that day because, by eight and a half minutes past eight
quite a lot of people around the shores of the Østersfjord were
echoing them.

Lohemeyer lurched excitedly towards the wheelhouse too.
'*Gefechtstation!* Action Stations . . . !' He saw the Cox'n's white
face staring at him from behind the wheel, reflecting the glow
from the twin fires of Oksenes and Hæl-en. '. . . Maximum
revolutions. Starboard ten the wheel!'

Krupinsky said, 'Don't be bloody silly!'

Lohemeyer gazed at him incredulously. '*What* did you say,
Krupinsky?'

The Oberbootman's leathery face wore an expression of irritable
patience. 'I said – don't be bloody silly . . . Leutnant. Look, son,
that ship out there, she's mounting more guns than you've had
years in the Service. You never seen a Naval action, have you?
But I have, an' I tell you we don't . . .'

The Leutnant drew himself to his full height and looked at the
older man very hard. Just for a moment there was a lull in the
bombardment and it seemed very quiet up there on the little
trawler's bridge, with only the sound of the wind in the rigging
and the muted rumble of the single screw threshing with ever-
increasing vigour as the ship's speed built up.

Krupinsky noted softly that the boy's mouth was trembling,
then the lips tightened with determination. 'I'm giving you an

order, Oberbootmann. I intend to take this ship into action . . .
now!'

The shelling started again from the sea. The old man listened
quietly, and the boy nervously, and the old man knew then that
they were going to die. Then the boy said hopelessly, '. . . *please*,
Krupinsky.'

Krupinsky looked at the Leutnant for a moment longer. And
then the sadness faded from his eyes to be replaced by the old
sardonic grin. He saluted Werner Lohemeyer, but this time he
really meant it.

'Aye, aye, Sir!' he said.

He joined the trawler's gun crew running forward just as the
ersatz little warship's bows steadied on the enemy destroyer in
the middle of the fjord. He noticed that the two youngest ratings
were so excited at this prospect of real adventure that they had
even forgotten to put coats over the thin Kriegsmarine blues to
protect them from the bitter Norwegian wind, and momentarily
felt sad again.

Then he snapped briskly, 'Target – warship! Range – one
thousand metres! Bearing . . .'

Because Krupinsky, when he had to be, was a fatalist too.

*

The solitary round returned by the Oksenes Battery, fired by
Voss's hatred, Kruger's bewilderment and the bloody-minded
gallantry of two Naval Artillerymen, was on its way towards
H.M.S. *Hystrix* just as Rear-Admiral Braddock-Tenby was
glancing at his watch and straining vainly between ear-splitting
salvos to raise the approaching drone of the scheduled Blenheims.

Stainless steel Rolex time read precisely eight minutes and
fifty-nine seconds past eight.

Leading Seaman Docherty's first pom-pom shell exploded
beside the weapon pit of his brand-new wife's ex-suitor at exactly
the same moment.

Right then Unteroffizier Zentner didn't give a damn *what* time
it was.

*

The Cooked Man and the Ice Man drifting in a Luftwaffe-yellow
raft over the far horizon might – had they been watching – just

have been able to detect the flash of guns, or even faintly heard the rumble which announced the coming of the Commandos to Ålvik.

Of course, then they would have known that the dinghy was sinking too. Slowly, hardly perceptibly, but still settling ever lower into the North Sea as the buoyant air trickled from countless pricks left by the same shellburst which had created that young widow in Bremen.

But to two dead men who had already fought *their* particular war, that didn't matter either.

Chapter Five

'Geneva Convention . . . ? Shit! Let's hit the
bastards hard, then keep on kickin' them while they're
down . . . !'
Unknown German Soldier. Wehrmacht Armeekorps H.

During those last sixty seconds before the British landed on the
shores of the Østersfjord, the rest of the War was going very well
indeed. But wars always go well for somebody, somewhere – it
largely depends on whether you're doing the killing or the dying
at that particular time.

For instance, it was going well for those units of the Red Army
who were, at that moment, driving Kleist's stumbling, frost-
bitten divisions back along the roads from Rostov to Taganrog
and Mariupel. Though it wasn't going quite so well for their
comrades to the north, still awaiting burial after the successful
German assaults on Vyazma and Bryansk some six weeks before,
while the Ålvik Raid was only a Top Secret twinkle in MO9's
eye.

The War was promising to go very well indeed for the mariners
and gallant aviators aboard certain aircraft-carriers now well embarked on a Pacific voyage, though they weren't scheduled to
arrive at their destination until the 7th of December. They flew
the Imperial Flag of Japan and they were looking forward very
much to visiting a place called Pearl Harbour. Certainly, they
weren't actually *at* war – or at least, if they were, they hadn't
mentioned it to anybody.

At that moment it was going well for the sweating men of the
British 8th Army, now driving for the second time against
Rommel's armour defending the Cyrenaican ports around the Gulf
of Sirte, but the future looked rather more bleak for Major-
General Maltby's six battalions preparing to hold the island of
Hong Kong.

It was the end of a good month for the Axis Navies in the
Mediterranean. The Kriegsmarine U-boat Arm had just an-

nounced the sinking of the British carrier *Ark Royal*, the battleship *Barham* and two cruisers, while Italian frogmen had penetrated the Alexandria Harbour defences to damage seriously H.M. Battleships *Queen Elizabeth* and *Valiant*.

British Bomber Command were temporarily benefiting from the lull while the Luftwaffe perfected its ground control and airborne radar systems. R.A.F. aircrew casualties were still perfectly viable and bearable – which meant that only two and a half men out of every hundred committed were dying from burns, bullets or impact.

At nine minutes past eight on the morning of 31st November, 1941, fourteen British merchant seamen were busy dying while a U-boat machine-gunned the only life-raft to escape from their torpedoed freighter.

Twenty-one French children were being cremated alive after a 100-lb. bomb from an R.A.F. Stirling over the port of Brest – originally intended for the sheltering battleship *Prinz Eugen* – missed its target and landed on their orphanage in the northern suburbs.

A Danish solicitor – or doctor or industrialist or librarian – gratefully ceased to breathe at that specific moment in the Shell Offices of Copenhagen. His Gestapo interrogators who now occupied the building never actually found out what the man did before he joined the Resistance. But then, he didn't tell them anything else either.

The gas-contaminated cadaver of a Jewish poet burst into flames inside an oven in a place called Dachau.

And two Royal Army Service Corps drivers finished kicking a Malayan schoolboy to death in the Changi suburb of Singapore, 'Because he looked like a fuckin' Jap, mate!'

A pretty Belgian mother of three eased quietly out of the bed in which she had spent the night with two bronzed, athletic young *Waffen S.S.* troopers. Before she left the room she ever so carefully placed a grenade under the pillows between the sleeping heads. And then pulled the pin.

It was a good dawn for a day of war. For somebody.

*

It was a bloody lousy day for Gefreiter Scherer.

Fortunately for him, H.M. Destroyer *Salamander* just didn't have the fire power of the Flagship and, consequently, the installations on the northern, Hæl-en pincer of the fjord entrance hadn't received a pounding comparable to that which the Battery was still undergoing.

Not that the sole Kriegsmarine representative of the area would have agreed, seeing he was now scrabbling on hands and knees among the remnants of his first command – in between salvos – and trying to find his elusively-interred bloody RIFLE *DAMMIT. . . !*

Another shell exploded in the middle of the searchlight emplacement with an ear-splitting crash. Scherer hit the deck again, feeling the hate rising within him until he was shaking uncontrollably. Rolling over on his back he raised a frustrated fist, waving it vaguely in the direction of the smoke-obscured British ship. Then he couldn't stand the inactivity any longer and, waiting for the next ripple of concussions to die away, scrambled painfully to his feet and started to stagger towards the path leading to Ålvik.

More than anything else in the whole world, Gefreiter Scherer wanted to see a British soldier right now.

Or as soon as he could find another weapon to shoot the bastard with, anyway!

*

In the clinical atmosphere of *Hystrix*'s main galley, Petty Officer Chalk surreptitiously glanced over to where his friend and mentor cast a critical eye over the sandwich makers – then speared only the minutest morsel of cake-mix on the end of his little finger and conveyed it secretly to his mouth feeling, as he did so, all the deliciously illicit pleasures of childhood days long gone.

The ship jolted again as the deckhead lights flickered. Cook Chief Petty Officer Lumley noticed the youngest rating's hand tremble slightly and moved casually over to the table. 'Not long to go, son,' he said gently. 'Then we can all nip back 'ome an' tell the kids what we done to Jerrie, eh?'

The youngster grinned nervously. 'I don't have no kids, Chief P.O.'

Lumley nodded solemnly and patted the boy's shoulder. 'Then you're even better off than most, lad. I mean, you can go 'ome an' start *making* yourself a few!'

He glanced at his watch – only another minute of the inter-ruption left to go – and turned towards Herbert. He noticed the pleased look on Chalk's face and knew why, too, because he'd been a chef for a long time and knew every temptation of the trade. He grinned understandingly, took one step forward, and started to say, 'You reckon there's enough dried fruit in there, 'erbert . . . !'

The shell from the Oksenes Battery entered the port side upper deck of the Flagship while Cook Chief Petty Officer Lumley was still smiling. And Herbert was just thinking it was probably the best birthday cake he'd ever made in his life.

*

Ironically, probably the most placid German reaction to the gun-fire took place in one of the most unlikely spots of all – in the wheelhouse of the slowly manœuvring Baltic trader *Wismar*.

That wasn't to say no one was nervous, far from it. But the presence of the elderly, unflappable Captain on the bridge seemed to have a calming effect on Deckhand Strobe and Second Mate Bögel which would have been more than welcome in many of the nearby military installations.

When the lights had switched on the Old Man had just wandered into the rattling wheelhouse, given a brief glance up through the smoke from his polluted briar, and said thoughtfully, 'Aye, Bögel. I don't think we'll be sailing to-day after all.'

Bögel wriggled uncomfortably inside his pyjamas inside his jersey inside his stained blue reefer, and glanced at the dark shore-line, dimly seen through the starboard door. 'P'raps we could get alongside, Kapitan? Less exposed . . . an' we'll be a bloody sight nearer dry land.'

The Old Man stared at him expressionlessly, still puffing as though they had all day and the nearest British ship was on the China Station. 'Why, Herr Bögel? I should be glad to hear your reasoning.'

Hans Strobe absently corrected the ship's tendency to swing under the kick of the propeller, and listened intently. For some reason he felt quite detached from all this – almost as if, by being a Jew and a little different from real people, he wasn't on one side or the other. More like his mother and sister in Nienburg, who didn't know whether the British bombers or the Blackshirts presented the greater menace. . . .

The Second Mate scratched his head, tipping his battered cap to one side. 'I . . . er . . . well, I reckon . . .'

Then First Mate Krupp charged up the starboard ladder yelling '*Auslug! Feindlicher Kreuzer in Sicht. . . . Raus! Raus . . . !*'

He stopped dead and looked a bit embarrassed as he saw the Old Man staring back at him curiously. Chief Officer Krupp didn't like to be caught displaying a humiliating burst of panic, especially when that hook-nosed little Hebrew was ogling over the Captain's shoulder. It was about time they stopped those filthy cretins from following the good, clean seamen's trade. . . . 'We're being *attacked*, Sir!' he finished weakly.

The Captain puffed at his pipe and looked at the lights and the explosions and the milling, panic-stricken ships of the convoy. And the British warship now pouring a stream of fire against some hidden shore position.

And said dryly, 'Thank you for your expert assessment, Herr Krupp . . . though I would suggest your cruiser is only a destroyer.'

But then, the Old Man didn't like Krupp either.

Then he turned to the Second Mate at the telegraph. 'Full ahead, Bögel. . . . Bring her round to port, Strobe. Steer on the middle of the fjord entrance.'

Krupp stared at him in disbelief. 'That's where the *Tommies* are, f'r . . .'

Strobe eased the wheel as the ship's head swung on to the gap between Oksenes and Hæl-en. It was easy to see now – there were fires on both sides of it. And a grey 'V' shape with a sparkling white bone in its teeth to betray the position of the warship. Strobe glanced uneasily through the wheelhouse door and noticed another small ship, probably the trawler escort, steaming practically alongside and to port of them. He could see the vague silhouettes of men clustering around her forward gun and thought with a spasm of surprise, 'They're going for the Tommy. They're going to *fight* . . . !'

The Old Man gestured to Bögel and then at the little flag locker on the after bulkhead. 'Look out the Swedish courtesy ensign, son. . . . Quickly, please!'

He turned back to the First Mate. 'As you say, Mister – we are heading for the British. But as we are undoubtedly well within range of her guns wherever we decide to run, the point would appear to have very little merit . . . steady as she goes, Strobe. Nothing more to starboard.'

Krupp still looked disbelievingly towards the destroyer, now neatly bisected by *Wismar*'s rusted jackstaff. 'My son would never credit . . .'

'Your son happens to fight *his* war from a tank, Krupp!' The little Captain eyed him coldly and with distaste. 'And at this moment I am supremely indifferent to any opinions held by an absent member of the *1st S.S. Panzerdivision Leibstandarte Adolf Hitler!*'

He puffed furiously a couple of times then swung away towards Bögel, leaving the First Mate with a vacantly hanging mouth and a surreptitiously grinning Jewish audience. '. . . if you wish to do something more practical, Herr Krupp, I would suggest you look for your lifejacket and then muster the rest of the crew beside their life-rafts. . . . Bögel.'

'*Ja, Herr Kapitan?*'

The Old Man allowed just the faintest suspicion of a smile to crease the corners of his eyes. Strobe thought incredulously, 'The old bastard. The old bastard's actually *enjoying* himself!'

'Run the Swedish Flag up to our main truck. Then illuminate it with the signal lamp.'

The Second Mate blinked. 'Pose as a non-belligerent, Sir? The British'll never believe it!'

A whiff of tobacco smoke and cabbage lingered in the tiny wheelhouse as the Old Man stepped out to the wing. 'I know,' he said placidly. 'But she's my ship, and I'm damned if I'll abandon without even trying to save her. . . .'

Strobe bit his lip and stared at the fires ahead without really seeing. Only the seaman in him still kept the tired old ship on her course, because now Hans Strobe was beginning to feel frightened.

Then he heard a movement behind him and a lifejacket was slipped over his shoulders. He felt the Second Mate's fingers pull the tapes tight, then tie them across his chest. Just for a moment the eyes of a pure Aryan met his, then the young officer grinned at the Jew.

'Good luck, Hans . . . and f'r God's sake, kick your boots off before you go over the wall.'

Then he was gone, and Hans Strobe was left alone in the

Wismar's wheelhouse, just waiting for the moment when he knew the British must blow the ship from under him.

But he didn't mind quite so much now. Not when he wasn't entirely friendless any more.

*

Aboard the other ships of the embryonic Convoy XJ23, the reactions to the British presence in the Østersfjord were varied and colourful.

The Master of the *Käte Hass* – who had already declared to Leutnant Sur See Rex his intention to have a good voyage to Bremen, God willing, and the Tommies – decided very quickly that apparently neither were and, accordingly, kept right on going across the fjord to run his ship aground on the southern shore.

The Captain and crew of the *Pökel* abandoned ship even before *Muscadin*'s midships pom-pom had irritably replied to Zentner's opening volley. They were heading for the Sørenson Factory jetty in the ship's boat at that particular moment, completely oblivious of the fact that so were the ninety Commandos of Major Bert Stenhouse's Group Four. They'd also forgotten that the *Pökel*'s unenlightened Chief Engineer was still down in her engine-room, waiting patiently for manœuvring orders from a deserted bridge.

Alongside the Sörsund jetty itself, the crew of the fish-oil tanker *Bluthund* were filing resignedly back down her still rigged gangway. Being a practical, if somewhat less than aggressive complement, each sailor carried with him an already packed suitcase. Most of them were wondering how long it would be before they found another berth because they had the feeling that the *Bluthund* would be paying-off very soon now.

The same tanker's Master and First Mate, however, were damned if any bloody Englishman was going to sail past their ship unmolested, and spent the last minute before the landings in stripping off the canvas cover from the single First World War machine-gun mounted on her bridge wing.

The *Staatsman*, still approaching Ålvik from the head of the fjord, thought *Muscadin* was a German warship on exercises. They just kept on steaming towards her while the standby quartermaster was sent aft to be ready to dip the Ensign in salute as they passed.

Her Master considered the Wehrmacht had made a simply

splendid job of simulating a real battle, over there on Oksenes Point.

*

At nine minutes past eight, six JU88s were scrambled from Stavanger in response to an urgent call from *Luftflotte Fünf* Operations – they had just received a garbled signal from Ålvik which suggested enemy activity in that area. All serviceable fighter aircraft at Herdla were already airborne and it was arranged that the Stavanger bombers would be able to refuel there before continuing north.

Less than ten seconds later the duty controller at Herdla glanced from the tower above the snow-covered field and saw, with understandable surprise, twelve bombers coming in from the west, all in perfect line astern and shaping up for a landing approach on the planked runway.

He decided to obtain the Station Commandant's permission for this unscheduled visit and had just moved out on to the balcony to fire the red 'stay off' flare, when the first Blenheim from R.A.F. Sumburgh opened its bomb bay and laid a stick of 250-lb. H.E. right up the middle of the road.

By the time the twelfth Blenheim had battered across Herdla at two hundred feet, and added a sprinkling of incendiary to the mixture, there wasn't any runway left for a JU88 to refuel on. Or, for that matter, any fuel, or dispersal point. Or duty controller.

Fliegerhauptmann Eicke's *Schwarme*, returning from their abortive southern patrol four minutes later, had no alternative but to force-land with empty tanks, and try and avoid the largest of the craters which now dappled Herdla like a nightmare lunar landscape.

Eicke's left leg was torn off when his ME109 upended. He died from loss of blood seconds before his plane burst into flames as the gases in his upside-down seat tank ignited.

The Squadron Adjutant, Gerhard Lusser, died too. He had just managed to crawl underneath the wreck and release Eicke's seat-belt when the fighter exploded.

It now meant that Paul Fichte and Söhler were flying the only German planes within range of the Østersfjord for the rest of that morning.

*

That garbled telephone message from Ålvik was actually made by
the Wehrmacht Narvik veteran who didn't trust the judgment of
those thick bastards in the Norske Hotell. He made it from a
public call-box. It was cut short because he ran out of small
change and, for some inexplicable reason, the Norwegian telephone
operator in Princessebrønn didn't seem to understand what he
meant by a 'Collect Call', abruptly cutting him off from *Armeekorps H* the moment his money had expired.

Unterfeldwebel Oehlschläger proved once and for all that he
really *was* a thick bastard. He forgot all about telling anybody what
was happening to Ålvik.

Not that he was too sure himself, right then.

*

Leading Seaman Alfred Docherty, R.N., released his grip on the
pom-pom's trigger and the eight water-cooled barrels fell temporarily silent. Alf let his eyes travel hopefully along the shoreline
towards the town and felt an intense glow of satisfaction. He
started wondering what his wife Edith was doing right then. Or
was she still in bed with her long black hair trailed casually across
the pillow, just like it had been on that first night?

He frowned momentarily. Sometimes, just sometimes, he was
aware of a faintly niggling doubt – no more than a suspicion,
because he didn't know a lot about these things – but a slight
apprehension that Edith hadn't been quite straight with him. That
some time before their first blissful, perhaps too easily accomplished union, there had been another man. . . .

Or was it just because he'd been pretty expert at it, having had
quite a bit've practice while shoreside in Singapore an' Kowloon,
an' Pompey an' Melbourne an' down The Gut. . . . 'Course that
was different, wasn't it? What with him bein' a matelot an' that.

Walter Zentner was dead. The top of his skull was still inside
his steel helmet, twenty yards away from where the MG34's crew
huddled untidily under their inverted, silent weapon. A little
farther up the road a shocked, disbelieving Corporal was scrabbling
round on his hands and knees beside his wrecked bicycle, looking
for his upper denture and still whispering repetitively through
bloodied lips, '*Fliegerwarnung . . . in Deckung gehen! Fliegerwarnung . . . !*'

But you couldn't have heard him, not even if he'd been able to shout. Because the air-raid siren on top of the Norske Hotell was making far too much noise.

*

On the Nordkai, straining his eyes into the gloom in an agony of Impatience, Leutnant Sur See Rex waited anxiously for the Commandant's launch to return. He could still see the squat, slab-sided shape of the *Käte Hass* and the white water kicking up under her counter as her propeller threshed convulsively through the freezing black water. He thought she seemed to be heading a bit too far to the east – her course to form up with the still invisible *Patzig* should be bringing her head round in a much tighter sweep – but right then he was more concerned with the whereabouts of Major Rhöme.

'Hurry, Döring! For God's sake hurry man. We'll look a bloody fine crowd if we maroon the Area Commander in the middle of the damned fjord while his own Garriso . . . !'

Someone from the other side of the town started firing wildly into the fjord. Rex twisted involuntarily, wincing as the pain from his crippled leg speared into the base of his spine. '*What* the . . . ?'

Momentarily the fires on Oksenes flickered as something big passed between them and the Leutnant. Then whatever it was out there opened up on the source of the Wehrmacht tracer and, abruptly, the shore position ceased firing. Rex screwed his eyes up, trying to make out the ship in the fjord – that weapon she was using so damnably efficiently had one helluva rapid rate of fire. A bit like an Oerlikon . . . except Lohemeyer's trawler didn't *have* an Oerlikon. In fact, it was almost like a British pom-pom. . . .

Christ! Maybe they were all going mad around here? German troops firing at ships, and German ships firing at troops. And not only from the seaward side of the Point now. . . . But even if the outlandish idea of a Royal Navy vessel in the fjord had any foundation he would have been well warned in advance. Hell, Gefreiter Scherer up there in the Signal Station – or the Signal Station that presumably was, before the bombardment commenced – he would have signalled to the Harbour Office twenty minutes ago. Scherer was a sadist and a bloody menace, but he was Proper Navy through and through, and would undoubtedly have seen a warship if it had passed right under his broken nose . . .

apart from that kid Balke, and the two fruits Hopp and Specht, relieving the watch . . . !

A dog started barking in the distance, only vaguely discernible over the wail of that damned siren and the rattle of the anonymous gun in the fjord. Then the gun ceased firing at last and Rex, desperately anxious now, traced the barking to a point somewhere to his left front . . . Rhöme! Major Rhöme and his damn great alsatian. Arriving back at the Nordkai just in time to land in the middle of the biggest bloody shambles since the word 'Panic' was deleted from the Nazi dictionary.

Rex was half-way to the top of the ladder when he saw the returning launch. It seemed a little farther down the fjord than he would have imagined, but maybe Döring had taken the Commandant on a tour of the town's waterfront first.

And then Rex saw *two* launches approaching in the growing dawn. And then three . . . and bloody *four*, f'r God's sake! And they weren't even built like Naval launches, because they were bluff-bowed and slab-sided and more like assault craft than anythi . . .

Jesus Gott!

Assault craft. . . .

Rex started hobbling frantically towards the Harbour Office and the rack which still held the Schmeisser. He wasn't even aware of the pain from his deformed hip any more.

But he was the first man in the Ålvik Garrison actually to see the approach of 22 Commando.

*

The leading L.C.A.s were only ninety yards away from their landing-places now. In the bows of every craft men strained to see the details which – according to the latest recce photographs – should be exactly according to the briefings of the day they left Sollum Voe.

More or less! But it was those lesser things, the details which either the high altitude cameras or the eagle-eyed R.A.F. Intelligence Officers had missed, which could cost lives.

The Commandos in the Colonel's Headquarters Party were peering over the barrels of their Thompson Guns, trying to pick out the most likely corners and rooftops from where a hastily organised defensive fire could come. They already knew about the two weapon pits to the west of the town, but they didn't anticipate any more inconvenience from them.

Mike Seely was gazing abortively through the cordite smoke drifting sluggishly across the water from the still exploding Battery above him. He had been warned to expect wire across the exit from the beach and it was a cardinal rule of defence that one always protected one's wire with fire power.

Mike had just started to hope that the fire power wasn't going to be from the wrong damned side. He wished to God the Colonel would send up the Vereys – they were getting too close to the Flagship's target area for comfort. One thing f'r sure . . . no birthday cake ever had candles burning like the ones up there on Oksenes.

Troop-Sergeant Arthur Henderson had started thinking about that knife he'd dropped over the side, and feeling a little touch of regret about it. Then he thought that Ginny would have been horrified by the very idea of it, and felt better. A movement beside him and he turned to see Corporal Loomis passing the end of the bamboo scaling ladder forward. Henderson nodded, catching the brief flash of teeth against blackened features, then eased the ladder up so that its legs rested on the ramp of the L.C.A., ready to be raised into position as soon as they were alongside.

Bren Gunner Tyndal watched the armed trawler churning towards the fjord entrance until she was almost abeam of their position. His poacher's night vision could faintly detect the crewmen scrambling round her forward gun, but it also showed him, with a surge of regret, that the Jerrie would now pass well away from them. The little Scot fought off a ridiculous urge to stand up and wave, and yell, 'Hey, youse . . . come ower here if ye's wantin' a richt meltin'!'

Then he settled the Bren more comfortably into the pad of his shoulder and forgot about the bloody German boat, and optimistically scanned the approaching quayside for more promising game to flush.

All Danny Williams could see was the vomit-splashed bottom boards of his L.C.A., now approaching the shingle beach beside the Sörsund jetty. That and Charlie Smart's backside, which was even more bloody revolting. He still knew what was going on outside, though, because the Mad Major was standing fully erect up in the bows – in complete defiance of his own orders – and giving the lads a highly professional running commentary on the Ålvik scene.

'. . . there's a tanker alongside, just ahead and to the left, chaps. There's . . . yes, there's a couple of blighters up on her bridge, fiddling with a cover. . . . S'all right! They can't see us. . . . Hah! It *is* a machine-gun, cocky devils . . . eh? . . . Yeah, well they can't see us against the darkness yet but they're all lit up like the Fifth of whatnot – some bristle-cropped squarehead's left the wheelhouse light on. . . . Bren Gunner! Where's the Bren Gu . . . ? Ah, good man, cover them there's a dear chap. Oh, and if they get a little presumptuous – *do* blow their fucking heads off. . . .'

Number 22 Commando was now like a tightly-wound spring. Less than a hundred yards ahead of them were the places where that tension would finally be released.

But it was still a new and comparatively untried metal. No one could yet be quite certain of whether all the flaws had been removed in its forging.

*

There were no flaws in His Majesty's Ship *Hystrix*. Those men of the Clyde who had shaped the steel used in the building of the cruiser were craftsmen supreme. Yet even their artifice and dexterity could never be proof against the impact of a 105-millimetre round fired from a gun designed specifically to lay against warships.

The round which had felt so cold against Soldat Kruger's prickling skin was a *Panzerbrechend* – armour-piercing. It was constructed with a fuse-controlled mechanism which would delay detonation for that millisecond of time necessary to penetrate even the armoured skin of a battleship.

And *Hystrix* wasn't a battleship.

The shell struck the cruiser on her port side, just aft of the catapult valve chamber which formed part of the Walrus Amphibian's launching gear. It was at this stage that the soft metal outer cap of the projectile began to collapse, acting as a shock absorber and preventing the inner fused cap from fracture.

Had that point of impact been situated almost anywhere else on the catapult deck, then the round would probably have ricocheted off *Hystrix* to explode harmlessly in the North Sea. But it wasn't. And it didn't.

Instead – glancing off the outboard face of the compressed air reservoir – the shell's path was deflected slightly, causing it to nose downwards at an angle of some forty degrees from its original trajectory. It then entered the upper deck with a velocity of over one thousand feet per second leaving an elongated almost smooth-edged wound of less than twelve inches in length.

The rogue A.P. round then passed clean through the shipwrights' workshop without detonating, its outer cap collapsing only a little further as it struck the bulkhead of the adjacent Royal Marines' wash space aft. It then penetrated its second deck level, punched an equally neat semi-circle through the deckhead of the compartment below and, still slamming downwards, impacted against that space's overhead fire main.

The outer nose cone now disintegrated entirely. The inner fused cap eventually fractured, and the only shell from the Oksenes Battery finally exploded two feet above the stainless steel preparation table in the cruiser's main galley.

It happened at that precise moment when Cook Chief Petty Officer Lumley was still taking his first step towards his surreptitiously sampling friend and assistant, and smiling tolerantly, and saying, 'You reckon there's enough dried fruit in there, 'erber . . . !'

The eight men in the compartment died instantly, the fat melted out of their still erect bodies by the superheated flash of the exploding shell. Within milliseconds of the detonation, the purposely thin skin of paint on bulkheads and fittings had also blazed, stripped and disappeared under the searing expansion of the white-hot gases.

The main galley of His Majesty's Cruiser *Hystrix* ceased to exist, along with Cook Chief Petty Officer Lumley, late of the Savoy, Herbert Chalk, P.O. – still with a fragment of glacé cherry in his mouth, six young ratings in white aprons, and three thousand, two hundred and twenty-two and a half roast beef and pickled onion sandwiches.

The birthday cake mixture in the metal bowl warmed, baked, crisped and then incinerated in less time than it takes for a matelot to blink.

Just before *Hystrix* shuddered again as she fired another salvo towards Oksenes. Very few of the sweating seamen manning her turrets even knew they'd been hit.

*

Dieter Balke sprinted past the last few trees which lined the road between Ålvik and Hæl-en. He was nearly exhausted now but the only sense he was conscious of was a feeling of relief that, at last, he was nearing the end of his mission, and very soon he would find Hafenmeister Rex to tell him about the warship.

Had any of the Wehrmacht machine-gunners in the weapon pits beside the path been left alive they would probably have heard the Leichtmatrose a hundred metres away. Even if the pounding of his too-tight boots on the powdery snow hadn't warned them, then the rasping of tortured lungs would have been quite detectable.

Except for the siren, of course.

Actually Balke didn't know what had happened to the weapon pits because, when you're running like hell, you can't really hear a pom-pom half a mile away. And he hadn't seen the gunfire from the fjord because of the trees. In fact, the only thing which finally suggested something might be amiss was that, as he stumbled past the first position, he was quite surprised to see that the road was all pitted and scarred, with great black smears of earth dappling the virgin snow.

The soldiers in the trench didn't seem quite right either, somehow – the way they lolled against the edges of it as though they didn't have a care in the world, and that the British were safely on the other side of the German Ocean. He smiled at himself and felt a bit silly – seen through the weak dawn light one could almost imagine that wasn't a man's head projecting over the lip of the pit there, but that it was an inverted leg . . . and a foot . . . still inside a *boot* . . . ?

Dieter Balke stopped running, the impetus of his charge having carried him on to the second position, nearest the town. This time, before he had even skidded to a halt, his mental defences were up and any sense of impending horror repelled in anticipation.

Which was why, when he did look down at the machine-gunner without a top to his head and the other two Wehrmacht corpses, all he felt was an overpowering – if slightly bewildered – sense of curiosity.

Because opportunity, according to the philosophy of Dieter Balke, could present itself in many guises.

And he'd always wanted the chance to fire an MG34.

*

A light machine-gun started firing sporadically from the other side of the fjord. Nobody was hit, and nobody seemed to know where the bullets were coming from or going to.

But it showed that the German Garrison – or part of it, anyway – was beginning to realise what was happening.

*

Muscadin's Number One dropped his night glasses from his eyes and swung round urgently. 'The armed trawler's swung towards us, Sir. Looks as though they've seen us.'

The Captain glanced briefly over towards the *Patzig*, now discernible even to the naked eye through the rapidly swelling dawn light, and chewed his lip thoughtfully. So far they'd been lucky. Only that one brief engagement up to now and, quite incredibly, no follow up to it.

He glanced at his watch – thirty seconds before the Troops would land, assuming they were on schedule. And perhaps it wasn't really so surprising that Jerrie hadn't got into top gear yet. In actual fact the bombardment had only been in progress for just over four minutes, and a covey of six-inch shells on your breakfast table takes a bit of digesting. They should still have the advantage of surprise on the British side.

A second, and this time concealed, light weapon opened up from somewhere past the town. Willie heard several shots clanging and sparking from the swept top of 'A' Gun shield and ducked involuntarily. It was a nasty, helpless feeling to know someone was shooting at you and you didn't know from which direction. He looked peevishly around the men on the destroyer's bridge, just daring them to grin, but they were all coming back to the vertical with sheepish pretending-not-to-notice expressions too, and Willie felt better again.

The starboard lookout, Jackson, called shrilly, 'Vessel bearing green one oh, Sir! Not the trawler . . . another one!'

Willie raised the glasses. 'Merchantman! Just about abeam of the Jerrie escort and on the same heading, towards us.'

Number One looked at the *Wismar* too. 'Looks as though she's making a run for it. Poor devils must be scared stiff.'

The Captain glanced at him strangely. Somehow he'd never suspected the First Lieutenant of such sympathetic feeling. But neither had any of the ratings either. He stared back at the approaching merchant ship and frowned – it didn't add up yet. To reach the mouth of the fjord they would have to pass within two hundred yards of *Muscadin*. And surely no German Master could ever imagine Willie would let him go with a wave and a smile . . . ?

Number One looked towards him anxiously. 'That trawler . . . she's liable to engage us any moment, Sir. They could just be crazy enough.'

Willie came to a decision. Who was it that once said, 'Let sleeping dogs lie'? And obviously very few of the defenders were really aware of what was happening yet. While the assault craft would be touching the ground within another twenty or thirty seconds now, so far virtually undetected. . . .

'We'll hold our fire a little longer,' Willie said, purposely not seeing the expression of anguished doubt on his deputy's features.

'Oh Lord!' the First Lieutenant muttered. Very, very quietly indeed.

*

'C'mon, c'mon, c'*MON* . . . !'

Ian tore his eyes off the blurring water passing below and glanced across the Blenheim's cockpit. Johnny Prescott was hunched slightly forward over the stick, peering ahead through the scarred perspex and screwing his eyes up in an agony of frustration.

The Navigator licked dry lips. 'You mean the greens, Skipper?'

The plane dipped fractionally and Johnny hauled her back up on to the rails with the sweat beading his forehead in little shiny runnels, reflecting the light from the fires now less than two miles ahead.

'If they don't fire them soon we'll have to go round for another run-in over the bloody target. . . . How long to go?'

Ian hauled his cuff back, irrationally grudging every moment lost of that almost masochistic anticipation of disaster he had experienced while staring hypnotically forward. 'Thirteen seconds to go. . . . *Chri* . . . !'

Johnny hit the rudder bar and the Blenheim skidded back on course. God, but it was hard to judge height and distance over the sea, especially when you didn't hardly have enough light yet to read a bloody newspaper. . . . He smiled tightly. 'Sorry!'

The Navigator didn't smile back. 'Eleven seconds. . . . Ten . . . niner. . . .'

Johnny wondered how Alley was feeling in the upper turret, going into battle backwards. And whether Dai Evans was still out there on their tail. But he didn't dare relax his concentration long enough to glance aft. Then Ian called urgently, 'There's the ships . . . there . . . *MARK*! One mile to the entrance now, Johnny. . . .'

Prescott was only vaguely aware of the black shapes as they rushed crazily towards them across the surface of the sea. But it wasn't the ships that were rushing – it was he, Johnny Prescott. And at a speed which, if they dipped too far too abruptly, would send both him and his crew spinning and cartwheeling across the reaching wavetops in a starfishing ball of flame.

A crazy glimpse of masts and funnels below, suddenly crystal-clear through the gloom. Then the long raked bow of the destroyer pushing a white bone in her teeth as it appeared to swing madly through the arc of their passing. Then the ships were gone and there were only the great black cliffs marking the entrance to the fjord, and the flames reaching out towards them, and the still continuing explosions. . . .

And suddenly Ian was screaming excitedly, 'The greens! It's the *greens*, Johnny . . . dead ahead!'

He lifted his eyes momentarily from the altimeter, and saw them. One soaring, beckoning finger against the distant mountains at the head of the Østersfjord. One green, then two . . . then three . . . !

The signal had been given. Now they were irretrievably committed. He thought, 'Please, God! Don't let me die . . . please.'

Then deliberately eased the stick forward until the Blenheim was blasting towards the rushing cliffs with the Mercury VIIIs echoing back from the white-capped rocks and the prop wash whirling the sea astern into leaping, angry fingers.

None of them saw the fighters dropping down towards them through the hole in the clouds above Ålvik.

*

The Colonel gazed up at the Verey flares he'd just fired, watched the last one burst with a high-altitude pop while the ghostly light momentarily washed the drab netted helmets of the men in his craft, then swung back towards the approaching Nordkai with a faintly ridiculous sense of relief.

Someone in the stern of the craft said tightly, 'Wonder if they'll come?' and the Colonel wasn't quite sure whether he meant the Blenheims or the Germans.

Seventy yards.

The Colonel glanced quickly to his right and left. There they were, now pulling alongside with thirty feet separating them – L.C.A.s Three and Four with, in the second wave, Five, Seven and Nine. Tail-End Charlie was Lieutenant Endersby's Support Landing Craft – a Commando innovation which was basically an armoured L.C.A. but mounting twin machine-guns and a three-inch mortar, and radio-linked to the assault groups by a standard 18 Set. John Endersby's somewhat buccaneering role was to cruise close inshore, lending both anti-aircraft and ground support wherever required.

Duncan smiled bleakly – during the next few minutes they would need all the support they could get while the Headquarters Party went ashore over the Nordkai. He noticed that Troop-Sergeant Henderson's L.C.A. Three already had their scaling ladder raised over the bows and reflected sombrely that the tall, sad ex-grocer probably faced the most dicey disembarkation of all. His Troop would first appear over the edge of the quay nearest to the Harbourmaster's Office, and any alert Jerrie with a sub-machine-gun wouldn't even need to step out into the cold to inflict bloody slaughter.

The distant rattle of light MG fire ceased briefly and the Colonel strained his ears for the drone of the planes. They should be entering the fjord now – if they were coming at all. And if they weren't, then all his Group would have as cover would be the fire from the S.L.C. . . . .

He stared ahead again, trying to detect any sign of movement along the wharf, now clearly seen, but there was nothing. Only the silvery glint of black water lapping against the weed-skirted stone and, above it, the high-pitched jumble of rooftops that was the skyline of Ålvik. Just for a moment it seemed very quiet and peaceful, except for the wail of that damned air-raid siren somewhere in the town.

Then a Trooper called softly, 'Listen!'

The growl of another salvo – the last salvo, the Colonel hoped –

died away from the Point and then, faintly above the siren's cry, they could detect a distant whisper. Then the whisper grew to a muted grumble approaching from the west. And then to a roar of power, racketing and reflecting around the shores of the Østersfjord.

The Colonel saw the tight grins as men smiled at each other from strained faces. Until there was a sudden terrible groan of agony from beside him and, startled, he swung his head to see that it wasn't a groan of agony at all but that – with all need for secrecy gone – it was Pipe-Corporal McLusky standing up in the bows of the craft like a great kilted image of his Highland forbears, and breathing the first breath of life into the bladder of his pipes.

And then they couldn't hear the pipes. Or the siren. Or even the pumping of their own hearts.

As the Blenheims of the Royal Air Force came blasting in from the sea.

*

Oberbootman Döring heard the aircraft and saw the L.C.A.s ahead of the harbour launch at one and the same time.

He didn't even feel the dog's fangs slash at his leg, or see the Commandant's shocked eyes staring up at him, as he hurled himself aft over the thwart shouting desperately to the white-faced helmsman, '*Steuerbord . . . !* Hard to starboard, man!'

And then helplessly watched as the launch's head swung towards the little beach to the east of the town, and wondered which one of the two hundred and twenty British soldiers in those dimly seen boxes would start to kill him first.

He didn't know that quite a lot of those khaki-clad men in the assault craft nearest him were Norwegian, or perhaps he would have been even more frightened than he was already.

*

Some of the officers on the cruiser's bridge had hardly faltered when the round from the Battery exploded in the main galley aft. The Captain, the Captain's Secretary and the ship's Navigating Officer, engaged in conning the cruiser from the forward end of the compass platform amid a litter of extra Army radio equipment, Army Signallers and lookouts, were almost entirely protected even from the blast.

The men at the after end of the bridge – including the Admiral, the Brigadier and the Force Navigator, Captain Rutleigh – had been rather more exposed. All Braddock-Tenby could remember was glancing at his watch, and the next thing being down on his hands and knees on the deck while the guns hammered out another salvo.

He looked shakily round, feeling a bit ridiculous but, irritatingly, unable to say or do anything at all until the fuzzy singing sensation in his head cleared. There was a numbed, cold feeling in the small of his back too, and just for a moment he wondered vaguely if he'd been hit, then the man lying on top of him rolled off with a muttered, 'Blast an' dammit to hell!' and the Admiral realised that he'd merely been struck a glancing blow by the rim of Rutleigh's steel helmet.

Rutleigh said, 'Oh, terribly sorry, Sir,' in the kind of voice one normally reserves for accidental collisions in crowded tube stations and, not to be outdone, the Admiral smiled politely at the deck and answered, 'Perfectly all right, Rutleigh!' as though he was quite used to being knocked down by 105-millimetre shells every day.

Then, as his head cleared, the incongruity of it dawned on him and he gazed into Rutleigh's apparently still floating features. 'John! The Brigadier. . . . Has he been hit?'

The Captain shook his head as Aubrey's voice called out breezily, 'Over here, Arthur. Take more than a Jerrie round to . . .'

Aubrey's voice suddenly broke off and the Admiral clawed himself to his feet urgently, using the after halyard cleats for leverage. Summoning all his reserves he shook his head, willing it to clear, then opened his eyes again to see, with a surge of concern, the Brigadier bending over a still, small form on the deck at the foot of the standard compass pedestal.

One of the lookouts said quietly, 'It's the Middy, Sir. Copped a packet.'

Someone else snapped, 'Get the Surgeon Commander to the bridge immediately!' and then the Admiral was looking down at the hunched, almost relaxed figure on the deck. He didn't feel anything right then, because there wasn't any time for grief, but he knew that the lifejacket which the Chief Yeoman was ever so gently placing under the child's head wasn't really necessary.

The little hole where the shell splinter had entered the Midshipman's brain, just under the too large steel helmet rim and behind the pink, slightly protruding ear, told him it wasn't.

He said anxiously, 'What time is it? How long . . . ?'

Then the Blenheims roared overhead just as the cruiser fired again, and he knew that only seconds had passed since the hit, and that they could expect the green Vereys from Duncan at any moment. The Brigadier grasped his arm and pointed upwards. 'Only two, Arthur. Only two damn planes . . . !'

Braddock-Tenby nodded grimly – it meant that somewhere, somehow, the planning had gone wrong, and that very soon some men would be fighting their way ashore without any screen to cover them after all. He asked anxiously, 'Which Groups . . . ?'

'Seely and Courtenay. We decided that if anyone had to lose the cover of smoke, then it was better to be the chaps following immediately after the bombardment. . . . The R.A.F. will miss out on both sides of the entrance.'

The Admiral frowned. 'That still leaves three landing points.'

'Ålvik itself, and the Sörsund Factory area will be the targets. The ambush party at the head of the fjord were to do without it anyway . . . try and retain some element of surprise if they're needed.'

Braddock-Tenby nodded again, his mind racing to catch up. It was funny how everything happened at once, and usually when you needed a clear brain to cope with the stresses which were already being forced on it. But perhaps having the ability to function under those conditions was why the Admiral *was* an Admiral.

He swung quickly aft. Already he had dismissed the shoreside-difficulties and was concentrating on the more immediate local problems – the lifting of the bombardment and the damage to *Hystrix*. The ship shuddered again and the cordite cloud hid the body of the boy momentarily. The Admiral thought irrelevantly that they must approximate a tableau of Hell, those tense, concentrating figures around him on the cruiser's bridge. Smoke, flame and the fumes of noxious gases while, in the midst of it all, ghostly figures still went about the mundane business of death.

'Call me as soon as you see the Vereys from the fjord.'

He leant out over the wing of the bridge, gazing astern past the starboard multiple pom-pom and the high forward funnel to where the ship had taken the hit. The pom-pom itself seemed to sit drunkenly on its mounting, barrels now pointing idly and in the air. Beside it, staring up at him with vacant, idiot eyes, two ratings lay still and unmoving while another leading seaman just sat with his back against the gun, not even trying to stop the blood which traced dark tributaries down the side of his ashen face.

The catapult deck was gone – only the jetting flames and twisted edges of buckled steel plate now indicated where it had been. The Admiral could see the shattered remnants of the recovery crane trailing down along the starboard side while the only other recognisable fragment was the after fuselage and tail-plane of the Walrus amphibian protruding from the crater. Then the fire licked higher, and glowed whiter for a moment, and even that was gone.

He passed an inexplicably shaking hand over his eyes and leaned farther out, ignoring the rushing black water below.

But already *Hystrix*'s damage control parties were converging on the scene. Steel-helmeted men moved swiftly and efficiently, crouching low against the roar of the flames as they ran white threadlines of hoses from the red-painted hydrants. Farther aft a sick-berth attendant knelt beside the body of one of the twin four-inch anti-aircraft guns' crew, blown from the cover of his thin protective shield by the force of the blast, and Braddock-Tenby wondered grimly how many more men were past all aid down there in the volcano that was the *Hystrix* midships section.

A Chief Petty Officer raised a soot-blackened arm and the leading hand of the hose party spun the hydrant wheel. The Admiral watched the first pulse of water wriggling along the flat white ribbon of the hose and automatically glanced at his watch – 8.09 and fifty seconds. It had taken the smoothly rehearsed machine that made up the cruiser's complement less than one minute to absorb, assess and tackle the body blow dealt to their ship.

The Admiral found himself nodding approvingly – already his own professional appraisal had shown him that the damage, while spectacular, was to some extent only superficial. No vital part of the cruiser was involved from a fighting efficiency point of view, and there would be no underwater fractures of the hull. And now he confirmed what he'd always known – that those crouching men around the crater were more than competent to handle the emergency without any help from an elderly, perhaps rather fractious Rear-Admiral who was only along for the bloody ride anyway.

He'd just turned forward when the lookout called excitedly, 'Flares, Sir. . . . Three. Bearing green eight five!'

The cruiser's broadside roared again and the Admiral waited for the rumble to die away, feeling as he did so the fresh Norwegian wind on his face lifting, capturing and dissipating the smoke of battle. He suddenly felt relief and elation – relief at the sighting of the flares, and elation in the knowledge that the Royal Navy had played their initial part to perfection.

Bracing himself stiffly he looked straight ahead, over the swinging bows of the ship as she turned towards the shore and into the dawn light. Then he called clearly, 'All guns – Cease firing!'

The smoke from the fires in *Hystrix*'s belly lay across the grey, heaving flanks of the North Sea. And in that smoke drifted all that remained of Cook Chief Petty Officer Lumley, and Herbert Chalk, and eleven more sailors who would never, ever go home again. Drifting and mingling with the carbonised atoms of what had been a young man's birthday cake.

And then the Admiral said sharply, 'Yeoman . . . make to *Salamander* immediately – PROCEED OSTERSFJORD IN SUPPORT OF HMS MUSCADIN. . . .'

He hesitated, thinking about the young boy. '. . . and add – GOOD HUNTING . . . message ends.'

Chapter Six

'Now would I give a thousand furlongs of sea for an acre of barren land.'

William Shakespeare.

On the fourth day of June 1940 the retreating British Army withdrew from the Continent of Europe. Reichsminister Paul Joseph Goebbels confirmed quite categorically that they were now merely a 'defeated, fleeing rabble!'

He must therefore have been a little disconcerted when – less than three weeks later, on the twenty-third night of the same month – the first of the rabble came back again.

Winston Churchill called them 'Men of the hunter-killer class'. Adolf Hitler called them 'Gangsters'.

The British Army called them 'Commandos'.

And from that night, the Commandos kept *on* coming back – to Boulogne and Plage de Merlimont, and to Guernsey and Stamsund and Vaagso and St Nazaire and Dieppe. . . .

. . . until, if you were a German soldier, you could never really rest easily in your bed at night. And you didn't dare leave even one kilometre of unscaleable cliff undefended. And you couldn't once afford to turn your back on the little bit of coastline you were guarding – which stretched from ice-bound Norway to the sun-washed Pyrenees.

Because if you did relax, even for a moment, then you were already a prey to the fear that those grim, silent, black-faced raiders would storm ashore out of the concealing darkness.

And kill you!

*

They would start to kill you at a moment in time called – *H-Hour*.

Not that the men of 22 Commando were able to arrive exactly unheralded and silent when H-Hour came to Ålvik. By virtue of the terrain, and the need to neutralise the Oksenes Battery before they could fire first, the raiders stormed up this particular hostile shore rather more with the roar of a British Lion than the whispering pad of a nocturnal leopard.

But it was also because of the five-minute warning from the Navy's guns that, by the time the assault craft touched bottom, there was at least some form of defence organised and waiting for them, mainly in the town itself and around the Sørenson Factory perimeter on the south shore.

For instance, while Leutnant Sur See Rex was still desperately hobbling towards the Harbour Office in search of a weapon, he had heard the clatter of running feet and whirled nervously to see three soldiers hurriedly, but very efficiently, setting an MG34 on its tripod at the corner of the warehouse. The point they'd selected would give them an uninterrupted field of fire over the edge of the Nordkai itself – just where the Colonel's Headquarters Party would appear in about twenty seconds.

Bending low, and wincing as the pain clutched his hip again, Rex altered course towards the machine-gun crew. 'They're coming, Corporal . . . less than fifty metres off the wharf.'

The gun commander glanced up and Rex recognised him as one of the combat veterans from the previous year's campaign. The man spat unemotionally into the snow and grunted flatly, 'We'll be ready, Herr Leutnant.'

'Who the hell's in charge in the town? Any officers?'

The Wehrmacht veteran glanced briefly at the gold rings on Rex's sleeve and grinned humourlessly. 'Not yet. But maybe the bastards haven't finished breakfa . . .'

He broke off and, deftly swinging the gun barrel experimentally, shrugged. 'There's a staff-sergeant-major organising back there – Stabsfeldwebel Leuschner. Most of the green squaddies're still down in the shelters, thanks to that bloody siren.'

Rex had just heard the first shouted commands from the main street, and gone back to wondering where the devil Major Otto

Rhöme could possibly be, when the roar of the planes drowned the metallic clatter as the Corporal cocked the MG34 and laid the air-cooled barrel right along the line of the wharf.

And waited without any sign of nervousness at all.

Just like Ordinary Seaman Dieter Balke, now also waiting a little apprehensively but quite coolly, behind *his* newly-acquired and restabilised MG34 in the shattered weapon pit beside the Hæl-en path.

One small part of Balke's fail-safe brain still found some difficulty in completely blanking out the horror of those tumbled, already stiffening bodies he'd dragged awkwardly out of the trench. Which accounted for the occasional twinges of apprehension – dimly he couldn't quite ignore the fact that when They finally came . . . and he didn't even know yet who 'They' were, he only sensed They were coming . . . then he, Dieter Balke, might just conceivably come under fire too.

His overstressed mind could not, however, possibly encompass the further logic that, once having been fired at, then he might be lying equally untidily and grotesquely in the snow, and without any top to *his* head either.

Which accounted for the coolness.

Balke started to whistle softly and, feeling in his greatcoat pocket, produced a stained white handkerchief with which he began to polish the splinter-scarred hardwood stock of the machine-gun. He started to think of many things as he rubbed – of his father, and how proud he would be if he could see his young son now. And of how he'd really always wanted to be a soldier, anyway, with a neat grey uniform and a machine-gun to fire against England. And of the dimly recollected Gefreiter Scherer, now presumably dead in the ruins of the Signal Station . . . which was quite an appropriate conclusion, really, because Scherer had been very unkind to him, what with the shouting and the stamping and the sneering an' that. . . .

Of course Dieter Balke couldn't possibly have been expected to understand that he was already a casualty of the Ålvik Raid too. That he was ill, mentally ill, because the stresses of Scherer's assault coupled with the traumatic impact of that horrific meeting with the dead men in the middle of the wood – all these events had snapped the few remaining strands of sanity that his previously unstable mind had desperately hidden behind.

Which was why, when he looked over the sights of the gun and saw a double line of assault craft crawling like great black water beetles towards the centre of the town, all he felt was a great sense of well-being and pleasurable gratitude to the British soldiers for being so good as to give him a beautiful machine-gun, as well as an overgenerous selection of targets.

Because, when you're as mentally deranged as Dieter Balke was by ten minutes past eight on that November morning, somehow you never think of yourself as being the most vulnerable target of all.

Of course Soldat Kruger was even more sick, being completely insane by then. Utterly demented, and lying all curled up under the barrel of the wrecked gun on Oksenes, and alternately howling like a lost wolf and snarling and grinning up at the drifting smoke still blanketing the murdered Battery.

Kruger was a shell-shocked lunatic. And the stubborn, veteran Feldwebel Voss was dead. And fat Woitke still lay in a hole in the ground with a grinning, paralysed mouth and pudgy hands which fumbled ineffectually to prevent his guts from slipping through the rip in his belly. . . .

Scherer was still bloody running! Still charging angrily and full of hate for the British, down the long winding path from Hæl-en, in the snow-impressed footsteps of Balke. He'd just breasted the steep slope leading down to the wrecked motor cycle and its obscene company, when the Blenheims came down the fjord and H-Hour had arrived.

In the Norske Hotell, Unterfeldwebel Oehlschläger was staring in utter disbelief at the platoon of infantrymen who had just doubled grim-faced into the lobby and immediately set about preparing defensive positions by smashing their rifle-butts through every pane of floral gilded glass in the place.

And at the no longer quite so reassuring Korvettenkapitän who was now frantically instructing three nervous S.K.L. ratings as to precisely which secret papers should be removed from the filing cabinets and burned first.

And especially at the thunderous expression of Staff-Sergeant-Major Leuschner who was now standing with a Schmeisser Machine Pistol levelled very deliberately at Oehlschläger's head, and roaring, 'You got two seconds, Oehlschläger! Two seconds to shut that fucking siren *OFF*!'

The big Corporal with the smashed face and the wrecked bicycle was still grovelling dazedly on his hands and knees near Balke's commandeered weapon pit, feeling for his lost dentures and croaking bloodily, '*Fliegerwarnung . . . in Deckung gehen! Fliegerwarnung . . . !*'

As the hands of the old brass clock on the trawler *Patzig*'s wheelhouse bulkhead crept up to precisely ten minutes past eight, her young Captain was gripping the sanded teak rail of her tiny bridge convulsively, and fighting to keep down the fear of the death he knew must come very soon.

But he was a German Naval Officer, and the one thing he feared more than death was the fear of being proved a coward. To the terrified cox'n at the trawler's wheel, however, Leutnant Sur See Lohemeyer looked the very epitome of Teutonic gallantry. Standing straight and tall, eyes fixed in a steel cold stare on the approaching enemy, the Kapitan looked so gallant and invincible . . . the suicidal, fanatical bastard!

The coxwain didn't know that Werner Lohemeyer was really so frightened that he didn't relax his numbing grip on the rail, and that he didn't dare turn away from the British destroyer because, if he did, he could never stop himself running away, and hiding all curled up for ever.

And that he kept on whispering to himself over and over again, 'For the *Führer*! I *will* attack . . . I will not scuttle . . . I . . . will . . . not . . . *scuttle* my Command! I will not . . . Please, God. Please. . . . But there *is* no God. There is only the *Führer* and the Fatherland . . . and I will not *scuttle*. . . . Heil Hitler! And . . . please, God . . .'

Twenty yards ahead of Lohemeyer, Chief Petty Officer Krupinsky turned aft to face the ridiculous little bridge, and called flatly, 'Range and bearing set. . . . Request permission to Open Fire!'

One hundred yards behind Lohemeyer, and steering the same course as the diminutive, stubborn escort, Hans Strobe kept the *Wismar*'s head firmly in line with the British warship. They were so close now that he could actually *see* the end elevation of her forward gun turrets directed straight at them, f'r Christ's sake. . . . But he still held the vibrating, smoke-belching old merchant ship on her course.

Hans Strobe should have been a hero – except that there weren't any Jewish heroes. Not in the Third Reich!

From the wallowing harbour launch nearing the little beach beside the Nordkai, the occupants were just watching and waiting, and feeling more and more sick with the tension and the helplessness of it all. But there *was* a difference in the attitudes of the two passengers – because, while Oberbootmann Döring was watching the assault craft now only a stone's throw from the wharf, and wondering when the British would finally see them and kill them, Herr Major Rhöme was staring stiffly and uncompromisingly ahead to where the water lapped so invitingly on the shingle, and planning quite coolly and precisely every move he would make from the moment he set foot ashore and rejoined his Garrison.

The dog Cuno was planning to snap at the rather unsettling Chief Petty Officer again the very first moment he moved!

Three thousand feet above everybody, Fliegerhauptmann Paul Fichte, with Söhler's ME109 apparently glued to his wing-tip, was hurtling down towards the two Blenheims now clearly seen against the water at the entrance to the fjord. Automatically, and without any hurry at all, Fichte allowed the leather-gloved thumbs of both hands to caress gently the twin firing buttons on his stick.

As the speed of the dive built up he felt the G-Forces clamp his head back against the sorbo rubber seat-rest. Gradually the airspeed indicator swung up to the 400 m.p.h. mark as he opened the throttle to full. He started to grin fiercely, aware of the excitement growing within his belly as it always did when the Tommies came. He called Söhler on the R/T.

'Got them?'

'*Jawohl!*' Söhler's voice sounded a note of anticipation, even across the hissing ether. '. . . *Heil Hitler!*'

Paul said 'Oh Jesus!' to the facia panel, then hit his radio link again. The A.S.I. now read 420 m.p.h. 'You take the one to the left, Jumbo-Two. Break . . . now!'

'Victor, Victor!'

'An' when you get to the bottom . . .' Fichte said to nobody in particular, '. . . don't bother to pull out, you sadistic little bastard!'

430 miles per hour!

The two Messerschmitts spread to left and right, peeling off with the distant sun glinting deceivingly warm on mainplanes and perspex canopies. Below and ahead of them the vulnerable Blenheims skimmed steadily down the fjord, even from this height the blast of their propwash quite visible against the velvet waters.

450 miles per hurtling hour! The oil temperature of Fichte's screaming engine started to rise while the vibration from the wing-tips transmitted itself to the taut muscles of his arms. His ears began to pop and he ripped the oxygen mask from his face.

460 . . . 470 . . . 475 . . . ! Blast it! He wasn't going to make it in time. Not before the bomber had completed its run over the town . . . and there was something else down there now. Just off the little wharf . . . assault craft? And others – over there on the other side of the fjord, and . . . Jesus . . . and *more* of them. . . .

Paul slammed the radiator cooling flaps shut. Anything to get that extra burst of speed an' the hell if the rad boils or the bloody engine seizes up . . . 480 . . . Thass it, boy! . . . 485 . . . 490 . . .

Now he was like a meteor falling through space. The pain in his eardrums filled his head and he felt the blackness fuzzing the edges of his vision. God but he'd have to start pulling out or . . .

The overpowering smell of boiling glycol seeped into the cock-pit just as the Messerschmitt passed through the five hundred miles per hour mark.

*

Willie Bradbury watched the green flares go up over Ålvik and glanced at his watch – four seconds after H-Hour. Then the heads on the destroyer's bridge turned aft as they heard the bombers coming in.

The First Lieutenant called, 'There they are!' and the men of *Muscadin* watched as the two Blenheims roared down the fjord towards them like great winged locusts skimming the surface of the sea, diverging slightly as they headed towards their respective targets on either side.

Someone started cheering down aft, carried away with the glorious drama of it all, and then someone else was waving like a bloody maniac until nearly all the men on the low, grey warship were grinning at each other behind gun shields and over weapon sights, and across stacked racks of ready-use ammunition.

The Captain stared quickly down the fjord towards the 'V' shape of the now clearly visible trawler steaming towards them, and suddenly he didn't feel quite so elated any more, because now he knew there wasn't anything left to wait for, and that there were men on that ridiculous little counterfeit warship – brave, fanatical or perhaps merely very stupid men nevertheless – who intended to attack his ship at any second now.

The sleeping dog just couldn't risk sleeping any longer.

'Enemy planes, bearing red . . . wun five, Sir!'

Willie caught one fleeting glimpse of the ME109s boring in – black falling crucifixes against the grey overcast – and of the green-and-brown camouflaged Blenheims thundering down the length of the destroyer, fifty crazy feet above the sullen water, with the red, white and blue rondels of the Royal Air Force still shiny with a varnish of ice.

Then he whirled abruptly. 'All guns. . . . Open Fire!'

*

Lohemeyer saw the enemy planes coming from his stiff-legged stance on the *Patzig*'s bridge. Almost immediately he realised what really *was* happening in the Østersfjord, and whirled too late to search the gloom astern for the landing craft he now knew must be there.

And – if he hadn't been such a blundering fool and a prey to the blind, unthinking myth of Nazi glory – the British soldiers against whom he could have inflicted such slaughter during the past few minutes of their utter vulnerability.

He didn't feel anything any more. Only the empty hopelessness of a man who could have done everything – and had accomplished nothing. He hurled himself towards the wing-mounted machine-gun, conscious only of the snarl of the approaching bombers, and the white faces of the gun's crew staring curiously aft at him. And of Krupinsky's resigned, leathery features waiting for his inadequate young captain's order.

'*Feuerlaubnis* . . . !' Lohemeyer screamed. '. . . Permission to Open Fire!'

*

The high, rust-scarred bows of the tanker seemed to swing over L.C.A. Eight as they passed literally underneath the overhang of the German ship. Looking up, Danny Williams could even make out the peeling, once white-painted letters stencilled above the massive anchor – B . . . L . . . U . . . T . . . H . . . U . . . N . . . D!

'Bloodhound.' Corporal Hanson said learnedly.

'Bloody *hell*!' Charlie Smart muttered, wiping his mouth shakily with a grubby khaki hankie and looking whiter than the paint above them.

Danny didn't say anything. He just gazed anxiously through the growing light along the length of the jetty, and hoped to Christ Jerrie would give them the extra few seconds they needed for the L.C.A. to run up on the allocated patch of shingle twenty yards ahead. At least they were now out of the field of fire of that machine-gun up on the tanker's now concealed bridge. Thank God they'd had to struggle with the gun cover, or . . .

The plane slammed in low behind and to the right of them. Looking at it nose-on it didn't seem to be moving at all, just hanging there above the water like a bloody great buzzing dragon-fly – not that Danny had ever seen a dragonfly, but that's just what one must look like. He ran his eye nervously along the piles of the jetty, and over the pitch black freezing sea below. It was getting lighter all the time now – too damn light – and he could clearly make out the weed-skirted tide-line round each baulk of timber.

He could make out the buildings on the shore now too. Black and menacing – everything was either black or white or grey in the Østersfjord, it seemed – but it was still too dark to detect any movement amongst the apparently haphazard jumble of timber huts which made up the Sørenson Fish Oil Factory. But they must *be* there, f'r God's sake. . . . The Jerries. Waiting and watching, and holding their fire until the Commandos had to come out from behind their thinly armoured shields with the whole depth of the bloody foreshore to cover.

Damn the R.A.F.! Damn them, damn them, damn them . . . ! Why couldn't they have been earlier? An' now the way that bloody lumbering old crate was holding off looked as if Danny would have to get up that exposed beach and into the buildings without any smoke at all. . . .

Twenty yards. The Naval Cox'n throttled back the engines and the bows of the L.C.A. dropped fractionally as the way fell off her.

Then, all the more unbelievable by its sudden impact, the Blenheim was thundering overhead at fifty feet, so low that the men in the L.C.A.s ducked involuntarily. Danny gave one frightened glance upwards, caught a brief glimpse of the plane's belly as the slipstream blasted down on him – then the bomber was gone, the snarl of its engines bounding and rebounding around the white-dappled slopes of the mountains.

And all it left was the swaying, plummeting shapes of parachute-stabilised smoke floats, descending in a neat line across the front of the tensely crouching men in the first wave of assault craft.

Almost immediately, perhaps desperate at the thought of losing vision before the British exposed themselves, a machine-gun opened up on the landing craft from the shadow of the main building.

A calm voice from the bows called sharply, 'Keep down in the boat, there!' just as Hanson stuck his head up to take a last, brief sit-rep of the ground before the smoke finally closed in.

Danny heard the bullets drum terrifyingly along the length of the craft, then Corporal Hanson sat down abruptly in the bottom of the boat, amid a slop of bilge water and oil scum and with, incredibly, a spatter of blood speckling the vomit – and Danny saw that Hanson didn't have any left shoulder-blade or neck tendons any more.

Charlie said, dead shattered, 'Oh Christ!' Then they both forgot about Hanson as the L.C.A. bounced once, and jolted, and the ramp went down with a splash and a rattle of chain just as the smoke closed in around the already running men.

The Bren Gun in the bows started to slam deafeningly as Danny followed Charlie through the gap and over the ramp. Keeping his eyes glued to Charlie's backside and the crossed web straps of his equipment harness, he felt the freezing water knee deep. Then the shore took a sudden upward slope and, unprepared, Danny tumbled full length, half in and half out of the tide-lap.

Charlie turned, grinning like a silly bastard, and yelled, 'C'mon, Danny Boy. I never been abroad before!' and Danny howled back irritably, 'You was less trouble when you was sick, Smart!'

Then he scrambled hurriedly to his feet just as two or three other machine-guns started to chatter from the factory, punctuated by the crack and rattle of British Lee Enfields and Tommy Guns. Danny thought irrelevantly that it was a pity Hanson had copped it before he'd even had a chance to try out his Norwegian, then he started running after Charlie again, into the crazy, smoke-blinded confusion beside the Sörsund Pier.

The first British soldier had landed, and the first British soldier had been killed.

The time was H-Hour plus nine seconds.

*

Johnny Prescott's Blenheim had two thousand yards farther to go before it reached its release point over the Ålvik landing area. He was still completing his bombing run while Dai Evans's kite had finished the Sörsund drop and was now banking hard to avoid spreading Dai and his crew right across the face of the big mountain flanking the fjord.

They'd racketed through the narrow gap of the entrance virtually wing-tip to wing-tip, and so low that the dawn had briefly turned to night again as the shadow of burning Oksenes blanketed the two bombers.

Then they were into the Østersfjord, with the destroyer ahead of them and the elongated cubes of the assault craft just a little farther into the shoreline than they should have been. But there was still time, just enough time, to lay the smoke over the primary targets.

Johnny had broken R/T silence then for the first time since leaving Wick. But it didn't matter now. Not any more. 'You take the factory, Dai. We do the town . . . check?'

The two planes drifted apart, the waters of the fjord below a blur of speed. 'Roger, Johnny. Set one up for me in the mess!'

Johnny thought, 'There won't be one needed for poor bloody Ben, though. Or, probably, for D-Dog's crew . . .' then Ian shouted tightly, 'There's the target! Left, Johnny . . . to the left!' Automatically he touched the rudder and the nose of the Blenheim veered fractionally to port, settling on the very edge of the waterside houses.

'Steady, Skipper . . .' Ian called. 'Steady . . . steady . . .'

The bomb doors were already open, safety and selector switches thrown. Johnny held the plane straight and level. Easy, Johnny boy, easy now. . . . One thousand yards to go . . . nine-fifty . . . nine hundred . . .

He didn't see Ian staring rigidly ahead, or notice the tiny armed trawler which shot past under their starboard wing. He didn't see the tracer which suddenly and ineffectually curled lazily towards them from somewhere around the Sörsund Pier, then at the very last moment appeared to veer sharply and fall away astern.

He didn't even really see the squat shoe-box shapes of the landing craft approaching the Nordkai. All he was aware of was the reverberating snarl of the Mercury VIIIs hurling them towards the target, and of the vibrating control column between his knees, and of the cold sweat trickling steadily down his numbed features as the aiming point – not caring anything about the speed or the noise or the tension – slid so incredibly bloody slowly under the nose of O-Orange.

. . . eight hundred yards . . . seven . . . sixer . . . !

'*Fighter!* Fighter coming in from one-o-clo . . . !'

Alley's frantic scream was overwhelmed by the hammer of the turret gun, and the fuselage started to fill with the acrid fumes of the Vickers K as the bright brass spent cartridge cases tinkled unheard into the turret well. Suddenly Ian was twisted in his seat, craning upwards against the straps to see where the terror was coming from.

Then, 'Go right, Johnny! Go right. . . . Go *RIGHT*, Johnny . . . !'

. . . four hundred yards . . . three . . . two-fifty . . . !

A machine-gun on the jetty ahead. Three men in field grey with big coal scuttle helmets and white faces swinging the barrel frantically round towards him . . . the troops need the smoke. They *need* the smoke. . . . Our Father who art in . . . Two hundred bloody yards . . . Hallowed be thy one-fifty to go . . . !

'. . . go *RIGHT*, JOHNNY!'

His thumb caressed the bomb-release button.

Slam! Slam! Slam! Tinkle, tinkle, tinkle. Someone crying into the intercom.

Suddenly he felt very, very tired indeed.

*

Fliegerhauptmann Fichte hauled the stick of the rocketing fighter back hard into his belly, fighting the impulse to close his eyes and invite a blackout which would kill him as surely as a bullet. Hell, the glycol stench . . . ! Radiator boiling. . . . Pull out, you mad bastard! Pull ou . . . ! Throttle back. Oil temp still off the gauge. Wonder how the Gestapo's gallant aviator is doing? There's the Tommy now . . . damn nearly nose to nose. . . . Still too fast. Still too bloody hot. . . .

He saw the fjord drop away under the spinning disc of the prop as the ME's yellow-painted boss came up smoothly, fighting for the horizon above it. What a fantastic plane she is, Herr Messer-schmitt. And a strong one too, or else the bloody wings would've ripped off by now an' . . . Fichte suddenly realised to his surprise that he was shaking. And that had never happened before.

He leaned forward quickly and opened the radiator cooling flap again, then his thumb was back over the firing button just as the Blenheim swam into the ring of his gun sight. Twelve hundred yards off now, and a closing speed of over six hundred miles an hour. His fighter pilot's brain slammed into gear as everything started happening in the few milliseconds left.

Open fire at one thou! Make it a long burst. Just stroke the shells gently along the line of the fuselage as they passed one another . . . make it good 'cause you'll be a mile away from him before you can even start to turn. . . .

The Tommy was firing at him now. He was so close he could actually see the white face of the turret gunner under the perspex blister . . . and the blobs of the pilot and navigator in the cockpit. Cannon and both machine-guns . . . give them the bloody lot.

Why the hell doesn't he turn away? Anyone would turn away now. . . . Turn, Mister Smith or Brown or whatever. *Turn*, damn you . . . !

A flash of L.C.A.s and packed khaki bodies below. Now the whole bloody world was shooting at him – Paul Fichte. The destroyer in the fjord was shooting, her midships' pom-pom winking and sparkling. And a single L.C.A. lying off the quay . . . some kind of Tommy surprise weapon. . . .

Paul allowed the cockpit of the approaching bomber to creep dead centre in his sights. The Royal Air Force rondels looked big as dustbin lids now. . . . One thousand yards.

FEUER!

His leather-skinned thumbs squeezed the firing buttons and the Messerschmitt shuddered brutally under the recoil of three 20 mm. cannon and two 7.9 mm. machine-guns.

Three-tenths of a second later he was past, and climbing with a snarl of power into the grey overcast covering Ålvik. He didn't know if he'd even chipped the Tommy's varnish.

*

Leading Seaman Scherer hardly bothered to glance at the dead Wehrmacht Corporal still crumpled beside the wrecked motor cycle in the forest. Kneeling down he quickly ran searching hands over the blood-stiff greatcoat, found three clips of ammo which he stuffed in his own pockets then, allowing the corpse to flop back with one rigid arm pointing accusingly up at him, Scherer picked up the Schmeisser and hefted it with great satisfaction.

He didn't spend long looking at the thing which had been his relief either. He wasn't really sure of whether the mess was ex-Hopp or ex-Specht anyway, but neither of them had been particularly attractive specimens, not even when they were alive.

The extra blue woollen glove was intriguing, though. Scherer spat some more dirt out of his mouth and grinned reflectively – he'd earn himself a few litres of mess schnapps on the strength of relating *that* little sidelight on the death of a queer.

A twin-engined plane passed down the fjord, hidden from Scherer by the trees. Then the occasional bursts of firing spluttered into a steady crackle of small arms interspersed with the measured pom-pom-pom of a more distant heavy weapon.

The Gefreiter started running again, the machine-pistol pleasantly heavy in his hands.

He didn't want to arrive too late for *this* particular war.

*

A Norwegian Lance-Corporal called Kristoffer Bruen, kneeling on the starboard side of L.C.A. Four approaching the Nordkai, heard the rising scream of the power-diving ME109 just as the siren trailed to a groaning halt in the town.

Defensively selecting the more immediate danger, he glanced automatically to the right, away from the landing point – and saw, instead, a wallowing harbour launch full of fleeing *Bosche* heading desperately for the other end of the wharf.

Kristoffer had come to Ålvik because he hated the Germans. It was a hate which – unless the Wehrmacht actually marched into Birmingham or Manchester or Bristol – the average British soldier would be unable to match.

It was also because of this hate that Lance-Corporal Bruen didn't hurry. He didn't tell anyone else about the launch either, because he hadn't killed a German before, and very much wanted the pleasure of being the first man of the Norwegian Independent Company to do so on that satisfying morning.

Ignoring the thunder of the converging planes above him he

ever so carefully laid the sights of his rifle squarely over the stiffly erect and ridiculously dignified figure of what could only be a Wehrmacht officer, over there across the water.

The L.C.A. rolled sullenly, just as the chatter of cannon fire exploded above the snarl of aero-engines in the sky. It meant that Kristoffer now had to wait a few more anticipatory moments before he could pull the trigger.

*

Ian screamed, 'Oh *God*, Darling . . . !' because he actually *saw* the twinkling cannons speckle the leading edges of the fighter's wings, and the bright orange blink of the nose guns firing through the yellow spinner above him.

Johnny didn't see anything other than the blurred, staring men ahead, and the white tails of the assault craft, and the rigid crook of his thumb on the bomb release.

And the sight which told him there was only one hundred yards now. . . . Seventy-five . . . *fifty* . . . !

'Oh *God*, Darling . . . !'

. . . forty . . . thir . . . !

The first cannon shell entered the stressed metal skin of the Blenheim just forward of the windscreen, at over one thousand miles per hour. It passed through the instrument panel, tearing out the A.S.I., the turn and bank indicator and the artificial horizon dials on its way, and finally exploded between Johnny Prescott's legs, still splayed on the rudder bar.

He died looking tremendously pleased, having just decided that the moment had come to release the smoke floats, bank right and get the hell out've it.

In fact, Johnny actually did press the button. But it was only the uncontrollable, reflex contractions of the tendons in a dead man's arm. And by the time the circuits were made and the load fell away, the Blenheim was already skidding crazily to starboard in a blasting half-roll as the severed rudder and aileron cables ceased to function.

Alley stopped firing and crying and everything else as the ripple of shells traced across the cab top, curved neatly around the aerial mast when the bomber started to roll, and finally chopped him and the turret and the Vickers into a wind-torn, shrieking obscenity.

In the Navigator's seat, Ian wasn't hurt. He had all the time in the world to just sit and watch, and wait as the wing-tip fell away towards the fjord and O for Orange started to slip over on top of him. He didn't even try and get out of his seat because a Blenheim is a cramped, impossible prison anyway, and his parachute was somewhere down aft, all mixed up with parts of Alley an' the hole in the bloody fuselage. . . .

. . . Look after our son, Darling. I *know* he'll be a son. A boy . . . little boy who'll never know his Daddy . . . I love you, Darling! For ever and ever I'll alway . . . Johnny! Stop *looking* at me, Johnny! Stop staring at me with those wide idiot-blank eyes 'cause dying's private . . . and I can't stop myself screaming any more. I can't . . . stop . . . screa . . . CHRIST! . . . we're going IN! We're bloodygoinginnn*NNNNNNNNNN*!

*

Leutnant Sur See Rex had hobbled desperately towards the eastern end of the Nordkai, calling only briefly into his blacked-out office for his Schmeisser. Being a seaman and not a Wehrmacht strategist, he only had some vaguely formed plan to assist the machine-gunners by providing an enfilading cross-fire along the length of the quay. Or something.

He arrived at the little stretch of shingle beach flanking the wharf as the camouflaged bomber roared in just above the wave-tops. He remembered thinking, 'Reckless bastard!' then a shadow passed over him, the hammer of its cannons lost in the battering violence of its slipstream, while the bomber quite slowly rolled away towards the middle of the fjord like a suddenly tired albatross and dug its starboard wing into the water, cartwheeling hugely before dissolving into an elongating meteor of blazing fuel and skipping, splashing débris.

Rex positively hugged the Schmeisser and grinned like a silly devil at the vanishing shape of the Messerschmitt as it howled into a flat-bellied, skidding turn at the end of the fjord and, for the very first time in his life, thought, 'Thank God for the Luftwaffe!'

Then he half turned to see, first with a sense of shock and then with a surge of relief, his harbour launch approaching him very nearly bows on with the white water smashing in urgent clouds of spray under the tossing, wallowing forefoot.

He didn't see the single Norwegian soldier in the nearest L.C.A., just waiting for the craft to steady before re-aligning his Lee Enfield sights on the impassive figure of Major Otto Rhöme because, by that time, the leading assault wave was so close under the overhang of the Nordkai that they were hidden from the waiting defenders.

Being almost directly beneath them, he couldn't possibly have seen the line of parachute-stabilised smoke floats descending in a neatly spaced line either – and almost where they *should* have been – dropped by the still disintegrating Blenheim O-Orange.

Almost, but not quite. Because one bomb, the last in the stick, had been jettisoned slightly to the right of its release point as the dead pilot had lost control and the broadsiding bomber had veered crazily off course.

With an irony that could only happen in war that bomb – with its sixty-pound charge of lethally-fused phosphorus – was now plummeting in a pure-silk controlled parabola towards the precise dead centre of the Norwegian Company's L.C.A. Four.

Only twelve seconds – less than twenty pulses of a frightened man's heart – had now passed since H-Hour came to Ålvik.

*

The twenty-five Commandos of Group Three, under Lieutenant Denny, were the next to land. Immediately they spread out, running in quick, planned darts up the sloping beach towards the proposed ambush position beside the Princessebrønn Road, each section making their allotted ground, then dropping sharply to provide cover for others.

There were no Germans there to meet them.

Twenty-year-old Denny satisfied himself that his men were properly established and concealed to enfilade the 'Y' junction as required under the Operational Schedule. He gazed just a little hopefully down the rough track which served as the only route into the Østersfjord then, feeling a slight sense of anti-climax, walked back along the grass verge towards his signaller, already calling the Flagship on the 18 Set.

'Tell 'em – OBJECTIVE SECURED. NO ENEMY ACTIVITY OR RESISTANCE. . . .' The Lieutenant grinned mischievously, for he was a very young man and hadn't yet developed a proper respect for Brigadiers and Admirals. '. . . In fact, tell 'em – REQUEST

The landmine, laid three days before, exploded the moment his
boot unwittingly brushed the scatter of snow above it. It blew
most of his right leg and quite a lot of his left foot away.

Nine months before Lieutenant Denny became a paralysed
half-man he had completed his studies with great distinction, and
the assurance of a brilliant future ahead of him.

But then, he had trained very hard indeed for the approbation –
at the Royal School of Ballet.

*

Twenty yards offshore, half hidden in the smoke billowing down
from the Battery, the second L.C.A. of Mike Seely's Group Five
ground to an abrupt halt, throwing its thirty Commandos forward
in a cursing heap.

Its Senior N.C.O., Troop-Sergeant Knox, helped the R.N.
bowman to probe the depth with a boat hook for'ad. They estimated solid rock at less than three feet. Knox gestured urgently to
Corporal Black to nip over the side and check before they lowered
the ramp.

The L.C.A. was only hung up on a vertical shelf. At the point
where Black rather foolishly vaulted over there was some two
fathoms of water. The Corporal went straight down and never
surfaced again. The men staring in shocked silence at the place
where he'd entered could still see bubbles rising to the surface
and bursting in little twinkling gouts reflecting the fires from the
Battery above, even when the L.C.A. shuddered astern then swung
to starboard to follow Captain Seely's crowd ashore.

*

Troop-Sergeant Arthur Henderson watched the rogue smoke float
from O-Orange as it curved down towards the Norwegian L.C.A.
Four, on the other side of the Colonel's craft. He knew it was
descending right into the packed craft and felt a numbed horror
mixed, rather perversely, with an immense sensation of relief.

The relief was because he could already hear the other smoke
bombs exploding along the wharf above him, and his chances of
getting ashore and delivering the account for Ginny and the kids
were that much improved.

The horror was because he had seen smoke floats in use before, and he knew what sixty pounds of igniting phosphorus would do to men who couldn't even run away from it.

He had one brief glimpse of the Blenheim – engines still roaring at full throttle – as it dug one wing into the water three hundred yards away, then cartwheeled across the fjord like a high-speed crematorium. The bomb, swaying pendulously under its parachute, ever so slowly sank into the press of khaki bodies and ignited with a dull whoomf.

Then the L.C.A. collided with the harbour wall, bounced off and ran back alongside, and all Henderson could see was Lieutenant Dixon's gaitered boots clambering up the ladder above his head, and the lanyard of his revolver hanging down in an umbilical loop from its butt ring.

Forefinger already crooked through the trigger guard of his Thompson Gun, he reached for the bamboo rungs as Corporal Loomis grinned savagely and made a funny sort of bow. 'After you, Cecil. . . .' Henderson thought grimly that the B.B.C. had a lot to bloody answer for with their damn silly catch-phrases, then the noise of the battle swamped in over him as he started to climb.

The slam of the departing ME109 trailing away towards the fjord entrance and the still reverberating rumble as the bomber continued to disintegrate. The screams of burning men from L.C.A. Four and the harsh shouts of Platoon Commanders struggling to be heard above the bedlam. The rattle of a Tommy Gun over to the right – misfire? Or a target? – and the measured pom . . . pom . . . pom . . . from the destroyer merging with the nearer cannonade from Endersby's Support Craft lying off the quay. . . .

Lieutenant Dixon's right boot lifted as he swung it up and over the edge of the wharf. Henderson noticed vaguely that there was a smear of oil staining the blancoed gaiter which was a shame because the brass buckles were shining like a Guardsman's.

Someone below bellowed 'Bloody hold *on* for'ad, there!' while a grenade exploded with a crish-crack up and to the left. Suddenly, through the nightmare of noise, Henderson heard the first skirl of the pipes as they cut incredibly across the roar of the battle for Ålvik. Just for a moment he hesitated on the ladder, looking down to see Pipe-Corporal McLusky – as erect and as impassive as he would have been on an empty parade ground – standing like a Scottish fir in the bow of the Colonel's craft, with the pipes under his arm and the Black Watch kilt a blue-green splash of colour against the khaki.

The Commando soldiers looked at each other and some of them actually grinned and, even through the fear and the terror of that morning, no man on the British side was left completely unmoved by the gallant, stirring lilt of the Highlandman's 'Black Bear' accompanying them into war.

Then the smoke from the quay blew down around Henderson as he heard the chatter of a German machine-gun opening up on them. And Lieutenant Dixon fell back down the ladder in a slackly flailing bundle of arms and legs.

*

Kristoffer Bruen's rifle sight had just zero'd on the tall, stiff German officer in the launch again, when someone behind him screamed in a shocked voice, '*Ahhhhh Jøss! Pass pa . . . !*'

He just had time to feel the L.C.A. bump, and see the shiny white silk collapsing on the bright yellow cylinder behind him before there was a blinding sheet of flame and he started to burn from head to toe.

He was glad when the ten cases of grenades in the stern of the craft detonated and killed him properly.

*

From the armed trawler's forward deck, Oberbootmann Krupinsky unemotionally watched the Tommy plane smash into their wake astern, and listened with a heavy heart as all the bloody silly young kids around the ancient gun cheered madly, proud of their gallant Luftwaffe comrades.

Now he was being cynical again. . . . Gloomily he thought, 'Some you win, some you lose, Krupinsky old son!' then, even while knowing it was their turn to do the losing, he swung back towards the British warship, took a last deep breath of the wind so cold across his leathery seaman's face, and allowed his already raised arm to slash irrevocably downwards.

'*Achtung Geschützbedienung . . . FEUER!*'

At precisely the same moment as the P.O. Captain of the

Mounting in *Muscadin*'s 'A' Gun Turret opened *his* mouth and roared the command which had rung across the cleared decks of British Ships of the Line from Quiberon Bay to Cadiz.

'*FIIIIIIIIIRE!*'

*

The Colonel saw the smoke float explode in the next craft just as the Nordkai loomed above them and all hell let loose above. He only had time to shout to McLusky, 'Quick! A tune, man! Gie the lads a tune . . . !' when great sizzling, white-hot spinners of burning phosphorus scattered down among the Headquarters' Troop and Bren Gunner Tyndal was spitting weird Highland oaths while beating frantically at a flaring chemical gob lodged in the neck of his lifejacket.

McLusky slipped the chanter out of his mouth for a moment, looked haughtily down at the cursing Tyndal, and said dead-pan, 'Ah'll thank ye not tae fuckin' swear in front of the Colonel, ye ignorant wee bastard!'

Then just stood there skirling the 'Black Bear' and tapping his foot in time to the lilt of it, not even deigning to notice the fury of battle which ranged around. But McLusky came of a strange breed of men whose forefathers had already fought the Germans. And when there weren't any Germans to fight, they'd fought the English. And when the English weren't handy . . . then they'd just spent their free time fighting each other.

There were a lot of Jocks in 22 Commando.

A heavy machine-gun started to clatter over to the Colonel's left, sweeping grey chips of concrete over the edge of the wharf.

Then the smoke rolled over the top too, and he thought, 'Thank God for the R.A.F.,' while at the same time trying anxiously to see the extent of the casualties in the now blazing Norwegian L.C.A.

There were heads in the water around the listing craft, heads still incongruously wearing steel helmets as soldiers, many of them terribly burned, just leapt overboard and away from the holocaust. The Colonel noticed with a sad stirring of pride that a lot of the Commandos still clung to their weapons, though.

The enemy H.M.G. fell silent, possibly because the smoke had started to do its job by concealing the landing places, then it opened up again, firing in controlled, staccato bursts which told the Colonel they were up against unruffled veterans and not panicky recruits.

A last, helpless look at L.C.A. Four – helpless because at this time his responsibility was to the direction of the whole attack and not to the individual agonies of men already neutralised – and his own craft was alongside with the ladders slamming towards the wharf and the first tense faces staring upwards as they scrambled into the drifting ceiling of smoke.

A Commando Corporal ran crouching along the edge of the quay, his mouth wide and savage against the black features as he fired his Tommy Gun from the hip. Someone else was sobbing out of sight, 'Oh ye bastard. . . . Oh ye lousy bastard, I cannae see . . . !'

A man, blazing from top to bottom, rose impossibly out of the fire that was L.C.A. Four and tumbled without a sound into the oil-covered water. Another voice yelling 'The hell with the bloody swimmers . . . get the bloody radio!' and then Bertie Torrance's L.C.A. Five, leading the second wave, nosed through the outstretched arms and pleading faces staring up from the fjord while khaki figures leaned so far over they were nearly toppling in too, to reach the burned clawing hands.

Tyndal went up the ladder like a two-year-old with the back of his lifejacket still trailing smoke and the heavy Bren slung over his shoulder like an illicit salmon. Another Commando came running along the edge, firing and yelling like a madman, then a bullet caught him and he kept on running over the wharf and into the water between the L.C.A.s. Tyndal stepped back to let him pass then stuck his head over, stared accusingly at Pipe-Corporal McLusky, and bellowed, 'Hey youse, McLusky. . . . If ye'd stop blawin' and start shootin' maybe they Germans'd no' be so bluidy bad-tempered!'

That was the moment when the Colonel knew, beyond any doubt, that 22 Commando were going to take the town of Ålvik.

*

Second Mate Bögel clattered up the bridge ladder and ran back into the *Wismar*'s wheelhouse, grabbing for the signal lamp. Plugging it in he leaned both elbows on the rail and pressed the trigger. Behind him Hans Strobe gazed along the inverted white beam to where the yellow-and-blue merchant Flag of Sweden now fluttered sullenly in the breeze of their passage.

'Instant Neutrality,' Bögel said gloomily.

Strobe smiled tentatively. '. . . or instant immortality?'

'Starboard five,' the Old Man called placidly, leaning over the bridge wing as though they were all alone on an empty sea.

They could hear Krupp bawling from the after deck, and the squeal of blocks as the old ship's lifeboat was swung out and lowered to deck level. Hans wondered where his friend Katzmann was, and hoped he'd remember to collect Strobe's personal gear from the foc'sle locker for him before going to his boat station.

They watched the British bomber plough into the fjord with tight grins of pleasure, then all hell seemed to let loose along the Ålvik waterfront astern while a fighter plane – a Messerschmitt, Strobe thought – slammed over their foremast so low that the blast of its slipstream snapped the illuminated Ensign out like a frozen board before allowing it to fall slackly and dispiritedly against the halyards again.

Everyone was shooting at everyone else now, in a mad world of half light and distant explosions and the thunder of receding aero-engines. For a brief space of time it seemed that the straggling pattern of vessels in the middle of the fjord was silently detached from it all, from the violence and savagery of the morning ashore.

Then the roar of nearby guns rattled the bridge windows and Strobe gripped the spokes of the wheel in fright while the Second Mate ducked rather ineffectually under the level of the sill, both of them anticipating the obliterating smash of a shell against the bridge.

But nothing happened, and nothing could be seen. Only the vague shapes of the two ships ahead of them – the little *Patzig* and the rakish enemy destroyer – still racing towards each other on an unswerving, head-on collision course.

'David and Goliath!' Strobe thought . . . except there weren't any gallant Davids now. Not in Hitler's Germany. . . .

Then the rounds exploded simultaneously, one from the impracticable trawler and one from the improbable warship. And the silent seamen watched from the fleeing *Wismar* as only the winner fired for a second time. And a third . . . and it didn't seem very long after that before the first shocked ratings were jumping heedlessly towards the dark, wreckage-fouled water lapping already sloping decks.

Most of them would die before twenty minutes past eight. The sea temperature was only a few degrees above freezing.

*

Captain Mike Seely's Group Five grounded under the lee of the Oksenes Battery at twenty-two seconds past H-Hour. Or the first L.C.A. did, at least. Sergeant Knox's craft, now already short of one drowned man, took a few moments longer, but it didn't really matter because nobody fired at them anyway.

Mike cast one hurried glance towards the Sörsund Pier, seen from his position half a mile away as a grey blanket of smoke reflecting the occasional flashes of exploding grenades, then his ramp went down and he was running towards the equally indeterminate skyline which concealed the Battery.

It seemed odd, almost eerie, to be struggling ashore with the only local sounds the scatter of boots amongst the snow-patched gravel, and the harsh breathing of men on either side of him as they advanced, bending low and with weapons tucked well into the hip.

A low voice to the right called urgently, 'Wire! Mind the wire . . . !' then the forward line of running men fell forward quite deliberately across the viciously barbed coils while the second wave just kept on racing up and over the prostrate backs with hardly a break in the pace.

Mike thought tensely, 'Machine-guns! Where the *hell* had Jerrie put his defences?' but still no sign of movement from above, only the soft crackle of something burning to the right – presumably a legacy of the bombardment – and the distant keening wail of a man in torment. Undoubtedly a result of the bombardm . . . !

The figure of a German soldier appeared on the top of the hill, running transversely across their path, and Mike thought ridiculously, 'Thank God *somebody's* still alive round here!' while Corporal Dick on his left took brief aim and squeezed off a single shot which dropped the hurrying man like a poleaxed rabbit.

Someone else behind them muttered, 'Mean bastard, you could've afforded two rounds!'

The destroyer's main armament opened up from the fjord, the

sharp cough of her 4.7s echoing time and time again round the dark, silent mountains on either side. Something else was firing down there too, another ship, but it was still too dark to make out details from here.

Still no movement at all. Seely felt the cold sweat jogging in abrupt little trickles down the side of his face as he ran. It was a horrible feeling, like bursting into a wrestling match and finding you'd arrived in a mortuary instead.

Just as the first wave breasted the skyline the firing began. A sub-machine-gun chattered from a dip ahead, then stopped abruptly as a grenade bounced over the low earth mound and exploded with the characteristic crish-crash of a Mills Bomb. Another light weapon opened up on the flank and Mike could hear the bullets whip-cracking over their heads until they were lost in a fusillade of Thompson fire as the Commandos replied.

Suddenly a man – just a white staring face under a flat sailor's cap – appeared from a hole in the ground ahead of Seely. He only had time to register that he'd nearly run full tilt down the entrance to a German bunker when the gun in his hand seemed to fire itself and the white face disappeared again with a scream.

Corporal Dick hesitated as he passed, bending low and lobbing something straight through the open door, then the grenade went off with a muffled thump and Mike felt the ground shudder slightly below his feet.

Another two figures materialised out of the smoke, not really presenting a menace so much as stumbling drunkenly in a circle, but someone shot them both anyway, then the firing stopped altogether as the initial impetus of the attack was lost, and the Commandos went to ground with a vague feeling of having been short changed and that, if this was a war, they might as well have stayed at home.

Cautiously Seely lifted his head and gazed with a mounting sense of shock at the carnage before him. While he'd been running it hadn't really dawned on him just what havoc the bombardment from *Hystrix* had inflicted. Now he could see more clearly, despite the dawn light and the still drifting smoke, and he suddenly realised why there had been very little opposition.

Because, above ground amid the shambles of the Oksenes

Battery, there were only the wounded and the dead, and the half mad and the totally mad left to oppose them.

*

Group One, landing on the Hæl-en side of the fjord, found virtually the same thing. Any defence offered was largely by shell-shocked men who still didn't even know what was happening. The flak tower, the searchlight post and the Naval Signal Station had all gone, pounded into fragments by *Salamander*'s guns.

Leaving one platoon of men to search the area for intelligence information and stray still-lively Germans, Lieutenant Courtenay led the rest of his Group at a fast double down the road towards Ålvik, in support of the Colonel's hard-pressed assault.

It was that same road which Gefreiter Scherer had taken.

And the one at the end of which young Dieter Balke patiently waited, complete with new-found MG34 and the incredible self-assurance of the mentally unbalanced.

H-HOUR plus 1 MINUTE

'It's bloody ridiculous,' Rex thought nervously. 'The Tommies landing less than thirty metres away on the wharf an' I'm standing here like a bloody welcoming committee, waiting for the Commandant. It's carrying Inter-Service formality a bit too far. . . .'

Hugging the buttress of the quay to keep out of sight, he watched grimly as the blazing L.C.A. Four drifted down the fjord. The pain in his leg had started again and he knew what war could be like, and what it could do to people. He saw the burning man leap into the water and felt a terrible sympathy, then the grenades went up with a flash and a roar to blow the stern off the assault craft which then sank hissing and bubbling in a great writhing cloud of steam.

Yet even then the Norwegian L.C.A. didn't want to be forgotten because, down through the dark water, Leutnant Rex could see the submarine glare of the still white-hot phosphorus. Until the smoke from the battle above blew down over the little beach and left him with only the firing and the cursing voices and the screams of the wounded for company.

'Thank God for the R.A.F.,' he muttered. Which was a bit of an odd thing for a German Naval Officer to say, but he really meant the smoke which was better than a miracle right then, to protect the launch during its last surreptitious dash round the flank of the British assault force.

The MG34 continued to slam deafeningly from the other end of the Nordkai, and Rex thought about the stolid Wehrmacht veterans who were manning it, and felt proud to be a German. Then he remembered the way the majority of the Garrison had been caught literally napping, with the lookouts – his *Naval* lookouts – not noticing a destroyer they could have thrown bloody stones at, and half the infantrymen probably still playing skat in the air-raid shelters as if they didn't know the difference between a damn bomber an' a Commando soldier. . . .

At last he caught the sound of the launch's engine approaching the beach. He still couldn't see anything because of the smoke but, tensing his back muscles in anticipation of a burst of Tommy Gun fire, he started to hobble down the shingle towards the tide-line, eyes desperately searching to pierce the gloom.

He was frightened now, really frightened, but he had to keep going. To meet the Commandant and the others and to direct them up the beach and along the only route into the town that he knew was still safe. It was his duty . . . but Jesus, he was scared. And the nerves down the back of his neck were cold and tingly waiting for the smash of shots that would mean he was dead and the attackers had gained a foothold on the Nordkai just a little too soon.

Move, leg! *RUN*, damn you. . . . Try an' *run* . . . !

Ever so slowly the launch came out of the smoke. Rex saw the tall, poised figure of Oberbootmann Döring standing in the bow with his Schmeisser, prepared for a last suicidal burst should the enemy be waiting. But the enemy were still pinned down fifty yards away, and the only reception committee was a crippled sailor with a dedicated sense of responsibility towards his friend and his men and his senior officer.

Rex hurried just a little faster, waving his arms to attract attention and dragging his twisted, deformed leg uncaringly. He didn't realise that the Chief Petty Officer with the wary respect for the British and the cradled sub-machine-gun was still half blinded by the smoke that Rex had been so grateful for.

Not until Döring shot him full in the chest because he thought the menacing, wild-eyed figure running towards them was a typical berserk British Commando. Just like the Reich Ministry of Information had described them.

Leutnant Sur See Rex wasn't really killed by a friend, or even by the men of 22 Commando.

He was cut to pieces by a wartime weapon called a Propaganda Machine.

*

The first Royal Air Force Beaufighter sortie arrived over the Østersfjord at H-Hour plus ninety seconds. From that moment on, until the ground troops withdrew, there would be British fighter cover for the ground operations.

Paul Fichte learned about the R.A.F.'s appearance shortly after he had rocketed low over the Oksenes Battery before skating skywards again in a tight, screaming turn which blurred the edges of his vision and caused the main spar to thrum under the strain.

A brief sideways glimpse looking down of one assault craft beached behind the Point, a second churning in to land ahead of a curving white tail of foam and, a little farther along the southern shore, two or three more elongated boxes half hidden by the smoke floats from the Blenheim that got away.

And a spreading, still burning patch of stained water and high-octane fuel in the middle of the fjord which established that he was either a better shot or a luckier pilot than his more politically oriented wingman.

He caught the flashes as the Tommy destroyer and another diminutive, smoke-trailing vessel opened fire simultaneously below, then he eased the stick forward, leading the Messerschmitt into a second steep power-dive towards the British assault craft lined up beside the Sörsund jetty.

One half of his mind was still thinking about Leutnant Söhler. And the Gestapo. . . .

Whoomf . . . whoomf . . . whoomf . . . !

Something rattled terrifyingly against the fuselage aft and he jerked round in shock to see whispy puffs of flak hanging in the air down the angle of his approach. . . . 'Christ!' he thought, angry with himself for not having anticipated ground fire and been a little more evasive when coming out of the turn. Then he glanced towards the sea and for the first time noticed the long swept silhouette of the cruiser and the shorter, stubbier shapes of two infantry assault ships lying off the fjord.

The enemy warship sparkled again and *whoomf . . . whoomf . . .* ! while Fichte allowed the ME109 to break sideways just as the next bursts of ack-ack fire blotched the grey sky precisely where he had originally been heading. He started to feel the irritated frustration building up inside him but he knew he didn't dare risk hitting back at the ships, because a cruiser with its hackles up is far too formidable and impregnable an adversary for any fighter plane.

The R/T crackled and Söhler's brusque voice called, 'Jumbo-One, this is Jumbo-Two . . . Over.'

Paul flicked the button. 'Jumbo-Two . . . where the hell are you, Söhler?'

Söhler's voice now held a note of triumph. 'Right behind you . . . look in your mirror some time, Herr Fliegerhauptmann!'

Paul's eyes darted to the mirror and he felt the blood drain from his face with shock. The image of Söhler's Messerschmitt looked very near as it bisected the glass, sitting squarely across his tail. But it wasn't fear of Söhler that was so frightening to Paul – the Leutnant was a screwed-up little bastard, yeah, but he hadn't joined the R.A.F. yet – so much as the fact that, for the first time in his career, he'd allowed a plane, any plane, to slip in on his tail unnoticed.

It meant he'd just made the most elementary mistake a fighter pilot could commit. The unforgivable sin, and usually the last. He thought, 'Oh my *God*, Paul boy. This Gestapo business has really got you rattled . . . a rotten little amateur flier like Söhler . . . !'

He snapped, 'We'll take the barges off the town, Söhler. Get down here an' be a proper wingman.'

The R/T hissed as Söhler touched his presser switch, but he didn't say anything for a moment. Fichte glanced frowning into the mirror again, not trying to shake the Leutnant off though he knew that now, being fully alerted again, he probably could outfly the kid any time. Then Söhler finally spoke and his voice sounded rather odd.

'You have until my count of five, Fliegerhauptmann Fichte. . . . *EIN.*'

Fichte still stared into the mirror, absently thinking that he'd need to get his flight mechanic to check – the strain of that last power-dive was causing the surface to vibrate until he now had a double image of the Leutnant's fighter in the glass – and then the impact of what Söhler had just said registered.

He flicked the R/T disbelievingly. '*What* did . . . Say again, Jumbo-Two. I repeat – say again, Jumbo-Two . . . Over.'

The earphones cracked gently. Then Söhler, flat and deadly. '*ZWEI* . . .'

Paul automatically started to bank over the other end of the Østersfjord. Jumbo-Two stuck to his tail like glue . . . or should he have said Jumbos Two-and-Three because of that blasted mirror? Then the full realisation of what Söhler intended hit him like a physical blow.

Söhler actually intended to *shoot* him down!

'. . . *DREI.*'

It was incredible. Bloody *impossible*, dammit! But it was really happening, nevertheless. The crazy kid astern – but was he all that crazy? Or just a common-or-garden fanatic? – had actually declared a war within a war. The macabre incongruity of the situation was such that Paul's initial reaction was to grin. And what a fantastic treat for the British when they looked up to see the only two ME109s over the Østersfjord mixing it above their heads in a private, quite exclusively Luftwaffe dogfight. . . .

He said calmly, 'I hope I'm wrong, Leutnant Söhler, but the enemy is down *there*. Follow me down – and that is an order!'

Paul gave a tentative flick to port and the plane in the mirror disappeared. Then it swam back in again and he knew Söhler intended to stay put. But *why*, f'r . . . surely not because of a stupid argument in the mess? Not when Söhler had the whole of the *Geheime Staatspolizei* hatchet organisation behind him?

And then he suddenly realised why. Because the Gestapo hadn't yet got to the stage of desiring any more publicity than necessary when they found it expedient to execute an embarrassing senior officer. It wasn't good for their patriotic Nazi image. And it knocked the hell out of morale, too, whereas just another death in action. . . .

Söhler snapped tightly, '*VIER, Herr Fliegerhauptmann.*'

Fichte stopped grinning and shook his head wearily. He wasn't even particularly worried now. If they didn't get him up here they'd get him on the ground and to hell with the niceties. But there was one thing he just had to know.

He said, 'Why give me a warning, Söhler? You could've dropped me before you called . . . so why?'

He glimpsed the entrance to the fjord coming under his spinner for the second time and thought listlessly, 'How bloody ridiculous can you get? Cruising along up here, back and forward like an elastic-tethered tennis ball and chatting like the R/T was a private telephone, while down there . . .'

Söhler sounded nervous now and Paul knew it would come soon. He kept one eye on the double image in the mirror and leaned forward, waiting, as the Leutnant spoke tightly. 'Because I am a German Officer, Fichte. When I execute you it will be with honour, and as an act of war. . . .'

He broke off and Paul gripped the stick with every sense now alert, feeling the rudder bar vibrate gently under the sole of his flying boot. '*Honour*,' he reflected tautly. 'You poor, sick, mixed-up little Nazi. You don't know what real honour is, boy. An' the "Officer" bit must've come out of some old legend from the bloody Kaiser's war. . . .'

'. . . *FUNFFFFF.*'

Abruptly Fichte slammed in the methanol emergency booster and roared vertically into a howling corkscrew climb even as the guns winked along the leading edges of Söhler's wings. The kid, taken utterly by surprise, shot straight on under Paul's tail with the black crosses on the Messerschmitt's mainplanes standing stark against the white snow carpet of the mountains.

Paul said bleakly to the sky, 'That's one thing they *don't* teach you down at the concentration camp, Leutnant!'

Then glanced back as he slid the plane into a tight turn – and stared incredulously.

Because he suddenly found that the double image in his mirror hadn't been a double image at all, and that there *had* been two planes following him, one after the other. And that Söhler had been so damned wrapped up in the execution trade that he hadn't noticed anything either.

The R.A.F. Beaufighter opened up on Jumbo-Two just as Fichte started shouting, 'Break left, Söhler! Break LEFT, damn you . . . !'

From the other end of the Nordkai, Troop-Sergeant Arthur Henderson dimly heard the accidental burst of Schmeisser fire killing Hafenmeister Rex, but it didn't mean any more to him than all the other clamour of battle.

Lying prone along the edge of the wharf and squeezing deliberate, single shots off in the direction of the MG34 which was keeping them pinned down, he realised that, unless someone took the initiative pretty quickly, the whole attack would falter and, as the enemy gained time to give their defence some depth, the Commando could be driven right back over the quay.

A line of bullets scarred the concrete beside him, spanging and ricocheting into the smoke as a body crashed heavily alongside and he turned his head to see the sweat-smeared face of Corporal Loomis looking a bit shocked.

He snapped, 'You hit?' and Loomis muttered, 'No! Jus' bloody terrified, Arthur . . .' then another diminutive figure came belting down the quay from the direction of the Colonel's party, yelling like a maniac and firing a Bren Gun from the hip in a one-man horseless impersonation of the Charge of the Light Brigade.

Henderson said, 'Tyndal!'

Loomis watched in astonishment as the galloping Commando disappeared ahead of them into the smoke again, and spat 'Mad Scotch bastard!'

Henderson hauled himself to his feet and started running too. The initiative had been taken for them, all they needed now was luck and guts, and the discipline that the British Army had spent over two hundred years in forging. 'C'mon . . . !' he bellowed. 'Section will advAAAAAANCE!'

The German machine-gun started barking again, punctuated by the sharper rattle of Tyndal's Bren. Then suddenly other men were following, charging through the whine of bullets as they glanced off the warehouse walls to the right. Charging in grim, dogged silence or charging with wide-open yelling mouths while, all the time, the skirl of the pipes growing louder and even more stirring as the smoke curled round and the occasional flash of a bayonet sparkled through the man-made gloom blanketing the Nordkai.

Loomis pulled alongside him, wild eyes fixed unswervingly ahead and the rounded curve of his steel helmet jogging violently with every racing step. Another soldier swerved in across their path just as the MG34 clattered very close indeed now, and the Commando went down clutching his belly, but Henderson was running too fast by then, so he just went up and over the falling man in a crazy, flying leap. . . .

. . . and the smoke cleared under the blast of an erratically exploding grenade, while the hidden machine-gun broke off abruptly and Henderson burst out into the sick dawn light to see that by some outlandish patronage of the Scottish Gods, Tyndal had galloped so far past the enemy position that he'd actually outflanked them before turning hard back and using the Bren.

One machine-gunner was still up on his knees, half bent over and staring into nowhere – until the little man fired again, a short, vicious burst, and Henderson watched the suddenly listless grey body of the Wehrmacht Corporal kicking and jerking into the red snowdrift against the corner of the warehouse.

The excitement drained out of him and, skidding to a halt, he called hopelessly, 'Prisoners, Tyndal. We take prisoners!'

Tyndal looked back at him and the eyes were very hard under the chipped steel rim of the helmet. 'Aye, Troop-Sergeant?' the poacher answered. 'Then ye'd better be marchin' they three bastards back doon the wharf f'r a start!'

Then he was gone, and the rest of the Group were doubling past Henderson towards the main street of the town. The Colonel came up, striding out with his stick in one hand and a sub-machine-gun in the other. He stopped and looked down at the three dead men round the gun and there was a great respect in his voice.

'Thank you, Henderson,' he said simply.

The Sergeant shook his head. 'Tyndal! Tyndal was the one who led the charge, Sir.'

The Colonel glanced at him curiously for a moment, then smiled softly. 'I mean all of you, Sergeant. You all did well. . . .'

Then he was gone too, and Arthur Henderson was left listening to the new clamour of firing ahead, and someone calling sharply, 'Stretcher-bearer! Over here, stretcher-bearer!' from behind. And looking down at the first enemy soldiers he'd seen since Dunkirk, only they didn't seem so big now, or so masterful.

D.A.–G   193

He moved off after the rest. A Trooper passed him, going the other way back to the craft and the aid station, and holding a bloodied field dressing where his right ear had been a few minutes before. The wounded Commando stumbled slightly and swayed, and Henderson called, 'Can you manage, lad?' but the man just kept on going past because he had lost both eardrums too, with the blast.

The Sergeant remembered the dead German machine-gunners again and found he wasn't pleased or elated, or even a little bit frightened after that mad, hysterical assault. But he *was* conscious of a slightly guilty stirring of surprise – because he hadn't thought about Ginny or the kids once since he'd set foot in Ålvik.

*

Under the bows of the grounded launch Major Otto Rhöme watched silently as the big Chief Petty Officer knelt beside the sprawled body of his friend and officer. The dog Cuno whined for a moment then settled at his feet, ears alert and trembling slightly as the detonations from the Nordkai continued without a break.

He said quietly, 'I'm sorry, Döring. The war . . . you were not to blame.'

Döring looked up at him, not even feeling the icy cold water lapping at his knees, and the Major could sense the anguish in his eyes because, like the Commandant, Döring was a gentle, sensitive man behind the tough Service veneer. The Oberboot-mann said, 'You should go, Sir. The British will be here any time now.'

The dog started to whine again impatiently, almost as if it realised the danger they were in, but Rhöme still didn't move. Somehow he felt they owed a duty to Rex, a duty of responsibility towards the dedication of a crippled, self-sacrificing young officer. The soldier in him urged him to leave immediately, to join his Garrison in repelling the enemy, but the man in him told him to remain until he was sure they were only abandoning a corpse, and not a grievously wounded comrade.

The three ratings had already gone, leaving the launch as soon as it touched the shore. One of them was too frightened to think about anything, another felt ashamed but felt an even stronger sense of duty to his wife. The third, a leading seaman, hoped to

God the British would kill Chief Petty Officer Döring before he caught up with them again.

Döring muttered flatly, 'He's dead. His chest. . . .'

He stood up slowly then, hesitating, bent down again and picked up the Schmeisser. A Bren and a grenade slammed together from the other end of the quay and, abruptly, the MG34 fell silent. The dog whined louder and nudged the Major's arm with its soft black muzzle, then they heard the British soldiers cheering and the nerve-racking lilt of the pipes swelling out of the smoke.

They started running – the old man, the sad man, and the dog.

They were only half-way up the beach when the first khaki-uniformed men burst out of the gloom as they raced round the corner of the Habour Office to outflank the defenders in the town.

And it was quite light. They had no cover at all now that the wind was blowing the smoke away from Ålvik.

*

The shell from *Patzig*'s forward guns exploded just above the destroyer's hawse pipe. It folded a section of forecastle deck back like a giant origami flower, severed the Blake and screw slips inboard, shattered the cable holder and the cable itself just above its point of entry into the navel pipe and carelessly allowed the starboard bower anchor to plummet unfettered and irrecoverably to the bottom of the Østersfjord.

It started a small fire in the capstan engine flat. It caused the Captain to say 'Damn!' and it encouraged the seamen gunners in 'A' Turret to rather more descriptive heights of verbosity.

It caused no casualties to *Muscadin*'s complement. The destroyer continued to engage the enemy as if nothing had happened at all.

No one aboard the German armed trawler knew quite where *Muscadin*'s first round registered. One moment the little escort was trembling under the thrust of gland-popping, wide-open valves with the steam pressure gauge high in the red, and the racketing, oil-bright piston arms a blur of reciprocating movement . . . then a 4.7-inch shell had torn through her well deck, hammock-slung fish hold, crew heads, W/T room and radio operator to detonate finally in the tiny, black-grimed coffin of her engine space.

A high jetting lick of orange flame, ancient soot and expanding steam roared from her spindly funnel while the stricken ship immediately began to lose way, veering uncontrollably to port as her rudder quadrant and chain steering gear fell into the gaping crater of the after deck. The swing corrected itself for a few moments when the mizzen mast collapsed over the quarter, temporarily acting as a jury rudder, then with a fusillade of high-tensile cracks punctuating the thunder of blowing steam lines, the tangled rigging parted and *Patzig* sheered beam on towards her adversary.

And stopped, her forward gun now pointing uselessly towards the rattle of small arms fire which marked the Sörsund jetty.

Oberbootmann Krupinsky threw one resigned glance aft, saw the whirling fountain of shattered deck planking, ventilators and débris rising ever so slowly into the air, and thought, 'That's it then, i'nt it?'

Kross, the leading seaman gunlayer and the only other real seaman aboard, said calmly, 'What now, Chief? Over the wall before the next one comes in?'

Krupinsky hesitated, looking down at the sullenly heaving water of the fjord. Already it was fouled with a slowly spreading mess of coal dust and wreckage, and he knew it was cold – bloody cold – in there. Too cold for it to matter much whether they were in or out of it when the destroyer fired again.

He turned towards the little bridge, trying to see if Lohemeyer was still in command, or had the blast from that first explosion left the decision to him already? One of the loaders, the youngest kid without a coat, started crying softly with cold and disillusion-ment. Krupinsky noticed absently that the boy still hugged the brass shell in his arms like an evil, metallic corruption of an only recently forgotten Teddy bear.

Then, incredibly, a machine-gun started to chatter wildly from the scarred bridge, and Krupinsky stared aft in amazement to see the Captain leaning back from the open sights and swinging the stabbing, tracer-spewing muzzle towards the enemy warship in a last, hopeless gesture of defiance.

And it *would* be the last. Krupinsky knew that. Because next time the British wouldn't cease firing until the trawler was a shattered, sinking hulk.

Kross said philosophically, 'Shit! That means we're heroes!'

While Krupinsky – tearing his eyes away from the sight of a young man who had suddenly been transformed from a conceited, frightened boy to a hate-filled fighting machine – hit the training handles of the gun, traversing the barrel to the right and on to the enemy again.

He roared, 'Reload! *Schnell . . . !*' just as Kross opened the breech and the spent case clanged out in a belch of ejecting cordite fumes to roll clattering and tumbling down the already sloping foc'slehead. The ship lurched heavily as something blew in the engine-room and the young seaman started yelling hysterically, 'Abandon ship . . . Abandon *ship . . . !*' until Kross hit him savagely across the mouth, snarling 'Pull yourself together an' bloody load, Eyssen!'

Krupinsky thought coldly, 'When it comes I hope to Christ I get it in the head or in the chest 'cause I couldn't stand finishin' up a twisted, deformed cripple like that Hafenmeister Rex over there . . . !'

The ship jumped as something else tore away and the tracers over the gun crew's heads dipped sharply, then rose again to disappear into the grey, rushing shape of the destroyer. A man started screaming from aft in a horrifying, inhuman key, and Krupinsky swung round in shock to see a figure, burning like a torch, scrambling from the blazing engine-room companionway and half rolling, half clawing his way blindly to the rail.

Then Kross howled, 'Ready on target!' while the steam and the flames roared even higher abaft the bridge, and the machine-gun in Lohemeyer's hands slammed even more hatefully, and the first panic-crazed young Kriegsmarine rating went leaping and bawling down the deck and into the water. . . .

. . . and the second round from *Muscadin*'s 'A' Gun Mounting exploded under the starboard wing of the *Patzig*'s bridge, blowing the funnel, the machine-gun, Leutnant Sur See Lohemeyer and the last hopes of survival into the fjord.

The time was o8.12 hours and fifty-two seconds.

Less than eight minutes had passed since a British cruiser had started shooting at Norway.

Chapter Seven

'*RAID* (*rād*) *n.* a hostile incursion depending on
surprise and rapidity; a foray; surprise visit . . .'
Collins New English Dictionary.

The Commando soldiers were raiders. But they were not, and
made no claim to be, supermen. As a group they were neither
large in stature or loud in their public conduct. Nor were they
unthinking automatons any more than undisciplined louts.

They were just ordinary, supremely fit men from all walks of
life. They were all volunteers, most of them were very brave, and
quite a few of them enjoyed a sense of *esprit de corps* which they
had never felt in any other previous vocation.

They were resolute, dedicated men. But they were basically
infantry soldiers, and human. They did most things a little more
skilfully, a little more efficiently, and very much faster than their
contemporaries in the Line Regiments.

Anyone would tell you that. Especially a man with a 'Commando'
flash on his shoulder.

And the Germans.

H-HOUR plus 5 MINUTES

The Admiral watched anxiously as the Brigadier took the signal
pad from the Corporal kneeling beside the master set tuned to the
Brigade Net ashore.

Behind him the crisp, urgent commands of the damage control
officers echoed above the crackle of the flames in *Hystrix*'s wound,
yet Braddock-Tenby found himself listening only to the distant
sounds of battle, and trying tantalisingly to read the reaction in
the Brigadier's face.

Then Aubrey looked up at him and, merely allowing his features
to relax slightly, for he was an old soldier and knew how the tides
of war could turn abruptly, said, 'From Colonel Duncan . . .
BEACHHEAD ESTABLISHED BUT HEAVY RESISTANCE EN-

COUNTERED CENTRE OF TOWN . . . SITUATION UN-
CERTAIN . . . CASUALTIES MODERATE . . . end of message.'

The Admiral wondered how moderate was moderate while, at
the same time, feeling a glow of relief that now they had heard
from all the groups in that so far away and hostile place.

The Brigadier stared wistfully across the sullen, ever-lightening
sea, and Braddock-Tenby knew where his friend would rather be
at that moment. Then the soldier's lips moved softly.

'They're ashore, Arthur. At least they are ashore!'

*

668497 Trooper Williams, D.H., was ashore, an' that was f'r
certain. But it was about all that Danny *was* sure of, because right
then he didn't know where Charlie was, or the pier or the rest of
the blokes or even the bloody Germans.

All he knew was that he'd gone up that exposed stretch of beach
like a dose of salts, with his heart in his mouth and the blood
pounding in his ears so loud that he wasn't really aware of any
firing, or shouting, or anything. Then the sand on one side of him
had started kicking and leaping in vicious, explosive little spurts
and Charlie had bawled, 'Machine-gun!' and, followed faithfully
by himself, had veered off to the left – and disappeared!

Which was bloody typical of Charlie Smart.

Then Charlie had appeared in front of him again, looking scared
rigid, until Danny saw that it wasn't Charlie at all but a fat little
man with glasses and a coal scuttle helmet holding a rifle like a
stick of rock. So Danny snap-shot him while still running, and
the fat little German flopped back on his bottom with the shocked
eyes behind the glasses staring up at him in surprise and a red
flowering stain on the front of the baggy uniform.

Danny smashed him under the chin with the butt of his rifle
as he tore past, and it wasn't for another twenty galloping yards
that he suddenly realised he'd killed his first man.

He stopped abruptly and was sick all over the frozen snow
while thinking how Charlie would have grinned like hell with the
irony of it – if Charlie had been there. Then he started running
again.

Until a leg caught him in mid-leap and he crashed heavily to
the ground to see another khaki-uniformed man lying prone
behind a corner of a building.

Desperately Danny wriggled into cover, listening nervously to the smash of bullets suddenly rattling against the wall above him. A grenade exploded somewhere to the right, lost in the still cloying smoke just as he realised that, if it hadn't been for the other bloke he, Danny Williams, would have been lying a bit farther along instead, and with more holes in him than a bath sponge.

He muttered, in between pants, 'Ta, mate! Oh, *bloody* Norah...!'

The man said unnecessarily, 'There's a nest of Jerries down there...' just as the hidden machine-gun opened up again and the two of them were hugging the ground and feeling the splinters of timber from the wall rattling on their helmets. The M.G. hesitated and Danny snarled miserably, 'Down *there*? Far as I knew they could've been back the way... din't even realise any of our crowd had got this far.'

His companion shrugged a bit oddly and Danny screwed himself round, feeling the first pangs of unease. Then the man said, looking a little embarrassed, 'I wouldn't know, Trooper... personally, I'm from British Movietone News.'

The camera he hugged so bloody concernedly didn't look half as reassuring to Danny as a Tommy Gun would have done.

*

Group Five had started to advance silently and with a slight feeling of stunned awe, across the bleak, shattered landscape which had been the Oksenes Battery. Those men with rifles had now fixed bayonets and, to Captain Mike Seely glancing down the steadily moving line, the scene held an eerie, timeless quality which could equally have reflected the cold shining steel of Caesar's Legions before Pharsalus, or Attila's hosts carving their bloody way across the Byzantine Empire.

Or their own fathers before them, grimly advancing against the very same enemy over the wasteland that was Mons. And dying as they did so, because they were determined that their children should never have to do the same.

And now these children were men. And *they* were advancing.

So the World hadn't learned a damn thing. Not in over two thousand years of agony.

Those members of the German Battery who still thought there had been an air-raid were now starting to surface. Most of them, as they emerged, were immediately prodded back through the line towards the waiting L.C.A.s. Stumbling, dirty men with disbelieving eyes and bowed heads, yet all wearing the same dazed expressions of relief that, for them, the attack was over before it had really begun, and that they were still alive. And that the British Commandos – against all warnings from Herr Doktor Goebbels to the contrary – were actually allowing them to leave their bunkers voluntarily, and not on the periphery of a grenade blast.

Most of them. An occasional muffled thump indicated that there were still Germans who were either too frightened or too stubborn to surrender.

Like the youngster who appeared in the entrance to his dugout just ahead of the approaching Captain Seely, took one incredulous look at the line of khaki-clad visitors, and disappeared back down again despite Trooper Belling's command to 'Hände hoch you bastard!'

Belling turned to the Captain and shrugged, fumbling inside the belly of his lifejacket. Mike said hopefully, 'Wait a minute, Belling. Give him a chance. . . .'

Then the German came back up with a rifle, threw two shots at Mike which plucked the sleeve of his battledress, and Belling looked all disgusted as he shot the youngster, saying, 'Now you can trust 'im, Sir!'

Mike rolled a grenade down the steps himself in case there was anyone else below. It was funny how quickly you learned things in a war. He started to jog-trot forward to catch up with the line, listening coldly as he ran to the sound of the man – or at least he thought it must be a man – still howling in a high, monotonous keen from the shattered gun positions ahead. Corporal Dick was beside him again now and the two of them hesitated only briefly at the first emplacement, noticing the wrecked weapon without a barrel and its smashed crew lying untidily around it as if scythed to the ground by an enormous flail.

Seely wondered with half his mind where on earth the massive barrel of the gun could possibly have got to, while the other half thought that maybe those broken artillerymen were still luckier than that distant, demented German who wouldn't stop screaming.

Abruptly Corporal Dick sheered off at an acute angle, skidded to a halt on the edge of a rubble-strewn crater and muttered bitterly, 'Oh *hell!*'

The Captain joined him, followed his gaze – and found that luck was really all a question of degree. Because you couldn't possibly get much more unlucky than the fat Wehrmacht Unter-offizier with the paralysed face and the eviscerated stomach who sprawled at the bottom of the hole. Not if you were mutilated like that *and* still alive.

Mike felt the Corporal's eyes switch questioningly towards him and gripped the butt of his revolver until the tendons of his fingers ached, trying desperately not to show the helplessness within him. Dick said quietly, 'Stretcher-bearers, Sir? Or . . . ?'

The German bubbled horribly and the Captain thought, 'What a bloody awful birthday,' and stared with the masochistic fascina-tion of a man who had never seen what shellfire could do to people. He found, with a surge of surprise and a certain guilty pride, that he didn't feel terribly sick, not right then anyway. But he did see that it didn't make very much difference whether you scrubbed yourself all over before a battle or not.

He kept his voice level. 'Or what, Corporal?'

Dick lowered the muzzle of his rifle almost imperceptibly, and slowly so that the wounded man wouldn't see the gesture. Mike started to snap 'I'm damned if I'll allow . . . !' then he found that the dying man in the pit *had* registered the British soldier's intent when the tortured eyes filled with such unmistakable gratitude and longing for the peace which the attackers could provide.

If he, Michael Seely, would allow it. As a gesture of . . . good-will?

He thought, 'I should be the one to do it,' and felt ashamed that he only turned away when the Corporal said softly, 'You go on, Sir. I'll catch up in a minute.'

He had only walked three paces when the solitary shot rang out. He didn't turn round again because there wasn't any point in it, and he had a job to do up ahead. The distant rattle of firing rose to a new high from the direction of Bert Stenhouse's Group, obviously hard pressed around the Sørenson Factory area, and Mike started to run again. The quicker they finished this filthy task of scavenging among the Battery's remains, the quicker they could become fighting men again in support of Group Four.

It really was a bloody awful way for a chap to spend his birthday.

And he did wish they could do something to stop that poor tormented devil howling like that.

*

From *Muscadin*'s bridge Willie watched grimly as 'A' Gun's next few rounds tore into the armed trawler ahead until the enemy ship was a listing, burning hulk. He hadn't wanted to continue firing – the first shot should have been enough to discourage any opposition – but even after that the little German was still using her light armament so she didn't leave one much choice.

Willie Bradbury was really a very humane man – apart from which, he had rather anticipated being able to board the enemy warship in the hope of saving her code books and confidential papers for analysis later. . . . 'A' and 'B' Guns slammed again, simultaneously, and the ship seemed to hesitate in her passage through the water, almost as if they had touched something below, while the acrid muzzle-blast swept back over the men on her bridge just as the fall of the shot sparkled briefly from inside the shroud of smoke ahead.

The Captain called sharply, 'Cease firing!' and lifted his binoculars to the other approaching ship, the old merchantman which seemed to still be proceeding as though *Muscadin* didn't even exist and that nothing untoward was happening in the Østersfjord at all.

Number One said thoughtfully, 'Swedish Ensign.'

Willie shrugged. 'German name, though . . . *Wismar*.'

'D'you think she could be genuine, Sir?'

'Do you?'

'No.' Flat and emphatic.

The Captain glanced at his First Lieutenant in surprise. They had both changed imperceptibly, even since the action had begun less than five minutes ago. He knew that he, himself, was beginning to feel the strain of constantly sifting and assessing the ever-changing situation. Of selecting targets then, almost as quickly, discarding them again in favour of other threats which loomed abruptly from a new quarter. Like the hidden shore-side weapon position which gave its priority up to the armed trawler which, in its defeat, made way for the 4.7s to engage a distant, panic-stricken merchantman. . . .

Number One, on the other hand, had appeared to blossom since the destroyer had swung into action. No longer was he the nervous, slightly hesitant young officer of before, loath to voice any opinion which wasn't called for directly by his Captain. Now he seemed to move more confidently, to emanate an air of competence and casual self-assurance in direct contrast to his former self.

When the shell had struck *Muscadin*'s bows the First Lieutenant had taken off like a rocket to lead the damage control party but, after assessing the rather more spectacular than critical damage and issuing his orders, had then returned to the bridge instead of doing as Willie had anticipated and flapping around the men working forward.

And now an instant opinion. More than that – a positive, uncompromising statement which, if it proved wrong, could reflect most unpleasantly on the First Lieutenant's career as a regular Naval Officer when the heat had died down and their Lords of the Admiralty were casually flicking back through the post-war records in search of likely candidates for bowler hats.

And firing on a neutral ship *could* prove a little awkward to justify. Especially if she claimed to have been held in Ålvik under duress, and merely to have been seeking freedom under what she thought was the timely protection of the Royal Navy. . . .

Come to that, Willie rather liked his job too, and had always wanted to be an admiral in preference to being a commercial traveller, R.N. Retired.

But even commercial travellers had to make decisions.

'Pom tiddely om pom . . .' said Willie philosophically. '. . . Starboard ten to zero nine five! Commence firing . . . !'

*

Gefreiter Scherer galloped past the weapon pits and the waiting Dieter Balke with hardly a sideways glance. It was quite light now and he didn't need to look closely to tell that the British guns had already been at work there. He didn't see his ex-assistant either, but even if he had done he wouldn't have stopped. The rage which had slowly been building up in him since *Salamander*'s opening salvo had demolished his first command was now a white-hot flame in the Leading Seaman's belly and all he wanted to do was to kill someone. Anyone. Just as long as they wore a khaki uniform and came within range of his Schmeisser.

But Scherer, enraged or not, still retained one facility which enormously increased his chances of survival over those of the happily unbalanced Dieter Balke. Because the big seaman was guided by one instinct which coldly and calculatedly refused to be overwhelmed by any fires of patriotism or hatred or bruised pride, and that was the need for self-preservation.

Which was why, as he came to the first house on the outskirts of the town, he slowed to an easy jog-trot and warily kept to the shadows while, all the time, his eyes scanned the half light ahead for the British soldiers to appear.

Suddenly he stopped dead as he saw a movement ahead. Curiously, just for a moment, the hate gave way to a surge of panic which left him feeling uncomfortable and a little shakier even than before. He brought the muzzle of the Schmeisser up frowning uneasily – this wasn't quite as he'd anticipated, not now the Tommies were so near, because he suddenly found he was starting to feel frightened and that didn't conform to Scherer's image of himself as a man of steel.

The thing moved again, about twenty metres away on the other side of the street. Scherer's heart gave a sickening flutter and he swung the barrel of the weapon hurriedly just as a flash from the other end of the town lit up the scene, and the thing croaked weakly, '*Fliegerwarnung . . . in Deckung gehen! Fliegerwarnung . . . !*' and Scherer saw with a great heave of relief that the terror in the shadows was only a Wehrmacht Corporal with a smashed face and a fixation about air-raids.

'Silly ignorant bastard,' he thought. 'Typical, of course. Typical bloody Army. . . .'

Ignoring the wounded man, he started to move cautiously forward again. Not quite so enthusiastically this time though, because Scherer was just beginning to find that facing an enemy at close range was a very different thing to facing them across the reassuring width of the North Sea.

And even being bombarded by a destroyer from over a mile away was rather less personal and frightening than the anticipation of being shot at point-blank range by an angry British thug who didn't even care about the Geneva Convention.

Not according to Reichsminister Goebbels anyway.

*

The Colonel, several hundred yards away and on the opposite

side of the town to Scherer, was rather more worried about tanks than about the niceties of war.

In fact, he was so concerned with establishing a defence in depth around the landing area before the enemy had time to deploy the three self-propelled 38(t)s which Intelligence had warned him of that, when he turned a corner to see his forward line of Commandos pinned down by fire from the other end of the street, he just kept on striding forward without glancing to right or left while, from either side, horrified British voices shouted 'Fire-swept area, Sir . . . !' and 'Get yer effin' heid doon oot the wa . . . Oh, sorry Colonel, Sir!'

The Colonel just waved his stick irritably and retorted with some heat, 'No damn time for that. . . . Move forward! Keep moving forward there!' while, at the same time, one half of his mind was hoping the Germans were poor shots and the other half was trying to orientate itself in relation to the position of the Norske Hotell and their primary objective within – the Kriegsmarine S.K.L. Headquarters.

He decided that the hotel must lie off to the right, some one hundred and fifty yards ahead, just as the fire from the British troops rose to a frenetic slamming and crackling as they covered their Commanding Officer while small groups of men, bending low and shooting as they ran, again started to double quickly from one doorway to the next. Group Two – this time led by the example of their Colonel – had once more broken the stalemate.

But by a quarter-past eight enemy resistance was growing rapidly as the element of surprise wore off.

Marching stolidly behind his Colonel, Pipe-Corporal McLusky saw the stick grenade come curving towards them from a window to the right, said resignedly, 'Bluidy Germans . . . !' kicked the grenade back towards the pavement while at the same time ripping off a burst of Thompson fire which folded the thrower untidily and finally across the brightly painted sill.

Then he politely but firmly shoved Dougal Duncan into the cover of a nearby open door and followed down on top of him with no regard for rank at all, just as the grenade exploded fifteen feet away.

When the dust and powdered snow cleared the Colonel gazed up at McLusky's blackened features with an icy stare and said accusingly, 'Pipe-Corporal McLusky! Where are your pipes, man?'

McLusky pulled his kilt down over his exposed buttocks with great dignity, and answered without any disrespect whatsoever. 'Sir,' he said most reasonably, 'Ah'd have had a gey hard job tae shoot yon aggressive wee bastard wi' the mouthpiece o' mah chanter . . . *Sir*!'

Three Commando soldiers bolted past the open door just as an apparently newly established MG34 opened up in the middle distance. Bullets started to scream and ricochet from the iced cobblestones in the street and the Colonel thought, 'Damn!' and hoped that one of the sections advancing along the waterfront would outflank it pretty quickly. He started wondering about those tanks again, and where they were and why the Germans hadn't brought them into action yet. Then he glanced at his watch and saw with a surge of surprise that they'd only been ashore for five minutes. . . .

A charging Trooper stopped charging right outside the door and went down without a sound, crashing headlong over the ice in a flail of arms, legs and equipment. McLusky hurled himself into the street, grabbed the wounded man's leg in one great paw and plucked him unceremoniously under cover. Then another running body hurled itself into the doorway, fell over McLusky, rebounded off the bullet-splintered frame and cannoned violently into the room itself with a muffled 'Dammitall!'

An enormous explosion from the eastern side of the town shook the windows in their sockets. The Colonel looked up from the field dressing he was preparing and said equably to the newcomer, 'Do come in, Dicky. I hear your chaps have started on the warehouses.'

But he couldn't help wondering just how stable the thirty-pound pack of plastic explosive strapped to his demolition engineer Lieutenant's back really would be, if the young man insisted on bouncing around the room like a snooker ball for very much longer.

*

Major Otto Rhöme and Oberbootmann Döring had stopped helplessly facing the first British soldiers as they tore around the corner of the Nordkai buildings. Both of them knew there was absolutely no point in trying to reach the cover of the low wall which flanked the road and, especially to the Major, there seemed something terribly undignified about being shot in the back.

No one noticed as the dog Cuno loped several paces farther up the beach then, aware that its master was no longer following, hesitated with the black ears erect and the first rumble of a low growl directing itself towards the approaching strangers. They were unfamiliar figures to the dog, unfamiliar and noisy and full of menace. The alsatian lowered its head between splayed forelegs and allowed the soft muzzle to curl back over vicious teeth in a snarl of hatred.

The leading Commando, an officer, skidded to a wary halt twenty yards away and shouted, 'Don't move . . . *Hände hoch*, eh?' then a Corporal with eyes white against a terrifyingly blackened face dropped to one knee, swinging the muzzle of his Thompson gun to cover the shocked Germans. Death, and an awful violence, hovered very near.

Bertie Torrance moved forward very cautiously indeed. Even through the dim grey light he could tell that one of the tensely poised Germans was a field officer, and that made him a prize worth taking alive if possible. But typical Nazi, of course – the complete *Junker*, standing there haughtily erect with that arrogantly impassive stare and those damnably polished jackboots gleaming softly under the flare of the smoke floats . . . though the other blighter looked a lot more immediately threatening, holding that Schmeisser and just waiting for the chance to use it. Navy, eh? Regular square-headed Kriegsmariner, cold as ice and just about as hard. . . .

He snapped brusquely, 'Drop it, laddie . . . the gun! *Tropfen* and *hände hoch, ja?*'

Döring thought bleakly, 'Typical bloody Britisher. Cold as ice and just about as hard. Arrogant and superior as hell . . . !' Then the Tommy Corporal lined his sub-machine-gun impatiently, even a little wistfully, on Döring's belly and the Chief Petty Officer slowly, ever so reluctantly, allowed the muzzle of his Schmeisser to dip in bitter acknowledgement. He still kept his finger casually inside the trigger-guard, though.

Furtively the alsatian inched forward, belly flat, towards the men who were threatening his master.

Major Otto Rhöme felt his shoulders sag wearily as the sick

humiliation flooded his throat with the bitter taste of defeat. Abruptly he drew himself up once again and stared calmly and, he hoped, with dignity at the British Officer before him. He was surprised and a little hurt to detect an expression of dislike on the Commando Major's face, almost of contempt, in fact. But then again, he didn't know that the last time Bertie Torrance had seen a German was when his regiment was being virtually decimated by the Wehrmacht at St Valéry.

Torrance jerked the barrel of his .45 towards Döring. '*Sprechen sie Englisch?*'

Rhöme said politely, 'I do, *Herr Major* . . . a little.'

'Yeah? Well you tell Admiral Doenitz there to drop his bloody gun. Chop, chop . . . *Raus!* I won't ask again . . . *verstehen?*'

Bertie waved the revolver pointedly at his opposite number. It was too much for the dog Cuno. One moment he had been tensely awaiting a command, some guide from his beloved master while his low rumbling growls were lost in the almost continuous whip-cracks of the battle for the town. Then the poised menacing figure of the stranger was making a threatening move towards the one person Cuno adored. It was too much.

The alsatian sprang, hurtling towards Torrance in a rippling trajectory of snarling hatred.

Bertie's Troop-Corporal, taken utterly by surprise, was only aware of the huge dog as a terrifying airborne shadow coming in from the right. Swivelling on one knee he squeezed the trigger of the Tommy Gun through sheer fright. The stream of nine-millimetre rounds virtually cut the dog in half while still suspended in mid-air.

Oberbootmann Döring must have known he didn't have a chance. But he still hurled himself to one side, away from the Commandant, and desperately swung the Schmeisser forward. The Corporal however, being a man of some perception, continued firing as he turned and – also being a man of some considerable marksmanship – succeeded in placing four rounds in a six-inch group centred on the Kriegsmarine eagle decorating Döring's breast.

Bertie Torrance, shaken to the core, only fired once. His warning bullet ploughed into the shingle beside the Commandant's feet and suddenly the beautifully-kept jackboots were dulled by a spatter of dirty snow and animal blood. It seemed symbolic, somehow, and rather shocking, yet the tall Major never even flinched. He just stared at Torrance through bitter, expressionless eyes before quite deliberately turning his back and bending over the sprawled body of the Chief Petty Officer.

The Commando said tightly, 'Get up. . . . *Move!*'

Rhöme turned to the dog. Just for a brief moment he allowed his hand to fondle, ever so gently, the soft fur behind the animal's ears while the alsatian gazed up at him through glazed, unseeing pupils already dulled in death. And then the lonely old man stood proudly erect, lifted his chin and, with immense dignity, marched slowly towards the waiting L.C.A.s. And captivity.

Bertie Torrance watched him go, trailed warily by the Corporal, and shrugged thoughtfully before swinging to follow his Troopers up the beach. My God but there was a real Prussian for you, a real Nazi. A man shot down beside him and not one bloody spark of emotion.

Cold blooded. Like the damned animal.

It didn't worry him a bit, though. Because, just for a minute, he really had thought the bastard was crying!

*

There was a lot of crying going on in the Østersfjord.

Krupinsky could hear them all around him as he clung to the old gun on *Patzig*'s shattered foredeck. He couldn't see very much because of the smoke from the fires and the jetting steam and the great pall of coal dust obscuring all but a patch of black water immediately below his dangling legs. But he could hear them.

She was going over, he could feel that much. Lying farther and farther to starboard with the brass shells from the ready-use ammo lockers bouncing and tumbling over the side, and the severed shrouds hanging away from the foremast like black-oiled tentacles.

And the crying, and the coughing, and the retching and the splashing. All around him.

Ahhhh, what the hell . . . !

Kross said conversationally, 'C'mon then, Krupinsky! Do we stay or go?' and the Chief screwed his head round and upwards to see the Leading Seaman sort of half standing, half lying against the sloping deck with his feet braced against the angled pedestal of the gun.

Krupinsky looked down at the water again just as a head bobbed past supported by a slab of hatch cover. The head stared up at him, just a shiny black globe with two white-marble eyes and a red slash of a mouth. Then a pair of arms came out of the smoke, clawing for the support of the wood, and suddenly there were two disembodied heads mouthing and coughing at each other underneath Krupinsky, both fighting for the one chance to stay afloat.

They drifted out of sight under the overhanging flare of the bow, but Krupinsky could still hear them choking and screaming with a frenetic outrage, each at the utter selfishness of the other, so he waved a hand at Kross and said positively, 'We stay, Kross. . . . Gimme a lift!'

It only struck him in a detached sort of way that the British had apparently ceased firing when the Leading Seaman's hand gripped his wrist and he was struggling to lift his knee up to get a purchase over the now almost horizontal barrel of the gun. Then Kross gave a heave and Krupinsky felt the corner of the sight vernier dig agonisingly into his groin before he was topside of the mounting too.

Kross grinned shakily, holding his arm. 'You're puttin' on weight. Too much beer in that gut of yours.'

Krupinsky rubbed his groin tenderly, already planning the next stage of the survival game. 'Just you gettin' old, Kross. Old an' feeble!'

The ship gave another shudder and lay five degrees farther over.

Leading Hand Kross grabbed at the bollard now almost above his head and screwed his eyes shut against the smoke-grimed features. Then, when they didn't turn right over, he cautiously opened them again and looked surprised. 'Old . . . ? Jesus but I'd give my old woman f'r the bloody chance to get a bit older. What now, Chief?'

The British destroyer opened up again from somewhere to the left and, just for a moment, Krupinsky braced himself for the slamming roar of the shells as they punched in through the smoke. Then nothing happened and he lost interest in other people's problems and concentrated on their own.

'We go up an' over, on to her hull,' he snapped urgently. 'Maybe she'll float long enough belly up, an' if she doesn't . . .' He shrugged – it didn't make a lot of difference except that the pool would be a little less crowded when they finally went in, '. . . you go first.'

Kross shook his head, wincing. 'I think I sprained my wrist last time. You go, pull me up after.'

The trawler lurched again and Krupinsky knew they only had a few moments left before she finally turned turtle. There wasn't time to argue. Glancing down he could see the water now lapping over the starboard rail and swirling sluggishly against the angle of the rusted scuppers. He stretched out his hand. . . . Blast! Just not tall enough to get a grip on the stanchion. . . . Kross gave a heave with his shoulder in against Krupinsky's backside and the Chief felt himself left with the wooden deck slimy cold against his cheek and the pain in his groin piercing deeper and deeper as he struggled to raise his foot towards the bollard. . . .

. . . then his fingers closed around the metal socket, and Kross gave another final heave as Krupinsky scrabbled to get his leg over the edge until he was virtually hanging horizontally under the angled inboard side of the rail.

And then he was up, and through, and over and lying on the port side plates of the ship with a red haze in front of his eyes and the rasping choke of heaving lungs pounding in his ears. Urgently he screwed himself back towards the rail, feeling the razor-sharp flakes of rust spearing under his fingernails, until he was looking down at Kross's white, upturned face and reaching desperately for the hand that stretched towards him.

But both of them knew there wouldn't be time. Not even to be brave any more.

Kross cried, '*Please* help me, Chie . . . !'

Krupinsky's palm slapped against the Leading Hand's wrist just as an explosion from aft shook the ship like a recalcitrant child. He felt her going over, slowly at first and then faster and faster as the water in her took charge. Under him Kross screamed in agony as the strain came on his injured arm, but the old Chief held on while knowing, even as he did so, that they were too late. Then, as the cold sweat poured over his screwed-tight eyes and the screech of tearing metal boomed in the hull below him, he felt Kross's wrist bones slide ever so finally through his grasp.

And Kross was gone.

Krupinsky opened his eyes again in time to see his friend falling backwards across the barrel of the gun. Slowly it seemed, almost in slow motion with Kross's eyes wide and disappointed against the grime and the blood, and then he pivoted forward round the steel fulcrum and dropped, all splayed and broken, face down towards the water.

The Østersfjord received Kross with a great gouting swirl of white, oxygenised foam as the ship rolled sullenly over. Krupinsky got slowly to his feet and, without any hurry at all, walked up the side as it came down to meet him until he was treading through the weed-slimed barnacles which encrusted the trawler's double-bottoms.

Then the *Patzig* was upside down on top of Kross and Lohemeyer and poor, frightened little Eyssen and most of the others who'd made up her complement.

Krupinsky squatted wearily down and patted his pockets thoughtfully. He pulled out a pack of cigarettes and lit one, then just sat among the barnacles waiting for someone to come, and watching the bronze curve of the silent propeller projecting above the far end of the upturned hulk.

He didn't feel at all heroic. He didn't even feel like a proper survivor.

But then, Oberbootmann Krupinsky hadn't even got his feet wet.

H-HOUR plus 7 MINUTES

Trooper Danny Williams, still lying doggo beside the cameraman under the corner of the Sørenson Factory, heard the sound first. Distorted by the smoke and occasionally lost in the echoing explosions he knew, nevertheless, that it was coming closer. Coming his way. A distant menacing rattle and squeak which gradually increased in volume.

He muttered 'Oh *Christ*!' and started to wriggle backwards, away from the corner. The Movietone News Man stared at him in growing concern. 'What is it?'

Danny stopped wriggling and stared hopelessly ahead, towards the lighter patch of smoke which, being free of shadow, indicated the end of the alleyway. He fumbled resignedly inside his pack for a grenade – hell, *two* grenades f'r what good they'd be – and wished Charlie was with him.

'Tank,' he muttered, then stared aggrievedly at the cameraman thinking that, out of all the calibres of weapon carried by the four hundred and odd blokes in the Commando, *he* had to go an' pick the one nutter who went to his particular wars armed with a thirty-five-millimetre roll of bloody celluloid.

'Jerrie Tank,' he said again, placing the two grenades on the ground before him then, feeling a bit responsible for the Movie-tone Man who was, when you came to think of it, a sort of guest, added doubtfully, 'You keep behind me, mate. For protection.'

The cameraman looked pleased. 'I've never filmed a tank in action before.'

Danny glared at him. 'You don't meet all that many people who *have* . . . not outside a cemetery!'

The MG34 rattled again, drowning the sound of the tracks until there was a sudden explosion and the gun stopped abruptly. Danny lifted his head cautiously, hopefully – all of a sudden he didn't feel quite so alone now he knew the rest of the Troop hadn't sneaked back to the L.C.A.s and gone home without him. Thank God that MG had been neutralised. . . .

He heard the tank again, much closer now, and went back to feeling lonely. There it was, dead ahead and coming down the gap. He couldn't see it yet but he'd heard that terrifying squeal and rumble often enough before on training films. . . . Danny's hands began to shake and he savagely snatched at one of the grenades, fumbling with his finger for the pin ring.

Another alien sound whispered beside his head. Screwing round he stared disbelievingly at the Movietone Man with the great Mickey Mouse ears of the camera magazine held steadily towards the approaching menace, and the mechanism already whirring to record Danny's moment of dying for posterity.

Rumble . . . squeal . . . no sound of motors yet. He always thought you'd hear the motors this close . . . rumble . . . squeak. . . .

The smoke thinned fractionally and he lifted the first grenade ready to lob. Please God let the conning hatch be wide open. He tensed himself ready to run for it just as soon as the grenades were on their way. Wait for it . . . wait for it, Danny Boy . . . let it go past an' then . . .

A dark shape loomed ahead of him through the fog. Oh *Christ* . . . !

The camera stopped whirring just as Danny started to frown. It did seem a pretty *small* tank, f'r . . .

He stopped the grenade in mid-throw. It was probably just as well because he only then realised he'd forgotten to pull the pin out anyway. The cameraman said disappointedly, 'You sure they train you blokes properly before they send you on these things?'

Danny didn't answer. He just rose stiffly to his feet and levelled his Lee Enfield hopefully at the little German with the fat stomach and the rimless glasses who appeared out of the smoke, stood docilely before them, and said cheerfully, '*Mein freund Kaput! Verwunded. . . . Boom, boom, boom! Ja?*'

All the same, it wasn't a very efficient wheelbarrow the pacifist little German had commandeered to transport his wounded friend in.

And to Danny – marching grimly behind his rather uninspiring prisoners in search of the British Aid Post – the rattle of the steel-rimmed wheel over the cobbles and the squeak of that ungreased axle could *still* have been quite easily mistaken for the tracks of a bloody great Panzer!

*

H.M. Destroyer *Salamander* moved slowly through the narrows between Hæl-en and Oksenes with her Battle Ensign flapping haughtily over already swivelling gun turrets as the ranges and bearings of her first selected targets flashed down from the Director.

One mile away they could see their sister ship cutting rakishly through the patches of smoke hanging over the Østersfjord as she engaged a small, squat merchantman with a spindly funnel and an apparent death-wish. A signal lamp flickered cheerfully from Willie Bradbury's bridge just before the destroyer fired again.

Salamander's Yeoman turned to his Captain and grinned. 'From *Muscadin*, Sir . . . WELCOME TO THE SHOW . . . I HAVE RESERVED A FRONT ROW SEAT FOR YOU . . . end of message!'

H-HOUR plus 9 MINUTES

It hadn't been stripping the canvas cover from the tanker *Bluthund*'s wing-mounted machine-gun that had taken the time so much as reading the Kriegsmarine-issued weapons manual to find out how to fire the bloody thing.

The Master and Chief Officer of the German ship had watched

in raging frustration as the three assault craft bearing the British Commandos had virtually cruised alongside the Sörsund jetty, right under their noses, while all they could do was thumb grimly through the index for the section entitled 'Loading – *Cartridges, cartridge belts, locking system and tab*'.

And, even when they'd found it – and the smoke-laying Blenheim had come and gone and the British were ashore and that bloody useless ex-escort of theirs had been battered into a flaming, topsy-turvy wreck – even *then* they weren't really ready to declare war. Because merchant seamen of any nationality aren't terribly familiar with such martial terms as recoil increaser and feed pawl and cannelure, to say nothing of interpreting '*Engage the hook on the front end with the lug on the rear end of the lower part of the feed plate. . . .*'

Which was why, when at nineteen minutes past eight they were finally ready to shoot at something, they watched with considerable surprise and satisfaction as the second wave of British troops sailed providently out of the smoke still lying over the water. Directly towards, and right under, the sights of the machine-gun.

The *Bluthund*'s Captain squeezed the trigger, tentatively at first and then with growing confidence as he watched the Tommies rising in the boat, clutching at bloodied, caved-in chests before toppling screaming into the Østersfjord.

In fact, he only stopped firing when the open craft was an empty, colandered hulk . . . and when his Chief Officer noticed the distressingly Germanic legend – s.s. PÖKEL. EMDEN – painted under the lifeboat's drifting bow.

But perhaps it was rather poetic really, because the crew of the *Pökel had* left their own Chief Engineer all alone in the engine-room of their virtually doomed ship.

And then a real British Commando appeared straddle-legged in the tanker's wheelhouse door, and shot the *Bluthund*'s Master and Mate right over their own bridge wing before they'd even had time to feel sorry.

*

For Paul Fichte, cramped in the shoulder-wide cockpit of his Messerschmitt, time had passed even more hectically since the Royal Air Force Beau had zeroed in on his homicidally inclined wingman.

Eight minutes, to be precise. Eight minutes of weaving and climbing, and spiralling down again to blast belly-flat along the shore of the fjord in search of a target. Anything or anyone British which fired or ran, or just threw themselves headlong under cover when the snarl of his exhausts homed in on them.

Yet they had also been the most frustrating eight minutes he'd ever spent as a fighter pilot because, every time he hauled the plane round to line his cannons on the new mark, either a whispering twin-engined shadow would fall on him from above or his windscreen would fill abruptly with those vicious warning puff-balls from the pom-poms of the two destroyers now leaving curving white tails across the Østersfjord.

'Jumbo-One to Base! Jumbo-One to Base! This is Jumbo-*One* f'r Chris . . . Jumbo-*ONE*! How do you read me . . . ?'

Savagely he ripped the oxygen mask from his face and gave up trying to call an ominously silent Herdla Field. A cold glance at the ME's fuel gauge then back up to the rear mirror for any sign of what he now assessed as the three British fighters currently in the air over sector Berta Ludwig.

Doing that made him think about Söhler again.

He still remembered his automatic warning to his wingman, '. . . left, Söhler! Break LEFT, damn you . . . !' Then a brief glimpse of the Leutnant's white, incredulous face twisting round and up to stare at him through the perspex canopy just as the Beaufighter fired.

Almost immediately Söhler's starboard wing fell off and went spinning and flailing astern while the Messerschmitt peeled over and started to go down vertically with long feathery streamers of venting fuel hanging above it. Fichte momentarily lost sight of the two planes as he roared into a half-roll at the top of his loop, then he was diving earthwards again whispering 'Get out, kid! Jump for it . . . !' just as Söhler's canopy jettisoned in a twinkling, tumbling flash of reflection.

The Beaufighter had swung sideways into his sights, the two huge Hercules XVI engines flanked by red, white and blue rondels bright against the camouflage. He stabbed the firing buttons urgently and the ME shook hammeringly, but the speed of his descent was too great and the Beau vanished above him.

The R/T crackled and he heard Söhler say quietly, almost

apologetically, 'I can't make it, Fichte. My shoulder . . . I can't mo . . . !'

Then Söhler's plane blew up just before it hit the fjord and Paul watched the creamy white-foam flower spreading with little bits of wreckage still splashing in run-away skips around its edges. His earphones hissed continuously but there was no one there any more and, quite ridiculously, Paul Fichte started to feel lonely.

But he wouldn't be lonely for long. Not once he'd got back to base. The Gestapo wouldn't want him to feel left out of it.

He'd said 'Heil Hitler' to the flower in the water and started to try Herdla again – there wasn't any point in going back but he should really tell them about the Beaufighters. And then he'd just stay around until his fuel ran out because it would be better to go in the cockpit of his plane than in the screaming limbo of a Berlin cellar. . . .

. . . and all that was eight minutes ago.

He watched bleakly as the Beaufighters gathered for the kill. For that matter he didn't really think that running out of fuel was going to be his main problem, anyway.

H-HOUR plus 10 MINUTES

Having got tired sitting behind the machine-gun and just waiting for something to happen, Leichtmatrose Dieter Balke had started idly raking around the wrecked emplacement in search of further diversions. He'd just found a half buried stick grenade when the firing from the seaward side of the town increased sharply and the first dark shapes of men appeared along the narrow path beside the water.

Vaguely he realised that the British must have already out-flanked the defenders but he wasn't too interested in the tactical aspects of the day. All he knew was that, when those crouching, running shapes came just a little closer, then he'd have the opportunity he'd always wanted.

To fire the gun and be a Hero.

His mind refused to anticipate what the Tommies might consider the right and proper thing to do in retaliation. Like shooting back at him with some considerable vindictiveness.

Absently he stuffed the grenade into the cavernous pocket of his greatcoat, then settled comfortably behind the MG34 again, sighting along the barrel experimentally. He wondered where Gefreiter Scherer was now, and how ashamed he would feel if he could see his assistant doing something so tremendously gallant and correct. And his father – wouldn't he be surprised and proud. And, when it was all over and the British had gone, perhaps they'd even give him a medal. A real, shiny black cross to hang around his neck over the brand-new Petty Officer's uniform. Maybe . . . maybe even presented by the *Führer* himself, with all the admirals and generals watching approvingly, and the bands and the flags, and the people clapping in delight. . . .

He smiled wistfully over the gun sights, without any animosity at all towards the approaching soldiers. Ever so carefully he slipped his finger inside the trigger-guard. He still remembered the manual instructions quite clearly for firing – upper trigger for single shots, lower for fully automatic.

The crook of his finger caressed the bottom of the metal stamping. After all, a machine-gun just wouldn't *be* a machine-gun otherwise. . . .

*

Troop-Sergeant Henderson knew he must have gone wrong somewhere because, instead of following the main body of the attack towards the centre of the town, somehow he'd managed to veer right until he found himself running along a small path with the foreshore on one side of him and silent, brightly-painted fishermen's houses on the other.

He wasn't the first Commando soldier to pass this way, though. Out of the corner of his eye he caught sight of a khaki body huddled close beside a garden fence. Dropping to one knee he turned the man gently over and recognised him vaguely as a corporal from the Norwegian Company. He also saw with a faint surge of shock that the Corporal had been shot neatly through one eye and shook his head bitterly, feeling sad that Death had been the only welcome for a man's coming home.

But then it had welcomed him too, the last time *he'd* returned from the war. But with him Death had been more subtle, more sophisticated, in that it had only struck at Ginny and Jim and the children and then, ever so cleverly, had drawn back to watch its real victim die while still staying alive.

So maybe the Norwegian corporal was lucky in a way, because now he didn't feel anything any more whereas Arthur Henderson, Grocer and Florist, lived on with an awful emptiness and would never be able to love again because he didn't have anything left to love.

Rising, he speared the man's rifle bayonet-point into the ground then placed the bloodied steel helmet over the butt plate. The one-eyed Scandinavian stared blankly up at him and he couldn't bear to look any longer so he slipped the identity discs from around the already cold neck and, stuffing them in his pocket, started running once more. It seemed different now, though, because having thought about Ginny again was making him all empty and numb inside like it had always done, and the exhilaration of that mad charge down the Nordkai had faded into a brief memory of the past.

He listened to the sounds of battle echoing over the high-pitched snow-covered roofs and looked anxiously ahead for some way to join it. Men were killing each other over there, only a few yards away from him, and suddenly he'd found that old desire for revenge and for the chance to square the account just a little. He started wishing he hadn't thrown the knife away after all. . . .

. . . so he was quite glad, really, when a German soldier seemed to rise out of the shadows and stand rather foolishly holding a rifle in his path. In fact, even as he stared at him the Sergeant couldn't help wondering why the man just stood there and made absolutely no attempt to defend himself, almost as if he didn't even know Henderson was there.

He fired while still on the run, a snap-shot from the hip which spun the strangely hesitant figure into the snow even as it called out pitifully, '*Hilfe! Ich bin verblenden . . . Meine Augen tun mir . . . !*'

But Sergeant Henderson couldn't understand German, so he couldn't possibly have been expected to know that the enemy soldier was already a seriously wounded man. And that he had been blind for several minutes before he'd met the lonely Commando on the path beside the Østersfjord.

And it was then, or very shortly after that, that a very strange thing happened to Arthur Henderson. Because his wife Ginny spoke to him.

It happened just as he passed the writhing man in the snow. He'd glanced down, still holding the Thompson barrel warily, and stepped around the German intending to cut right at the next path between the gardens in search of the Troop. He'd felt a bit sorry, of course, about the mistake, but it didn't really matter because Jerries were Jerries and the way that bloke was retching and gasping it wouldn't be very long before he was the best kind of enemy – a dead one.

And then Ginny said softly, and quite clearly, in that voice she'd used so often to guide him when she knew he was doing the wrong thing, 'Don't leave him, Arthur. Don't leave him all alone without anybody. Because *he's* far away from home too, and he won't ever be able to see the ones he loves again either . . . !'

So Arthur went back, and knelt down beside the dying man, and he didn't really know quite what Ginny had wanted him to do so he just spent the next few moments staring curiously down at the face of his enemy. And gradually, ever so gradually, he began to see just what it was that Ginny meant him to understand

For despite the blood and the grime and the jagged wound which disfigured the pallid features, this face below him was the face of an ordinary man. It was the face of a homely man, a kindly man. And it was the face of a man who was very frightened because he knew he was going to die and, unlike Arthur Henderson, would be leaving behind the most precious things on earth.

It could have been Arthur Henderson himself. If he'd been lying there and Ginny and the kids hadn't already been lost to him.

He said softly, 'Easy . . . take it easy, lad.'

The blind face turned fractionally, painfully. The cracked lips moved slowly. '*Eng . . . Engländer?*'

Arthur said gently, 'Just a friend. *Freund* . . . ah . . . you *verstehen? Ein freund!*'

The lips relaxed and a little shiny bubble of blood trickled down the inverted jaw. The Sergeant thought, 'Hurry up and die, you poor bastard,' and said again, '*Freund!* To look after you?'

Below him the face eased slightly, and whispered '*Freund . . .*' as though it was the most important thing in the world. Arthur Henderson thought how tremendously clever Ginny was to realise just how much it would mean to the dying man to have someone close while he did.

Yet it was a dangerous thing too, for Arthur. Because his reactions and his reflexes as a fighting soldier had, up to now, been conditioned very largely by his hatred for the enemy. And his conviction that they were, in some remote way, different and inhuman and not at all like ordinary people.

Until now.

Then the wounded German moved his arm with a great effort and, seeing that he was trying to reach something in his breast pocket, Arthur very gently undid the button and eased it out. It was a wallet, a brown leather wallet softened and cracked by years of carrying it close. Feeling a little awkward at this invasion of a lost man's privacy he opened it carefully and found a little, rather fuzzy photograph and, in a side pocket, a tiny silver crucifix.

He asked, 'Photograph . . . is that it?'

The face nodded, starting to go grey very quickly now. 'Foto . . .? *Lichtbild.* . . . *Ja, ja.* . . .'

The Sergeant opened the slack fingers and ever so gently closed them again over the cracked pasteboard square. Then he took the little silver crucifix and placed it on the man's breast, feeling just a tiny bit embarrassed but knowing, somehow, that this was important too.

The German turned his blind face towards Henderson and made a slight movement with the hand. Almost imperceptible it was, however, an unmistakable gesture of giving, of offering something very dear to him.

He whispered so faintly that the Sergeant had to bend low to catch the words '*Mein Frau* . . . *Mein kleiner kinder* . . . *Danke.* . . .'

Then more dark blood seeped out of the slack mouth while the German Eagle under the crucifix on the soldier's breast stopped heaving altogether, and Henderson knew his enemy was dead.

Thoughtfully he prised the photograph from the still hand and looked down at it frowning. It was the first time he'd ever been left anything by anybody and that made it a sort of rather special legacy. Unless, of course, you counted memories.

It was a picture of a woman kneeling on a blanket with a mountain behind her and tiny Alpine flowers all around. Beside her sat two children, a little girl and a little boy, and they were all holding hands and smiling at the camera. The mother wasn't as pretty as Ginny was . . . had been . . . but the children were so like Barbara and little Tommy that just for a wistful moment . . .

222

Troop-Sergeant Henderson blinked a couple of times. Then he got to his feet and, only for a few seconds, stood looking down at the dead German. He remembered something he'd heard Marlene Deitrich say in a film once so he murmured softly, '*Auf Wiedersehen*, mate!'

Then he started running again, but this time he wasn't quite so invulnerable – because now, having met an image of himself on a path in the middle of a battle, he'd lost that essential determination to kill the enemy on sight.

H-HOUR plus 13 MINUTES

They found Kruger under the barrel of the gun over on Oksenes Point, but he was so utterly demented that they didn't really know what to do with him so, like soldiers the world over, they called on the nearest officer to shoulder the responsibility.

By the time Captain Michael Seely had reached the position there were flecks of foam mingling with the caked blood and grime around Kruger's mouth. The lips themselves were drawn tight-back exposing whitely gleaming incisors which snapped hysterically at the three Commando Troopers struggling to hold him down.

The first Trooper had recently lost his mother and father when a hit-and-run Luftwaffe bomb blew a gap in a suburban Liverpool terrace more than four miles from the nearest strategic target. He wasn't being very gentle. In fact, the only reason Kruger wasn't already dead was because the other soldiers had got there first but, on reflection, the Trooper was quite glad now – it was only trapped rabbits and injured cats and run-over dogs which warranted that kind of favour.

The second Trooper was impatient. He'd come to Ålvik to fight Germans, an' that didn't include wet-nursing some kind of Wehrmacht nutter who just couldn't take the same kind of treatment that, until now, the Nazis had been pretty generous in dishing out. But *he* had once watched a panic-stricken refugee column, mostly French women and children, being decimated by a leisurely strafing Messerschmitt on his way to the beaches near Dunkirk, so perhaps he did have some grounds for cynicism.

The third Trooper was a man who, before the war, had played a

trombone every Sunday for the Salvation Army in the slums of
Leeds. He just kept saying 'Easy, son . . . everythin'll be O.K.!'
even though he knew that, for the insane German, it never would
be again. But, to him, a soul in that special kind of torment didn't
have a nationality any more.

Mike Seely looked down at the animal, and the animal growled
back with a blank-eyed stare. The Captain thought tiredly, 'That
poor bloody creature's no good to us, no good even to them any
more. He's not a soldier now, or even a proper prisoner. . . .

He said coldly, 'Tie him up and make him comfortable as you
can. Then leave him where they can find him after we've pulled
out.'

He hoped they wouldn't find the creature until the next morning.
It was very cold on Oksenes. Too cold for a man to live a whole
night without being able to move about.

Not unless he was a film hero, of course. Like Errol Flynn. . . .

The young Captain glanced at his watch. The time was precisely
eight twenty-five and he had to smile a bit to himself, thinking
about his mother. She'd always told him that he'd been born at
8.25 in the morning.

He was exactly twenty-six years old this minute.

H-HOUR plus 15 MINUTES

Still concealing himself carefully in the shadows of the timber-
framed house flanking Ålvik's main street, Scherer watched the
Commandos advancing towards the Norske Hotell – crouching
alien silhouettes running for a few moments then, abruptly,
melting out of sight again before the beseiged defenders could
zero-in with anything but pot-luck accuracy.

The Gefreiter knew he should be fighting too. In fact, *especially*
him, one real Kreigsmariner being worth ten poncy Wehrmacht
squaddies. But unlike Dieter Balke a hundred metres away with
his machine-gun and his dreams of fame, Scherer was gradually
becoming more and more aware of the consequences of being a
Hero.

Like being dead rather shortly afterwards.

Because the blind rage had evaporated completely now. Oh, the
hate was still there, but even that had died to a gently simmering

resentment distilled with the caution which had camouflaged all Scherer's impulses throughout his career in the Navy. The conviction that it didn't matter what you did, or to whom – so long as you made bloody sure you would get away with doing it.

It meant that the big Leading Seaman's previous blind determination to kill a Tommy – any Tommy – had now to be tempered by one slightly restraining influence; it would also have to be done with discretion. And with one's back against an appropriate escape route.

Holding the Schmeisser at the ready he started to hurry between the houses forming the first passageway down to the waterfront. He could see the fjord waters heaving sullenly fifty yards ahead, just past the corner.

He didn't realise that, only a few moments before, a party of British soldiers had already passed across that entry, heading towards Dieter Balke's welcoming field of fire.

Even more important – Scherer didn't know that there was still one straggling Commando also running for that particular corner, and roughly equidistant from it. He was a Troop-Sergeant. One half of his mind was thinking about a dead German, and the other half remembering a girl called Ginny.

*

A long way away from the explosions and the dying and the terror a grey little wave slopped over the edge of a yellow rubber dinghy. And then another, and another and quite a few more until the raft was virtually awash.

Inside the dinghy its occupants stirred as the water rose, the lifejackets around their shoulders gradually assuming a positive buoyancy under the lift of the encroaching sea. Before very much longer, the two dead airmen were sluggishly moving back and forward, back and forward with ice-coated heads bumping gently against the deflating cushion encircling them.

Their chariot still didn't sink, though. It would take a long time for all the air to escape yet.

Not that they were in any hurry, anyway.

Chapter Eight

'In war, whichever side may call itself the victor,
there are no winners, but all are losers. . . .'

Neville Chamberlain.

The Planners of MO9 considered it inadvisable that 22 Commando
should outstay their welcome in Ålvik. The deployment of the
wounded Lieutenant Denny's Group Three – now commanded
by his Troop-Sergeant – around the Princessebrønn junction
could merely be expected, at the most, to delay for a short period
the arrival of reinforcements from a stunned but only temporarily
ineffective *Wehrmacht Armeekorps H.*

And there couldn't be anything other than an equally brief
reprieve from the attentions of *Luftflotte Fünf* before they overcame the tactical and logistic problems presented by the craters
in the Herdla runway, and longer-range bombers roared towards
the Østersfjord from the direction of Stavanger and Trondheim
instead.

Then there were those Kriegsmarine destroyer squadrons under
the control of Admiral Saalwächter at Naval Group Command
West. He would be very upset indeed about the enthusiastic
destruction of his Ålvik S.K.L. sub-section and, being an astute
strategist, would quickly plot courses for the interception of
Force King during its withdrawal. It was therefore felt desirable
that the British ships should be well away from the Norwegian
coast by first light on the following morning because, as well as
being dangerous and hostile, the North Sea can also be large and
very concealing.

For these reasons 22 Commando were allotted just over four
hours to complete their business of the day before re-embarking
for home.

But that was where the planning had to stop. Because the first
essential task during the minutes following H-Hour had to be the
killing, the capturing or the neutralising of the German Garrison
as a preliminary to the destruction of that Garrison's warehouses

and oil tanks and ammo dumps and pretty well anything else with an eagle stamped on it. And the snag there was that it *is* rather difficult to persuade an enemy soldier to die in the strict chronological order demanded by operational necessity, no matter how reasonable it may appear to the planners of the event.

But a norm had to be set. A completion target. An estimated time for killing. Oh, the violence would continue sporadically during the whole of that four-hour period because a Commando raid is, through its very conception, a concentration of human outrage. It has to be a distillation, the very essence of war and, particularly during its initial phase, a high-speed crushing of all organised resistance.

The crushing norm set for 22 Commando was thirty minutes. There were still fifteen of them to go.

H-HOUR plus 16 MINUTES

The crushing of the Oksenes Battery and the Hæl-en installations had gone very well indeed – for the British. Yet to Captain Michael Seely and his men now doubling urgently to join up with the fighting around the Sørenson Factory it had been a great disappointment, an anti-climactic end to the months of training and conditioning which had brought them to the Østersfjord. They weren't relieved as one might think because, to them, a lack of action now could only mean frustration and bitter disappointment.

It was perhaps understandable then that, on breasting the last slope leading towards the Sörsund jetty, a certain relief could be detected on the faces of those Commandos that Jerrie had been bloody-minded enough to hang on until they arrived, and that he was undoubtedly fighting back with accommodating persistence.

Too much persistence, according to Trooper Danny Williams who was a little nearer to the factory than the approaching enthusiasts of Group Five. Though he'd at last found Charlie Smart again after having delivered, a little diffidently, his first prisoner plus one wounded Hun in a Mark One *Panzerwagennach-bildung* Wheelbarrow and then gone back into the smoke hoping to God there were other people around here apart from bloody movie-makers. . . .

. . . and found, with horrific suddenness that there undoubtedly were when two German soldiers hurtled towards him out of the gloom, whereupon, before Danny had even realised it, one of them had obligingly impaled himself on the automatically out-thrust point of the Lee Enfield's bayonet.

The transfixed man went down with a scream, dragging the muzzle of the rifle with him, while Danny just stood there and stared in disbelief as the second German, skidding to a shattered stop past him, started to swing and aim all in one frightened reaction.

It was a funny thing but, for some inexplicable reason, perhaps that was the moment when Danny Williams stopped being nervous and really started to become a soldier. It did seem a little late though because, quite coldly and calculatingly, he knew that he could never withdraw his bayonet from the clamping vice of the spitted Jerrie's ribs before Hun Number Two had ended his military career with half a dozen 98k Carbine rounds.

He still tried though, pulling the trigger of the Lee Enfield and blowing a hole in the German's chest amply large enough to withdraw the bayonet. Then starting to pivot even while feeling the first wild shot rip away the buckle of his belt and the second round sear numbingly through the Commando flash against his upper arm. . . .

. . . while the third didn't seem to go anywhere at all. Until he realised that the second German hadn't fired again because he was lying all twisted and writhing on the ground, and that it was a bullet from Charlie which had saved him from a fate worse than a Troop-Sergeant-Major's displeasure.

He said shakily, 'Thanks, Charlie!'

Charlie knelt down and began to saw an epaulette from the German's shoulder as a souvenir. 'S'all right, mate . . .' he nodded generously, '. . . hang on a minute, though. I promised the kids . . .!'

Then a heavy calibre round ricochetted from the wall beside him and tore away Charlie's hip and, ever so slowly, Charlie fell over sideways and lay staring disbelievingly up at Danny with the white ends of bone sticking out of the hole.

It seemed to suggest that there was still a bit of crushing to be done around the Sörsund jetty.

*

Across the fjord in Ålvik itself the Colonel was feeling quite pleased. He'd set up his Command Post in the house on the main street and, even from the preliminary reports he was now receiving from his section commanders, he felt fairly optimistic about holding the town until noon at the earliest.

22 Commando already nearly surrounded the perimeter and, with the additional support of the Group Six reserve now en route from *Hystrix*, he hoped that, within the next half an hour, they would divide the main body of the Garrison into smaller, more vulnerable units which could be dealt with while their primary task of demolition and the ferreting for intelligence went on with a minimum of interruption. And coincidentally, of course, with the recruitment of local citizens for the exiled Norwegian King's Armed Forces, and the embarkation of refugees and female volunteers for the Norwegian Red Cross in London.

And then there were the Quislings to be dealt with. Those few Norwegian members of the Nazi-sympathetic *Nasjonal Samling* Party plus one or two others among the local populace who, according to information received, could well tend to convert to the Teutonic way of life. The hard-liners would be arrested and taken back to Britain and detention. The others . . . ? The Colonel smiled grimly. That was one of Bertie Torrance's allotted duties – to persuade them to remain firmly on the Allied path of righteousness.

Another heavy explosion rattled what windows there were left in their frames and the Colonel hoped that his somewhat over-boisterous demolition engineer Lieutenant had shrugged the pack of plastic explosives from his shoulders before he detonated it. Then the firing from the direction of the besieged Norske Hotell slammed into a fresh intensity which proved that the German Garrison counted several very brave and determined veterans among its complement. It also showed that they weren't out of the wood yet, not by a long chalk.

Because there were still those three tanks. The enemy hadn't, for some inexplicable reason, brought *them* into action yet. . . .

*

Colonel Duncan was to worry consistently about the three tanks for the rest of his Commando's stay in Norway. But he didn't really have to, as it so happened.

Half a mile away in the middle of the Østersfjord the merchantman *Wismar*, having failed in her attempt to bluff Lieutenant-Commander Bradbury into believing she was a non-belligerent, was currently being battered into a flaming hulk under the fire of *Muscadin*'s main armament.

One of the ironies of war was that, among the many items detailed on her cargo manifest, were Consignments Numbers 8 to 10 inclusive – three self-propelled guns, type *PzKpfw 38(t)*. They had only been loaded aboard the day before for the first stage of their transhipment to the Russian Front.

The German High Command had considered they would be far more usefully employed against the Red Army than just sitting idly in a backwater town in the virtually dormant Norwegian Theatre of Operation.

H-HOUR plus 16 MINUTES

A Bristol Beaufighter carried the heaviest armament of any aircraft in the world flying at the latter end of 1941.

It could project 780 lbs of high explosive, tracer and ball ammunition per minute towards a target, through six .303 Browning fixed machine-guns and a further four 20 mm. Hispano cannon harmonised to converge at two hundred and fifty yards. It was a very lethal weapon indeed.

So when one manœuvred inevitably on to Paul Fichte's tail, and began firing at just over two hundred and forty yards, it immediately confirmed what he'd already anticipated – that his rapidly disintegrating fighter just wouldn't have enough time left in the air to run out of fuel anyway.

It happened right after he'd roared in above the tops of the grey waves, the Messerschmitt shuddering under the recoil of her guns as he watched twin lines of white-hanging water cutting towards, across and over the assault craft lying off the Oksenes landing area. A brief glimpse of a British Bren Gunner lying flat along the casing of the nearest L.C.A. and a blue-jacketed Naval rating tumbling forward into the troop space, then he was hauling the stick back and rocketing up the wire-strewn slope towards the cliff-tops and the sea.

Until, without warning, there was a shocking drum of fire behind him, the armoured back of his pilot's seat punched into his spine with terrific force and the cockpit filled with flying shards of plexiglass splinters as the starboard rear window panel fell in under the canopy mounting.

The Beau fired again and the great twin-engined image now in his mirror disintegrated as he watched. He said bitterly, 'Oh Jesus!' and wrenched the plane into a left-handed spiral which flung him hard against the side of the cockpit just as something ripped the instrument panel out and threw it into his lap, slashing the leather gloves into gaping, bloody weals of pain.

Then he was climbing and twisting all at the same time while the Beaufighter streaked across his vision, travelling fast towards the fjord. A blast of freezing air was plucking at his flying suit, all down the right side of his leg and, glancing calmly below, he saw a gaping hole in the fuselage with the torn skin vibrating and slamming under the compression.

There was something burning too. He could sense it in the sudden odour of hot oil and glycol and less specific things which seeped into the enclosed space. He thought, 'So what the hell *now*, hot-shot?' and swivelled aft to try and find the other enemy fighters. . . . One way over there, cruising protectively above the town . . . another – probably the bastard who'd jumped him – now banking in a tight turn about a mile and a half away, black against the white carpet of mountain snow. Yet there had been three not long ag . . .

Whoomf! Whoomf! Whoomf . . . !

The third Beau never appeared in his mirror because there wasn't any mirror left, but it was still there, hanging on to his tail in a four hundred mile an hour stalk. The ME109 shuddered as though a steamroller had run into the fuselage then, ominously, the note of the engine faltered, cut and then unexpectedly roared into life again just as three great holes appeared in the port wing.

He was lucky. Even that fractional hesitation on the part of the Daimler-Benz had been enough to reduce his airspeed with an abruptness which caught the R.A.F. pilot off balance. The over-shooting Beaufighter slammed above his head, still firing viciously and with an intensity which made Paul automatically if somewhat pointlessly duck his head, then the shadow was gone and the crippled Messerschmitt had cleared the cliffs and was heading out towards the sea.

And the British ships. The cruiser and the two troopers.

He knew *they* were ready for him when the very first puff-ball tore away part of his tail section. The plane started to turn over just as the flames ate through the engine compartment bulkhead and reached for his face.

H-HOUR plus 20 MINUTES

The British soldiers had seemed to take much longer to reach Dieter Balke's position than he would ever have believed. It was still quite entertaining, though, as during the waiting time he'd watched groups running from one door to the next, kicking them open then, Thompson guns at the ready, darting inside with the wary tension of men skilled at the in-fighting techniques of house-to-house clearing.

Only one building seemed to hold Germans, however. That was the one where, as soon as the khaki figures moved in through the doorway, a rattle of shots shattered the local silence and no one came out of the house again. Then a second group of Commandos moved in, crouching low under the windows, and someone tossed something with a tinkle of breaking glass just before the whole window frame spewed out on the end of a jet of flame and the firing stopped abruptly.

The young Ordinary Seaman thought approvingly, 'Those Tommies are good, very good indeed,' and wished he could fire too, just to show them that the Kriegsmarine weren't exactly slow at adapting themselves to land-bound hostilities. But he didn't, because he'd made up his mind to wait until the Commandos were just in line with a stunted, rather pathetic-looking tree about fifty metres away. He was almost certain it was fifty metres because he'd had ages to estimate the distance. In fact, he felt quite disappointed now that he hadn't actually paced the range out to make absolutely sure, the British having been good enough to allow him so long to prepare.

He still couldn't envisage what might happen to him once the tree had been reached and he'd squeezed the trigger of the gun. That protective mental shell of Balke's was as invulnerable as ever. Those fast-moving, alien street fighters held no more menace for him than a row of plastic duck targets at a *Bierfest* shooting stall. He did feel one slight spasm of guilt, though – that he never actually did tell Hafenmeister Rex that there was a British destroyer in the fjord. But he thought the Leutnant would probably know that by now, anyway.

Then the first soldier passed the tree and Dieter Balke became a Hero.

Or nearly a Hero, at least. It was all very disappointing in a way.

The trouble was the MG34. Never having actually fired one before, he just never realised how much they kicked back into a chap's shoulder and, because he wasn't prepared for that, the machine-gun immediately commenced to judder sideways on its bipod while Dieter Balke's so keenly anticipated dreams of glory vanished in a stream of tracer some fifteen degrees to the right of dead centre.

And dead centre was a Scottish ex-poacher with a dislike of Germans and a 23-lb. Bren Gun which he'd been using for the past twenty minutes as easily as most people carried a rifle. But far more efficiently.

Tyndal's reflexes were very good too. He was launched into the prone position and returning Balke's fire before the disconcerted young seaman stopped squeezing the trigger – both top and bottom – and started wondering instead, with understandable confusion, why his bullets were knocking absolute hell out of the windows of the local residents' houses while doing very little to those suddenly earthbound British soldiers under the stunted tree.

And then Balke, with the abrupt loss of concentration of the mentally disturbed, decided to forget all about his medal anyway. Really he'd only been interested in finding out what it felt like to fire a machine-gun, but that part of it had proved a pretty frustrating experience altogether and not much better than just being a sailor.

So he listened detachedly and without the slightest resentment to Tyndal's rounds as they slammed into the earthwork above his head until, getting bored with that too, he tied the white hankie – which he'd used earlier for polishing the stock of the then prized MG34 – to a stick.

Then waved it gaily in the air while, at the same time, calling in a clear, friendly and unflustered voice, '*Kamerade! Ich möchte übergeben, bitte . . . ?*'

And it was only natural that Leichtmatrose Balke would like to surrender, please. Because for him the war was over and he considered that any further unpleasantness was completely unnecessary. After all, they were gallant adversaries who'd fought nobly and with dignity and it wasn't as though there had been any suggestion of a personal vendetta because he quite admired the British in many ways.

So that was why, when Trooper Tyndal's Bren suddenly stopped firing, Dieter Balke stood up without a moment's hesitation and with complete equanimity started to walk towards the Tommy soldiers.

He didn't realise, not being an infantryman, that it takes a few seconds to replace the empty magazine of a Bren Gun. Even for an expert who could tie a whisp of a salmon fly with the same facility which he applied to the science of killing Germans.

*

Curiously enough one German soldier *was* being killed quite deliberately, and at that particular moment of time. But not by either a British or a Norwegian visitor. It was happening in the gilded, but now rather bullet-scarred, ground floor lobby of the S.K.L.'s Norske Hotell Headquarters.

Staff-Sergeant-Major Leuschner interrupted his unflagging direction of the Wehrmacht defenders just long enough to shoot a panic-stricken and hysterical Unterfeldwebel Oehlschläger in the back of the head.

But Stabsfeldwebel Leuschner realised that the British were too strong for them to hold out very much longer, and that he and his grimly resisting men would very soon be dead as well – while that gutless little bastard Oehlschläger *had* been warned twice before about trying to sneak out of the hotel's back door.

In fact he'd actually saved Colonel Duncan's men a job because, at that moment, two Troopers were already kneeling close into the rear wall of the building, just where the late Oehlschläger should have appeared.

Being men of considerable resourcefulness the two Commandos carried cans of petrol. And the Norske Hotell, like most of the other buildings in Ålvik, was constructed of timber.

Very dry timber.

*

Much drier than the piece of wreckage that Hans Strobe, late helmsman of the Baltic trader *Wismar*, was balanced across.

He still remembered with horrifying clarity that second in time when the British destroyer fired at virtually point-blank range, and her first round exploded with a shattering roar against the *Wismar*'s side. He remembered the way the wheelhouse windows had caved in on him under the blast, and the shocked look in the Second Mate's eyes above the rumpled, projecting pyjama collar.

Then the old Captain, still puffing just a little faster on that pipe of his, had turned towards the wheelhouse door and called sadly, 'You may go, Strobe. And you, Herr Bögel. . . .'

He'd hesitated as the second round went through the four-metre space between the after end of the bridge and the high spindly funnel like an express train, without even scratching the rust, then continued calmly, '. . . give my compliments to the Harbourmaster when you get ashore and apologise to him for me. Perhaps I should have run her ashore like the *Käte Hass* over the . . .'

Muscadin's third salvo tore into the old ship's starboard wing, just under where the Old Man was standing, and by the time Strobe and Bögel had picked themselves up there wasn't anything to see outside the sliding door other than water and wreckage and a sheer drop to the fjord.

The Second Mate screamed, 'Get out, Hans! Jump f'r it, kid . . . !' then flung himself towards the engine-room voice pipe. He was blowing frantically down it to call the engineers on the whistle, cheeks swelled out like rosy red apples, when he caught sight of Strobe still hesitating at the other door. And then everything changed for the young seaman.

Because Bögel snarled, 'Get the hell out've it, Strobe! Or are your lot fatalists too, like the Mohammedans an' the bloody Chinks . . . !'

Strobe walked numbly away from the bridge, still hearing Bögel's urgent warning into the voice pipe. 'Chief? That's it then, boys. . . . Abandon ship! I said – Abandon *ship* f'r . . . !'

He was numb because now he knew that even the fresh-faced Second Mate had been playing out a lie, had only been kind to him in the way that people are kind to lame dogs and blind men and lepers. Because he was a German Jew. And he was different. He always would be. . . .

The fourth, fifth and sixth shells exploded on the bridge. The blast threw him head first down the after ladder and skittered him along the boat deck until he was lying face down and staring at a great white whale below him in the water. Then he realised that it wasn't a whale but that it was the upturned bottom of Chief Officer Krupp's lifeboat which must have capsized as they tried to let go the falls. There was still one crushed man lying across it, splayed out like a crucifix with the washed-out rivulets of blood forming excited little tributaries down the curving lines of the hull.

Quite slowly and without any feeling at all, Strobe leant out over the water and captured a sullenly swaying lifeline. He allowed himself to swing free until he was hanging over the side of the doomed ship and – just as another British shell toppled the remains of the funnel on to the remains of the Second Mate – he went down hand over hand into the freezing water.

He didn't feel anything because – like even the Second Mate thought – Hans Strobe wasn't really the same as the rest of his shipmates.

*

A few minutes before Dieter Balke gave up being a machine-gunner and declared Peace and Goodwill towards the British Army a rather curious thing occurred on the corner of the alleyway leading from Ålvik's main street to the lonely fjord path.

It happened because both Troop-Sergeant Henderson and the murderously inclined Gefreiter Scherer arrived at the corner at precisely the same moment in time and, rounding it in opposing directions and at a fair trot, collided with an abruptness which afforded no time at all for anticipation.

In fact it happened so fast that, just for a fraction of a second, neither man was any more aware of the other than they would have been in a chance encounter during a city rush hour. Actually, Scherer probably received the worst of it, his Schmeisser being knocked clean out of his hands and sent skating across the ice leaving him completely unarmed and defenceless.

Had he collided with any member of 22 Commando other than Arthur Henderson he wouldn't even have had time to look surprised before he died, but in selecting this particular opponent Fate had given him a second chance. And then it gave him a third.

Because the Sergeant, still utterly preoccupied with the startling similarity between his own dead children and the images on the legacy of a blinded German corpse, just picked up Scherer's gun, handed it back to him saying vaguely, 'Sorry, mate!' and then started to run again towards his Troop and where his duty lay.

Scherer, on the other hand, being equally dazed, only forgot about his intention of finding a lonely Tommy in an isolated place for long enough to snatch the Schmeisser irritably, snarl ungratefully *'Dummkopf . . . !'* and turn away from the stupid bloody idiot who didn't even bother to look where he was going. . . .

Realisation had dawned for both of them – the British soldier and the German sailor – just one split second later.

They both swivelled as one, each wearing precisely identical expressions of shocked surprise and utter disbelief, each swinging the muzzle of his sub-machine-gun up and on to the man facing him. There was, in fact, only one vital difference between the two.

Perhaps it was because Arthur Henderson was a far too gentle man. And he just couldn't forget that he had already unnecessarily killed one father and husband because he'd fired automatically, and without even thinking about it.

Or maybe it was less complicated than that. Maybe, for one fraction of time, he was thinking about Ginny and the kids. Or maybe he didn't care any more. Or maybe he just wasn't a very good soldier because, even in the Commandos, it was hard to tell the real strength of a man until the killing time came around.

So Scherer shot the Sergeant with the greatest pleasure in the world. And when he'd done it, and waited a few moments to make sure they were still alone, he walked slowly over to where the British soldier lay staring up with sightless eyes. And kicked him.

Then he looked up to see the flames rising straight up into the grey sky from the direction of the Norske Hotell, and Scherer realised he didn't have a lot of time down here. Shouldering the Schmeisser he moved quickly towards the little path which led out of the town and up the mountainside. He passed through the last gap in the cordon which 22 Commando were throwing around Ålvik only two or three minutes before it finally closed.

Half-way up the slope he rested behind a protective rock and looked back towards the town. They wouldn't find him here. And as soon as the real fighting men arrived from Princessebrønn – or as good a mob as they had in the Wehrmacht – then he'd be able to go back down and tell 'em what a Kriegsmariner tiger was made of.

A *proper* German warrior!

Scherer lay back and closed his eyes. It hadn't been such a bad day after all. In fact, it was shaping up nicely for being a bloody good War.

The only thing was . . . well, it did make him wonder just a bit . . . but, when he'd looked down at the British Sergeant's face after he'd killed him . . . he could've *sworn* the bastard was actually smiling!

H-HOUR plus 22 MINUTES

Willie Bradbury called flatly, 'Cease firing!' then lowered his binoculars from the listing *Wismar* and looked around the rest of the Østersfjord with a sense of faint surprise. It seemed very quiet out there right then with the destroyer's guns silent for the first time in – he glanced at his watch incredulously – in only twenty minutes!

Half a mile away the recently arrived *Salamander* was still engaging the merchantman which had steamed straight for the other side of the fjord – the one whose master must have decided to run her aground rather than risk her being taken as a prize. Willie decided it would be most unsporting of him to butt in at this late stage so he started to look hopefully for another target.

But they were a little short on hostile targets in the Østersfjord by half-past eight on that November morning. The troops were still busy, certainly – he could still hear heavy firing going on from both Ålvik itself and the Sörsund area – but apart from those enemy ships which had already been engaged there appeared to be nothing else at all which presented either an opportunity or a menace. Even the ME109s had disappeared from the sky overhead. . . .

He turned as the signalman appeared at his elbow. 'Signal from the Flagship, Sir – TO MUSCADIN . . . PRIZE CREW WILL

BOARD GERMAN TANKER ALONGSIDE SÖRSUND JETTY . . .
SAIL PRIZE DESTINATION KIRKWALL EARLIEST SITUATION
PERMITS . . . end of message.'

Willie glanced up and saw his First Lieutenant watching curiously. He smiled. It was a lovely smile because it had been a lovely old day. Almost as much of an event as that time at Scapa when the Parliamentary V.I.P. got wet. . . .

'Starboard ten to . . . Two one five degrees! Number One.'

'Sir?'

'Get your toothbrush . . .' Willie said considerately, '. . . you've just been given your first command!'

*

Captain Mike Seely had led his men at a fast double down that slope from Oksenes. Even before they'd linked up with Group Four they had come under fire from an enemy M.G. post somewhere to the right of the factory, the rounds whip-cracking over their heads in a tattoo of frenzied retaliation, but the Commandos kept on advancing while a fusillade of covering shots rattled from their opposite numbers already entrenched below them.

But they'd definitely found themselves an action at last. There would be no disappointment now, or frustration, because this was the thing which they'd come all the way across a sea for. For the first time since landing, Group Five were doing the tasks of soldiers and not of scavengers among the maimed and the mad, and the dead.

So Mike Seely grinned with nervous pleasure as he threw himself headlong into a hole and, twisting quickly round, observed Major Bert Stenhouse's battered, blackened and rather homely features staring at him from behind the sights of a Tommy Gun.

Bert waited until the grenade which someone had thrown at him exploded with a flat report and covered them both with tiny clods of smoking earth, then he nodded as casually as if people tried to blow him up every day of the week, and said hospitably, 'Mornin', Mike! Nice of you to drop in. . . .'

He stuck his steel-helmeted head over the edge of the hole just long enough to rip off a burst of fire which showed the Germans that they were bloody awful grenade throwers, then slid back down again and stuck out his hand. There was a little Iron Cross in it, still with the ribbon attached.

239

Mike saw there was also a hole through the middle of it, almost exactly nine millimetres in diameter.

'I've been saving it. It's a present,' Bert murmured generously. 'Well, a *sort* of a present anyway. . . . Many happy returns of the day, old boy!'

Then the first of the oil tanks blew with a roar and a climbing rolling column of flame, and Captain Mike Seely thought warmly, 'Maybe it isn't going to be such a bad birthday, after all. . . .'

*

Corporal Loomis didn't think that Bren Gunner Tyndal should shoot Dieter Balke as he wandered towards them from the direction of the bullet-pocked MG34 emplacement with his hands clasped firmly and in a very proper attitude of surrender above his head.

Instead, Loomis cautiously rose to one knee under the stunted tree and, covering the approaching sailor with his weapon, said warningly, 'Leave him, Tyndal! The Colonel wants prisoners if possible.'

Tyndal hesitated with his finger round the Bren's trigger. If it had just been Loomis goin' soft then he'd 've squeezed half a dozen rounds intae the wee bastard first, then looked awfy upset an' said 'Sorry, Corporal! Ah must've slipped on a root . . . !'

But it was what the Colonel ordered that mattered, and the Colonel was a braw man – an awfy bonnie sodjer. He nodded regretfully and muttered, 'Aye, O.K. Corporal! You get the wee lad a seat an' I'll away and find a motor car so's he'll no' have to walk all the way tae the wharf, eh?'

Leichtmatrose Balke, on the other hand, wasn't at all put out by the hostile expression on the little Bren Gunner's face. Certainly he could see the British soldiers weren't quite smiling in welcome, but he felt sure that as soon as they could see he was intending nothing other than camaraderie and good fellowship, then they would all be quite pleasant company for each other.

But he did wish they wouldn't point those guns at him in quite such a mistrusting manner. He continued walking towards the tense soldiers, a weird Chaplinesque figure with his greatcoat-tails flapping around muddied legs and the faintly ridiculous coal-scuttle helmet square across his brows. Anxiously he started wondering how he could make some sort of gesture towards them, something to break down that completely unnecessary barrier of suspicion. . . .

. . . and then Dieter Balke had an idea.

He remembered the stick grenade which he'd picked up earlier and thrust into his coat pocket. He could still feel it in there, bumping awkwardly against his thigh every time he moved. Actually he did have some vague plan about saving it until after the war and then giving it to his father as a sort of souvenir – for the mantlepiece perhaps, or to hang on the wall beside his medals. But he didn't think he'd get all that many medals now, so. . . .

The youngster lowered his hand and thrust it into his pocket. He'd give the British soldiers the grenade instead, then they'd see that he had absolutely no intentions of being aggressive. He pulled it out and smiled reassuringly, holding the offering invitingly forward.

Loomis dropped flat even while he was shouting warningly, 'Grenaaaaaade!'

Tyndal didn't drop. He just swung the belled muzzle of the Bren upwards until it was centred on the Jerrie sailor's chest. He certainly wasn't surprised – they were a' the bluidy same, they Nazi lads. An' stupid too, dead thick. . . .

And for the very first time in Dieter Balke's life his mental fail-safe circuits refused to function. Until that particular moment in time his distressed mind had simply refused to recognise any menace or any threat presented by the British soldiers. Like Scherer before them, and the mutilated motor cycle Corporal and the impacted Gefreiter Hopp, they had been switched off a long time ago.

Until now. Because even a deranged simpleton can detect the face of Death when it leers at him.

He screamed urgently '*Nein* . . . *Nein!*' down the barrel of the Commando Bren.

Tyndal glanced pointedly at the grenade clutched in Dieter Balke's woollen-gloved hand, said reprimandingly, 'Oh, *ja* bluidy *ja*, Adolf!'

Then shot him.

Under the shadow of the Sørenson Factory wall Trooper Danny Williams had tried desperately to stop the flow of blood from Charlie's shattered thigh, but he didn't really know what to do, so he just stuffed all his and all Charlie's field dressings into the hole, then held Charlie's hand while screaming 'Stretcher-bearers . . . ! *Stretcher*-BEARERS . . . !'

Charlie was breathing a bit queer now, the air sort of hissing through the white lips in little quavering sighs, and Danny saw with a terrible helplessness that his colour was changing quickly, going chalky and pallid, almost grey in fact.

He whispered, 'Hold on, Charlie boy. Only another minute or two before the lads come f'r you.' Then Charlie looked up at him with such a frightened, anguished look that Danny knew he must be in terrible pain and started fumbling in the pocket of his B.D. blouse for that pack of morphine tablets one of the R.A.M.C. blokes slipped him on the boat coming over.

He pulled them out then dropped them in the dirt and the blood, but then Charlie squeezed his hand so hard he panicked and just picked one up along with a pinch of wet snow. He said foolishly, 'Can you manage it without a drink've water, mate?' but Charlie couldn't speak because of shock so he just stuck his tongue out a little bit and Danny placed the tablet and the snow and the dirt all on it together.

Then he put another one on it because he wasn't even sure how many you should take and Charlie was hurting awfully bad. . . .

And another bloke from their section came blundering out of the smoke so Danny choked, 'Look after my mate, will you?' then rolled away quickly and was violently sick in a corner and turned back, wiping his mouth shakily on the back of his sleeve, just as the other Trooper said curiously, 'What're you givin' him pills for . . . he's dead, Williams! Sorry an' all that, seeing he was your mate, like.'

Danny picked up his rifle and stood looking down at Charlie for a minute. Then he bent down and gently took the sawn-off German epaulette from Charlie's hand and put it in his own pocket. Perhaps, some day after the war, he'd be able to visit

Charlie's kids and give it to them, and tell them how brave their Daddy had been.

Standing up again he looked ahead, into the smoke to where the Germans were, and worked the bolt of his Lee Enfield so that the spent cartridge ejected on to the ground beside Charlie's body and a shiny new one slipped into the breech.

He sniffled a bit, not caring whether the other Trooper saw him or not, then he set the steel helmet square on his head, took one last look at Charlie, and said grimly, 'C'mon then! Let's go an' find the bastards!'

He led the way into the smoke himself.

668497 Trooper Williams, D.H., had finally become a Commando.

*

Still balanced precariously across his own piece of wreckage, Hans Strobe, late of the Baltic trader *Wismar*, watched disinterestedly as one of the few heads left in the water bobbed and struggled towards him.

He knew it couldn't be deckhand Katzmann because he'd been that face-down corpse on the upturned lifeboat, but it didn't really matter any more – Katzmann and the Second Mate were just like the rest. None of them wanted to be seen or associated with an officially different animal like Strobe.

He started to feel cold as the sea-water gradually froze so that his clothing crackled gently every time he dared to make the slightest movement. The head was much nearer now, coughing and choking in a last desperate effort to stay afloat long enough to reach the wreckage and temporary safety, so Hans just tried to forget the cold and concentrated on thinking about his mother and sister in Nienburg while he waited for the head either to sink or to reach him.

And when it finally did he saw it was on top of the shoulders of First Mate Krupp. Krupp the Nazi, Krupp the man who hated Strobe more than anyone – or anything – else in the whole pure Aryan world. Krupp, the man whose major claim to Hitler's approval being that he had fathered an S.S. son. . . .

Krupp spluttered tentatively, 'Strobe! Hans Strobe! By God but I'm glad to see you made it, kid. Jus' give me your hand and we'll make out togeth . . . !'

Hans kicked the First Mate in the face. Krupp went under with a disbelieving shriek and when he surfaced he had started to drown. Hans kicked at the blood-congested features again and again with great deliberation, and finally Krupp didn't come up at all.

Then he said politely, and without any trace of feeling, 'Sorry, Herr Krupp. You see, this raft is for Jews only.'

But you *did* get a bit fed-up. Especially if you've been pushed around for the last two thousand years!

*

When the flak from the cruiser had turned Paul Fichte's Messerschmitt virtually upside down he thought, with an oddly detached sort of resignation, that it was the end. In fact, as the flames started to eat into the legs of his flying-suit and occasional stray firelets stroked his face with agony-laden fingers he was quite glad in a way, because he knew the plane would blow up as soon as the tank below his seat overheated. And then it would all be over and the Gestapo could do whatever the hell they liked with a grinning corpse in a burnt-out cockpit at the bottom of the North Sea.

Curiously the British ship passed sideways above his head at four hundred miles an hour – or was it below him or what? – and even despite the fear and the pain he couldn't help noticing how magnificent she looked with her guns sparkling and rippling, and the White Ensign streaming above her bridge while the wriggly worms of hoses surrounded a smoking black crater between her funnels. . . .

And then another burst of ack-ack fire exploded somewhere under his inverted wing and the plane incredibly tipped over through one hundred and eighty degrees until she was flying straight and level again, and Paul thought bitterly, 'By *God* but dying's slow. . . .'

He felt inordinately grateful for one thing, though. The fire was still there but now the flames were being forced downwards and away from his face as the blast of air from the shattered rear window panel turned the inside of the cockpit into a howling, sub-zero wind tunnel.

The ships were past now, somewhere astern as he rapidly flew out of range of the guns. He wondered disinterestedly where the Beaufighters were, then decided that only madmen or upside-down suicide pilots would fly through a cruiser's air-defence barrage like he'd just unwittingly succeeded in doing.

Which left him, Paul Fichte, all alone and heading farther and farther into the North Sea at some six miles per minute. Tentatively he touched the rudder bar – nothing happened! He kicked a little harder and the fighter rolled sluggishly, but his heading remained pretty well the same as before. He chewed his lip thoughtfully, obviously his rudder had been shot away by that first burst of flak – or the Beaufighter – so now he couldn't even manœuvre with anything other than the inefficient ailerons . . . but what the hell! He wasn't going anywhere, anyway!

Then everything seemed to happen together.

A muffled explosion under the engine cowling and he saw it rise vertically before blowing up and aft in a fluttering, flailing spinner of torn metal. Then the airscrew note rose to a shrieking pitch of torment – and stopped! He thought, 'Oh Jesus but that's *it*, boy!' just as the oil sprayed back over the windscreen in a thick hot treacle while, at the same time, the flames came back up through the floor and all he could see below his knees was roaring, crippling fire.

He tried not to scream. He knew it couldn't last very long because the plane was already rolling over with a finality which no miracle could ever prevent this time, but the primary instinct of self-survival still made him scrabble for the canopy release handle while his other hand was somewhere down in the fire snatching in agony-laden desperation for the safety-belt catch.

Then all of a sudden the perspex canopy had jettisoned just as the Messerschmitt lurched forward and started to plunge sickeningly towards the sea.

Fichte felt his legs start to burn even as the slipstream dragged him half-way out of the open cockpit. He wasn't even aware of releasing the straps as he kicked frantically with one charred flying-boot at the stick which was jamming hard into the muscle of his other leg . . . then his leg tore clear and the pressure blasted him flat back against the rear of the seat yet he *still* couldn't get FREEEEEE F'R . . .

The ever-increasing slipstream battered at him with numbing ferocity, clamping him immovably half in and half out of the diving plane. He was screaming now, shrieking against the wind which tore his mouth wide open and inflated his cheeks to great tearing balloons of agony while plugging his nostrils with a spearing suffocation. All he could feel was the racketing, disintegrating fighter holding him and the red clutch of the flames as they roared up and round and past his body towards the shot-away tail.

With a last superhuman effort he dragged one arm free, felt the hungry blast clutch at that too, smashing it helplessly aft against the canopy seating and snapping it like an irrelevant twig. . . .

He screamed, 'Please God! Please . . . God . . . *Pleeeeease* . . . !'

Then the flames were gone, and the pressure and the pain, and he was tumbling clear and actually staring at the fuselage of the plummeting fighter as it passed him ten metres away, and thinking quite ridiculously that it'd definitely have to go into workshops for another tail unit before he rode *that* bucket again. . . .

. . . then he blacked out just as his parachute streamed above him in a great climbing column of bleached white silk. . . .

The next thing he knew was the sea embracing him in its icy blanket, breaking over him and smashing against his inflated life-jacket while the chute started to drag him down and down into the blackness. Foolishly he noticed that the water tasted very salty as, almost without being aware of it, his one good hand hit the quick-release catch on his harness.

He thought dazedly, 'You're a fool, Paul boy! Just a complete gutless bloody fool for persisting in staying alive. . . .'

He still thought that when he saw the rubber dinghy which floated so impossibly less than twenty feet away. He knew it couldn't be there, and that he was much better to stay in the water because he would be dead a few minutes faster doing things that way. But he still swam towards that non-existent hope of life which towered high above him one minute and then fell in a smother of white water to float a long way below him the next.

It was only when Paul Fichte had hauled his tormented body over the ominously soft cushion of the raft, and saw the eyes of two dead comrades staring blankly at him through their little lenses of ice, and realised that they had already been there a very long time indeed, that he really appreciated the irony of his purely temporary salvation.

The last thing he sobbed was 'Heil bloody Hitler!'

And then he started to laugh. . . .

From the cruiser's bridge the Admiral watched the Messerschmitt flying upside down through the curtain of fire and thought, 'There's one German boy who bears a positively charmed life.'

Then a burst appeared under the fighter's wing and, quite casually, it flipped back over and continued out to sea as if the pilot didn't even care enough about the British guns to bother to weave.

Someone said admiringly, 'He'll go far, that chap,' while someone else retorted cynically, 'He's going to bloody have to if he keeps to that heading – the nearest land's three hundred odd miles. *And* it's British!'

The Brigadier pointed shorewards and nudged Braddock-Tenby. 'L.C.A.s! Coming out of the fjord.'

The Admiral forgot about the lonely German flying on a dead straight course for nowhere and raised his binoculars. Even from this distance he could see them, bank upon bank of stretchers lining the sides of the sickeningly spiralling assault craft.

'The first wounded,' he said quietly. 'I'll send word to the Surgeon Commander. We'll look after them in every way possible.'

The Brigadier nodded, his features expressionless. 'Thank you, Arthur.'

The Admiral shook his head slowly and watched the L.C.A.s again. 'Not me,' he murmured softly. 'It's them we want to thank, John. . . . Those very brave young men under the blankets!'

H-HOUR plus 30 MINUTES

In the room which now served as the Ålvik Command Post the Colonel's signaller said loudly, 'Looks like Bertie's declared a one-man war on Norway, McLusky!' then, when he caught sight of the Colonel looking up reprimandingly, the Signals Corporal huddled back over the 18 Set with a guilty red flush spreading under the rear rim of his steel helmet.

Dougal Duncan couldn't resist the temptation. Ever so carefully, so that nobody would notice, he raised his head to a level with the shattered window frame and glanced out into the street.

Bertie Torrance stood right outside the C.P. Or at least the Major wasn't so much standing as leaning easily back on the prop of a shooting stick . . . the Colonel blinked disbelievingly, but yes it really *was* a shooting stick, dammitall! And Torrance resting with the casual aplomb of a gentleman at Royal Ascot while all the time stray shots whistled and ricochetted over the rooftops and into the snow-covered main street.

The Colonel watched a little longer, starting to smile despite himself. There were civilian figures grouped in a confidential little semi-circle around the Major. Suspected Norwegian Quislings who, for lack of evidence, were to be allowed to remain in Ålvik, but only on sufferance and after a severe warning from Bertie. And it didn't really need an interpreter to understand what Bertie meant.

The Major waved his .45 admonishingly at the crowd of jumpy locals and said in a sincere and gentlemanly way, 'Now look, you bastards – if I hear any more about you collaborating with Jerrie I'm gonna come back here all on my own and personally blow your bloody thick Nazi heads off! D'you get me? *Comprenez vous . . . ?*'

Then the local telephone exchange blew up in the next street and the terrified civilians flung themselves flat as baulks of timber and shattered equipment landed all around, while Bertie looked down a bit surprised from the top of his shooting stick and said reassuringly, 'No, no – not *now*, chaps. I said "Next time" . . . and only then if you're naughty.'

The Colonel turned away from the window just as a Sergeant came in with a bloodied bandage round one arm, snapped to attention and saluted saying matter-of-factly, 'Hotel's on fire now, Sir! We should winkle Jerrie out in a few more minutes.'

The Colonel nodded, reaching for his helmet and stick. There was still firing going on from the eastern end of the town, but he knew now that they would accomplish everything they had come to do because the real violence was over and the target had been fulfilled. He glanced at his watch – it said 8.40 G.M.T. 22 Commando had been ashore on enemy-occupied territory for precisely thirty minutes.

It was nice to hit back for a change. And one day, one very special day in the far-distant future, they would come back again. To stay!

He said quietly, 'Thank you, Sergeant Eames. Nip off and get that arm of yours seen to before you go back, will you?'

Hesitating, the Colonel turned to his Signals Corporal. 'Make to the Flagship – ÅLVIK NOW SECURED . . . CASUALTIES STILL MODERATE . . . INTEND TO IMPLEMENT PHASE TWO TASKS IMMEDIATELY . . . DUNCAN!'

Then he stepped out into the street. There were several bodies lying farther down, just where the smoke from the blazing hotel was beginning to swirl in sluggish eddies. Some of the dead soldiers wore field-grey uniforms and quite a lot of them were dressed in khaki. 'It's strange,' the Colonel thought gently, 'how all their faces look the same in death.'

Pipe-Corporal McLusky moved protectively behind his Colonel as they strode briskly down the street. He still carried the Tommy Gun instead of his pipes, but the kilt was there, and the pride and the courage and the dignity.

And the COMMANDO flash gleamed very bright against his sleeve.

LONDON. 1ST DECEMBER, 1941 – Yesterday a
small-scale raid was carried out against enemy land
and sea forces on the Norwegian coast. Combined units
of the Royal Navy, Army and R.A.F. took part.
Norwegian troops were also involved in the landings.

The operation was entirely successful in all respects
and all of our ships returned fit for immediate
service. Casualties were light.

Official British Communiqué.

BERLIN. 10TH DECEMBER, 1941 – Last month
British Naval forces attempted a surprise attack on a
desolate stretch of the Norwegian coast. After brief
engagements the British landing detachments were
ejected by small local patrols of the Wehrmacht
and Kriegsmarine.

German coastal batteries sank a cruiser and two
destroyers of the fleeing enemy formation. A further
two cruisers were severely damaged by German
bomber units.

No casualties were sustained by our forces but several
Norwegian merchant ships engaged on peaceful
coastal traffic were viciously attacked and sunk by the
British.

Official German Communiqué.

Endpiece

'. . . I conned the ship close alongside the object which was then observed to be a German Luftwaffe mark of rubber dinghy. The dinghy was awash and contained three bodies, none of which appeared to show any signs of life. I did not make any attempt to recover the men as, in my opinion, stopping my ship in those waters would have constituted an unjustifiable hazard. . . .'

Extract from Captain's Confidential Report.
H.M.S. Muscadin.

Colonel Duncan never did go back to Ålvik. He died at the head of his Commando on a Normandy beach. Pipe-Corporal McLusky fought all the way to Berlin, and the very first thing he did when he got there was to play a lament for the Colonel. Bren Gunner Tyndal was with him too. And Corporal – or by then – Sergeant Loomis, but McLusky was the only one who actually cried, though perhaps it was just the whisky which made a man a wee bit maudlin – that, and the infinite sadness of the pipes which stir memories best left forgotten.

Soldat Kruger is still alive, and still mad. He resides in a Bavarian nursing home and tells everybody his name is Flynn – Errol Flynn. The cold of Oksenes didn't manage to kill him after all, so perhaps he did gain a little of that celluloid immortality he so craved.

That same cold did kill Deckhand Strobe, though. They found him firmly welded to his raft after the British had left the Østersfjord. But even if he had survived, and gone home to Nienburg, he would have found that his mother and sister had left the town a week before. Aboard a cattle-truck bound for a place called Belsen.

Trooper Danny Williams is still in the Army. He's a Regimental Sergeant-Major now. Occasionally, when he rummages in a drawer, he comes across an old Wehrmacht epaulette, faded and torn. It keeps on appearing every time he moves to another posting, and he always means to look up the records to remind himself of the name of the bloke who died in his arms on that violent morning beside the Sörsund jetty.

Oberbootmann Krupinsky is dead. He died much as he had lived, with great coolness and fatalism. The last time anyone saw him he was leaning casually back in the gun-captain's seat of 'X' Turret, and lighting a final cigarette while the battleship *Scharnhorst* began to roll over and sink. Maybe Krupinsky decided that saving himself from one capsizing ship had used up all the luck a Navyman was entitled to.

Captain Michael Seely is dead too. He was a full Colonel by the time a Chinese mortar round landed beside him on a Korean hillside. It exploded exactly ten years to the day after he'd led Group Five over the wasteland of the Oksenes Battery. It meant that he was killed on his thirty-sixth birthday.

The Admiral will probably live for ever. He still tends his roses in his little Hampshire garden, and thinks that it was a great pity that John Aubrey passed away so young – Dammit, the Brigadier was only seventy-eight when he went!

Bertie Torrance went back to the Østersfjord. It was something he felt he really had to do after the war. And rather an odd thing happened while he was there, as he was standing silently looking down at the little line of British graves which are now the only reminders of Number 22 Commando's visit. One of them – that of some vaguely remembered soldier called HENDERSON A, TROOP SERGEANT, KILLED IN ACTION, 31ST NOV 1941 – lay very close to that part of the cemetery which holds a rather larger section of German dead and, when Bertie glanced over, he noticed a very old, very erect Prussian gentleman standing just as sadly and just as silently among them.

Bertie didn't speak to him because he knew his memory must have been at fault but, just for a moment, he could have sworn that the elderly German was the spitting image of that bleakly impassive Nazi Major he'd captured down there beside the Nordkai many years before. Still, it was intriguing to speculate on why the old chap had made this particular pilgrimage. And about the young black alsatian which sat patiently waiting by the visitor's side. . . .

H.M. Destroyer *Muscadin* was lost with all hands during a night action off Malta, so nobody really knows how Willie Bradbury died but, whether it was with the suddenness of a high-explosive burst or more slowly under the Mediterranean waves, one can be sure that Willie went immaculately, and with great aplomb.

No one knows quite what happened to the missing Blenheim D for Dog either. Its crew must still be under the North Sea somewhere, in company with Paul Fichte and the Ice Man and the Cooked Man, and a host of other souls who had lost their particular bit of War.

And Gefreiter Scherer . . . ? The Kriegsmarine gave him a medal for conspicuous gallantry in the face of the Enemy, and a Chief Petty Officer's rate to go with it. He had a lovely war, spent mostly in various Naval Headquarters around the Mediterranean sunspots until, after it was all over, he wangled himself a coveted job with the Allied Occupation Forces.

Since then he's never looked back. He has two cars, a yacht, a private aeroplane, three mistresses and a favourite anecdote about a blue woollen glove. He is the most Anglomaniacal German you'll ever meet. Perhaps that's partly because he now owns a travel firm which specialises in, among other delights, cut-price holidays from the United Kingdom to Scandinavia.

One of the highlights for British followers of the Scherer Tours itinerary is a one-day visit by ship.

It's to the town of Ålvik. In Norway. . . .